HEALER, HEAL THYSELF

Dion's mind spun to the left. There was a dizzying drop of thought, and images rushed by like a fall from a mountain cliff. There was a jumble of color and scent—the fragments of memories and bodies and wounds and then of flesh torn and blood vessels ripped apart. There—the tendons curled into balls where they had snapped from the bones, and Dion reached into herself with her mind, aiming her energy, touching here, there, until the tortured oozing of her blood stopped . . .

By Tara K. Harper
Published by Ballantine Books:

WOLFWALKER
SHADOW LEADER

SHADOW LEADER

Tara K. Harper

A Del Rey Book
BALLANTINE BOOKS • NEW YORK

In memory of Brent E., who taught me how to finesse a climb, and showed me that one of the greatest challenges is that of facing your fears.

Chapter 1

In gray tones, speak the wolves;
The whisper of their hunt is soft.
But when the poison masa walks
Even the wolves flee the woods.

Aranur staggered to a stop and caught his breath. The rustlings behind him grew louder, and the coils of the poison masa were already creeping along the branches overhead. He half straightened and threw a glance over his shoulder. If those sucker vines got any thicker . . . With a curse under his breath, he pulled his long knife from his belt—his sword would be useless if he became tangled—and shoved himself away from the tree. Longear's scouts could be on his trail even now, he knew, but that was not what worried him—the masa was stirred up enough to keep the scouts from his footprints for days. No, it was the wolfwalker for whom he feared.

He broke into a jog. The hungry vines snaked through the trees above him as he ran, and the feeder roots were as thick as his wrist. Dion had never seen poison masa before. If she stepped into a masa coil unknowing . . .

He ducked under a low branch and vaulted a rotten log, slipping on the loose bark that scattered under his boots before he caught himself again. He glanced around for signs of the wolfwalker. Thank the moons he was close—cleanly cut stems still oozed with fresh sap where Dion had sliced off the wild herbs with her knife. But then the wind rose briefly, and a new scent hit his nose. Fresh water. A lake? Or a stream hidden in

1

a gully he had not seen from the ridge? His knowledge of this county's border was scant. If there was a pond here, there would be clear bands of soil near the banks—and that would be ripe hunting ground for the masa . . .

He doubled his pace, ignoring the branches that caught and snapped on his mail as he ran. A deadfall leapt up under his feet, and he jumped it without thinking, sliding down on the other side as the ground fell away in an unexpectedly steep slope. The soft earth piled into his boots, and rotting sticks stabbed his legs where the studded leather slid up to his hips. He landed with a grunt, rolled, and came up running, the humus scattering like chaff.

The ground became marshy, and the softness of the sweet dirt gave way to mud. His feet drove deeply into the ground with splucking sounds as he shoved his way through, one hand holding the hilt of his sword so it did not catch on the brush, the other in front of his face to ward off the branches that stabbed at his eyes. Before him, a tiny hillock served as a dike to the mountain runoff. He charged up it until his weight collapsed one of the rodent tunnels that honeycombed the dike and he slammed to the ground face first at the top of the hill.

Wait.

He froze.

That voice—it was Gray Hishn, the wolf that ran with Dion, the massive creature's tones husky in his mind. *Watch,* the gray wolf said softly.

Motionless, Aranur caught his breath. What was going on? Where was the wolf? And where was Dion? He glared across the lake over the top of the dike, his narrowed gray eyes stabbing each shrub that hung out over the silent water. He could see no sign of the enemy scouts that patrolled the borders in greater numbers than ever. But there—to the right—he located the wolfwalker before spotting Gray Hishn hiding behind her. The woman's worn, leather mail melted so well into the brush that she was nearly invisible, but the silver headband, which marked her as a healer, glinted dully in the sun. It gave away her position and turned Aranur's angry apprehension into puzzled curiosity. He hardly noticed the chill where the mud soaked his leggings. What was that fool woman doing now? She looked frozen in place, like a statue, her hands out in front of her as if she had been turned to stone in the middle of clapping. Behind her, three small, neat piles of herbs testified to the gathering she had done. He squinted, shifting silently to a better position. But he could see no danger around her—and, too, the wolf would not be lying in the brush behind Dion if she sensed anything wrong—so what in the name of all nine moons was going on?

Suddenly Dion let out a short, sharp yell and brought her hands together with a clap that echoed across the water.

"By the gods—" Aranur almost jumped into the nearest tree as the banks of the lake—on every side—erupted, and thousands of startlingly green lizards leapt up from where they had lain, perfectly hidden, in the mud of the shore. They were a full meter tall on their hind legs; they ran like half-size men toward the water and then, to his amazement, rushed out on the surface of the lake as if it were a mirage and solid as the banks he stood on. Frantically they sped toward the center of the lake in a spattering thunder, tiny wakes cutting back from their webbed feet and chopping up the water like a thousand knives. And then, just as suddenly as they had appeared, they sank out of sight. And then there was—nothing. Just the lake, the banks, and the wolfwalker standing there with a foolish grin on her face.

And she had the audacity to giggle. Aranur closed his mouth with a snap and got to his feet, stalking down the dike. It did not help that he slipped twice and caught himself only once. By the time he reached Dion, who had already picked up her herbs and motioned for the wolf to join her, he was wet, muddy, humiliated, and coldly enraged. He wiped a last handful of marsh mud from his scabbard and flung it on the shore.

"All right, Dion," he snapped. "What the hell was that all about?"

The wolfwalker, her violet eyes sparkling, gestured toward the lake. "Green tobi lizards. Did you see them take off for the water? There must have been a thousand of them lying on the shore."

"Dion," he said in a quietly dangerous voice, "why are you out here alone this far from the trail?"

She looked at him then. "I was gathering herbs, Aranur. I told my brother where I was going before I left."

He wiped another streak of mud from his scabbard. "Rhom hardly knew you would be gone this long or this far."

She gave him an irritated look.

"Look, Dion, you weren't scouting trail, so no one knew where to find you. It took me half an hour just to locate the spot where you left the rocks back near the main path, and now I've left traces there, as well. We're too close to the border of Bilocctar, Dion. You don't realize what can happen."

"Gray Hishn's with me," she protested quietly. "She sensed no danger—"

"That wolf doesn't know everything about these mountains, and neither do you. What if these tobi lizards were venomous? What if this little trick of yours drew the attention of a badgerbear or worlag or one of Longear's men instead of me?"

"Aranur—"

"Gamon sighted a group of scouts barely an hour after you'd gone."

In spite of her irritation, Dion was startled. "But we're still two days from the border. And we've been a long time crossing the mountains from the coast—they could not know where we are yet."

"I don't know how they did it, but they are in these hills just as we are. And if they catch sight of us—or of you," he reminded her sharply, "then all this—" he gestured at his worn boots and stained leather mail. "—will be for nothing."

Dion was silent for a moment. "Hishn and I would not have been seen," she said finally. "The Gray Ones are seen only when they wish."

"Moonworms, Dion," Aranur exploded, "you're not a wolf. You're a woman, and as easily seen as the rest of us." He ran his fingers through his hair and forced his voice to be calmer. "Look, Dion, if it were merely Zentsis's soldiers who were after us, I might not be so concerned. But Longear's men—like their master—are far more ruthless and cunning. You're a good scout as long as you keep your mind on what you're doing, but you get so caught up running around with that wolf that you forget the dangers that could take others as well as you." He gestured sharply. "You've got to stay closer to the group. If you ran into trouble out here, we would not even know it."

Dion gave him a strange look. "You might." She did not explain, but instead turned on her heel and stalked back toward one of the trails that led away from the lake.

"Dion—"

She did not turn. But the wolf, with a sly smile at Aranur, trotted after her. With a flick of her tail, Hishn sneezed just as she came even with Aranur so that he had to move his boot from her path, as well.

"Dnu droppings," he muttered. "Dion, wait there," he ordered. "I will go first. There is masa growing down here."

"I know," she said shortly. "I went around it."

But she paused for him to step in front of her on the path. Hishn, also waiting, cocked her head at him and panted. Aranur, still reeking with the mud of the marsh, glared at the Gray One and snapped, "And wipe that grin off your face, you gray-skinned mutt."

Dion touched his arm. "You didn't have to hurry so, Aranur. We did scout the area before we came down to the lake."

"Paths can change in a matter of minutes when there's masa around, Dion." He ducked into the game trail the wolf had indicated and catalogued at a glance the tracks that lay on the path. Even though he was keeping his voice low, it still seemed loud.

"What do you mean, 'paths can change'?"

"Masa walks. Haven't you ever heard that?"

"Yes, but it's not that thick here," she returned, brushing her hair back from her face.

Aranur glanced over his shoulder at Dion. Her straight black hair heightened the color in her cheeks, and her violet eyes, so like those of the moonwarriors of legends, were quick and clear. She was slender, but tall enough to come up to his shoulder. Tall enough, he reminded himself, to stand up to him when she took issue with his words. He snorted, making his way around a deadfall that blocked the trail, but as Dion slipped silently after him, he nodded to himself in approval. In spite of her slimness, she was strong and quick with her sword— something that had surprised him until he learned to count on it—and fought as well as any of the men who rode on his venges back in Ramaj Ariye. An odd woman, he thought. One who knew the woods as well as another woman would know politics. Where most women were content to run the businesses and act as elders to the councils, Dion preferred the forest and the stark heights of the mountains. She would have been a master healer in any city, but she chose instead to take her healing skills to the tiny villages that perched on wispy cliffs and the scattered towns that squatted in the remote valleys of Randonnen. Not all wolfwalkers were healers, he knew, though most of them had skills in that science. But this need to run the ridges with the wolves—he wondered if all wolfwalkers were like that.

The thought of the woods brought his mind back to the

masa, and, edging around a bush, he listened carefully for sounds of creeping runners as the vines threaded their way through the brush. The masa was closer now, but the trail ahead seemed to be clear. He motioned for Dion to hurry.

"Masa does not grow in your county," he said in a low voice, pausing to clear a branch from his own dark hair. "It's the altitude. But we're only a hundred meters off sea level here, and the masa grows thickly. Larger than I've seen it before."

Dion looked down the path. "We had to go around two major growth circles before Hishn found a clear path to the herbs I wanted."

Aranur bit back an acid comment. "The problem is, Dion, that the masa is large enough here to attack creatures our size and bigger. Look, see that root over there?"

She nodded. "It's as thick as my forearm."

"I saw vines as thick as that gathering on that other game trail."

"They were not there when I went by."

"That's what I mean. Masa walks." He scowled as the trail faded out and left him facing a wall of brittle peatrees. Only tiny paths led through the dense growth before them, and Aranur pulled his sword from the sheath with a mutter and began hacking his way through. "Each growth circle sends out feeder roots along the ground," he said, grunting as he slashed through a thick clump of blackwood stems. "At the same time, the vines creep out over nearby trees before they kill the other plants." He took two steps and bashed another wall of sticky brush. "When the runners find a spot with clear space beneath the branches, they coil up like snakes on the upper limbs. Then they wait for the feeder roots to sense pressure and movement." He slipped between the thick shrubs and made his way for another ten meters before he had to hack at the brush again and stop, forced to clear his blade of the clinging growth after just two more cuts. "Then, when an animal comes by that weighs enough to tempt the plant, the vines drop, and *kapow*. You're history." He paused for a moment and looked back. "It's a good thing we're taking another trail back. By now, that first path's a death trap."

"But how could the trail change so fast? Even if you took your time, I went through barely twenty minutes before you did."

"I didn't take my time," he said shortly. "Close to the lake,

I went through barely five minutes after you. It's like this, Dion. If the feeder roots sense more motion in one direction than another, the plant shifts its vines over there. You and the wolf must have been pretty tempting fare."

Hishn cocked her head at the healer, and Dion paused, hearing the gray voice easily in her head. "To the right," the wolfwalker said. "Another trail opens up."

Aranur glanced back, then to the right. "How far?"

"Five meters, maybe more."

He cleared his blade, wiping the steel on his leggings and shoving it back in his scabbard. Clambering over the peatrees, he forced his way through the heavy bushes till the tangled brush suddenly halted and he stepped abruptly out on a thin trail, just as the wolf had said. But as he saw the tracks that littered the path, he halted. Behind him, Dion froze. She waited silently while he examined the tracks, but even at a glance he could see that the largest tracks were old. The last predators on that trail had been a band of beetlelike worlags that had passed days before, and the marks of their long, insectoid claws had already been partly filled with dust and caved in by the other prints of rabbit and grouse. He motioned for Dion to join him.

"There are few animals using this path," he commented. "And it is running in a fairly straight line toward camp."

But she hesitated and pointed along the trail. "All the large animal tracks are old here, Aranur. Only the small ones are new." She shook her head, and the Gray One bared her teeth slowly.

"And masa walks," he said softly to himself.

"Would the masa let the small animals through so that larger ones would follow?"

He shook his head slowly. "A trap like that implies intelligence, Dion."

She chewed her lip, a vague uneasiness making her unwilling to set foot on the path. "Let's think on this a moment, Aranur. What if this masa is intelligent? It's not native—the ancients brought it across the stars when they came. And they did a great deal of crossbreeding before they developed the plants we use today. They could have bred these vines the same way."

He snorted. "For what purpose?"

She motioned, and the wolf snarled deep in her throat. "This masa is an almost perfect barrier," Dion said softly. "Better than the thornbush, since that cannot move or chase its prey. If this masa grows throughout the foothills as thickly as it does here, it would keep anyone from invading across the mountains."

"Maybe." Aranur stood up, glancing down the trail one more time. "But I think if the ancients could cross the stars and tread on worlds as easily as the legends say, they would not have used something like masa to keep them from each other's throats."

"Who's to say it was themselves they were guarding against?"

Aranur smiled grimly. "Whoever or whatever worried them, the ancients left these hills long since. This masa now . . ." He looked down the trail again and frowned. "We will never see the feeder roots on the ground in all this brush. If there are coils up in the trees big enough to haul us up, we will have to be fast to avoid them before they catch us." He squinted. "They are not quick so much as they are unexpected. And strong. You can get snagged and caught before you know what hit you, and the toxin in the vines' suckers is just like that in water eels—it works fast." He took two steps forward, paused, and looked back over his shoulder. "Watch the trees overhead. You'll hear the leaves rustle just before the coils drop."

Dion shivered. She looked around again, but this time the forest seemed dark, not shaded, and sinister, not silent. The few birds that flashed through the leaves were fearful of making too much noise, and their songs were short, sharp warnings of things that moved too dangerously close. The thickets of silverheart trees that leaned against the game trail were guards who slept so that the poison masa might pass. Dion could not suppress the chill that crawled slowly down her spine, and her hand tightened on her sword. Under the crowded canopy, where the sun was rebuffed by the dark green of the trees, the trail crept away from them in both directions, hemmed in by the shrubs and branches of black willow and blowweed. But the blowweed twigs looked more like vines now, and the open space of the path was suddenly small and claustrophobic. She dropped her hand to the gray wolf's scruff, alternately scratching and gripping the thick fur. The massive creature echoed her apprehension, and Aranur could almost hear them talk, the gray tones faint in his mind like a dream he could not quite remember.

Can you smell it, Hishn? Dion's gaze sharpened as a bird flew suddenly up from a tree.

The wolf growled low in her throat. *Thick in my nose like an onion*, she sent back, snorting softly to clear the cloying odor from her muzzle.

Something rustled to the side, and Dion tensed, but it was another eelbird darting across the path, its beak full of the sour berries that the jackbush carried in a dry season. She glanced at Aranur, then back at the forest. *Where is the masa now?*

Another animal moved in the brush behind them, and the wolf's lips snarled suddenly back from gleaming teeth. *Go. Go on the trail now and do not wait.*

Aranur was regarding them with a strange expression. "I heard," he said quietly. He cleared his sword one more time of the sap that clung to the blade, but left the weapon bare and ready. "Stay close," he ordered.

Dion hid a wry smile. She was not going to be farther away than his heels. Not if masa walked. She drew her own sword, making sure her long knife was loose in its sheath, as well.

Almost touching, the two fighters worked their way down the path, the Gray One slinking first in front of them, then behind, but never more than a step away from the woman who followed Aranur like a shadow. And Aranur, with the grace of a dangerous cat, moved always so that his sword arm was free. There were few men who could match him in the woods, Dion realized. Few, too, who had as much skill in weapons as he. And although her brother, Rhom, would not yet admit it, she suspected that Aranur could best Rhom quickly in both hand-to-hand fighting and weapons. She shifted to the side to keep her sword arm clear of Aranur's cutting path. As the tall, lean man moved silently across a tiny clearing, the sun flashed briefly on the mesh of his warcap, then hid again, as if ashamed to be caught peeking through the trees. The shadows on Aranur's face grew dark under the trees. His bones were too angular for him to be handsome, Dion thought, but there was a power in the strong chin and slate-gray eyes that would make any woman look twice. She slipped through the branches of another deadfall and looked back, gauging the movement that chased them down the path. Vines as thick as her forearm? Moonworms.

The sway of the upper branches in the breeze added soft sounds to the rustling that grew behind them, and the tiny sounds of the low twigs that brushed against the ground in the same wind tightened the muscles across Dion's back. Was it masa or imagination that dropped the leafy arbor closer to their heads? Aranur seemed to ignore the way the trees reached down for their hair and clothes, but the wolfwalker felt a chill. The dark clumps of the deadfalls could hide anything. If the grasses and weeds that choked the path harbored the masa's feeder roots, she would never know. Even the tiny meadows she and Aranur crossed were haunts that the sucker vines could hide in. Hide and wait until the prey was too far from the safety of shrubs to escape back into the woods.

The path is clear, the gray wolf insisted. *Clear.*

But Dion could not shake the feeling. Her nose was too full of the sweet, rotten scent of the plant. And Aranur's sense of smell was no better. He paused continuously, but only his eyes and ears told him where the rustling followed; the smell of the masa was too thick even when the breeze brought a cool touch of water to the air.

Suddenly the wolf's hackles rose and Dion froze.

"Wait . . ." she breathed.

Aranur became motionless midstep.

Dion eased her knife from the sheath so that both of her hands held blades. "It's here," she whispered. "Around us."

He nodded imperceptibly.

The wolf touched a cold nose to Dion's hip.

"Ahead, and to the left."

He eased his step to the ground, raising his sword slightly. The sound was too loud to mistake.

He was several meters ahead of her now.

"Aranur—"

He did not look around. "Watch my back."

He eased forward half a step. Then another. The brush became suddenly silent. Then—

"Moonworms—"

"Look out!" Dion shouted.

Hishn snarled, Dion jumped forward and hacked, and Aranur lunged back while a sudden rain of vines clutched at his body. He dodged left, between two evilly snaking runners. As he threw himself back over a root, he landed with a *thwumph* at the healer's feet. Dion scrambled out of his way, slashing at the last thin growth that dragged at his ankle.

"Light of the moons . . ." Dion quickly flipped a thick vine over a solid branch and cut across another's reaching tendril.

Aranur, rolling to his feet, stabbed at a drape of several runners before clearing the air of the sticky vines. "Moonworms," he muttered again.

The sap from the vines slid down Dion's blade onto the pommel and stung her skin where it mixed with her sweat. She pulled her hand free, wiping it on her leggings; Aranur, glancing up at the trees, yanked her abruptly back from a vine that dropped suddenly down. It swayed back and forth, searching blindly for its prey. The buds at the ends of its runners opened to expose suckerlike mouths. They smacked obscenely in the air as they twisted to and fro, curling up as they sought out their meal above the ground as well as on it.

The wolf growled at the growth, her mind primal with the instinct of a hunter, and Dion stared at the shuddering brush. "The whole grove around us is alive," she said in disbelief. "The whole hill."

Aranur shook his head, looking back as well. "Damn, but that's impressive," he returned as he faced the hungry green curtain.

The Gray One whined, and Dion gripped its fur while she glared at Aranur. "What's impressive is the way you take chances," she said sharply. "Those vines were as thick as my wrist. They could have dragged you up before I could have cut anything."

He grinned. "They're hungry. The game must be almost gone from this area. Besides, you're hardly one to talk, Dion. You're the reason we're out here anyway."

They wasted no more time trying for silence. Instead, they quickly shoved and cut their way through the brush. Hishn led and the two fighters followed, ducking into game trails and then cutting across the rocks and rises that blocked their way. Finally they strode up a steep hillside of thick needles and dead ferns that was shaded from the gray sky by the deep canopy of evergreens. There they stopped. Before them, a rounded cliff of granite rose thirty meters, covered in a blanket of moss.

Aranur looked quickly around, gauging the movement of the masa behind them while searching for a way around the cliff. But Hishn whined and raised her paws up against the moss. Dion, soothing the gray beast, moved up beside the wolf and scraped a chunk of the greenery off the cliff. Underneath the growth, deep cracks edged smoothly back into the cliff where the water had run down for thousands of years. She made a face. The moss was thick with bugs. Even as she stripped another quilt of soft growth from the hidden crack, a clump of beetles blew suddenly out from the naked stone and buffeted her cheeks and hair before diving back into the undisturbed moss to the side. "Moonwormed bugs," she muttered, snorting and blinking to get them off her face. She tore another chunk of the green away and, with a grimace, reached into the crack.

"Can you climb it?" Aranur did not glance over his shoulder, watching instead the evergreens that hung dangerously close overhead.

"It's smooth. Give me a minute."

"There are runners in the trees."

She did not answer, but jammed her fist into the crevice and wrenched it sideways so it stuck, her knuckles crammed together to make a wedge of flesh and bone. Behind her, Hishn growled, but Dion ignored the Gray One. She tugged on her fist once, then pulled herself up easily. "Got it. I'll clear the crack as I climb."

"Hurry."

"I know." She jammed her other hand in the crack and pulled herself up, stepping into the dark crevice with her feet and twisting them into the same type of wedges as her hands, standing up on them until it looked as if she were climbing an invisible stone ladder. *Hishn, go around,* she sent as she glanced down. *We'll meet you at the top.*

The wolf whined as Dion climbed another meter up, then growled. *Motion,* she sent. *A hunger greater than my own—*

"No," Dion commanded out loud. *Leave us,* she continued silently as she wedged the ball of her foot into the crack and eased up another half meter. *We have no way to carry you up with us,* she sent. *Go around the ridge. Meet us along the trail if you can't find a way to get back to us at the top.*

The Gray One snarled again, this time louder. *Hunger. Danger growing, closing in . . .* The wolf turned and snapped at the woods beside Aranur, then turned back and, still snarling, placed her paws on the rock and stretched toward the wolfwalker.

No! Get out of here, Dion ordered sharply, cutting through the Gray One's instinct-blurred images. As the wolf's emotions took over, the images colored Dion's thoughts as well and made it difficult to see through human eyes. *Go,* she commanded, urgently. *Go!*

She hung out, away from the granite, and tore another blotch of green from the face, then swore suddenly and swung into the moss on one side of the cliff crack. A rude chittering answered the sudden light that hit the stone where she had bared it, and a family of tiny brown mice scampered out and around, one of them biting the wolfwalker on her arm, though its tiny teeth made little impression on the leather. "Sorry—I'm sorry," she muttered to the creature. She scraped more moss from the rocks, then jammed her fingers into the narrowing crack, clinging easily to the granite. But her legs began to tremble.

"Easy, Dion," Aranur urged quietly from below.

"It's okay. I'm okay."

He noted the movement in the upper branches of the trees below them and turned to the cliff himself. "Hishn's gone."

She tossed down another wedge of moss. "Watch the beetles. They're nesting under this overhang."

Her voice shook slightly, and Aranur tightened his jaw. For a climber to be so afraid of heights . . . But this was nothing compared to what he had seen her do before. He spared only one more glance at the evergreen canopy before starting up the rocks. The crack Dion exposed was dirty with roots and rotten growth, but it was clear enough to follow, and Aranur took as little time as she did, jamming all his fingers, then just two, and then one into the smaller and smaller holds. Above him, the woman leaned out and kicked her right leg up shoulder-level so that her ankle caught and scraped the moss off the edge of the ledge that struck out into the air. "Almost clear," she said under her breath.

She paused a moment, clung with one hand and foot to the face, and shifted her sword back with the other hand so that the hilt would not catch. Then she lunged up and over the edge in one smooth move, grabbing at a tiny crack far above. Her momentum swung the rest of her body up till she came face-to-face with the rock. She poised, suspended in time with Aranur's breath. Her thighs touched the face of that smooth and threadbare cliff; her body fell back into the air as her momentum left her. Aranur froze. Could she hold? Time stopped, as if to give her a chance to find another hold before she fell. One of her feet crept to the right, her toes crawling along a ledge that was not even as wide as her fingernail. The other foot was trembling off a small, triangular spur that stuck out of the ragged crack to her left. Her right hand was plastered to the ridge where her little finger drove itself into the tiny, shallow hold she had lunged for. Her left hand trailed the rock face with her balance until both caught up with the rest of her. For an instant, Aranur heard the echo of a silent scream in his head. Then Dion's harsh breathing smothered her scream, and

Aranur could only imagine he heard her chanting, "It's just me. Me and the rocks. I'm doing fine . . ."

He eased out from the ledge after her and glanced down at the forest to see the masa runners. They were stretched out in confusion as their prey no longer triggered their roots. He took a deep breath. It was not the narrowness of the ledge that made it dangerous, or the moss that clogged its holds, but the sheer smoothness of its face and the masa waiting below. Like Dion, he was not wearing climbing boots, but instead rough-cut leather moccasins. And after a ninan of hiking through the mountains, the leather was so thin he might as well have been barefoot. It was so loose now that it shifted between his foot and the rocks and slipped him off the holds. And if he fell, he reminded himself, the masa would drop on him like a starving lepa on a sleeping dog.

"Top's clear," Dion called down unevenly from over the edge.

He nodded without answering. Bracing his left toes in the now-tiny crack, he reached up and barely got a hold on the edge of the out-thrust ledge. The wolfwalker had smaller feet than he did, and only half of his big toe carried his weight on the rock where two of her toes had given her the leverage she needed to lunge up. The rest of Aranur's foot hung out over thin air, and he had to lean away from the rock, bracing himself off his toe while he pulled back with his left hand. He edged out, then pulled up ever so slowly until his elbow was even with the rock and he could ease it over onto the ledge. Finally his arm took his full weight, and he breathed out heavily. A minute later, with both hands on the edge of the next overhang, he heaved and got one knee above the slab. After that, the rest was as easy as Dion had said—only a few more meters, and they both stood at the top. The wolfwalker's chest rose and fell with her quick breaths as she clenched and unclenched her hands, while Aranur eyed the trees whose tops were even with their gaze. He could actually see the movement of the masa in the canopy, and it was not slow. He shot his glance up the steep hill that thrust up from the ridge, looking for a trail they could follow or a looseness in the brush that would admit them more easily.

Dion could hear the masa behind them, but the threat had paled next to her fear of heights. As she tightened the laces on her leather jerkin, the cold sweat in it pressed against her shoulders and chilled her. She shivered.

"Okay?" he asked quietly.

"I'm fine," she said, too sharply.

"Let's go then."

She nodded silently, not trusting herself to speak, but her hand, where it gripped the hilt of her sword, was steady. She reached for Hishn with her mind. *Gray One,* she called, *have you found a way up?*

I come.

Dion glanced up, judging shadows. *We run with the sun at our backs.*

I run with the sound of your voice.

Dion's worry—that Hishn had not yet escaped the reach of the masa—reached the wolf, who bared her fangs and snarled a reassurance deep in Dion's mind. The growl was more real to the wolfwalker than the sound of the creepers below her. She resisted the impulse to bare her own teeth in response.

In front of her, Aranur stripped the last tendrils of moss from his sword's pommel, then started up the vertical hill on his hands and feet. But he went up fast for all that. Dion was right behind him, stepping awkwardly in his sliding footsteps rather than trying to make her own stairs in the soft humus. Minutes later, they reached the top of the hill where they stood, hands on burning thighs, doubled over to catch their breath.

Aranur was the first to stand straight. "Masa walks," he said, "but it might also climb." He glanced at the canopy below them, then at Dion. She might be tired, he knew, but she would be beside him as he forced himself back into a jog.

The wolfwalker sucked a last deep breath of air, then fell into step, far enough behind Aranur that the branches he whipped back did not snap at her. She was glad she had left her pack at morning camp with her brother. As thick as the brush was and as fast as they were moving, a pack would only snag and trip her on the boughs, leaving signs for everyone to see. *Gray One,* she called, *are you near?*

The pack runs, the wolf returned. *I lead.*

Hishn's voice had a shadow of its own, and Dion knew that the wolf had been joined by another of her kind. *Tell the Gray One that he honors us—* Her thought broke off as her ankle gave out suddenly in a soft patch of earth, and she shut her mind abruptly to the sharp senses of the wolf; she could not tell, with both pair of eyes, which branches and stones would trip her first. She must be more careful. If Aranur was right and Longear's scouts were near, Dion's tracks could be the ones that betrayed them.

Hishn growled. *Run toward the second moon. The brush is clear, the path well worn.*

Dion nodded. "Aranur," she called. "Cut over to the east. The ground should be more clear."

She could not tell if he nodded his own answer, but ahead of her he was already cutting to their left, leading the way beneath trees that grew taller with each stride they took. There the shade deepened again, and the brush grew sparse until a dim trail crossed their feet in a fork. One path led north, the other northeast. But at last the air was clear of the cloying scent of the masa, and Aranur spared only a glance at the trees. If there was no danger of masa to the wolves, there should be none to the humans, or Dion would have warned him. He paused and looked back, waiting for the wolfwalker to catch up. He nodded at the path.

"That way," she said, pointing at the northeast fork and having time to catch her breath only once before he led off at a quicker pace. She glanced back. Hishn was near: she could sense it. Of the masa, there was no sign.

They could see almost twenty meters through the trees, and Aranur jogged only to the top of the next gully before stopping again. His eyes took in the forest right and left, and he listened carefully, while Dion, coming alongside, again caught her breath. "We can walk," he said finally. "Hishn?"

She glanced east, her eyes unfocused for a moment. "A few minutes away," she said finally. "But the Gray Ones say that the last growth circle of masa is two gullies behind us."

"If the masa was this thick here, there might be more along the way, and Gamon probably went on ahead with the others. He might need us."

Dion said nothing at the unspoken criticism, but when Aranur began to hike, she set her feet in a jog again, and he, with a glance at her face, did the same.

It took him several minutes to realize they were being shadowed, but even as he became aware of the hunters, he caught a glimpse of gray fur and realized it was Hishn and another wolf who paralleled them along the hill. A moment later, the second wolf was gone, and Aranur wondered if Dion had sent it away.

As Hishn drew closer, Dion's eyes took in the wolf's images along with her own. With the wolf in her mind, she saw the trail from two heights and smelled through a nose more sensitive than her own. And Hishn, whose yellow eyes sent both memory and speech to the woman, stretched her legs to leap up the steep slope and join Dion.

The hunger was strong, the gray wolf sent with a memory of the masa. *Strong, like the badgerbear who wakes in spring and finds his stomach six months' empty.*

Dion smiled, her teeth clicking together as she jumped off a log that angled its way down the hill. *It is behind us now, Hishn. But if there is any more masa between us and the others, let us know now.*

There is more than masa to make my nose curl here.

Dion glanced behind her, then peered past Aranur through the woods.

Men, the wolf added, stopping suddenly and sniffing the ground, then turning around and sniffing again. *Old tracks— old by days. But tracks of men who run silent. Men who hide their tracks on stone, and stink of stealth, not speed.*

"Aranur," Dion said. "There have been other men along this path since the last rain. These could be patrols, not just isolated trackers."

"If there are patrols here, we have more to worry about than I thought. Stay sharp," he warned. "We tempt all nine moons by traveling so fast."

The game trail went up the hill more steeply, and Aranur finally dropped to a fast stride. His long legs took him over the jutting rocks and brush quickly, but Dion's thighs ached and burned until she was lifting them by rote, not feeling. She stumbled twice, the second time landing on her hip before catching hold of a low branch and pulling herself to the side of the small avalanche of needles and dirt she had started. Hishn, close enough to lose her footing as well, snarled and leapt to the side and then up above the slide path where a log kept more dirt from rolling down.

Aranur glanced over his shoulder as he realized that Dion was no longer behind him, then hesitated and turned back.

"Go on," she muttered. She struggled out of the branches and grabbed a handful of needles to throw over the narrow slide. When the next rain came, the scrape would wash out as erosion. She stepped over the slide path after Hishn, but Aranur waited. "You don't have to stop," she said sharply as she reached the top of the hill.

But to her surprise, Aranur shook his head. "I'm sorry, Dion," he said quietly. "I'm pushing too hard."

Her burning legs made her want to rub them until they

stopped screaming at her, but she stood straight. "It's not as if I'm not used to running the hills, Aranur."

He looked her over carefully, noting the shadows of exhaustion under her eyes and the lean, almost gaunt way her cheekbones were pronounced in her clear face. There was only muscle on her long, slender legs, and her tunic hung loosely beneath her stolen leather mail. As she caught her breath, Aranur wondered again at the bond of the wolves. Few could take the strain of scouting as Dion had done for him and his group. Did the Gray Ones give her strength of will as well as the use of their senses? He shook his head and met her eyes. "You've been driving as hard as any of us, Dion. And you've been out scouting with Hishn every night for the last two ninans while the others caught extra sleep. You've had even less rest than I."

She took a last deep breath and shifted her sword forward on her hip. "As you said," she returned, "we're close to the border of Bilocctar. We can't afford to be seen."

"You'll be less use to yourself and to us if you're worn out."

The wolfwalker flushed slowly. "Is that Aranur the weapons master speaking, or Aranur the man?"

He gave her a strange look. "Perhaps both."

It was Dion who turned away first, the flush fading so that only two high, red spots were left on her cheeks. Hishn, who panted and sniffed the air around them, fell in beside Dion as the woman silently picked up Aranur's pace and followed along the trail.

Breathe, step, step. Half a kilometer passed. Then another. They had to be getting close to Gamon and the others, though it would take Dion and Aranur longer than Dion had at first thought. Her feet padded quietly on the dirt in their worn boots, but her legs were again numb. The pouches of herbs at her belt made a soft syncopation with her stride until it was thrown off as she clambered over a set of logs. Hishn brushed through the branches like a ghost, and Dion ducked after. Her ankle twisted again. It nearly threw her, but she caught herself like a thought and ignored the shooting pain, knowing that it, like the other aches, would dull in a few moments and disappear.

Breathe, step, step. Hishn snorted softly and faded into the brush, and the taste of dust clung suddenly to Dion's tongue. The wolfwalker spit to the side, clearing her mouth and mind of Hishn's images. Only the gray thread of their bond held strongly between them.

She crossed a shallow gully. Her legs burned and her lungs ached for deeper breaths as she forced herself to plod up the other side. She damped her thoughts to the path. Ahead of her, sharp deer prints cut across the trail, and she ran around them to keep them clear; the droppings were scattered and fresh, and there, where one deer had turned suddenly, the whole herd had bolted. Her feet kept a rhythm with the Gray Ones running beside her. There were two voices now. Hishn's voice was strong and clear; the second one a faded gray that crept into her mind as if by mistake.

Two kilometers. Then three. A wide circle, nearly complete. They had to be close. Dion frowned. Another wolf had joined the other two, and their thoughts were not silent anymore. She could hear them, and then the scent that rose suddenly to Hishn's nose spoke more sharply to the wolfwalker than the snarl that Hishn sent.

"Aranur," she whispered urgently. "Get down!"

He froze, catching himself midstride, and shot a look over his shoulder. Behind him, Dion leapt to a thin log, stepped across to a small rock, and disappeared into a flat stretch of grass that grew only a few sparse handspans high. Aranur shoved his half-drawn sword back into its sheath, then jumped from the path into a shallow dip behind an upended tree's rootball. Flinging himself down, he pulled a redfern across his chest, then stretched a loose branch over his face.

Ten meters away, Dion lay flat against the ground. She had pulled her healer's band off, and it lay cool against her warm skin inside her jerkin. The grass, half brown, half yellow, covered her but barely, but her leggings and mail were so worn that they blended in with the dirt. She pulled a clump of short grass from the ground and set it on her hip; it would help hide the space her body made in the clearing. In her mind, she heard Hishn growl again and knew that the wolf had retreated up the hill to stand in shadow. But the scent of men remained, and Dion breathed silently, knowing that the Gray One was right. There were scouts on the path.

One minute. Two. Would Aranur stay down? At this distance, she could not reach him through the wolf. Even her brother Rhom could not hear the Gray One until he looked into those yellow eyes. But Dion worried. Four minutes passed, and then five. A pair of junko birds flew back to a branch over her head, and a minute later a rabbit crept back to nibble on a half-eaten leaf.

Gray One, she sent. *Do you see them?*

Like clumsy deer, Hishn sent back. Her lips curled back and the bristle on her back was raised. *They come.*

The woman sorted out the sounds of the birds, then the sounds of the wind in the leaves, and finally the steady pounding of her own heart and lungs. And then the faintest sound of something else reached her ears. She relaxed. She breathed with the earth and stretched her senses like the wolf, listening as each step brought the hunters closer. And then the sound came again, and she knew it for cloth and leather rubbing together.

The scouts. They would pass Aranur first. Had he left a track on the trail? No, he was as careful as she was. Now she could hear them clearly, and there were at least three. *I hear them, Gray One,* she told the wolf.

There are more behind those that you hear now. The image the wolf sent was of three men, one of them carrying a basket, and then the sharp sounds of two more. Dion resisted the temptation to hold her breath. In the first group, one of the men paused, his soft boots losing their rhythm as he scanned the brush, but his eyes passed over the flat meadow and went to the trees and shrubs instead. The wolfwalker did not move. Then the junko birds, scolding at the man on the path, dropped down to a lower branch, and she heard his soft snort of humor before his feet moved on.

Dion remained still. Another four minutes. Ten. The gnats found her legs and then her face and hovered overhead, but she did not wave them away. As another pair of junkos joined the couple on the branch above, Dion watched them as they watched the trail. A moment later she heard the pair of men padding after the first three. She wished she dared to raise her head to see them, but Hishn warned her again.

They run with purpose, the gray wolf sent. *They run with the others, I can hear the steel against the leather from here.*

Dion hid her smile. Hishn's voice held as much disdain as dislike. *Are these the last?*

I hear no more along the trail.

Dion broke off their silent speech, holding still as the new scouts' footsteps became audible and padded by the clearing.

She waited until they had faded to silence before querying the wolf again.

It is safe, Hishn sent back.

They do not scout behind them, sent a second wolf, who appeared on the trail as Dion sat up quietly.

The woman met the strange wolf's eyes. *Gray One,* she sent softly, *you honor me.*

You run with the pack, the other wolf returned. It trotted after the scouts and disappeared.

Hishn ghosted down from the hill as Dion carefully replaced the clump of grass she had pulled out and made her way back to the path. She glanced around but could only sense Aranur through the Gray Ones; his hiding place was perfect to her. Aranur, seeing that she was up, appeared suddenly from beside the rootball, and she grinned.

"Another game you learned from your Uncle Gamon?" she asked softly as she returned the healer's band to her forehead and settled her warcap firmly on top of the rest of her loose hair.

The lean man looked after the scouts. "My uncle has taught me many things," he returned soberly.

The look on his face . . . the way his hand gripped his sword . . . Dion's eyes shadowed, and she turned away from the pain of his memory. One of his girl cousins had died from a raider's sword not three ninans before. And a merchant—another of Aranur's friends—had died that way, as well. Neither the speed of Aranur's sword nor the edge of his will had been able to save them. Nor the healing skill of Dion's hands. She stared at the man, but her eyes did not see. There were ghosts in her past, too, that haunted her skills, souls whose faces were both old and young. She could not carry his ghosts, as well.

The wolf nudged her hand and whined softly.

"Come on," Aranur said harshly. "Let's go."

Chapter 2

Question of the elders at the Test of Abis:
  If you took Danger
  And distilled it
  And drank it,
  What would it taste like?

An hour later, Aranur and Dion had found fresh signs of Aranur's uncle, Gamon, and the others. The wolfwalker was leading. With Hishn to send her Gamon's scent, Dion moved quickly, glancing and choosing trails unerringly while the tall man behind her kept a keener watch for scouts. Dion's gaze was distant, as if she were sensing the trails more through the gray wolf than her own eyes, but it sharpened when the sound of a twig snapping brought her up short. It was only a fleeing treecat, and Aranur shrugged wryly. Hishn, who snorted at the two humans' alarm, trotted on ahead, and Dion smiled briefly. The Gray One was getting hungry, and the treecat had been a reminder that hunger was a drive that could not be ignored. The wolfwalker promised Hishn a hunt in half an hour or less. Hishn, looking longingly after the treecat, whined softly and paralleled the healer along the trail.

A few meters later, Dion paused and chose one of the paths that forked before her. She had been right; Gamon had taken the group along the rocks to hide their prints, then across a clearing and into the forest on the other side. The tips of the grass were still bent back from their passage. Aranur jogged up beside her, and she pointed to one side where they could cross the same expanse without leaving as many marks.

Hishn, taking the chance to join them and cadge a petting, nudged Dion's hand. *The tracks are fresh,* she offered. *I can smell Gamon's sweat.*

Dion scratched the wolf's ears absently. *And I can smell his temper from here. He and Rhom are not going to be happy about carrying our packs this far without us.*

Rhom should not complain. Your pack weighs less than a ninan-old pup.

It's not my pack I'm thinking of, Dion returned. *And it would not be Rhom carrying my pack, but Gamon, since my pack is lighter and Gamon is older. My brother would be carrying Aranur's pack, and that piece of luggage weighs half as much as you.*

The wolf looked at Aranur and her yellow eyes gleamed, but Dion gave her an admonishing look. Hishn licked her long teeth instead.

Ten minutes after that, Dion knew they would come upon Gamon and the others any time. The breeze had not even dulled the edges of the footprints of the two younger girls, and Dion carefully crumbled dirt into the prints, then brushed the marks from the trail with a low-hanging branch. If the light wind held, the tracks would be gone within half an hour, and what was left would look as if the wind had brushed the branch across the path by itself. Hishn told her that the Gray Ones would chase some deer across the trail after they had passed, which would hide the faint prints even more, so Dion stepped carefully across the softer spots in the trail and continued. Aranur, who waited silently while she cleared the trail, gauged the sounds in the woods and then followed, cutting his stride to match hers, while the gray wolf loped ahead.

They had slowed their pace to jog up one last hill when Hishn stopped suddenly. Dion and Aranur froze, then faded back into the brush as Hishn raised her head and sniffed the wind. But it was the image of Dion's brother that the wolf sent to the healer. Smiling, Dion answered silently, and Hishn grinned, disappearing into the brush for her promised hunt.

Dion smiled faintly. "Up there," she said softly to Aranur. "It's Rhom."

Her brother, as if called by the wolf's warning, got to his feet at the top of the hill. He smiled as they stepped forward, though his glance was sharp as it took in the mud on Aranur's mail. "What took you so long?" he asked, waiting for the two to climb the hill before leading them into a dip that was hidden from below.

"Masa." Aranur gestured behind him with his chin. He nodded a greeting to his uncle, Gamon, as he crested the top of the dip, then smiled briefly at his sister and the other two youths.

"Was it bad?" Rhom asked quietly.

"Bad enough," Aranur returned noncommittally, and the blacksmith, with a glance at the others, nodded without questioning further. He would ask Dion later what had happened. If Aranur did not want to mention the masa in front of the girls, he understood. The young cousins had not grown up in the forest like Dion and Rhom. Rhom did not want to add more fear to their dreams than was already there.

Behind him, Dion looked back over their trail once more before joining her brother in the hidden meadow. There was no obvious trace of their passage, but she frowned. That the scouts were concentrating on this area—had there been something left behind, something crucial that told the scouts where to look for them? Not even the youngest, Tyrel, was sloppy on the trail. All of them knew the risks of being so close to the borders of the county of Bilocctar. What with Longear's scouts and Zentsis's soldiers cutting them off from their own county, they had been doubly careful. But, she admitted silently, the scouts were here. The trail of seven people was not an easy thing to hide. And if Dion could follow the trail as easily as she had, then Longear's scouts could see it, as well.

She glanced around the hidden gully. If they were already within the borders of Bilocctar, they would be considered spies. Longear . . . it all came back to Longear. They knew from the letters they had stolen that it was he, the head of the Lloroi Zentsis's secret service, who was directing the raiders against Aranur's county, Ariye. Longear, not Zentsis, was paying slavers to steal women and children like Aranur's sister and cousins. And it was Longear who had forced them to flee when they stole the letters and learned of Zentsis's war plans. But how Longear could have anticipated their trek across the mountains Dion could not understand. Yet there were signs of scouts all along the borders—the very borders that Aranur and the others would have to cross if they were ever to get back to Ariye. And if even one of their camps had been located . . .

No. She shook her head. She had chosen most of their camps herself. Picked places in the middle of bramble patches and unexpected clearings in rock piles far from the game trails. She would bet that it was not from campsites that the scouts had found them—if, indeed, they had been found yet. Dion reached in her mind for the Gray One, but found no solace in the distant lupine mind.

She sighed and dropped to the ground. The throb of her exhausted feet beat at her with every pulse. Rhom glanced across the clearing and grinned. "Footsore?"

"Stepped on a sharp rock."

He motioned at the leather soles that were thin as paper. "You need new boots, Dion."

She quirked her eyebrow. "When we get to a shoemaker, I'll have some proper ones made. Until then, it's loose leather and calluses for me."

He chuckled.

Dion glanced around the clearing. Besides her brother, there were two men: Gamon, the eldest; and Aranur, his nephew. Then there were the two girls and the boy. It was strange, the wolfwalker thought, how Tyrel, at fifteen the youngest in the group, seemed so much stronger than his older sister. Sandy hair, clear blue eyes, a smattering of freckles across his nose. He was already taller than Dion, but certainly lanky; his strength lay more in his stubborn will than in his shoulders. He was the son of Aranur's Lloroi, the leader of Ramaj Ariye. And it would be Tyrel who would one day lead Aranur's people. If, Dion reminded herself soberly, the boy stayed alive long enough to earn that post.

Tyrel's sister, Namina, was barely as tall as Dion, but she was as slender as Tyrel was lanky. She had brown hair as dark as Tyrel's was light. Their blue eyes were the same, but where Tyrel gave off the brash confidence of youth, Namina had an air of depression—the aura of a person who did not care whether she lived or died. She was barely seventeen, the Age of Promising, but she walked like an old woman. Her eyes were deep and withdrawn.

And then there was Shilia. Aranur's sister was as bright as Namina was dark. Her hair was light brown, and her eyes green. She had the same straight nose as Aranur; her cheeks were high and fine-boned, and there was a lightness and grace to her step when she walked. Dion had noticed long before Rhom that Shilia was interested in him. The blacksmith had finally caught on. Since then, he and Shilia had become close—perhaps closer than Aranur would have wished. But Shilia was also twenty years old—three years past the Age of Promising—and Aranur had no right to judge her friendships.

Gamon looked to be three times as old as the others. His gray hair, left long and braided in the back and cut short on the sides in the style of old-times weapons masters, bristled out from under his warcap. His nose, once straight like Aranur's, was bent and ridged from both fists and blades. He had gray eyes, too, but where Aranur's seemed young, Gamon's eyes were as old as the moons. He was as tall as Aranur, but his shoulders were less broad, and he tended to favor one knee when he ran. Dion knew that her pack was light, but carrying it along with his own had taken its toll on Gamon. When she looked at him, settling his single pack on his shoulders and urging the two girls to get up again, she could see the dull burn of pain that was written into the fine lines of his face. His knees were no longer as strong as hers, yet he had carried her pack for her without complaint. She owed him a healing.

And then there was Rhom. Dion smiled slightly as she looked at her brother. He was standing beside Aranur, and watching the two men together, she was struck again by their similarities. It was not their physical looks, though they both had dark hair. Rhom, her twin, was violet-eyed like herself, though his eyes were darker and his face craggy and weathered where hers was smooth. He was burly like an ox; Aranur was tall and lean like a straight line of steel. Dion's smile widened slightly at the comparison. Not even the hands of the two men were the same. Rhom's hands were thickly muscular and scarred by burns and cuts from the smithy, and his shoulders were broad and thick, as well. Aranur's shoulders were broad but not heavy, and his hands, strong and lean like the rest of him, wore only the long straight scars of the blades that had cut through his gauntlets some time in the past.

No, what made the two men alike was not their coloring or build. It was the aura of power that clung to each man's shoulders. Rhom's power: tense and silent, as if it was contained by his strength. And Aranur's: taut and yet relaxed, as if it lay like a pool of light, waiting only to be focused into a lancelike bolt of lightning. Yes, she thought, it was the way they shifted—the way they watched the woods around them, aware of each sound and smell. Their very movements spoke of a quiet danger that could be unleashed before their thoughts called them to action. Dion smiled again to herself. As the others returned to the trail, she followed her brother, silently slipping through the brush like a Gray One herself. She was unaware that she wore that same aura of distilled danger like a cloak, her eyes quick and clear as she catalogued the sounds around her, and her hand resting easily on the hilt of her own sword. The three of them—Aranur, Rhom, and Dion, their leather mail and leggings dark and dirty from the ninans it had taken to cross the mountains from the sea, and their faces lean and worn and wary with the long journey on short rations—moved as one down the path, their steps silent and their passage as faint as the mark of a winter fog on a wet wharf.

Two kilometers down the trail, Hishn joined them again, first as a shadow that seemed to melt from shrub to shrub, and then, as she loped closer to the small group, as a solid image, still silent, but now in sight. Gamon, who was leading the group, was glad it was not him that the Gray One hunted. He had seen enough of the wolves to realize that the Gray Ones could be a greater threat than most men knew. And they guarded the wolf-walker as if she were one of their own pack—something that Gamon did not completely disbelieve of Dion. He smiled to himself. There was the same wildness in Dion that there was in the wolves, a wildness he glimpsed only as a storm that pulled at the wolfwalker when the Gray Ones ran. And Dion was young. She had not yet learned the depth of that storm.

Hearing the woman's soft feet pad along the path behind his nephew, Gamon glanced back and saw her eyes unfocused with the sense of the wolves. He wondered if, had he been given the chance, he would have run with the Gray Ones, too.

It was barely an hour later when he called the group to a halt to make camp for the night. The stunted blaze that Rhom and Aranur built against the exposed rock of a ridge let them cook the game birds Gamon had shot down, but it would still be a slim meal.

"Try one of these," Shilia offered, handing Dion a tuber.

Dion accepted it with rueful thanks. "I think I've eaten my weight in these things in the last ninan." When Shilia laughed, Dion added, "It's getting so that when I see one of these plants, I run the other way."

"No wonder you stay out in the hills so long," the brown-haired girl teased. "You're trying to avoid the potato plants. And I thought it was because of Aranur's bossy ways."

Dion chewed noisily on the root. "He's only bossy with you

because you're his sister," she said sourly. "He's just plain arrogant with me."

"At least he notices you." The girl looked pointedly at Namina.

The wolfwalker followed her gaze. "Namina will pay more attention to life in time, Shilia," she said quietly. "She will get better once we get her home to Ariye."

Shilia looked unconvinced. She opened her mouth, but her stomach growled just then. She stared at her stomach, looked at the root in her hand, and made a face. "Even my stomach is tired of these things. There's Rhom," she said suddenly, getting up.

Dion smiled as Shilia crossed the clearing to join the black-smith. But the thought of food stayed with her. That their bellies growled was nothing new. There was little large game here; hunting had already taken them too far out of their way four times. It was as if something had frightened the bigger animals away. There was not enough masa to account for the lack of deer, she mused. What if Aranur was right? If Zentsis's and Longear's men were already thick in these hills, they would have killed enough game for themselves in a ninan to move the rest of the herds south into the mountains. Dion scowled. The Gray Ones were not thick here either, she realized. Where she now saw one or two at a time, just nine days earlier—one ninan—she had run into packs of eight and ten.

Her eyes absently followed Namina, who had left to go to the stream with Tyrel, and she blinked as Gamon came up and squatted beside her.

"It's quiet," the older man said.

Dion stirred, and Hishn's head fell off the healer's lap with a *thwump*. With a soft growl, the wolf shoved her nose back under Dion's hand. Dion, smiling to herself at the Gray One's command, scratched the creature under the chin. "Too quiet," she said in answer to Gamon's comment. "And yet too noisy."

"She senses this, too?"

Dion nodded slowly. "There's not enough big game. And the small creatures are uneasy."

"Well, we're close enough to the border that we should expect it."

Dion hesitated, and Hishn got up, stretched with a toothy yawn, and trotted down the gully into the night. The wolf-walker stared after the wolf and chewed her lip. "I want to scout back along our trail tomorrow, Gamon."

Aranur, standing nearby, looked over at her, gauging the weariness of her eyes against the strength of her voice. He shook his head as he joined Gamon beside her. "After what you ran into today, Dion? No. Look, if the scouts are following us, there's little we can do about it except be more careful on the trail. And waiting for you to return would put us all that much closer to the scouts' blades."

"You'd not have to wait for us. Hishn and I can catch up."

"And if you run into trouble by yourself? Take Gamon with you. Then you'd be safer and we wouldn't have to wait."

She shook her head. "Gamon—no offense—" she said hastily to the gray-haired man, "would slow me down."

The old weapons master chuckled. "And that gray-eared mutt of yours would chew my butt for falling behind if I did."

She grinned.

But Aranur frowned. "Then stay only a half hour behind us, Dion. That would give you enough distance to know if Longear's men are actually trailing us or just patrolling this side of the border."

Dion pictured the trail as they had run it that day. "Staying a half hour behind you won't make the difference, Aranur. If it did, you and I would have picked up whatever it is the scouts are following when we trailed Gamon back earlier."

Gamon nodded at his nephew. "You followed us long enough to see what marks we left."

"The marks were slight," Dion stated. "And Hishn helped us find them."

The wolfwalker's tact made Gamon smile.

"It will take much more time than half an hour to find out what the scouts are doing, Aranur," Dion continued.

Aranur considered that. "How much time?"

"Four hours, maybe five. If I don't find traces by then, the scouts must have a way to track us that I won't be able to see. Carrier birds, perhaps."

Aranur shook his head. "Not out here. The forest is too dense, and the lepa and other aerial predators too fierce. Carrier birds can get a message through to another post, but would not be able to circle or glide to watch our steps from the air."

She shrugged. "Well, I won't be gone more than half a day. And besides, with Hishn's help, I'll be able to see any scouts before they see me."

He smiled without humor. "And what if you're seen anyway?"

"This gully isn't safe either, Aranur. Do you want to wait here until the scouts find us?"

He chuckled. "Gamon is wrong about you," he said with a sideways look at his uncle's raised eyebrows. "You couldn't be a moonmaid. You're far too practical." He ignored Gamon's guffaw. "A moonwarrior, perhaps," he added, "with those violet eyes and the sword at your belt, but not a moonmaid." He looked at the sky to judge the time. "You have the last watch," he pointed out. "If I sit in for you, you can take off early, before the rest of the group is up and before any scout hits the trail. With luck, you should be back by the time we are ready to leave. As long as you don't stop for nonessentials," he added sharply.

"I was gone only a few hours today."

Gamon gave her a measuring look, cutting off Aranur's acid comment before his nephew could speak. "You were gone six hours before that, Healer," he said quietly. "And then another two this afternoon before Aranur came after you."

Dion sighed.

Aranur nodded. "I don't need to worry about you day and night, Dion. For this, you can just let the Gray Ones do the tracking. You shouldn't have to go more than a kilometer yourself."

The slender woman raised her eyebrows. "The wolves are not the guides you think they are, Aranur. I can see through Hishn, yes. But the others—I can speak with them only. They are not pets, to be ordered around." She frowned at him. "They work with me as a favor to Hishn and as an honor to the ancients who gave them the Voice in the first place."

Aranur shrugged. "I've seen you bond with other wolves, Dion. Remember when you called that pack in the mountains? And that time Rhom and I saw you healing the Gray One off-trail? And Rhom says you did that many times in the mountains in Randonnen, your own county."

"That is not bonding," she objected. Gamon raised his eyebrows again, and Dion shook her head. "That is merely a merging of thoughts and senses."

"It seems to work as well as your bond with Hishn," Gamon said.

Dion was silent for a moment. "There is no love or loyalty in a merging," she said finally. "There is respect, but respect is not enough to let them break a merging right away. They have needs that I feel as a wolfwalker. And when there are more than two or three, their needs are ten times as strong because they are combined." Aranur frowned at her, and she added, "Running with them is like a merging, Aranur. And to track with them, I will have to run with the pack."

Gamon gave her a thoughtful look.

"But you can call them?" Aranur asked.

She shrugged. "When there are more than four or five, I don't call them so much as they call me." She looked up at him. "And the call is strong, Aranur. To run with them, that will take some time."

He snorted. "If it takes too much time, you could very well run into the scouts that are running after us."

Gamon chuckled. "The healer might not be able to call the wolves herself, Aranur, but I'd bet a month's pay that if she ran into Zentsis's scouts, the scouts would turn tail and head the other way. And they'd have a pack of Gray Ones at their backs howling the hunt all the way to Breinington."

"Being a wolfwalker has its advantages," Dion admitted with a grin.

Aranur was not smiling. "I realize that, Dion." He gave her a sharp look. "Sometimes I can hear Hishn as well as you."

"Like Rhom," she admitted, "when you meet Hishn's eyes, and when she opens her mind to you, then yes, you can hear her. But you don't feel as I do. You don't smell from her nose or see through her eyes. If the link between you and me was not so strong—" she blushed at Gamon's sly look "—Hishn would not hear your voice in her mind either."

"The question is, Dion," Gamon returned, sober now, "not whether they can take care of you on the trail, but can they take care of Longear's traps? Zentsis and his man Longear have driven us far from our home to keep us away from Ariye. They want us badly. With the seven of us dead, Zentsis's war plans would remain a secret, and our elders would be ignorant until he marches across our own borders with the raiders leading the way. The closer we get to Bilocctar—if we are not already within its borders—the more traps there will be." He ran his hand through his silvered hair. "Remember Sidisport? And Red Harbor?"

Aranur frowned. "In a few more days, Longear's scouts could have us pinpointed within a few kilometers."

"Longear's scouts, no matter how good, are still men," Dion returned.

He gave her a sharp look. "And you run like a ghost," he

said flatly. He stared into the darkness. "All right," he said finally. "You'll have two hours before dawn. We'll wait until eight for you to return, so you will have another three hours to find out how close Zentsis's and Longear's men are to finding us." He got to his feet.

"Zentsis's men should not find us before that, Healer," Gamon added.

Dion turned away to lay out her bedroll, but Aranur leaned down and touched her arm.

"Run safely tomorrow, Dion," he said quietly. He opened his mouth to add something else, but Tyrel called to him softly from across their camp. He turned and strode away.

She looked after him for a long moment, then shook her blankets out and lay back as Gamon had already done. As she waited for Hishn to return from hunting while the moons crawled slowly across the sky, her ears followed Aranur and her eyes took his image into her dreams.

She wakened to the sense of someone moving beside her. Her hand tightened on her long knife, and she opened her eyes, but she knew at once that half the night had passed. There were six moons in the sky, and beside her, her brother was rolling out his blanket and readying himself for his own watch. She must have been tired to sleep so soundly. She had not even noticed Hishn returning. Had it not been for the warmth against her side, she would not have known where the Gray One had settled for the night. Rhom, hearing his sister's breathing change, paused for a moment. Hishn stirred, and Dion sleepily scratched the wolf's neck behind her ears to soothe her back into her dreams.

"You have last watch?" Rhom asked quietly as he squatted beside his sister and strapped his sword to his hip.

"Wake me a little early," she murmured, burrowing further into the gray wolf's warmth. "Hishn and I are going to scout the trail before dawn. Aranur will take last watch instead."

He grinned. "You probably just tell the Gray Ones to do your scouting for you while you sit in a hidden meadow and daydream."

"You know perfectly well it doesn't work that way," she retorted. "As if you would notice anyway. Once you hit the ground, you snore like a badgerbear."

He chuckled, but his tone was softer when he answered. "Get some sleep, Dion. I'll wake you when it's time."

It was almost exactly two hours before dawn when Rhom

woke his twin. He touched her gently under her ear, and she stopped breathing for a second, then resumed, her eyes opening sharply as she smoothed her breath automatically. To one who could not see her eyes, she had merely caught her breath in a dream.

After rolling to her feet, Dion took only a moment to wrap her bedroll and strap it to her pack. Rhom, knowing that she had what she needed in her belt pouches, wordlessly bound her thin pack to his own. As she slung her bow loosely on her back in place of her pack, eyeing her preparations, he silently pulled his extra knife from his belt and offered it to her along with one of his boot knives. The wolfwalker gave him a smile that did not reach her eyes, but she accepted them both. The boot knife was tucked into her right moccasin, where she had kept her own before losing it a few ninans earlier, and the longer sheath was snapped quickly onto her belt. Opposite her sword and her own long knife, the extra blade was a reassurance. Like Rhom, Dion preferred fighting with both hands when it came to blades. As their father often told them, better to parry with steel than flesh.

Hishn, watching the two, stirred finally, stretched, and got to her feet, yawning at their movements. But when Dion motioned, the wolf melted into the woods. The Gray One did not wake anyone else, though Dion's movements caused Gamon to stir in his sleep and Shilia to murmur. Rhom would have shaken Aranur before Dion left, but she held her finger to her lips, and her brother grinned tiredly. Aranur and Dion had spoken civilly to each other the previous night, but the two had been clashing lately. He knew his sister would rather be out of camp when Aranur rose to take her watch. Dion waved and followed the gray wolf down the gully.

The night is quick, Hishn sent as she trotted ahead of the healer. *You must run silent, or the prey will turn.*

Dion smiled. *Gray One, my prey are the hunters, not the deer whose scent tickles your nose. I want the ones who follow us so closely instead.*

The wolf paused and sniffed the air, and Dion, waiting, stepped into a shadow where the moonlight did not fall.

They are not yet near, Hishn told her. *There is no scent of other men.*

Dion nodded. *Then let's follow our trail back until we come to the place where we met up with Gamon earlier. Dawn will be close enough by then that we should be able to see our traces well.*

I can smell your tracks as easily in the dark as in the light, Hishn complained, looking back at the healer and panting softly. *And the deer are close.*

Dion shook her head. *I have to see our trail with the eyes of a human hunter, Gray One. Otherwise we'll never know how the scouts found us.*

Hishn growled low in her throat, but she led off again, her nose dipping occasionally to the ground as she loped. Dion, running behind, knew better than to follow too closely. The Gray One was not like a hound. The wolf continually stopped without warning and turned abruptly back to pick up the scents she had not caught as she ran. And Dion, watching her footing and the treacherous sticks that reached up ankle high, could trip as easily on the wolf when Hishn halted in front of her as on the branches that stuck out over the dark path.

The six moons lit the trail brightly, and they made good time. Although Dion worried at first that they could run right over a camp of scouts, the gray wolf reassured her that there were no men close by. According to the wolf, they were safe on the path for at least an hour. By the time the black shadows had become a light gray, the wolfwalker had reached the spot where Gamon said they had stopped for a break half an hour before she and Aranur had joined the others the day before. She glanced around. She was a few kilometers beyond where she and Aranur had met up with Gamon, and her legs had long since passed the state in which they complained about the pace. She was ready to rest.

We can wait for full light here, she told the wolf. She would need to be able to see Gamon's backtrail clearly from that point on.

Hishn's eyes gleamed dully in the gray light. *The field rats are thick in these clearings.* Her voice was wistful, and Dion, feeling the gray beast's hunger, smiled briefly and shoved the wolf away.

Go get your breakfast, she told Hishn. *I'm going down to the stream, and I'll be there for a while.*

The wolf disappeared without further urging. Dion, catching the edges of the Gray One's hunt, knew that Hishn's mind would soon be unreadable. The bloodlust of the Gray Ones was strong. She closed her mind to most of Hishn's thoughts, and thought instead of Gamon's trail as she made her way toward the small river. According to Gamon, Namina and her brother Tyrel had refilled their water bags there.

The place where Tyrel had chosen to reach the water was a pocket in a tumble of granite boulders. Once inside the pocket, Dion rounded a rock and found that the twisted path opened onto the stream suddenly. Back on the main trail, the ground had hidden the stone beneath a thin layer of soil, but here, where the ground was exposed to the wind from the cut in which the river ran, the rocks were dried and old, crawling beside the stream like ancient badgers. Crumbled stone formed paths that held no prints of wildlife, and the swathes of vines and shrubs that grew up the sides of the massive rocks hid lichen that was hundreds of years old itself, judging by the width of the orange and purple growth rings. The wolfwalker glanced around as the sky lightened. In spite of the exposed stone, there was enough brush there that even if Gamon had taken his whole group through, the shrubs would have sprung back and covered his trail within hours. She could see nothing that would cause another tracker to suspect that path.

But there had to be something. Even if they had already crossed Bilocctar's borders, Zentsis—and Longear—would have no reason to place scouts so thickly unless Aranur and the rest had been discovered. She found herself waiting impatiently for dawn's light. The moons were no help in the pre-dawn gray. They only made the shadows at the base of the boulders seem darker, and she wanted to run the trail quickly. But all she could do for the moment was wait.

She leaned her head against the cool stone as if it would clear her head by its touch, but a glint of light caught her eye as the sun finally broke over the top of one of the round rocks.

Dion glanced to her left, then frowned. Two long threads dangled from an overhanging branch at the stream, and she straightened and reached for them, untangling them from the limb on which they had caught. Her face was suddenly serious. Threads from Namina's tunic. The young girl had stood too suddenly, gotten caught, and yanked herself free. And Tyrel had missed it. Dion wound the threads around her finger until they formed a knot, then tucked the tiny bundle into one of her belt pouches.

It was lighter now, and Dion, after returning to the main trail, followed Gamon's path back another two kilometers until it led her to the creek again. From there, the path broke away from the stream. She dipped a hand to the water and sipped warily, watching the banks above and below her as she did so. She considered her position. If Namina and Shilia had been careless near the water, the scouts might be following the stream, not Gamon's trail, as Aranur had thought. If that was true, then she should stay with the stream. She had found little on the trail itself. Although, if she waded downriver, the noise of the water would make it more difficult to hear, and the reflection of light on water would trick her eyes into seeing movement in the forest when there was none. She would have to rely more on Hishn's ears and eyes than her own. After a moment, she dried her hand absently on her leggings, then waded into the knee-deep water, grimacing at its chill.

Around her, the water burbled at her calves, and she made her way over the river rocks easily, avoiding the few places where mud had settled between them. The current ran quickly, but though the few snails she disturbed would climb back on their perches within minutes, a footprint could stay in a sheltered pocket of silt for hours.

She saw no sign of Zentsis's scouts on the banks, but the creek was winding through an increasingly rocky canyon where debris cluttered the eddies that clung to the higher walls. Hishn, on the west side of the stream, had sensed no one nearby, but Dion was uneasy. She scanned the banks carefully.

Half an hour later, Dion was almost convinced that there was nothing in the river to betray Gamon's group. Aside from the two threads from Namina's tunic, she had found nothing amiss, and the water, deeper since another creek had joined the first, was cold and fast, prompting her to withdraw when possible. She had already climbed out several times to pass small falls. The last fall, a good five meters high, had forced her back upstream before she found a clear place to get out and make her way around. The overhanging trees and the steepness of the walls over what had become a widening river did not allow for quick passage, and once inside the rocky canyons, Dion had to allow for more time to retrace her steps. She paused at the edge of a deep pool, which she would have to swim in order to reach the next shallow stretch of rocks. She made a face at herself. Her leggings were already heavy and so stretched by the water, that she had had to stuff them deeper in her boots. If she continued, her tunic and jerkin would be in the same chilled state, as well. But, she admitted, it would take another ten or fifteen minutes to work her way back upstream far enough to go around again. Hishn appeared briefly as a silhouette at the top of the canyon, and Dion smiled. The wolf was not one to get herself wet if she could help it, and the Gray One's amusement at Dion's determination was clear. But Dion could waste no more time.

With that thought, she waded deeper into the pool until the cold water reached her thighs and threatened her footing. Beneath her feet, the river rocks shifted awkwardly, clacking and burping with suddenly freed air pockets. Above the water, Dion's teeth chattered to punctuate the rocks' rhythm. Best to get it over with quickly, she thought. She shook to rid herself of her shivers, then took a breath and knelt until the current pulled at her neck. The shock of the cold water forced her breath from her lips, but she struck out in a strong side stroke while the water pulled her along and the weight and drag of her sword and bow pulled her legs down awkwardly in the water. Kicking vigorously, she kept her head above water. A few seconds later, her knees hit stone painfully and she scrambled against the current onto a more shallow plateau, her breathing fast and deep with the exertion. Her jerkin hung down heavily, and the water that weighted it dripped off in steady runnels, but the sound was drowned in the rush and clutter of the river where it crossed rocks a few meters away and dropped again.

There were still no signs to indicate people. No cloth torn from a shirt in a crossing; no shards of arrows floating in the stream. No upturned rocks or shifted logs where a man had been careless or a young girl had slipped. Dion shook her head. *Gray One*, she called as she shivered in the wet chill of her tunic. *Do you sense anything on the path?*

Only Gamon's day-old scent. What my eyes see is not what you would recognize. No other human would know this trail.

The wolfwalker frowned. Finally she wrung out the edges of her tunic and waded toward the shallow rush of water that led on down the river. She had rounded a bend and reached open ground again when the canyon walls fell away abruptly on one side of the river and the water curled and boiled from currents that cut across each other over the hidden bottom boulders. Something caught her gaze. Tracks. And not those of Gamon or his group. She dropped lower in the water and made her way near enough to the shore that she could cling to a submerged log and hide in a shadow.

The footprints in the nearby mud were fresh. Dion, close enough to see the sharp edges of the tracks, stayed on her knees, leaving only her neck and face above the surface. She shivered constantly, but forced herself to memorize the prints. There had been three men, she saw, and they had come by this morning: their tracks obscured those of the night animals, and only a few morning bird tracks marred the freshness of the men's. Hishn, who was trailing from the top of a bald ridge, pulled her lips back from her teeth, and the wolfwalker smiled without humor, her expression like that of the wolf. The Gray One answered with another snarl, dropping to the ground and laying her head on her forepaws as she watched her companion below.

The current tugged at Dion's legs, and her scabbard banged gently against her thigh with each surge of the stream. From where she was kneeling, she could see the tracks clearly, and she stared at them until she knew them and their owners by heart. One of the scouts was tall and thin: his stride was too long for a short man, and the prints did not sink deeply into the damp soil. He turned his right foot out slightly. The wound that had caused his foot to turn out must have been old: he did not walk with a limp. The second man, the one with the burden, was of average height and build, but had large feet. Whatever burden he carried, it was in a basket rather than a pack; the imprint where it had been set down was sharp and round rather than dull and shapeless. Dion puzzled over the basket, but then turned her attention to the third set of tracks. This man was tall like the first one, but built more like Rhom, she suspected. Even though the scout was careful to place his feet where they would leave light tracks, his weight was heavier in the dry soil than it should have been. He had studied the river as she was studying the bank, and she looked around thoughtfully, wondering what he had seen.

She eased herself over the log and close to shore—and then halted. There, in an eddy not three meters away and barely a meter to the left of the tracks of the scouts was what she had been searching for. Not a careless track, a broken branch, or the silt from the upstream crossing, but something else. A washcloth. It floated against a branch in the water and called itself to the eye by its flatness where the branches and grasses were sharp lines in the water.

Dion splashed through the water, losing her footing once as she stepped in a hole. The river closed over her shoulders and dragged her along several meters before she could get her legs back under her. Then the stream tugged at her clothes, urging her past the eddy where the water ran slow and shallow, but Dion caught hold of a long log and pulled herself back. The thick cloth swirled and tucked itself under the edge of another branch, only to wash out again with the river's surge. Behind her, a river snake's head floated gently to the surface, but she paid no attention; only mud and stone-suckers were dangerous, and they preferred a wide or sluggish river or swamp to the clear running flow of this stream. No, it was not mud eels that worried her. It was the glint of light off Namina's washcloth that caught Dion's attention and fear.

She pulled the cloth off the log. The fabric had not been in the water for long—there was little dirt caught in its weave. If Dion had been one of Longear's men, she would have known that she was not far behind her prey. That clump of cloth was like a road sign pointing upstream.

Her face grim, Dion looked back up the cliff. *Gray One*, she sent urgently, *cross over. We must get back. These tracks are fresh from this morning.*

She broke off. Something brushed against her arm, and, looking down, she gasped and thrust herself back abruptly. The long, thin shape that had found its way to the river's surface was not a water snake as she had thought. There was an open ring of teeth where its jaw should have been, and it had no eyes.

"Ugh!"

She yanked her knife from its sheath. The mudsucker swirled. It avoided the knife easily and curled back at her naked hand. It was not a large sucker, but even a small one should not have been in a stream like this . . . The wolfwalker stumbled back, keeping her eye on the mudsucker and trusting her feet to find a way toward shore. She shoved the sucker away again, using the sleeve of her leather jerkin to thwart its sinuous dodge toward her bare skin. The water was still thigh deep, and she could wade only slowly, stabbing at the eel until her knees came clear and she could thrust her way to the shore. In a second, she was perched on a boulder a long meter above the stream, and the mudsucker, unable to find its prey, circled aimlessly before tucking its tail down into the rocks again, anchoring its length in the mud and letting only its head float to the surface. With its mouth closed, its head looked like a fish holding its position in the current; the suckers often fed on birds lured into trying their luck on such a fish. This sucker was only three feet long, but its anchor would hold against a pull of fifty times its own strength. A victim would be drawn down slowly and surely until the water closed over its head and it drowned, drained of blood by the rings of hollow teeth that spiraled down inside the sucker's gullet.

Dion swallowed her bile. There were few things that disgusted her as much as parasites.

Still clutching the wet washcloth, she made her way cautiously from one boulder to the next until she was far enough upstream that the mudsucker was out of sight. She did not understand what the sucker had been doing there in the first place. Mudsuckers should not have been able to find their way up or down this stream—there were too many rocks; it was too shallow, the water too clear, and the current too fast. They could live in clear water, yes. But they did not travel in such streams. They needed the mud to warm themselves and breed in. Glancing back once more to make sure the sucker had not eased its way after her, Dion shook her head. Perhaps a bird had caught it, flown a ways, and then dropped it again when it became too heavy. An easy explanation—but she was still disturbed.

Dion wrung out the cloth and tucked it into the same pouch that held the threads. With their lives at stake, that Namina could be so careless . . .

Worried, the wolfwalker tracked Hishn in her head, listening for a moment to the Gray One's thoughts as the wolf ran across the ridge rocks. *Cross where the river runs fast,* Dion warned the wolf. *If there is one sucker in this stream, there may be others, as well.*

Hishn, sensing Dion's repulsion, bared her teeth as she streaked across the trails.

It was an hour past dawn, and it had taken Dion three hours to get this far. But she had moved carefully. Now, having learned how the scouts had found Gamon's group, she did not have to move as slowly. The trail that had taken three hours to follow would take less time to retrace. By the time she got back, Aranur would just be ready to lead the others out of the gully. She dragged herself along a sharp, flat rock that stuck out just above the surface, then waded quickly upstream, keeping to the east side of the river where the shadows still stretched into the water. She could not help thinking that if she had found the washcloth and the threads torn from Namina's tunic only that morning, what else had the girl lost to mark their trail? The scouts would be close enough now that Dion would probably see them before she caught up with Aranur again. He would have to be careful.

And you also, Hishn sent, catching Dion's thoughts on the run and baring her teeth. *The pack is far away, and you run where the hunter can become the prey.*

I know, Gray One. But Zentsis's men should have been on the trail for an hour now. They will not cross back to the creek until they find where we camped. The wolfwalker glanced up at the sky and judged her time. It was more difficult to walk the creek against the current; where the water was deeper and the footing more treacherous, the river pulled her back two meters for every three she swam forward.

She was coming to the short sets of waterfalls that ran the length of the canyon. As she struggled around a small, deep pool, the creek took a sharp bend, and she came up against a row of rock stairs that splashed water across her face as she climbed them. Twice the force of the water almost washed her off the steps, but she did not have time to climb around. She made her climbing holds beneath the surface, her wrists disappearing underwater into the cracks between the stones while the river surged up her arms and blinded her with its changing course.

A kilometer away, Hishn paused on the trail. Her eyes gleamed. *Humans,* she sent, fading like a ghost from the trail.

How many? Dion pulled herself up and slipped over the edge of the waterfall into water that was chest deep. Her bow, still slung across her back, caught for a moment in a crack of the rock, but she eased it free and made her way along the rocks until she reached shallower water.

Two, Hishn finally sent back.

Stay hidden, Gray One.

They cannot see me. They could not see their own shadow in the sunlight.

Dion smiled, then slipped and cut her hand on a sharp rock. She swore silently, sucking at the ragged gash. The water was not cold enough to numb the pain as it had the bruises that marked her shins and knees. By the time she reached the fork in the stream, she had bashed one of her elbows against a stone, as well. Though her leather mail protected her from getting cut, she knew that her skin would be mottled black and blue for a ninan.

She examined the banks critically. Longear's scouts would

have maps, made by Zentsis's soldiers during their long occupation of the territory. So they would know that the river forked here. Unless they were following Aranur's trail exactly, and she doubted that, she should see signs of them where they kept close to the banks to watch for other telltale debris.

She waded upstream another half kilometer, not daring to take to the trail. The scouts were somewhere close, and her wet clothes would drip enough water on land to leave marks even a blind man could follow. She had to wait to go to ground until she found a place where there were enough leaves or rocks to let her run without turning the trail into mud.

In her head, the Gray One's thoughts had grown sharper, but Dion locked all but Hishn's surface thoughts out of her mind. The river had become a tumble of rocks again, and she could not risk the confusion of seeing through two sets of eyes and hearing through two sets of ears. The next kilometer would consist of knee- and thigh-deep wading through fast water, and her footing would be treacherous enough without trusting her weight to a rock that was not there except in her head.

The scouts—was she ahead of or behind them on the trail? In spite of her care, the rocks clacked softly under her feet. The shadows pulled back from the river and left it to the sunlight. Even though she could move faster in the shallower water, she kept her pace slow. At each new stretch of the stream, she stood motionless until she knew the natural movements of the trees and the sounds of the river. Only when she was sure that she did not share each stretch with the scouts did she continue.

Sunlight glinted suddenly in the corner of her eye, and glancing over her shoulder, she froze. There, not twenty meters behind her, were the scouts she thought she had been following. They were making their way along the river, and the only reason they had not yet seen her was that she was standing on the other side of a fallen and floating tree, and the branches of it were thick and tangled. The scouts' leather mail was, like Dion's, the color of the earth and trees, and Dion herself would not have been lucky enough to see them first except that the lead man, a left-handed fighter, wore his sword on his right hip, and the sun had flashed on it.

The wolfwalker sank slowly into the water until only her face showed, then pulled herself along by her arms as quickly as she could. They were coming directly toward the river, but she hoped the snag would hide her long enough for her to make it around the next sharp bend in the river, and by then Hishn would be near enough to help out. In her mind, the sense of the wolf had sharpened with her fear until it had a bitter taste of its own. Hishn had crossed the river and was coming, and coming fast.

Dion hesitated to watch in puzzlement as the scouts dipped their basket into the river, but she saw nothing she could understand about it, and could wait no longer. If the moons were with her, the scouts would go back into the forest and leave the river for a time; they seemed to be stopping only at the deep pools—where debris would be caught in the eddies, she reminded herself. She submerged again. She was chilled to the bone, but she still could not risk running the trail with the scouts so close behind.

She was forced to pull herself along the center of the river as it widened and silt began to build up. If the scouts downstream saw mud suddenly stirred into the water, they would not wait to hunt her down. But she had gone only another fifty meters when she came to another deep pool. She had forgotten that pool. And there was no cover on the opposite bank—there was no real bank, only a wall of rock against which the water curled and flashed away. Hishn, who was ghosting after the scouts, was uneasy as Dion had been earlier. There was an odor to Zentsis's men that brought a snarl to her muzzle, and Dion, reflecting the gray wolf's emotions, found her own teeth bared. She shook off the wolf's images and struck out for the near shore, where there were enough snags and rocks to hide among that even a sharp-eyed scout would miss her. She hesitated once, her toes bouncing her off the bottom of the river as she stood briefly in the sluggish flow, then chose the snags.

She kicked hard to bring herself off the bottom. But her mail dragged her back, and her weapons pulled her down. She was already tired. She ducked her head under the water and pulled the last strokes with the river blinding her eyes until she broke the surface with a silent gasp. Strangling her harsh breathing, she sucked in a breath and held it a second until she could release it more slowly and take another. The scouts? There. By the banks. Fortunately they were not looking in her direction; their attention was on the basket one of them had set down. Dion heard Hishn's snarl in her mind, but ignored it, pulling herself along a thin rubbery branch until her head was flush against the slimy trunk of a snag.

The shadow of a stretched-out log hid her and left a slit where she could watch the scouts from safety. Her legs slipped once on the slick underwater branches, and she cursed at the small splash she made, then pulled her legs as far under her as she could, crossing and tucking them under the log while she wedged her shoulder in tight at a broken bough. The underside of the log was slick with green tendrils that curled around her body, but she could hear the scouts clearly now, and she did not move.

". . . set another out here, Hartis." The man's voice carried easily across the short stretch of water.

"I don't see why we bother. We're close enough now that we'll have them by tomorrow evening."

"Longear will stretch our necks if we don't follow orders. You saw what happened to Errol—there wasn't a big enough piece of him left to pick up."

The third scout nodded. "Besides, ever since we found the hair from that girl's combings three days ago, we've known that they were out here. We hardly needed to see that cloth this morning. We can pick them up within days."

"Not without a lot of men to back us up," the shortest man said.

"Longear knows what he's doing," the first scout returned. "He'll have the manpower ready when he needs it. There's still too much chance our friends from Ramaj Ariye could slip away in the hills if we made our move now. No, Longear will wait till they're closer to the cities."

"And in the meantime . . ."

"And in the meantime, we put the suckers out. Then we keep track of our friends from Ariye. Once they get near Wortenton, we'll nab them neat as a chicken in a pie."

From beneath the debris, Dion was like a log herself, frozen in the wash of the water. The scout had said they would wait till Aranur and the rest of his group were closer to the cities. Did Longear know so much? And what did they mean about putting out the mudsuckers? Were the scouts hunting the eels? If there were any suckers in this water now . . . By the moons, she realized, her hand was still bleeding—a signal for a sucker's supper if ever there was one. And then an image flashed in her mind, and an answering picture from Hishn doubled the vision. Longear. The basket the scouts had been carrying. The pools. The mudsuckers where none should be . . .

Dion's hands crept to her tunic, pulling it tight about her at her waist and neck where it swirled about, exposing her taut flesh to the water. The scouts were not hunting the suckers.

No, Longear would not have ordered them to do that. But "putting the suckers out?" Gods, it could not mean that they were seeding the eels in the streams! She strained to hear the men's voices as they leaned over and muffled their sounds.

". . . only three left," she finally made out.

The tallest scout nodded. "We'll need only two for the last two pools."

"Why seed the pools at all if we're behind the Ariyens?"

"Because they've escaped Longear twice now. They stay close to the water to hide their tracks, and they backtrack almost as much as they go forward. The suckers are insurance. Those eels will keep the Ariyens from crossing the rivers as casually as they have been doing. Even if the suckers get only one of the Ariyens, it makes one less for us to catch. Watch your hand," he said sharply. "They're venomous." He paused, then snapped, "Careful with the lid. Once those things latch on, they don't let go."

"Like Longear," another man muttered.

"Let's just shut up and get this over with," the third man said.

A small splash reached Dion's ears, and she stiffened. She was upstream of the scouts by meters. Had her hand stopped bleeding? She twisted her jerkin tighter.

"Look at that sucker go," one of the scouts said, satisfaction in his voice. "What I'd give to see it latch onto one of those Ariyens. Bet they'll jump clear to the eighth moon when the suckers hit 'em."

"Better get the next one into the release chamber. I'm not going to run trail with the last two loose."

Something touched the wolfwalker's back, and she caught her breath audibly.

All sounds on the banks stopped abruptly.

On the banks, steel came free of its scabbards, and Dion froze. She could still see the scouts, and one of them motioned for the others to spread out. Their eyes darted from one side to the other. Dion glanced wildly over her shoulder. The thing on her back nudged her again, edging down toward her waist.

Hishn? she called urgently. Her neck—was it far enough out of the water?

I am near, the wolf returned quickly. *The scent of the scouts is hot in my nose.*

Come . . . Hurry . . .

In the water, the sucker mouthed her leather mail, testing it for flesh, then sliding around to her side. She hunched further under the log. Her warcap was too round—if the scouts got too close, they would see it for what it was. Or they would see that her legs were not the branches they pretended to be. *Hurry* . . .

One of the scouts stepped into soft mud, and his foot made a splucking sound. But she could not duck under the water. If the sucker found her neck or face, it would kill her. As if drawn by her thought, the eellike creature prodded its way to her stomach, then pressed against her arm.

Wolfwalker, I am here.

The scout stepped into the water.

The sucker touched her wrist. *Draw them away, Hishn. Hurry!*

And then something tore into her hand. She stifled a scream, ducking her face underwater to muffle the sound. The sucker's teeth gashed her clenched hand, and her flesh was sucked up around the hollow fangs. She could not move. Her lips peeled back from her own teeth, which clenched in a silent shriek, and the muscles on her neck stood out.

Hishn's mind grew chaotic. Dion could not read her thoughts. *No! Don't attack,* she cried out in her head. *Hishn, draw them away* . . .

The sucker's teeth ground down, and its tail whipped down to find an anchor in the silt under the log. Dion's hand was yanked from her tunic. No! She balled her fist onto her leather mail and wedged her shoulder harder back against the log. On the shore, the scouts searched the water with their eyes. She must not move. But oh, moons, her hand was being crushed . . .

The sucker yanked again, and Dion jerked, one of her legs hitting a loose snag.

One of the scouts pointed, and the others moved quickly. And then the brush snapped behind them, and they whirled.

"There—"

"In the bushes—"

Hishn streaked away, and the scouts burst after the wolf, crashing through the growth after the sounds of snapping twigs. Dion, her mouth streaming water, raised her head, then threw an arm around the log and unhooked her legs. As they touched the edge of a rock, they brushed against the rigid length of the sucker where its body was a line of steel that bound her to the bottom of the river. She drew her knife from its scabbard and cut at its body near the head. But the blade did not slice through, and the sucker's teeth chewed down harder on her hand, making her cry out even from between her clenched jaws. Fire seared up the veins of her arm. Her right hand opened involuntarily as she jerked, and the knife fell free, disappearing into the murky water as if it had never been. She grabbed after it. But the sucker pulled inexorably down until her legs slipped and her shoulder disappeared under the water again. She swallowed the soft taste of the river and spit it out, shaking her head. Frantically, she groped for the other knife. The sucker's teeth minced her hand and she cried out. She sawed at the eel. Not until Rhom's blade cut up under the scales did the water cloud up with a darker fluid. There was a last tightening of the mudsucker's jaws, and then the body was severed. The head remained locked on her hand. Her blood pumped out in steady trickles from the neck of the eel.

Wolfwalker—

She clung to the log with one hand, the knife washing itself in the river as the green tendrils underneath the dead tree lapped and curled at her with the waves. *Run, Hishn,* she sent. *Don't stop.* She could not stop shuddering. *Don't let them turn back.*

The gray wolf snarled.

Down the trail, Dion repeated, her mind's voice harsh with her pain. *They'll think it's Aranur or one of the others.*

The wolf listened for a second, then growled and dodged around a shrub and landed on another branch, rattling its leaves before leaping off and snapping another clump of twigs.

In the river, Dion dragged herself along the log with one hand, clambering over the draping branches until she reached shallower water, where she crouched, her eyes dark and her face gray with pain. The severed head of the eel still sucked slowly at her hand, each tooth a tiny pump and the fleshy neck a hundred lines of veins. She stared at it with a horrified fascination, finally forcing herself to wrap Namina's washcloth, which she pulled awkwardly from her sopping belt pouch, around the eel's neck so that the blood would not drip on the rocks and paint her trail red.

The fire in her veins reached up into her elbow, and her mind was becoming a blur. Her thoughts followed Hishn. The senses of the Gray One sharpened her own eyes where the fire blinded her. She stumbled along the banks where the water barely covered the rocks but where her wet boots would leave no tracks. She made it ten meters, then twenty, before the blood began to seep through the cloth. She stared at it. The crushed nerves of her hand tore at her senses. There was something in the bite of the suckers. She could feel it, crawling from each tooth like a slow poison up her wrist and into her arm.

"Hishn," she whispered, unaware that she spoke out loud. "Come back."

Wolfwalker . . .

"Gray One—lose them—I need you here."

The answering shaft of thought was like a gray arrow.

She fell to her knees, slamming into and slipping off the round rocks. She did not care. Her knees were numb. She crawled. There were shadows and pools among the boulders. She fell shoulder first into a pocket of the river, her mouth and nose filling suddenly with water until her legs followed and kicked against the rocks to find their way back under her. The wolf growled—or was it Dion? She could still see the river bank—but she could not seem to drag herself out of the water. The rocks were too steep. Too rounded. There was no color in her sight anymore. Movement was more sound and sense than light. She reached for the boulder again, but her arm fell back, listless, and her knees gave out. Was the Gray One near? Hishn's mind was cutting into Dion's thoughts like a knife. Rhom's knife. Was it still in her hand? No, she had dropped it. She reached for it and sank into the pool until she sat, her chest mid-deep in the water and her head lolling against the stone. It was cold. The water was cold like a glass tongue on her skin. It surged and shifted her body into a notch. She would be all right. The water was dark. The water was cool. The shadow was deep. Her knife was only a meter away. And Hishn would find her soon . . .

Chapter 3

There is a point
At which you cannot go further.
You cannot lift another step;
You cannot force your arms against the current;
You cannot suck air into your chest one more time.
Your fingers slip;
You cannot hold on—
And you know that
If you are to live—
To survive—
There is an instant;
A second;
A minute;
—A breath,
A step
Or a struggle;
And a terror that eats at your gut like acid.
And when there is nothing left
With which to fight,
That
Is where fear fails
And courage begins.

She did not know how long she had sat in the river. Her eyes cleared slowly so that she was not sure if it was day or night. But she was cold. The fire that had burned up her arm seemed to have died down, and she felt only a deep chill in her bones and the numbness of her skin pulsing sluggishly with the hammer that pounded her hand. There was a weight on her shoulder. She frowned, baffled by a whine in her ears until she reached up, and Hishn scrambled back.

Wolfwalker?

Hishn? Her mind was not yet clear.

The wolf nudged her softly. *The scouts are gone.*

Gone. Gone for how long? She should move—get away from the river, make her way back to the trail. But she had no strength. She told herself to move, but her head rested against the blunt stone and only turned to the side when she shifted. Her legs were stiff, and the skin of her hands was wrinkled and pale from the water. Cool currents washed over her legs and eddied around her waist. The shadows were gone from the riverbanks. Above her, there were only three moons in the sky, and the sun heated the small pool like a bath without warming her skin as well. The colors—they were wrong, washed out, without yellow to brighten their tones. And, too, the motion of the waves and wind was too sharp. The images were not Dion's. Her eyes could not yet focus. No, the wolfwalker was seeing through Hishn's eyes, not her own.

She shifted again, but the tip of her sword was stuck in the rocks and her bow was jammed against her back. She could not reach around to free it; her left hand clenched her jerkin where the mudsucker's head still hung onto her flesh. It took a sharp shrug to loosen the bow and a jerk of her right arm to yank the sword free. She did not try to get to her feet yet. Instead, she borrowed Hishn's eyes to look around. She was sheltered from the stream banks; she could not see the brush on the shore. To her left was a short wall of rock, to her right another shallow pool, and on the narrow band of stones that divided the pools lay Rhom's knife. With Hishn pacing the boulder above her, she let her body tilt slowly along the stone as she groped for the blade.

Hishn whined low as Dion replaced the steel in its sheath.

"It's all right, Gray One." Dion's voice was weak, even to her own ears, and she coughed, spitting to clear her throat of the odd taste that clung to her tongue. "The poison is nearly gone."

The scouts returned twice. They found nothing, but they are thick on the trails now like flocks of birds.

Dion nodded weakly. She tried to unclench the hand still locked on her jerkin, but her fingers had stiffened around the leather of her mail. When she tugged at the mail to free it, pain shot abruptly up her arm in a crushing sensation, and she cried out. Hishn was on her feet in an instant, and the gray bond between them snapped taut. The wolfwalker's face flung back and her teeth were bared.

Wolfwalker?

Dion forced her head down. The cloth wrapped around her hand was dark with the mixed blood and fluids of the eel. The fire had not burned down. The poison was only beginning to work its way out of her flesh, and the throb of it beat like clubs up inside her arm and shoulder and into her temple. She could not remove the eel's head. Each tooth had an inner anchor that splayed out into the flesh and could not be removed until its roots and nerves were severed. Something she could not do herself. "Aranur . . ." she whispered.

The time—how late was it? Hours past the time she should have returned. It must have been late morning already, and Aranur would be angry with her for taking so long. He and the others would be several hours on the trail by now. She would have to run quickly to catch up. She glanced at the sky again, blinking as spots of light burned away the darkness in her gaze. Time . . . She had to move. The water was too cold, and even with Hishn's bond to strengthen her, she could not wait longer. She braced herself against the boulder with her shoulders, then shoved with her feet until she pushed herself out of the water and sat, shivering, on the stone that had protected her from the sharp gaze of the scouts on the shore. After a moment, she struggled to her feet. But one knee buckled, and she barely caught herself.

Hishn shoved her shoulder under Dion's hand. *Wolfwalker?*

The woman breathed harshly, shivering in the sun. She gripped the gray pelt until her knuckles were lost in its thickness. "I need help, Hishn," she whispered.

Slitted eyes stared at her for a moment, then the wolf turned and jumped to the shore. *Follow.*

Dion slid down the back of the first boulder, lurching against the next stone as one foot slipped awkwardly into a crack between the rocks. With her left hand still clenched, she pulled herself around the next pool. She did not want to get her boots wet again; they had just stopped dripping. But their leather soles were slick, and as she jumped across to the next stone, she slipped again and landed on one knee. The flat smack of the stone was jarring, and the burst of pain stunned her so that all she could do was crouch for a moment with the new fire shooting up her thigh. Turning back instantly, Hishn growled. Dion, her jaw clenched, did not trust herself to speak, even to the wolf.

Finally she reached the bank from a large, flat stone that let her step into the brush from the river. As she moved, her eyes finally began to clear. She could see trees and open areas—but not scouts. She could not see detail through the fog that bound her vision. And she had to avoid Longear's men. She paused, and the Gray One looked back. "Get us to the ridges, Hishn. We can follow Aranur more easily from there."

The wolf growled low. *The climb is not gentle,* she returned with worry.

"Better that than a run-in with Zentsis's men."

Hishn nudged her softly, then faded through the bushes into a game trail that led away from the path. Dion made it half a kilometer before her mind began to blur. This time, she felt the weakness coming and stopped against a tree, letting herself sink down among the roots until her vision cleared again. The thread of nauseous fire that traced its way in her veins brought that moldy taste to her tongue again before it passed, and Hishn, whining, lay down at Dion's feet and put her head on her paws, her ears twitching. At last Dion forced herself up again. Aranur . . . How far ahead was he now?

"Hishn," she said softly, leaning on the tree, "I cannot run silent."

The gray wolf looked back, worried. *I will call the pack.*

Dion shook her head. "No," she said slowly.

They will guide you and keep you from those who hunt your tracks, Hishn insisted.

"The pack is too many."

It is what is needed.

But Dion buried her hand in Hishn's scruff. "Not the pack, Hishn. The poison of the eel has made your thoughts loud in my mind." She shifted her sword as she spoke. The long blade had become increasingly heavy, and its weight dragged on her hip. "No," she repeated. "Three or four others, and they would be too much for me."

I will be with you.

"Gray One," she said gently, "you honor me, but you are young, as well. Would you remember to run Aranur's trail? Or would you lead us with the pack until we both remembered my other friends?"

Hishn looked up, her yellow eyes troubled. *Two then. To guard,* she returned.

Dion hesitated. But she shifted, and the pain in her left hand blazed again, dimming her sight. "All right," she said finally.

Fifteen minutes later, the voices of the Gray Ones began to seep into Dion's thoughts, and she knew the wolves had come. By the time they had gone another kilometer, Dion's senses were half in the Gray Ones' world. Her ears were full of acute sounds, and her skin felt the breezes as if it were covered with fur. Her stride was a long lope. And her violet eyes had a gleam that, when caught in the light, seemed as yellow as the ring in the eyes of the wolves. Aranur . . . She forced herself to concentrate on his image. She would reach him soon, and he and Rhom would take the sucker from her hand. Aranur . . .

It was late afternoon. The sun had begun to spear the lower leaves on the trees, and Aranur, leading the group at a quick pace, jogged around a sharp bend and jerked to a stop.

"Dion—"

She stood in the path, her breathing ragged, her eyes unfocused, her shoulders hunched, and one awkwardly wrapped hand clutched at her middle. Hishn was at her side, head down and shoulders bristling.

"Dion," he repeated. He stepped forward. "Shilia," he said in a low voice over his shoulder, "get Rhom. Gamon, get the others back around the rocks." There was something about the wolfwalker's wary stance that gave him pause. "Dion," he said softly, "are you all right?"

She did not answer, but when he stepped forward again, her lips pulled back and she crouched lower, as if to leap or turn and run.

He held out his hands. "Stay, Dion," he said quietly. "I will not hurt you."

Her nostrils flared, then she breathed out quickly, as if to clear Aranur's scent from her nose. She frowned at his words. But her free hand was clenched around her knife.

Aranur, his eyes still on the wolfwalker, barely moved to the side as Rhom edged up. The blacksmith took in his sister's stance in a second, then narrowed his eyes.

"What is it?" Aranur asked.

"She's deep within the Gray Ones."

Aranur gave him a sharp look. "How deep?"

Rhom frowned, judging his sister's expression. "I don't know."

Aranur pointed at the stained and bulging bandage wrapped around her hand.

The other man nodded. "Dion," he said softly. "I'm here."

Hishn snarled. Dion's eyes narrowed, but she hesitated.

"She's weak," Aranur whispered. "I could catch her before she got far in the forest." He took a step forward, but Rhom shook his head sharply. Dion whirled at the movements, poised to run.

"No—Dion, wait!" Rhom snapped.

Her hand clenched and unclenched on the hilt of the knife, and her breathing was uneven, her violet eyes dilated. Beside her, the wolf backed up a meter, the yellow eyes glaring at Rhom, then Aranur. Rhom saw the way his sister was holding the blade. "She's got the speed of the Gray Ones behind that blade, Aranur," he said under his breath. "You'd lose your hands if not your life. I saw this happen once with another wolfwalker."

He eased forward again, and Hishn backed off, a low growl burrowing up from her stomach into her throat, until it became a steady grate against Aranur's ears. Dion twitched.

"Dion," Rhom said softly. She stared at him for a moment, then raised the knife. Hishn bared her teeth and reached forward, but he ignored her. "Dion," he commanded again. "See me. Look at me."

Dion blinked. And then her eyes lost their glow and became dark, and Hishn whined as the woman sank slowly down on her knees, her left hand cradled at her middle and her right hand still holding the knife, but now limp against her leg. Her eyes closed. The wolf, her long teeth gleaming, whined again at Dion, and Rhom knelt cautiously beside his sister.

"Rhom," Dion whispered. "I need help."

He put his arm around her shoulders and looked back at Aranur.

"Gamon has more experience with this than either of us," Aranur said, motioning for Gamon to join them.

As Aranur warily watched the forest around them, Gamon eased himself down beside Rhom. Dion, her forehead pulled against her brother's chest, let them reach for her stiffened hand. But when Gamon got his fingers around her grip, she gasped, and he stopped. Hishn lunged to her feet, and Dion's face drained of color.

No! Dion managed the command harshly in her mind. *Down, Gray One. I need their help.*

Hishn paced a circle twice, glaring at Gamon and the other men, then sat abruptly, her eyes not leaving Dion. Gamon glanced at the wolf, then shook his head slightly. Unwrapping the cloth on her hand, he peeled it away from the rotting eel head that covered the back of her hand. "By the moons—" he said involuntarily. "Sorry, Dion," he added quietly. "I just haven't seen anything like this for forty years." He dropped the stained cloth in the dirt and, after giving the wolfwalker a measuring look, examined the head of the eel. Behind him, even Aranur's lip curled.

Rhom, watching Gamon's work, tightened his grip on his sister's shoulders.

Aranur stared at the wound, his eyes narrowed with a frown. What had a sucker been doing in the mountains? And that Dion had happened to run into this one . . . He gazed thoughtfully at the wolfwalker, but he did not see her. His thoughts were tracing their path through the mountains, remembering their flight from that coastal city and the traps they had escaped there. How Longear could have found them so quickly he did not know, but somehow he knew that that was just what had happened.

Gamon peeled back part of the eel's skin, but there was too much tortured flesh to see clearly. He could not tell how old the wound was. "Do the teeth still pump?" he asked her.

Dion shifted, and Hishn whined, inching forward on the ground until she could put her head on the wolfwalker's leg. Dion forced the words out from between clenched teeth. "The first poison is—gone. The teeth have been in—about nine or ten hours."

Aranur dropped his pack, pulled his water bag from his shoulder, and began searching for a clean cloth. "We'll need fire," he said to Tyrel and the girls. The three youths nodded, and in a few moments a small, smokeless blaze had been built within a pocket in the rocks. It would be easy to hide later and, with the stone as reflecting walls, would take little fuel to make the fire hot.

"You'll have to burn away the back of the head," Dion told them with difficulty. "Expose the roots of the teeth. Then use my cutters to— cut off the ends of the roots." She stiffened involuntarily as Gamon shifted her hand again. When she continued, her voice was lower and breathy, and Rhom tightened his grip on her shoulders. "It will make the inner barbs relax so you can pull the teeth out," she said finally.

Gamon nodded. He took his knife and handed it to Aranur, who set both that blade and his own into the fire, then got Rhom's knife, as well.

"Aranur." Dion stopped him as he turned away. "The scouts are within hours of you."

"I know."

"They found the trail by watching the river."

"We can talk about that later."

"No." She lifted her head from her brother's chest and stared at Aranur. Her violet eyes were dark, and there was no hint of the wolves in her gaze. "That cloth—it was Namina's. And this—" She picked awkwardly with one hand at one of the pouches at her belt. "I found at another spot along the banks." She held out the now-dried ball of thread. "The scouts said they had found her combings days ago."

He looked at the threads and stained cloth for a long moment. "I see."

"Healer," Gamon said quietly. "I'm ready to begin."

Dion turned her head into Rhom's shoulder again and gripped Hishn's scruff with her free hand. "All right."

She made no sound as he burned away the eel's skin with one of the knives. She gagged once at the stench. Hishn, who growled continuously, was held down by the wolfwalker until she began to whine. Then Dion released her, and the gray wolf leapt away, scraping her paws over her nose until Dion ordered her to stop. The wolf slunk away a few meters, then dropped to the ground and laid her head mournfully on her paws. The wolfwalker found her free hand in Rhom's grip.

"Almost down to the teeth," Gamon said softly. "Just another minute."

Aranur glanced over his shoulder to find that Tyrel had retched. Shilia looked sick, too. Namina was pale, staring away so that she did not have to see, and it was to her that Aranur strode.

He hauled her to her feet. "Namina," he snarled, "this you will watch." She struggled against his iron grip for a moment, but he propelled her closer. "You, too, Tyrel," he snapped. "Get your head out of the dirt and get up here." He motioned. "We—I trusted you to use the river alone, Namina. Look at what your carelessness has cost." The horror on the girl's face was plain, and she twisted to free herself, but Aranur did not let her go. "This could cost us not only Dion's hand, but our lives, as well. The scouts have been following us by your signs."

Tyrel had stepped forward. He gagged again—a reflex—but held his stomach down. "It's not all her fault, Aranur," he managed. "I was with her at the river sometimes."

Aranur looked at him. "I know that, Tyrel," he said coldly. "And you had better learn from this, too."

"I can see the tops of the teeth now, Dion," Gamon murmured. He took the small cutters she had pulled from another belt pouch and held the tool gingerly. "Aranur, I'll need some help."

Aranur glared at Namina for a moment, then released her and she fled back along the trail until Shilia caught her and held her close.

Gamon glanced back only briefly. "Take these," he said to his nephew, "and cut the roots of the teeth when I pull the edges of the flesh away like this. There—try that one first."

Dion gasped. They both stopped for an instant, but Hishn had only whined, not leapt up to guard her wolfwalker. Dion had not moved her hand. "Go on," she whispered. "The inner barb just released."

By the time Aranur cut the last root, the sucker's teeth had begun to slide out of the back of her hand and the head of the eel was hanging off her mangled flesh. Aranur gingerly lifted the head away, his lips tightening at the sight of what was left of Dion's hand, and Gamon tossed the rows of cut teeth into the fire.

The wolfwalker did not lift her head. "Wash it," she said in a low voice.

Aranur motioned for a cup, which Shilia brought, leaving Namina to huddle on the trail by herself. Shilia poured the liquid and handed it back to him with another clean cloth, and he absently nodded his thanks, his eyes not leaving Dion. "I cannot stitch it, Dion," he admitted.

She laughed unevenly. "Nor can I." She pried her good hand free of Rhom's grip, and he shook his arm out where his sister's fingers had left deep marks. She gripped the elbow above her mangled hand until what was left of her flesh turned pale. The bones were laid open to the air amid the red and tangled flesh, and they seemed to shift as the flaps of torn muscle lay first over one, then the other. "Wash it," she repeated. "I'll deal with it later."

Aranur hesitated. "Will you have the use of it again, Dion?" he asked quietly.

Rhom's jaw tightened, and he could not help the glance he threw at Namina.

Dion shrugged as best she could. "I'm a wolfwalker."

The tall man looked at her steadily, then dipped the cloth into the water and began to dab at her hand.

"It will not hurt me, Aranur."

He looked up. Her eyes were still dark; her jaw was tight, and her grip on her elbow tighter. He knew what she was doing, and he knew that she was lying. Even a nerve pinch could not hide what she was feeling.

She looked at him. "If you don't do it, I will have to."

He hesitated again, but when Dion shifted, as if to take the cloth away from him, he shook his head. "I will do it."

She closed her eyes halfway through his work, and her knuckles grew pale, then whiter. Hishn, who whined constantly, paced the ground a few meters away, lay down again, then jumped up and paced again.

It will be over soon, Gray One, she told the wolf.

Hishn paused in her pacing, lips pulled back from her fangs so that it seemed as if she would bite the air to lessen the pain. But she finally sat, and Dion did not look at her again.

Aranur sat back at last. "That's the best I can do, Dion." She opened her eyes, and Rhom released her. Then she examined her hand dispassionately, as if it belonged to someone else.

"Rhom," she said. "The second and fourth pouches. There is a silver-lined vial, and a packet that smells like bitter smoke. Crumble one leaf and then pour two drops from the vial onto it. Mash it together and spread it as best you can over this." He nodded, detaching the pouches easily and pulling out the items. "I'll be ready to run in a few minutes, Aranur," she told the other man.

"Dion—" he started, then stopped. They had already spent a half an hour there. If the scouts were so close on their trail, he needed to keep the group moving at almost any cost. He nodded shortly.

"I'll keep your pack, Dion," Rhom said under his breath as he handed back her pouches. She did not argue, though she stopped Aranur before he rose.

"Aranur," she said, "stay as far from the river as you can. The scouts—they're Longear's. They're the ones that have been herding us to the north and west again. And they're seeding the water with mudsuckers. The water bodies east and north of here are already stocked. And they mentioned a swamp."

"I see," he said again. He did not speak to Namina as he strode back along the trail. "Gamon," he said to his uncle, "brush out our tracks. Tyrel will help. I'll want Rhom up front."

The weapons master met his gaze. "How is Dion's hand?"

Aranur shrugged, but Gamon saw the expression deep in his nephew's eyes. For a healer not to have the use of both hands . . . and for it to be the fault of someone under Aranur's leadership . . . The older man turned away and motioned for Tyrel to follow.

Chapter 4

Do you trust yourself
With your dreams?
There are images
That know they will not survive
When you
Wake

It was near evening. Four hours had passed since they last stopped to rest, and even Aranur's legs had deadened to the trail. The two times they had crossed running water, he had made sure it was where the streams ran fast and no sucker could find a hold. Dion ran as if her hand did not trouble her, but Aranur knew differently. There was a tightness to her eyes that had not been there before.

She should try the internal healing—Ovousibas—on herself, he thought. As a wolfwalker as well as a healer, she could do Ovousibas just as the legends of the ancients described it. For centuries no one had believed it could be done, until Dion had stumbled upon the secret and learned to focus her mental energy through the bond of the wolves to heal injuries and illness without touching an herb or a knife. Aranur had seen Dion use Ovousibas half a dozen times now.

But, he reminded himself, he had never seen her do it on herself. He glanced back. Was it possible for her to heal her own hand? Ovousibas was draining—the few times he had seen her use the skill, it had left her shaking and starved, as if the energy it required had been drained from her own body. And what if she needed both hands to do the healing in the first place? He frowned. Dion could not bend her fingers, and even he could tell that the tendons and ligaments themselves had been torn from her bones by the mudsucker's hold. If he suggested Ovousibas, he wondered, pausing to view a small meadow before crossing it, would Dion be willing to try it.

As he paused, Rhom caught up with him, and Aranur realized that it would not be Dion who hesitated, but her brother who protested the use of her skill. Rhom did not believe that Dion could escape the curse that had followed Ovousibas for the last eight hundred years. And though Rhom had seen his sister do the internal healing without contracting the plague afterward, he was still uneasy.

Aranur shook his head to himself, then shrugged at Rhom's questioning glance. "Let's stop here," he said. "We can climb the hill from here—the rocks will hide our tracks well, and that ridge will shelter us from any eyes on the path."

The blacksmith nodded. "I'll scout the other side."

But the wolfwalker, who had just reached them, disagreed. "I'll scout, Rhom." She motioned to the wolf, and had already taken two steps past Aranur when he stopped her.

"Dion, your hand—"

"Does not affect my sight."

Aranur frowned, glancing at Rhom for backup, but the blacksmith shook his head. "She's still a better scout than I."

"And as a fighter with one hand?"

Dion met his eyes. "It will be a brief run only, Aranur. I will stay out of sight and be gone no more than twenty minutes."

A moment later, she was on her way, and Aranur was staring after her, wondering if he should have ordered her to stay while the rest of the group made its way up the hill. She would do what she wanted anyway, he knew, and he smothered an oath of irritation as he turned up the hill after the others.

Dion and Hishn returned fifteen minutes later. They had not gone far, but there had been no sign of scouts within scent or sight. Dion was relieved. But Hishn, who sensed the wolfwalker's body as much as her mind, knew that Dion was fighting the pain of her hand with activity. The Gray One hinted at sleep for both of them, and Dion nodded absently. But she stopped in the darkening shadows of the trail before climbing the ridge to join the others. Above them, Tyrel was sitting guard in a pocket of stone overlooking the trail, his warcap removed, sandy hair fluffing lightly in the wind. Dion frowned. Tyrel did not see them.

His eyes are tired, not sharp, Hishn commented.

Dion absently rubbed her wrist where the throbbing of her hand broke into her thoughts like a fire pulsing against her nerves. She clenched her right hand against the pain of the left. It was easier to ignore the wound when she was doing something. Examining the boy's position again, she noted the way his view was blocked by a thick clump of brambles on one side. It was blocked by an outcropping on the other, as well, she realized. Tyrel had stood watch many times before. He should have known better. *We could get within meters before he saw us,* she sent softly.

Beside her, Hishn snorted arrogantly. *Even Aranur cannot see a Gray One at dusk.*

Dion gave her a sideways look. *You've been too long from the company of other wolves if you think you're that good on the hunt,* she teased ungently. She directed the wolf toward the bramble patch. *There will be a trail through there.*

Hishn snorted softly. *A belly trail,* she returned in disgust.

Dion smiled without humor. *You challenged, so I lead.*

She eased back into the woods until the bramble patch was between her and Tyrel, then ran in a low crouch toward a small game trail that led directly into the barbed brush. In a flash, she was on her stomach and worming her way inside. At her heels, Hishn's hot breath snorted in the dirt until Dion shushed her.

The trail led to the right, then branched, with one branch leading up the hill, and that was the one she chose. It was dim within the brambles. Only spots of light broke the shadows where the leaves accidentally let the evening sun trick its way inside. But the shadows were a blessing. Once out of the brambles, Dion and Hishn could use the shadows in the rocks to sneak closer. Neither Tyrel nor any of the others would see them—or any scouts, Dion reminded herself soberly—coming. She untangled her clothes carefully, without shaking the brush, and while Hishn grumbled behind her, she eased up the hill. It was a good thing that Longear's men would not look for tracks in this sort of game trail. She had been careful of using her hands, especially the left one, but her knees and elbows made marks she could not hide.

Moments later, she lay at the edge of the barbed vines, her eyes darting from side to side as she looked for signs of anyone watching. She stayed on her stomach to crawl out of the trail, then rolled into the shadow of one of the small boulders that littered the bald ridge. A second later, she eased closer to the boy until she leaned against the boulder behind him. Hishn, slinking up beside her, breathed silently, her ears twitching as she caught each movement the boy made. The wolfwalker cleared her throat.

Tyrel whirled. "Moonworms—" He shot a glance behind him to see if Aranur had seen how Dion and the wolf had appeared.

Dion brushed the dirt from her leggings as she watched him. "There are many trails to the top of a hill, Tyrel. Not all of them are obvious."

"But how—"

"The brambles, Tyrel." She shifted her sword back to a comfortable position, careful of her left hand. "But we could have come over that bulge, as well."

He glanced at both blind spots and flushed.

Moving into the camp, Dion paused and looked back. "When you are Lloroi, Tyrel, you'll have to think like all your people—those who work with you as well as those who work against your leadership. Only then will you understand all the possibilities of your actions." She stepped up to the camp, greeting Rhom and the others quietly. Behind her, Tyrel moved to a spot from which he could see both outcropping and trees, but his shame took a long time to fade.

"How is your hand?" Shilia asked as Dion picked up her pack and unrolled her blanket.

Dion shrugged.

"If you need help . . ."

The girl's offer trailed off, and Dion smiled briefly, her expression unreadable. It was not Shilia who could help her, she knew, but Aranur. He could hear the Gray Ones as Dion could. If Dion was to try Ovousibas on herself, which she was considering, she would need his strength, as well. Rhom could also hear Hishn, but Dion and her twin were too alike to work together in the internal healing. The touch of Rhom's thoughts against hers was a grating shock—like a baring of intimate truths she could not stand. Where Aranur's touch gave her strength, Rhom's burned, and she knew it was to Aranur, not her twin, that she would have to turn. She gripped her wrist again, pinching the nerves to deaden the pain. But the temporarily respite only made the throbbing more intense when she released the hold. She gritted her teeth.

Shilia glanced at Dion's tight face. "Gamon said it would be a dry camp again. He said there were too many scouts around." The girl prodded her thin blanket into a more comfortable pile and pulled off her equally thin boots. "I'll be glad to reach a road after this. I don't think I ever appreciated how nice they were to walk on, and how nice dnu are to ride—their six legs go a lot farther a lot faster than my two."

The wolfwalker nodded. Unslinging her water bag from her shoulder, she began unwrapping her hand. The wound looked worse than it was. The mangled flesh was scabbed over, and though the movement forced long needles of dull-red pain up her arm, she could wiggle her fingers.

Shilia got up and looked at the injured hand with a frown. "You couldn't do that a few hours ago."

"I worked it as I ran." Dion smiled briefly at the look of uncertainty on the girl's face. "I'm a wolfwalker, Shilia. I always heal fast."

Shilia nodded, then went over to her uncle and spoke to Aranur, who rose and came over to Dion.

"Can you try the internal healing?" he asked quietly, dropping down beside her.

Dion looked at him. "There is no record of a wolfwalker trying Ovousibas on herself," she said, voicing her fears.

"There was no record of the way to do the healing successfully, until you found one."

"That was luck."

"It was logic," he corrected. "The moons do not give gifts that are not deserved. Look at Gamon, Namina, Shilia. Even your own brother would not be here if you had not cured him of the plague."

She glanced at her hand. "But *I* was not in need of healing then, Aranur. It will be different this time."

He touched her arm, and in the dimming light, his hand was strong on her skin. "I will be here," he said. "And I will be the same."

She looked at him for a moment, then met Hishn's eyes. *Gray One*, she sent. *You feel this wound of mine?*

The wolf's eyes gleamed, and as she opened her mind to Dion's pain, she snarled silently. *Like a dnu pounding over my own paws*, she sent. *I would lick your hurt, but you cover it from my touch.*

Aranur's hands were on Dion's shoulders, and she glanced at him, then at the wolf. She smiled softly. *There was poison in the wound, Gray One. If you had licked it, the poison would have affected you, as well.* She rubbed the creature's ears.

*Aranur is willing, Hishn, and it is Ovousibas I need now. Will
you take me in?*

The wolf cocked her ears. *You want to walk within yourself?*

*I need my hand, Hishn, and the tendons are torn. They will
not heal by themselves, and I know of no other way to get the
use of my fingers again.*

Then walk with me, Healer.

She did not need to look at Hishn, but the yellow almond
shapes of the wolf's eyes followed her into her mind. For
Aranur, those gleaming yellow coals swallowed him until he
could hear Dion's and Hishn's voices as if they were his own.
And under his hands, Dion stiffened.

Her mind spun to the left. There was a dizzying drop of
thought, and images rushed by like a fall from a mountain cliff.
There was a jumble of color and scent—the fragments of memories and bodies and wounds and then of flesh torn and blood
vessels ripped apart. And then the pulse, the pound of the heart
far away and the cells forcing their way through the debris of
the wound, leaking away only to die. There—the tendons
curled into balls where they snapped from the bones, and Dion
reached into herself with her mind. Aranur's strength buoyed
her, and Hishn directed her focus while the nerves whipped and
frayed beneath her consciousness. The healer aimed her energy, touching here, there, until the tortured oozing of her
blood stopped and she could sense the damage that burned at
her as from a distance. Hishn was a gray wall that the pain
could not cross, and Aranur fed the wolf his own strength until
the wall became a solid thing.

Dion did not hesitate. She knew the wall would not last. She
seamed and placed the tissues. Each muscle to a ligament; each
tendon to a bone. She set them in place and welded them with
her thoughts until their bonds held like steel. There were pockets of brackish poison still hiding in her flesh, and the toxin
crawled as she forced her antibodies to crowd and crush it. Her
pulse grew loud. The gray wall was strong, but it thinned and
shortened until the Gray One began to withdraw, letting the
impulses from the nerves grind against it. The healer shuddered
within herself. She fought the pull briefly, then surrendered as
it warred with her own strength and won. Her pulse caught her
up and shot her away.

She opened her eyes. She was shaking, her hands trembling
as the one clenched the other, and Aranur sat back as she

shrugged herself free of the weight of his hands. Hishn's teeth were closed about her arm, and Dion, loosing that hold, realized that it had been Hishn's sharp touch that pulled her back from the healing. Other hands steadied her, and she looked up to find her brother beside her, his face lined with concern.

"Was it enough?" Aranur's voice was hoarse until he cleared it.

Dion nodded briefly. Her stomach cramped, and her hunger consumed her, and she did not trust her voice. She uncovered her hand instead, and both Aranur and Rhom stared. It had not healed cleanly; there were thin ridges and lines where the flesh had set back together without bonding, but beneath the transparent layer of skin that now covered the wound, they could see that the tissues were in place, and the muscles and bones rippled slightly as she worked her fingers.

Rhom turned his attention to his sister. "I thought you would tell me before you did this again," he said steadily.

She looked up at him, then clenched her good hand against her cramping stomach. "It had to be done sometime," she managed, "and better now, before infection set in."

Rhom gave her an unreadable look, then dug the last of his jerky from his wallet. He added the tubers Shilia had saved for her, and Dion accepted them without speaking. She felt starved, but she tore only half the jerky off for herself. The other half she offered to Aranur. Hishn, after nudging Dion and nearly tipping her over, trotted off into the shadows to hunt her own meal.

Aranur accepted his share of the tubers as well, but his eyes did not leave Dion. "Was it different?" he asked finally. "Doing the healing on yourself instead of someone else?" He watched her carefully. "I can only sense your thoughts, not what you do when I ride Hishn's strength to help."

She stared at her hand. "It was . . ." She paused and frowned, struggling for the words. "I . . ." she tried again, then shrugged helplessly.

He touched her thigh. "You don't have to talk."

"No, I—I want to." Meeting his eyes, she lay her hand on his. "It was . . . intimate, private, Aranur. But at the same time, more vast than—than the sky where it spreads across the desert."

Aranur frowned, trying to see the image.

"I was inside myself—in my own thoughts, my own heart," she tried again. "But the sense of it stretched beyond my body through Hishn, through you, through my own mind." She motioned at the clearing. "It was as if I was an extension of a sense that was not limited to what I can see now. As if I understood the motion of every cell, every molecule. As if the gray wall that shielded me from myself took me beyond thought to a—to a level that was pure life."

Aranur, watching her, smiled.

She caught his look. "You don't understand."

"No."

She shrugged and pulled away slightly.

"Dion—" His hand tightened on her thigh.

She looked at him unwillingly.

"It is not important for me to understand completely," he said softly. "What is important is that I am here when you need me." He touched her hand. "This—this is real," he said, squeezing her palm in his. "What strength I can give you is real. But what I feel and see when you do Ovousibas is like a dim candle compared to the light you see with. The healing is a gift from the moons, Dion. A gift only you can truly understand."

The wolfwalker stared at him for a moment, then leaned toward him until her forehead touched his shoulder, and his chin rested briefly on her hair.

Across the camp, Rhom threw a dark look at Aranur. Ovousibas was dangerous. And Dion knew that, but nothing Rhom said would give Dion more caution—especially when Aranur encouraged her to do the healing at every turn. She had not needed to do the Ovousibas—she knew Dion was a wolfwalker. Her hand would have healed eventually anyway. And the pull of the internal healing—he had seen it, and it was stronger than the pull of the wolves. He had caught it in her eyes before Hishn bit Dion's arm and pulled her back, and he knew that it could hold his twin if she tried it on herself again. He tossed fitfully on his blanket. He stared at the faded stars. Aranur merely gave his strength in the healing; Dion gave her soul. If she went too far . . . He tightened his jaw. Finally he forced his eyes closed.

The next morning, a light gray veil of clouds covered the sky, and the group went only a few kilometers before the wind rose, bringing with it a stagnant warmth. Aranur, in the lead again, climbed a rise and made his way carefully into a steep gully, following the wolf. Hishn picked the deer trails as if she knew them already, though Dion had told Aranur that the Gray One learned the trails from other wolves who had run that way in the past; the memories of the Gray Ones stretched far beyond their own lives. In front of him, Hishn paused, sniffing, before lunging up the hill. The path was a switchback so steep that even Aranur found himself climbing over the eroded rocks with his hands on his thighs, as if to force his legs to work. Sweat beaded on his temples. As he crested the ridge, the wind cut to the left and swept along the treetops, and he stood for a moment, waiting for the others to catch up. The smell became familiar, wrinkling both Aranur's and Hishn's noses. "Swamp," Aranur said as Tyrel joined him.

"At least it's a small one," his cousin said, peering down through the trees as he caught his breath.

"About a kilometer across."

"Should we go around?"

Aranur shook his head. "Look at the growth patterns in the valley. There are swamp trees at both ends; it wouldn't be any drier unless we went back into the ridges, and that would cost us a day and a half."

The boy lowered his voice and glanced at Dion, who crested the rise with her brother. "What about mudsuckers?" he asked. "Dion said the scouts have already seeded this area."

"Mudsuckers need open water."

Dion gave him a sharp look. "You want to cross the swamp here?"

Aranur nodded.

An odd expression crossed her face, and she turned away, standing with her back to him for a moment, until Hishn, who rubbed against her thigh, whined. Turning to face him again, the wolfwalker said flatly, "Hishn and I will go around the swamp, Aranur. We'll meet up with you again on the other side."

Rhom glanced at her, then nodded. "I'll go with you, Dion."

But Aranur shook his head. "No, Rhom, Dion. We'll stay together."

Dion stiffened. "You take this staying together too seriously, Aranur."

"If I didn't," he returned sharply, "some of us would be dead."

But the wolfwalker stood her ground. "I will not cross that swamp, Aranur."

"You would not have hesitated before yesterday," he said deliberately.

Dion clenched her teeth. "Even if I wanted to cross," she said in a low voice, "I would not be any good to you until you got to the other side."

He shrugged. "I'll take that chance."

She shook her head angrily, and Hishn bared her teeth. "You don't understand," she insisted. Shilia and Namina had joined them and were listening. Dion's face flamed. "From what the scouts said, this swamp was seeded ninans ago—and mudsuckers reproduce after every feeding. That's more than enough time for there to be dozens of suckers in that place— and long enough by now for some of them to be twice our size."

"The swamp is large, Dion. And there are tastier fish to feed on than leather and steel."

"And if they like leather and steel?"

"It's summer, Dion, and even though the clouds are thickening up, they will not bring rain before tonight. Right now, the water is low, and we can cross on the floating islands for most of the way."

"Even from here, I can see open water."

"And I can see that you're losing your nerve."

Dion's face stung, and no one else spoke. Even Rhom did not look at his sister.

"I'm sorry, Dion," Aranur said. "That was not fair."

She clamped her mouth tight and dug her hand into Hishn's fur until the Gray One glared at him as well. "All right," she said in a low voice. "We will cross with you."

He touched her arm. "I will be going first, Dion."

"That won't help you," she said bitterly. But she fell into line anyway, ahead of Rhom, who came last, brushing out the few tracks they left behind.

Ten minutes later, they trudged down into the tall grasses of the marsh, wading through the jagged blades and snorting at the pollen released by their passage. The ground, soft at first, quickly became soggy, and the mud began collecting on their boots and turning their feet into blocks of weight that became increasingly difficult to lift. As she watched the others carefully picking their footing ahead of her, Dion motioned to Rhom to pass her, and he gave her a steady look but went on.

At the edge of the deeper mud, Dion hesitated, but at Rhom's backward glance she clenched her jaw and stepped out into the fen. Hishn sniffed the rotting mud and snorted, backing away. Motioning for the Gray One to follow her, Dion forced herself on, but Hishn whined. The wolf paced along the muck, looking after Dion and stretching her nose.

Rhom glanced back. "She's as reluctant as you."

His sister gave him a cold look. "I'm here, aren't I?"

"Yes, but where's your better half?" He extended his hand to her and held it there, waiting for her to take it.

Dion stared at him, then laughed shortly in spite of herself. As she accepted his help to the next solid footing, she said sourly, "My better half is keeping dry while we get bogged down in this mud."

Rhom chuckled. "She'd better come soon if she's going to try it. We'll be out of sight in a minute," he said, stepping carefully to the next spongy island. The swamp grass grew taller here, and clumps of thick brush made islands of more-solid mud in the marsh.

Dion glanced up. "Since when has Hishn needed her eyes to find me?"

"Since you smell like the mud you're wading in," he teased.

"Well, you smell just as bad," she retorted. She looked at the mud and shuddered as she made her way through the next deep hole. "Maybe worse, with the way you're sweating on top of it." But she paused and looked back. The wolf had taken two gingerly steps into the marsh, then stopped. *Come on, Hishn.* Dion sent. *Hurry up.*

The wolf whined, then loped off to the east, returning in a few seconds to whimper and try the mud again.

Dion frowned. "She's beginning to panic."

Gamon, four islands ahead of them, turned and motioned for them to catch up.

"If you were out of sight, she might be more eager to come after you," her brother suggested.

But Dion hesitated. "The longer we're away from home and the more unfamiliar the land, the more she insists on staying close to me."

"Dion, Rhom," Gamon called irritably. "These islands aren't stable, and we can't wait all day."

"Moonworms," Dion muttered. *Come, Gray One,* she sent silently. *I agreed to do this for both of us. But you have to walk this path, too. Just follow my steps like you did as a pup. I am no farther away than my thoughts.* She turned and jumped to the next floating clump of grass, and the tall, yellow-green stalks abruptly cut her off from the wolf's view. The Gray

One's howl, however, followed them across the mud as easily as the hungry bugs that clouded the air over their heads.

Her brother swore under his breath at the wolf's long whine. "Why not let the whole countryside know we're here? Can't you tell her to do that in your head and not our ears?"

Gray One, I am here. Just follow my thoughts.

Rhom offered Dion his hand as she teetered on the edge of a muddy rock before jumping to his slippery island. "If we'd only left you behind as well, everything would have been fine," he teased ungently.

But as Hishn howled again, Dion turned back. "I'm going to have to go back for her," she told her brother. "Tell Aranur that I had no choice. We'll find a better place to cross, and then meet up with you later."

But Rhom snagged her arm and hauled her around. "That's no solution, Dion. Hishn's young, but she's got to learn sometime," he said sternly. "And so do you."

Dion shook his arm off. "She's scared, Rhom. She needs me."

"She needs discipline, not coddling, Dion. You're both old enough in your bonding to know that."

"But she'll panic—"

"She's testing your independence, Dion. And your courage."

Dion stared at him for a long moment.

"She's perfectly capable of following you. She thinks she makes it easier on you, and now she wants you to make it easy on her."

Dion stared back toward where the Gray One should be, then looked at Rhom measuringly. "You might be right," she admitted slowly.

Listen, Gray One, she sent sternly. *You've led me many places, but this time I must lead, and you must come after me.* The wolf's answering whine was a thin gray line in her head— one that made her want to reach out and take the line, reeling Hishn in.

Your scent is like a wisp. There is no track to your thought, the wolf told her.

Dion closed her eyes, and the shape of wolf became solid. *Feel this. Track me now.*

The line of gray in her mind became suddenly thick and, like a cord stretched between towers, grew taut. Then, behind her, she heard the sound of four feet galloping through the mud. Dion opened her eyes.

Rhom grinned. "Didn't take her long."

The wolfwalker leaned down to greet the wolf, who lunged across the mud and burst through the grass, her yellow eyes wild and her thick fur wet and slimy with spattered mud. Dion braced herself to meet the force of Hishn's arrival, and as the wolf hit her in the chest, the mud and loose fur transferred itself to Dion's mail.

"Okay, Hishn," she whispered. "You're with me now. Calm down." The wolf nudged her hard, hiding her head in Dion's arms. But Dion gripped Hishn's jowls and, looking into her yellow eyes, shook the gray head until the wildness left her and the Gray One's thoughts came more clearly.

The smells cling to my nose, the wolf whined softly. *I can only hear you in this place.*

"I know, but you can see me now, and I, you." And between the two of them, she told herself, maybe they would see the mudsuckers before the suckers saw them.

Rhom motioned for her to hurry, so she pushed Hishn away and stood back up. "Come on," she said, as if the words would make her brave. "Let's catch up."

It took a good half hour to wade far enough across the swamp to see the other side. If the grass islands had not suddenly given way to a mud flat, they would not have seen the other bank until they trod on it, but as it was, they got a clear glimpse of the last stretch of swamp before they had to cross it. By that time, they were covered in mud, and their faces were smeared where they had swatted at the bugs and scratched ineffectively at the bites. Even Hishn's gray fur was thick with drying slime. Dion, whose legs were like lead weights, the mud sticking to her worn boots like liquid rock, told herself that mudsuckers needed open water. They required deep pools to live in, not thin runs. They could not breed in a bog. She wished she had not thought of the suckers breeding.

The Gray One whined constantly, stepping distastefully into the marsh and sinking up to her chest in mud, then deeper into the thin brown water until she was swimming as she followed the wolfwalker. And Dion, her breathing shallow as she held back her fear, lifted her pack over her head like the others and staggered and slipped along behind Rhom, blinded by the clouds of insects that hovered overhead. "Put more mud on the back of your neck," she advised Rhom nervously. "It'll help keep the bugs off."

He made a face. "Great. By the time we get out of here, Aranur's sister won't even look at me, let alone walk next to me."

"She might think it an improvement," Dion retorted. The next instant, she found herself ducking a glop of mud he tossed over his shoulder.

By the time they reached the other bank, Dion was chilled and sweating. While Hishn leapt ahead of her to disappear into the dry grass on the shore, Dion hid the trembling of her hands by wiping them on her leggings and then in the grass until they were as clear of the swamp mud as they were of the shakes. She was afraid, and she was disgusted by her fear. That she had faced that fear made no difference. It had not faded. She looked at her hands, still trembling, and clenched them against her leggings.

Aranur, who had rested his hand on Tyrel's shoulder for a moment, looked around for the wolf. "Where's Hishn?" he asked Dion.

Dion did not look up at his question. "In the bushes. Rolling in the dirt. Making sure she gets as much of it ground in as possible."

He shrugged. "At least the dirt smells better."

The wolfwalker laughed shortly. "Don't be too sure. She's a wolf. She's probably rolling in deer droppings."

Aranur made a face, but turned to the others. "We'll go another half kilometer to the west," he told them, tying the top of his pack down and slinging it onto his back. "Then we'll cut back north. That way, we'll avoid those rockfalls we saw from the ridge. We'll be into the farmland by evening. And with the luck of the moons, we'll bypass any scouts on watch." He gestured at the second place in line, and Dion met his eyes with an unreadable look. But she fell in behind him, the gray wolf trotting noisily out of the brush, snorting and dropping once more to the ground to roll more of the sticky mud into the dirt and off her fur, before taking her place by Dion's side. Although Dion accepted Hishn's nudging with good grace, the wolf's images must have been strong; the wolfwalker's eyes grew unfocused as she listened to the forest through the beast.

. . . *damp mists rising from the soft dirt. Stench of a worlag's passing and marking the trail with its piss. A shift, a movement, a gather of birds scatter to their left. Eyes flash.*

Noise blasts through straining ears. Leaves close behind them.
The gray shades of motion are gone. Gray fur rubs against the
woman's leg . . .

They had crossed another hill before the sky became more
heavily overcast and the air turned cool. Dion, who had sent
Hishn out to hunt for supper, opened and closed her wounded
hand as she ran, ignoring the pain as best she could. They were
following a dry streambed, clambering quietly among the rocks
a meter below the level of the ground, when a bough slapped
softly against the back of her hand and she froze.

She held her hand up to halt the others and breathed,
"Aranur—"

They all dropped instantly to a crouch. To their left, a group
of men sat eating their lunch, two of them sleeping in the cool
precursor to the evening's rain. Another moment along the
streambed and they would have been in plain sight.

Silently Aranur strung his bow. He picked an arrow, checked
the feather for a clean flight, then aimed between the trees
down trail from where the scouts waited. A few seconds later,
the brush rustled, and one of the scouts stood up sharply. He
grabbed his sword and kicked one of the sleeping men. "Yarl,
Makks," he snapped. "Get up. We've got something down
trail." Grabbing bows, the scouts ran silently along the path,
and Aranur motioned for his group to hurry. Namina slipped
and snapped a twig off a branch, and Aranur whipped around,
his face thunderous, but he said nothing, and they did not stop
until they were far enough from the site of the scouts that they
could breathe without fear that someone would hear.

When Aranur finally motioned them to halt, Shilia dropped
to rest beside Rhom. She breathed quickly, her chest rising and
falling as she caught her breath. "Longear's men?" she whispered.

Rhom nodded.

The girl hesitated, her brown eyes worried.

Rhom wished he could tell Shilia that the moons would bless
them with a clear road to Ariye, but he scowled. It was not for
him to second-guess the moons.

She glanced at her brother, then back to Rhom. "Do you
think we'll really be safer once we reach the towns?" she
asked.

The blacksmith looked at her carefully. But she was not
questioning her brother's judgment so much as looking for
reassurance. He nodded. "If we can get to a town, yes," he

said confidently. "We can hide among the people—Longear will not guess that we would go through his own front yard to get home. It would take us six times longer to get back to Ariye through the mountains."

Shilia nodded. "And we have to get back before autumn."

"If Ariye is to have a chance to prepare for the raiders set to invade in spring, yes."

"And to give you and Dion a chance to get back to Randonnen to warn your own elders."

He brushed a lock of hair away from her shoulders. "Randonnen is close to Ariye."

She looked at him silently. A desert separated the mountains of Randonnen and Ariye, and it was not crossed lightly. She would not see him again if he went home to Randonnen without her.

But Rhom was glancing toward Aranur, and, seeing that the other man had already motioned for Dion and the wolf to follow him, got to his feet as well. He offered Shilia his hand, and she took it, but she would not meet his eyes.

On the trail, Aranur and Dion moved quietly ahead, followed by Gamon, then the two girls, and lastly Rhom and Tyrel. They kept to the streambed for another hour before it turned sharply and angled back toward the lower trails. Gamon glanced at the streambed regretfully. If it rained that night, the runoff would probably wash all traces of them away. But he was not sure it would rain, and the stream turned back toward Zentsis's scouts. He would rather risk the high trails than the scouts, and Aranur had agreed.

They had seen no signs of Zentsis's or Longear's men for the past three hours when evening sucked the light from the sky, and Aranur chose their camp. As he stood looking over the shallow valley, he found his eyes following Dion's silhouette as she hunted greens for their dinner. The man's jerkin and mail she wore disguised much of her shape. At a distance, he would not be able to tell she was not a man. He watched her thoughtfully. Shilia and Namina were girlish enough that they could probably pass as youths if they dressed like Dion. And he and Tyrel both had extra tunics—Shilia had been using his for several nights to keep the stingers from her face as she slept.

The wolfwalker, having gathered an armful of duckfoot leaves, stopped by him, and they stood quietly for a moment. Before them, only a ribbon of purple-orange outlined the horizon. The warm air chilled with dew, and the sky, still pale with the light of five moons, showed only patches of stars. Dion glanced at Aranur. His figure, broad across the shoulders, lean in the hips, was still, wary, as he searched the forest below for signs of light or movement. She wondered why he, and not Gamon, the weapons master, led the group. Then she shook her head. Aranur had not told her exactly what position he held in Ariye, but it was one of high respect, she knew. That the Ariyen Lloroi had sent Aranur, his nephew, to find and return with his daughters instead of going himself; that Gamon listened to Aranur's lead and followed the younger man without hesitation; that Aranur's fighting skills were already beyond those of most of the Randonnen fighters Dion had met—these things left little room for doubt. If Gamon did not lead, it must be because Aranur would soon be a weapons master on his own. Although, Dion thought uncharitably, the gray-eyed man acted often as if he already wore the weapons master's moon chain. She regarded him with curious eyes, chewing on her lip.

Aranur broke into her thoughts without turning his head. "Dion," he said softly. "Scout along the ridge, will you? See if Hishn picks up signs of Zentsis's men. If it's clear up here, we can run these bluffs until we get beyond this valley."

She waited a few seconds, then nodded abruptly, oddly disappointed at his words as she handed him the greens she had gathered. She turned away. As Hishn joined her, she tugged at the gray wolf's scruff and then dropped and buried her face in the creature's fur to hide the sudden watering of her eyes. What was her problem tonight? What had she hoped Aranur would say? Or was she just tired and hungry, sick of the people she was traveling with?

Hishn looked at her, and the yellow eyes gleamed.

Dion tightened her jaw and got to her feet. The Gray One was eager to hunt, and the wolfwalker nodded, making her way across the stones as Aranur followed and stopped by his sister.

"Shilia," he said, handing her the greens as Dion continued on, "I'd like you and Namina to dress like Dion from here on in."

The girl peered at the handful of leaves to see how much dirt clung to their yellow veins, then looked up. "Why?"

He shrugged. "A group of men and boys attracts less attention than a group of men and women, and we'll be in farm country soon."

That did catch her attention. "You mean that we'll see people soon?"

He nodded. "But they will want to know why you were traveling and where you were from. And Dion," he said, stopping the wolfwalker just before she slipped off, "you'll have to tell Gray Hishn to stay out of sight when we get to the towns."

Dion paused, frowning.

He saw her expression, but he was tired himself, and in no mood for her to question him at every turn. "It can't be helped, Dion," he stated flatly. "She can join you on the trail afterward. You could not explain her without exposing who you are."

"Hishn and I can circle the towns while you go through," she protested quietly.

He shook his head, his temper flaring so that he had to clamp it down hard. "We've gone over this before, Dion. You get into trouble when you're off by yourself. Look at your hand."

"I get into trouble no more than anyone else," she returned in a low voice. "Have you forgotten your run-in with that lepa flock last ninan? Or the time you stepped in quicksand and almost drowned? My hand will not get better just because I run through a town instead of a forest. And I can pass around a village in the same time it will take you to go through."

"No."

"Dammit, Aranur," she exploded. "Why not?" She remembered in time that her emotions were felt by Hishn, as well, and grasped the snarling wolf by its fur.

Aranur ignored the wolf. "Too much can happen, Healer Dione," he said deliberately. He took a breath and forced Dion to meet his gaze. "And I don't want to lose you."

She gazed at him, an unreadable expression on her face. "Yes," she agreed bitterly, her voice low. "A healer is handy to have along." Turning abruptly, she strode along the ridge with the wolf until she disappeared.

Gamon gave her a sharp look as she passed.

Aranur stared after her. He ground his teeth, then slapped dust off his thighs in frustration and strode over to his uncle. He took another breath to calm down, but his voice, when he spoke, was still angry. "I just don't get it, Gamon," he said, glaring after Dion. "Every time I pay that woman a compliment, she acts as if I've just insulted her."

The weapons master eyed his nephew in amusement. "Are you asking my advice?"

Aranur swore under his breath. "I've had enough of your

advice to last half my lifetime. And it hasn't gotten me anywhere yet but trouble.''

"Looks to me that, with Dion, that kind of trouble could be mighty fun,'' the older man said slyly.

Aranur snorted. "She'd rather be with that wolf of hers than with me.''

"Maybe Hishn has a softer voice.''

"And maybe I'm tired of her fighting me every time I ask for something to be done.''

"It seems to me,'' his uncle returned quietly, "that you order more than you ask.''

Aranur stared at him.

"You also command more than you make conversation. Perhaps all Dion wants is some consideration.''

"What do you think I've been giving her?'' Aranur demanded.

Gamon chuckled. "I don't think I'd better answer that.'' He changed the subject. "Where is she off to now?''

"I asked her to check the ridge to make sure Zentsis's men have not been up here before us.''

"It's not an easy route we've chosen,'' the gray-haired man commented. "I'd lay odds that the scouts will think we'll be keeping to the low ground.''

"I'd think the same,'' Aranur agreed, "but I've learned that I can't anticipate Zentsis's men with any accuracy.''

"I think we have Longear to thank for that.''

Aranur frowned heavily. "That Longear—I just can't figure him out. We jump in the least likely direction, and each time, he's there before us, like a cat playing with a mole. Why the mudsuckers? And how did they find us so quickly out here? It's as if they can't decide whether they want to kill us or capture us—indications point both ways.''

Gamon lost his smile, and his gray eyes were grim. "Or as if Longear is after more than just our group. There would be no other reason to seed the waters or set as many scouts out here as there are.'' He shook his head. "I can't seem to anticipate the man. I can't seem to get inside his head and figure him out.''

Aranur chewed his lip and went thoughtfully to the fire where Rhom was cooking. He was worried. They had avoided the scouts just barely each day. Unless they reached a town soon and found a fast road out of this part of the county, it was only a matter of days before they were forced into Lloroi Zentsis's hands. They had evaded the scouts twice already; Longear could not afford to let them slip through his fingers again. With a sigh, Aranur sat down to eat, but the bird meat was as tasteless as wood.

The next day, they trudged over two more small hills and around a meadow of itch grass before the thick brush grew sparse and they found a stream so shallow it could hide nothing except the water skeeters that skipped along its surface. Dion, seeing the slight depth of the water, slung her pack on the ground and took off her warcap to dunk in the creek. Gamon and Rhom made their way downstream, but Aranur stopped beside the healer and splashed his face in the creek as well. He glanced back at Namina, but Dion said she would keep an eye on the girl. Now that they were finally away from the scouts— as far as he could tell, he reminded himself—he did not want to risk Namina betraying them again. The girl had been crying again during the night; he could tell by her eyes. Whether it was from her guilt over their trail and Dion's hand, or because of her sister who had died, he did not know, and as the moons shone, he had to admit that he did not care. If she did not start taking an interest in her own life again, by the moons, he would— He stopped and glared at the woods with such intensity that he startled himself. Would what? He swallowed his frustration. He would do nothing, he knew. He would let Namina sort out her life on her own. And watch the girl waste years doing it. He splashed water down his neck to loosen the mud that had caked under his collar. Moonworms . . .

Dion's voice caught his attention finally, and he looked up. "What is it?" he asked.

"We'd like to bathe," she said pointedly, motioning with her chin at Namina and Shilia. The two girls had already dropped their burdens and were tugging their boots off.

His face dripping, Aranur looked around while Dion unbuckled her sword and lay the weapon on the ground next to her bow. She was careful of her hand, but he knew that she would not hesitate to pick up either weapon if there was need. "Where's Gamon and Rhom and Tyrel?" He asked.

Dion pointed downstream.

He nodded and started off.

"Don't you think you'll be wanting this before you get too far downstream?"

He accepted his pack from the wolfwalker with a grin. "Sorry."

"I'll bet," Shilia whispered.

He raised his eyebrow, and his sister giggled.

"Get out of here," she ordered peremptorily. "And don't come back till you're cleaner."

He grinned. "That'll take awhile."

"And don't bring Rhom with you until he looks like himself again."

He made a mock bow. "As you command, my sister." He glanced at Dion as he slung his pack back over his aching shoulders. "Shilia, Namina, don't forget to put on Tyrel's extra tunics when you're done bathing. They're in your packs."

"You mean we might see people by tonight?"

"If we're lucky," he returned. "Maybe even find a farm-house."

Shilia's eyes widened. "Does this mean we could actually sleep on a bed? Eat off real plates? Shower?"

He grinned before striding out of sight. "If you need anything, just yell."

An hour later, the girls looked even more like waifs than Dion, dwarfed as they were by their borrowed clothes. Aranur stared at them. But Shilia just laughed and braided her hair up under a cap.

"Come on, Namina," Shilia said ruefully. "Let's hide your hair, too."

"I don't want bugs getting in it," the other girl protested fretfully as Shilia went to unbraid her hair first before braiding it to fit under the warcap.

Shilia forced a smile. "No bugs," she promised.

Namina did not smile back. She looked thinner, Aranur realized. And the shadows under her eyes had not lessened. He watched his young cousin for several minutes before touching Dion on her arm.

"What is it?" the wolfwalker asked, glancing up, one hand full of short green twigs, and the other holding a soft brown pouch.

He motioned his head. "It's Namina."

She set the pouch back in her pack. "Yes?"

"Isn't there anything you can do for her? Say to her?"

"Something that hasn't already been said?" Dion shook her head and carefully wrapped the twigs in a fat yellow leaf, not looking up until she was done. Then she sat back on her heels and looked up at him soberly. "She's carrying a lot of guilt, Aranur."

"If it's about the trail—"

Dion shook her head. "Namina knows what she did on the trail, but that's only a small part of what's bothering her. The death of her sister is what eats at her so badly, Aranur. And everything about that has already been said."

"I can't let her continue like this. There has got to be something you can give her to make her right again."

"Guilt and loss cannot be treated with pills or lotions."

"What about Ovousibas?" he returned. "You've done miracles of healing with that. Why can't you do it again?"

Dion shook her head again. "That was a healing of physical, not emotional wounds. It's time Namina needs now, not miracles or orders or advice."

"No." He rejected her statement flatly. "She's had time. Three ninans—twenty-seven days—and she still won't look any of us in the eye. She needs help, Dion. The help of a healer."

Dion frowned. "Looking into someone's mind is not the same as healing someone's body, Aranur. Namina and her sister were close the way Rhom and I are close. The way you and Shilia are close." Dion shook her head. "When Namina lost her sister, she needed to be surrounded by familiar things, not strange valleys and glacier worms and poison masa and swamps. She's feeling lost and alone, Aranur. And she's on the edge. Don't judge her by Shilia or Tyrel—she's not like them. She's terrified by the death and the pain she's seen."

He stared down at the healer, his gray eyes cold. "She is the daughter of the Lloroi of Ramaj Ariye. She cannot escape life by ignoring it."

"You're wrong, Aranur." Dion gestured with her chin. To their left, Namina sat gazing blankly into the distance while Shilia fussed at her hair under the warcap. "Look at her. She's already escaped. She's so withdrawn that none of us have reached her in a month."

The tall man's eyes narrowed. "I won't allow it, Dion. She has no right—" He took a step toward Namina as if to catch the girl and shake her till she snapped out of it.

But Dion caught his arm. "She's young, Aranur. Young and inexperienced. Listen to me." She forced him to look at her.

"Namina was kidnapped by raiders. She watched two of her own friends die during the raid. She was sold into a harem, rescued, caught again, freed once more, and then forced to watch her sister die under another slaver's blade. Yes, we escaped from Red Harbor, but being shipwrecked wasn't a calming experience either, nor was crossing the glaciers or facing the plague at the dome of the ancients. Namina had no experience to prepare her for facing those things. She was taken from a sheltered village and thrown headfirst into a world of blood and pain and death. How do you expect her to feel? How do you think she should react? You can't expect her to embrace the things you've shown her?"

"I expect her to act like who she is," he returned coldly.

"And just who do you think she is?" Dion returned, her voice low but heated. "She's the daughter of the Lloroi of Ariye, yes, but have you ever understood what that means? Look at her. She's never had close girlfriends—her station in Ramaj Ariye prevented that. And she hasn't had a boyfriend in her life—they're all terrified of her father. Her only close friend was her sister. When that raider's sword fell, both her family and her only friend died, and she can't see beyond that. And so you, Aranur, have to look beyond what you expect her to be and let her be what she is."

"It's Namina who needs your advice, not me," he returned coldly.

But Dion stepped in front of him, blocking his path. "You deny your own grief, Aranur. It's how you deal with what you can't handle." He opened his mouth to reject that, but she cut him off. "Tyrel," she continued, "he re-creates his grief with his eyes every day, every hour, every minute. And Gamon wears his like a heavy cloak. Your own sister Shilia hides her pain and smiles and pretends she is brave, because that's what she sees her brother doing. And Namina—"

Aranur stared at her. "Namina withdraws."

"Yes." Dion said it forcefully, as if by her voice alone she could convince him. "Namina escapes to her memories. The only place where her sister is still alive. Aranur, don't you see—"

The tall man's face closed off, and Dion looked at him for a long moment.

"Can you even admit to yourself how you felt as a child when you saw your parents die?" she asked softly.

The question startled him.

"Do you remember?"

He nodded slowly, his face still and his gray eyes boring holes in hers, but seeing only his own memories, not the woman he stood before.

"Then think of that," she said softly. "Remember the way you felt at their deaths, and give Namina time."

Wordlessly, Aranur stared at her. Finally he turned and started slowly—almost like a blind man—down the trail.

Dion, with a glance at the others, fell in behind him, as the rest of the group dragged themselves to their feet and straggled after them.

The land began to roll into low hills covered with thicker stands of leafy trees, their greenery rustling continuously in the breeze that brushed the thicker clouds across the cooling sky. The sounds of the branches rubbing gently against one another kept Aranur company as he strode with that bleak look of silence on his face. He paid little attention to the wind. It would rain later, he knew, but not for several hours. The dark thunderheads that clumped over the mountains and billowed across the gray sky would take a long time to reach the far side of the valley in which they trekked.

As the ground grew drier, the stands of silverheart and blackthorn gave way to piletrees, the trees that dropped their branches each spring and fall to build up soft hills that sheltered the trunks and roots from summer drought and winter freezes. So they trudged raggedly among the trees, ducking under the dead lower branches that caught in their hair and broke off, brittle and dry, while Aranur paused every few minutes to take a new sighting and put them back on course.

Suddenly the ground at his feet erupted. A brown, spotted shape exploded from the dug-out hollow, and a badgerbear leapt out in an explosion of flying leaves and dirt. The man's startled heart froze at the bloodcurdling scream even as his arms fairly ripped his sword from its scabbard. A black hole, ringed by curving yellow teeth, led down the badgerbear's gullet in the middle of its red, dripping maw, and Aranur's instant thought was that he would be suffocated and torn apart by its brown spreading fur and sharp yellow fangs. Namina screamed as Gamon shoved her away from him and the creature. The old man shouted, and then two long knives sliced through the beast's flattened neck, jarring it midair. As it fell frantically toward him, Aranur stabbed the hard shell of bone in the badgerbear's midsection that cased its brain, the creature's claws catching on his mail and jerking him forward with tremendous force. He yanked himself free. As the beast shuddered, thrashing to the earth, he jumped back, careful to stay out of reach of its death throes.

"Aranur!" Shilia darted past Rhom, who let go of her when he saw that the bear was no longer a threat. "Are you all right?"

"Yeah, though I just about jumped out of my leggings for a moment. Thanks, Rhom, Gamon."

At the back of the line, Tyrel had his arms around Namina, but she thrust him away.

"I want to go home," she said tightly. "I don't want to follow game trails and sleep on the ground and cook on open fires and—" her voice was rising "—eat raw roots and dried jerky and get b-blisters on my feet and d-dirty hands and there was a—" Her voice shook and rose even further in pitch. "—a gellbug in my blank-ket this morning and the g-ground comes apart when you step-p on it and horrib-ble creatures jump out to eat you an-nd—" She sat down on the ground and put her face in her hands and sobbed.

Aranur looked down at his sword, which dripped blood and an entrail that clung grossly to the stained steel, and absently wiped the blade. He stared at her for a moment. "I'm sorry, Namina," he said finally.

Tyrel, his young face straight and grim at his sister's outburst, let her cry for a moment, then turned away, reshouldered his pack, and hefted hers to his thin shoulders, too. Rhom lifted the girl to her feet and placed his hand under her arm to steady her shaking body, but she shrugged him off, the tears running down her dirty face, and her hands, equally filthy, wiping ineffectually at them as she stumbled after her brother. After a while, she took her pack back from Tyrel without a word and followed him down the trail.

From the front of the ragged line, the old man glanced back. "Aranur—" he started.

"We'll stay at a farm tonight if we can find one," Aranur answered flatly. "An empty field if not."

Gamon dropped it. Aranur must have been twice as tired as the rest of them, but he was still driving himself like a demon, hunting twice as much trail, carrying twice as much weight, and the moons knew that the lean meals they had had through the mountains had given Aranur little enough energy to work with. As if he thought he could lead them like shadows out from under Zentsis's reach and back to the peace of Ariye, the old man thought to himself. He did not worry about Rhom; the young blacksmith was as tough as they came and, he reminded himself, knew when and how to take a break. But of the rest of them, Tyrel was still gaunt from the fever that had held him too long in its grip, Shilia had not the strength to begin with, and Gamon was too old to push his body like the younger men. Aranur was driving them all near collapse, especially the healer and her wolf, sending them to scout before and behind them as they hiked. Gamon looked after Dion for a long moment. Each day they struggled through the mountains left the violet-eyed woman ever more lean and dangerous, as if she became closer to her wolf with each passing hour. She would stand and wait sometimes for long moments, saying nothing, just sensing the trails through the Gray One, and then, when someone moved, she would start, realizing she was on the path with other people. He wondered how much she relied on the wolf now, and how much she relied on herself. He shook his head, rubbing his knee where it had begun to ache more constantly than before. It would be a long way home.

An hour later, when the sky sent its drizzle down to dampen their spirits as well as their skins, and twilight began to seep through the trees and strip the color from the woods, they straggled out of the last thick stand of forest and climbed the rude fence of a farmer's unused pasture. In the distance, they could see the tiny lights of a small house whose windows winked from the top of a low hill. From the edge of the trees, Aranur motioned wearily at the dwelling, pointing out the lights to Namina. The tiny glows were the cheeriest thing they had seen in a long time, and he could only thank the nine moons for seeing the group through the mountains safely.

Gray grass lay clumped in the fallow field, and the deep shadows that were flung from the tiny knolls left by dnu droppings turned the pasture into a patchwork of black-and-gray holes. The lean fighter strode a few steps, sank into the damp ground, stumbled over a harder knoll of dirt, and caught himself before swearing.

The Gray One at Dion's side nudged her hand, and the wolfwalker pointed toward a deep ditch that cut across the grass from northeast to southwest. "Fresh mud. Hishn can smell it from here."

"Probably just irrigation."

She nodded and would have continued, but he stopped her with a hand on her arm.

"Dion, Hishn can't go up to the house with us."

She shrugged. "It's dark, Aranur. I'll send her away when we get close."

He hesitated, then nodded. "All right." His muscles ached, his stomach cramped with hunger that refused to be relieved by the jerky he chewed continuously, and his pack weighed twice as much as it had that morning. Although he knew he should tell Dion to send the wolf away now, he was just too tired to argue. She was right: it was near dark, and who was there to see? So they trudged across the field, their feet slipping in the wet earth and the misty rain dripping from their warcaps and noses as it found its sly way like a thief into their clothes.

They reached the next fence and clambered over, and Aranur paused, taking Dion's pack as she vaulted the wire-and-wood structure behind him.

"Good strong fence," she commented, resting her hand on one of the poles and giving it a tug. "Whoever built it must have taken pride in his work." The wolf lunged easily over the fence beside her and landed with a muddy thump.

"If only my legs could jump like that at this time of night," Aranur muttered under his breath.

Dion took her rucksack back and slung it over her shoulder, shrugging the other arm through the straps and accepting Aranur's help gratefully when it caught on her thin poncho and the weatherized cloth began to tangle as well. "How many people live here, do you figure?"

"Looks like a small house, but there's a lot of land. The house must be bigger than it looks, or the fields end at the top of that hill."

"Will they accept us?"

He shrugged. "I don't know. If they recognize us, they'll probably turn us in to save their own skins from Zentsis's men."

"I don't think I care if they're friends or enemies as long as they feed us."

He chuckled mirthlessly. "I'm almost hungry enough to agree."

With the moons hidden behind the clouds, it was hard to see clearly across the pasture, but the lights in the house still beckoned, so they trudged obligingly toward the next fence. But suddenly, Hishn growled.

"Aranur—" Dion stiffened.

The tall man whirled.

A dark figure loomed out of the wet trench barely ten meters away. Aranur glanced at the forest, too far away, and the house, up the hill through another field. As the man's face turned toward them, he realized that there was no place left to hide.

Chapter 5

The healer's gift is free;
Offered when needed,
Given when asked.
    This do I swear
    By the gift of the band.
The Healer's Right is taken;
Used when needed,
Refused when not.
    This do I swear
    By the right of the band.
The healer's burden is silent;
Sung not.
Spoken not.
Life is cherished whether gained or lost.
    This do I swear
    By the moons of the band.
    This do I swear.

—Second stanza from the Creed of the Healers

The old man turned. Hishn snarled. Gamon half pulled steel from the sheath. Aranur shifted, silent, deadly.

Dion clenched his arm. "No," she whispered.

The wind died, and the tension stretched into hours. The farmer stood in the ditch, gauging their still, silent forms, their hands on their swords, the wariness of the wolf in Dion's eyes and the chill of a winter fog in Aranur's cold, gray gaze. Someone exhaled audibly.

"Let me give you a hand with that."

It was Rhom.

The elderly farmer, still motionless from straightening up with the bucket, looked at the burly man with narrowed eyes. His gaze traveled to Aranur, then to the slim fighter who held back the tall man's sword arm, then to Gamon, whose lean, seamed face was so shadowed by the twilight that the scars of his history were only edges to the dark hollows of his cheeks. The wolf, growling so low that the rumble never left her throat, slunk behind a clump of grass and dropped to her belly, disappearing from the farmer's view; if the Gray One had been a shadow in the mist, she would have had more substance than the memory she left the man. As they held their breath, the blacksmith stepped forward and lifted the heavy bucket up from the old man's hand.

"Irrigation?" he asked quietly with a nod down at the muddy trench.

The farmer gave him a speculative look, glanced up at the others, and nodded briefly. "That, and draining the fields."

Rhom set the bucket on the rain-sloppy ground. "You must have dropped the water table by what, a quarter meter?"

The older man nodded slowly. "Hoped to start in on the west sixty this year." He took his shovel from where it leaned against the wall of the trench, the thin mud dripping down its handle where water ran off the bedraggled grass at the edge of the ditch. He met Rhom's eyes squarely, then Aranur's. "I got to finish up here, but you all look like you could use a wash. Go on up to the barn. There's a pump on the east side." He stabbed the shovel back in the mud. "I'll be up in a bit."

Aranur exchanged glances with Rhom, who raised his eyebrows. With an almost imperceptible nod, Aranur answered his unspoken question, and Rhom shrugged off his pack and handed it to Gamon. The burly twin stepped cautiously to the edge of the ditch and jumped in, his leather boots sinking into the muck up to his ankles as the water seeped over his feet.

The farmer looked up slowly, but Rhom's hands were empty of steel.

"You shovel, and I'll toss it up," Rhom offered. He reached for the bucket and flung its heavy contents up on the bank, then set it back down for the farmer to refill. "Save you some time."

The old man eyed him without comment, then dug the shovel in and dropped a chunk of slippery clay into the bucket.

Up in the pasture, Gamon gestured for Tyrel and the girls to follow him across the ditch and beyond the field. Shilia hesitated, but Dion shook her head and motioned with her eyes so that the other girl went on with her uncle instead. As Aranur watched them cross the ragged grass, he shifted so that he could see both the farmer and his uncle at the same time, and the old farmer paused and glanced up.

"There's two more shovels back about twenty meters," the farmer said. Rhom tossed his full bucket over the edge again so that the mud landed with a thick splat. The farmer's eyes followed the motion with satisfaction before adding, "One of the tools is dull, but the other is sharp as the tooth of a lepa." He turned away and stomped the shovel back into the ditch, wedging out another lump of clay. "Long as you're here . . ."

Aranur hesitated, then shrugged out of his own pack and handed it to Dion along with his sword. Dion met his gaze briefly, then set his pack on the edge of her foot to keep it out of the mud as much as possible. He turned to the old man. "Are you shoring up as you go?"

The farmer shook his head. "Ran out of sacking nine days and fifty meters back."

"You've got plenty of silverheart growing around here. Why not use the poles instead?"

"What do you mean?"

Aranur motioned for Dion to get the shovels, then dropped into the ditch himself. He examined the walls of the ragged trench carefully. "Cut the poles about five meters long, then drive them into the sides, straight in." He pointed along the ditch. "Here, and here—about so far apart. It gives the wall stability. Then lash crosspieces to the ends of the stabilizers, and build a thick lattice along the wall. Instead of sacking sand or rock to hold the shape, you can spread the sacking out—even use tree bark. It'll go six, seven times farther. It's a good method where there's a lot of erosion."

"Maybe."

Aranur shrugged, stepped back to the edge by Dion, and gestured with his chin down the muddy trench. "How far are you taking this ditch?"

"Down to the tree line. Runoff goes into a swamp a hundred meters back."

The tall man nodded. "How many of these fields have you had to drain?"

"Only two, but Jack Scratch—we call him that because he's always scratchin' his chin when you talk to him—he's had to drain all of his. Course he lives in more of a hollow than we do here. Just over the hill there. The bottom half of all his land is swamp."

"So you own the fields to the top of the hill and east beyond that last fence?" Aranur took the shovel that Dion stretched down to him, but as she leaned down, her slender fingers on the handle, the farmer's gaze sharpened. She froze, then pulled her hood farther forward. Aranur and Rhom glanced at each other.

The old man looked at Dion, then leaned on his shovel and said to Aranur, "Are you wanting to know how far away my neighbors are, or just where the marsh lies?"

Aranur smiled, though the expression did not reach his eyes. "Both, if you'll tell us."

"Don't see why not. Jack's place is a quarter kilometer that way, and the marsh a quarter kilometer beyond that. Did you come in east or west of Masa Hill?"

"Masa Hill?"

"The saddle-back mountain north of the long lake."

"Over it, then west," Aranur returned. He shoved his own tool in the mud and sliced out a chunk of clay.

The old man gave him a sharp look. "I've heard a lot of tales, young man, but that's got to be the wildest." He snorted. "No one's gone over Masa Hill in fourteen years."

"We didn't have a choice."

"Hah." The farmer bent his aging shoulders into the shovel and heaved to loosen a particularly large clump of clay. "You always got a choice, boy."

Aranur smiled slowly. "What do you call the lake back in there?"

"Silver Lake."

"Not Lizard Lake?"

The old farmer looked sideways at the gray-eyed man. "So you did go through. Wouldn't have thought even Zentsis's scouts had the balls to do that."

Dion became very still at his words, and Aranur's smile was suddenly cold. "Why do you say we're scouts?"

The farmer paused and leaned on his shovel. "Listen, son. I've lived here sixty-two years. I know every man who's lived in this valley for the last eighty. You got troops in town and scouts swarming the outer county for the last four ninans. Now the troops—they're the ones who swagger and brag, eat the tonnis root, cut up the taverns, and start fights." He pointed at the three fighters. "You scouts, now you're different. Quiet. Like a lepa before it leaps. You all look the same, dress the same, wear your weapons the same way, and got the same look in your eyes.'' The old man slid his chunk of clay into the bucket and sliced the shovel back into the clammy soil. ''The only difference between you and the others I've seen is that you're down here in the mud with me instead of up in a tavern with the rest of them when it rains.''

Rhom grinned and flung the contents of the bucket over the edge. ''We figure if we're polite, we'll get to eat something besides roots and lake larvae for dinner.''

''Thought you city boys took rations with you when you went out.''

''There are city scouts, and then there are scouts,'' Aranur returned with a slow smile. ''City scouts take rations, and run for the inn when it rains. The rest of us,'' he finished with a shrug, ''keep on walking.''

The old man chuckled. ''Seeing as how it brought me some help, I ain't complainin'. Sure, you're welcome to stay for dinner. We can knock off for now. We've reached my marker.''

Rhom threw the last bucket of mud over the edge. ''What do we call you?''

''Jaime neKohler.'' The older man set the shovel against the slippery wall and caught his breath. ''But you can call me Jam.''

Aranur set his shovel next to the farmer's. ''I'm—Shull. That's Devlin—'' he pointed to Rhom ''—and that's . . . Deats,'' he added with a gesture at Dion.

''It's a pleasure.''

''Likewise.''

''Want to give me a hand up?'' the farmer asked Dion, holding up his hand. ''My ladder's back quite a ways, and it's too slippery down here to be tromping around looking for it.''

The wolfwalker hesitated, her dark eyes going first to Aranur, who quickly cut in. ''Before you go up, Jam, where do you want these tools?''

The old man turned his head, and Rhom stepped up to Dion instead, letting his sister pull him quickly out of the ditch. He met her eyes with amusement as she moved away from their work and let both the shadows and her sleeves hide her hands again.

''Just hand them up to me when I'm up top, will you?'' Jam said to Aranur as he turned back to Dion.

Aranur nodded. But when Jam reached up to take the healer's

hand, it was Rhom who offered his arm, and the old man's eyes twinkled momentarily as he grasped the blacksmith's wrist and let himself be pulled up. "You've got a strong grip, Devlin."

"Comes from working in a smithy."

The old man glanced across the fields at the small house that sat on the hilltop. "We better hurry. Knowin' my mate, she's liable to be holding a bow on your men."

Dion took the tools Aranur handed her, while Rhom helped the tall man out of the ditch.

"The troops have been causing trouble here?" Aranur asked.

"About what you'd expect when you turn fifty soldiers loose in a small town."

"If anyone bothers you while we're here," Aranur said quietly, "we will take care of it."

The old man shrugged. "No offense, Shull, but we'll be glad when you boys find what you're looking for and get out of our valley."

Aranur fell in step with the farmer and let the other two trail him across the now-dark pasture; he wondered if the wolf was shadowing Dion as Dion and Rhom shadowed him. "Well," he said to Jam, "if we have anything to say about it, it'll be sooner than you think."

"Givin' up?"

Aranur shrugged. "We'd be wasting our time to hang out back there any longer," he said honestly.

"What were you lookin' for, anyway?"

Aranur smiled slowly. "You know we can't tell you that, Jam."

"Well, it don't hurt to ask." The old man gestured around the field. "Watch your step from here on up. There's jack rabbit burrows everywhere."

"How long has this field been fallow?"

"Decade and a half. Ever since my two youngest died." Aranur glanced at him. "I'm sorry."

The old man shrugged. "The moons take who they will. Himali and Attim, I named them, after my father and his brother. Attim was the serious one, always studying. Wanted to be a chemist. Himali, now, he was the wild one of the bunch. He could run the woods like a ghost. Would've made a good scout, too," he added with a speculative glance at Dion.

Having reached the end of that field and the clean line of a well-built fence, the farmer stopped, stomped mud from his boots, and unhitched the gate, glancing back at Aranur with a speculative look. "The missus, now, she's had bad luck, as well. Got caught out in Grover's Gully pickin' herbs when the lepa were flocking." He closed the gate after his guests and motioned them up the field, stomping ahead of them a few steps without looking back. "Them knife-faced birds were so thick they looked like a thunderstorm. And me too far away to help. Took me nigh onto two days to find her," he muttered, more to himself than them. "Footprints wiped out by the scavengers. Bones all over the gully . . ."

"She was all right?" Rhom's question seemed to startle the farmer, and the old man glanced back at them.

His eyes finally focused. "They marked her, some, but she gets around now." He paused. "I'd appreciate it if you didn't mention it when we get to the house."

Aranur nodded. "Of course."

The old farmer pointed at the building sitting west of the house. "If you want to wash up first, the pump's on that side of the barn. I'll tell the missus you're here. Looks like your friends are waiting for you."

Aranur nodded again, and Jam made his way over to his home while they joined Gamon and the others at the stable.

Looking after the old man, Dion asked Aranur in a low voice, "What do you think?"

"Seems safe enough. What does Hishn say?"

"She senses no intent from him. His scent is clear, not sharp, like that of a hunter."

He frowned slightly and nodded to his uncle as they rounded the corner of the barn. "Gamon," he said, "did you meet Jam's wife yet?"

Gamon shook his head. "We stayed here and checked out the barn. There seems to be only two people living on this place—there's sleds and saddles built for children, but they haven't been used in years. There are only two sets of footprints anywhere near the barn. No sign of Zentsis's troops."

"Yes, but would they leave sign in the rain?"

Gamon chuckled without mirth. "Zentsis's men, yes. Longear's men, no."

Dion gazed back at the forest through which they had come, her ears hearing night sounds through the wolf's senses, not her own. "Gamon," she said slowly, "you haven't been able to figure Longear's moves, have you?"

The older man's face grew suddenly still. "No. There's something I keep missing about that man. Something that isn't right . . . "

Hishn growled low at Dion's thoughts, and the wolfwalker turned and looked at Gamon's frown. "What do you mean?" she asked softly.

"There's something not logical about the way he sets his scouts out, what he has them do. Even his traps—like the mudsuckers—they don't ring right." He shook his head with a puzzled frown. "It's as if . . . "

"As if what?"

Gamon shook his head silently and stared across the muddy barnyard at the house.

Dion studied the older man, then glanced at Aranur as he scrutinized each person in his group.

"Dion, is your headband hidden?" Aranur asked sharply. He did not wait for an answer. "Shilia, Namina, make sure your hair is up under the warcaps. And don't stand up so straight. Slump a bit. It'll help hide your chests." He gestured at the pump, which Rhom, still dripping from the cold water, had just vacated. "Go ahead, Dion. I can wait." Looking around, he scowled. "Gamon, they must keep carrier birds around here. Have you seen them yet?"

Shilia tucked her loose hair up into the cap. "They have a carrier bird pen up by the house," she said, "but we didn't go near it."

"What kind of birds?"

"I only heard the pigeons, doves, and falcons," she said slowly. "But they might have hawks, as well, since they're good hunters, too."

He nodded, waiting while Dion splashed water on her face and neck and then scrubbed her hands under the pump's steady stream. She hesitated as she tucked her hair back up into the warcap and looked wistfully at the pump.

Aranur shrugged. "If this farmer's on the level, you can wash it tomorrow. Right now we can't take the time."

"He seems decent enough, Aranur."

"Some of the worst raiders have pleasant faces, Dion," he returned shortly, looking around. "Where's Gray Hishn now? Did you send her back to the forest?"

The wolfwalker patted her face dry with her one semiclean cloth and avoided Aranur's gaze. "No, but she's out of sight."

"What do you mean, 'out of sight'?"

"Well, it was dark, and I didn't think Jam would notice . . ."

He frowned at her. "Where's the wolf now, Dion?"

She sighed. "Over there."

Aranur looked to his left. "Where?"

Shilia and Rhom exchanged glances, and Dion heaved another sigh. "You really can't see her in the dark. Jam will never even know she's here."

"Where is she, Dion?" His voice was cold, and Dion knew it was no use to argue. She pointed slowly.

"Come on out, Hishn."

There was a slight brush of fur against dirt, and then the wolf stood up and poked her nose out from under the steps of the barn. Aranur stared at the wolf, incredulous. "You had her sitting under these steps? Sitting at the very door of the barn?"

"Well, you stepped over her twice and never noticed."

The lean man glared.

"Look, Aranur, it's only for the night. And Jam thinks we're Zentsis's scouts anyway, so what does it matter?"

Aranur opened his mouth, but Gamon chuckled. "Ease off, nephew. If the old man thinks we work for Zentsis and Longear, and the Gray One disappears before dawn, there's no harm done." He peered at the younger man. "How did you manage to make him think we're scouts?"

Aranur quelled his irritation and shrugged. "He guessed it. I just didn't correct him."

"He guess how long we were out in the hills, too?"

"We told him we wouldn't turn our noses up at a dinner invitation if he gave us one."

Gamon nodded. "Good. I was getting tired of Shilia's cooking."

The girl made a face. "If you'd catch something other than rabbit, you'd have something better to eat."

Just then the door to the house opened, and light scattered across the porch. Jam came out and looked toward the barn.

"Quiet," Aranur ordered in a low voice. "Dion—"He gestured behind him. "Hishn."

Dion nodded, and the wolf slipped back under the steps of the barn, settling silently into the dust and snorting only once at the dirt in her nose.

"If you're washed up, come on in," the farmer called.

Aranur waved. "Give us a few minutes more. We've got a lot of mud to clean off."

Jam nodded and stepped back inside.

"Aranur," Gamon said as his nephew washed his face and hands. "I didn't see any riding beasts in the stable, but this farm is far enough out of the main county that Jam'll have to have some kind of dnu here. They may only be working beasts, but he might let us buy one or two to ride out of here, and it would save time on the road."

Aranur let the water drip from his face as he shook his hands dry. "I know, but let's see what kind of welcome we get in the house. Rhom, keep your blade loose."

The blacksmith nodded. Aranur caught Shilia and Namina by the shoulders.

"Don't talk in there, all right?" he said quietly. "Your voices will give you away. And try to eat more with your fingers than your forks. It'll look less—dainty."

Shilia made a face. "Can we at least use napkins?"

He grinned and shrugged. "Follow Tyrel's lead."

"Then we'll look like dnu," she retorted.

"Better dnu than dead," the boy returned shortly. But as they climbed the two wooden steps to the porch, the door opened again, and they fell silent, Jam stepping back so they could enter easily.

"This way. Come on in. Supper'll be ready in twenty minutes."

Aranur passed him, glancing around the room and noting the painfully neat furniture and spotless tabletops that greeted them. The farmer's mate was not in sight, but he could hear the sounds of a pan clanking down on the stove and the shuffling feet of someone in the kitchen. He stepped aside, and Rhom entered behind him, then Tyrel. But when Dion got to the door, the farmer put his hand on her sleeve to stop her.

"Ma'am," he said quietly. "Could I speak to you for a moment?"

She stopped, looking up at him with wide, startled eyes like a water cat caught suddenly in the light. Over Jam's shoulders, Aranur stiffened; and Rhom half turned, his own violet eyes dangerous as he judged the farmer's next words.

Jam glanced at Aranur, then back at the wolfwalker. "I figure I'm not supposed to know you're a woman, and I'm not meaning to get you in trouble, but the missus ain't had women folk to visit in over a year. If you'd talk with her, keep her company a bit, she'd be rarely pleased and I'd be sorely grateful."

Dion looked helplessly over the farmer's shoulder at Aranur, and he, though his eyes narrowed, nodded.

She smiled ruefully at Jam, then reached up, let her hood fall back, and took off her warcap so that her glossy, black hair fell out around her shoulders.

"Well, nail my hide to a bullion tree," the farmer exclaimed. "You're more of a sight for my eyes than I'd have guessed in a well-lit ninan."

Aranur hid his involuntary smile.

"Byra's in the kitchen. Just go on through there." He turned to Rhom with a shake of his head. "Don't that beat all? A woman lookin' like that bein' one of Zentsis's scouts. Why, she could knock the shine right off the first moon. And she's like enough to you to be your twin," he added with a pointed glance at the blacksmith.

Rhom shrugged.

"By the moons," Jam repeated softly, "don't that beat all." He shook his head again.

Dion, having reached the large opening to the kitchen, peered into the room. Against the back wall, the windows, dark with the drizzling night, added black silhouettes to the spotless, whitewashed walls and wooden cupboards. Long, clean counters edged their way along each wall, and a larger counter block took up its position in the center of the room. The whole room was lit with bright oil lamps. But what was odd in the oblong kitchen was a number of curved, wooden protuberances that stuck out of the countertops at hip level all along the workspace—some folded down against the cupboards, and some braced out—and the handrails that interspersed the hooks, as well. Dion frowned slightly, studying the woman who was stirring their supper in a large pot.

"Hello," she said finally.

Startled, the farmer's wife turned swiftly, and Dion realized why Jam had made the hooks that poked out of the counters all along the room. The older woman's skirt had hidden her legs, but as she turned, Dion saw that Byra leaned into the hooks to stand at the counters. The old woman's right leg dragged softly on the floor as she caught a handrail and supported herself while she looked around.

"Hello— Why, you're a woman!" The farmer's mate straightened and leaned back into the hip hook so that she could see Dion more clearly, and the healer's eyes flickered at the scars that raked the old woman's face and dragged the right cheek down in long, parallel lines.

"I'm afraid we dropped in on you rather suddenly. I hope you don't mind."

The farmer's wife stared at the younger woman for a long moment, taking in the thick, black hair and creamy skin, the slender shape, and the clear gaze of those violet eyes, and abruptly she turned her own scarred face back to the stove.

"Jam said we'd have company for dinner," the gray-haired woman said sharply over her shoulder, "but he said you were scouts."

Dion nodded slowly. "I'm—Deats," she said, remembering at the last moment the name Aranur had given her in the pasture.

"Not much of a name for a woman."

"To Zentsis's army, I am not a woman," she returned dryly. In her head, Hishn echoed Dion's amusement, stretching her lips into a lupine smile.

The other woman stirred the pot another moment, then lay the spoon down, wiped her hands on her apron, and rested both hands on the counter, her back hunched to the healer.

"I'm sorry," Byra said finally. "I've not talked to anyone but Jam in a long time. I've forgotten my manners." She turned. "I'm Byra. Forgive me." She looked straight at Dion, her old, washed-out blue eyes steeled for the repulsion she knew she would see.

But the wolfwalker merely shrugged. "There is nothing to forgive." She gestured back toward the living room. "You have a beautiful home," she said, changing the subject. "You must have a lovely view of the sunset."

The old woman drew herself up. "That we do. We've lived here most of our lives. Gave us a chance to fix the place up right proper."

Dion smiled and glanced around the room. "It shows. You must have a garden, then, too?"

"I do a wee bit. I've got banked beds for the vegetables, and Jam built me a greenhouse out back," she said, pointing toward the door that led from the kitchen to the yard, "so I grow the herbs I need in there."

Dion's attention sharpened at the mention of herbs, but she asked casually, "Really? What do you raise?"

"Oh, tarragon, ansil, chervil, dill—all the usual ones." The older woman bustled around the stove again, stirring the pot one more time before taking it from the burner and lifting the lid of the one next to it.

Dion fingered the countertops. "I'd love to see your greenhouse. I've an interest in herbs myself."

"Huh." Byra sniffed the pot and grunted in satisfaction. "Have you ever grown chervil or yellowdock?"

The wolfwalker laughed softly and her eyes got a faraway look as she gazed at one of the dark windows. "Yes, but a long ways, a long Journey from here."

The old woman's eyes softened as she looked at Dion. If she had had a daughter among her five sons, the girl would have been about Dion's age, she thought. She sighed. "You're homesick?"

"Sometimes."

"It must be hard, always traveling."

Dion shrugged. "It's interesting. Exciting, at times. It's something I've always wanted to do."

Byra hesitated, then met the younger woman's gaze with a strange, intense look. "Tell me everything," she said abruptly. "Tell me where you've been, what you've done—who you've seen—what they looked like . . ."

Dion laughed uneasily. "Where should I begin?"

The old woman's eyes got a faraway look, and she put her spoon down slowly as she stared out the rain-spattered window. "Clothes," she said, with a faint smile. "What is everyone wearing in town?"

The wolfwalker glanced down at her dirty leather leggings and thinly worn boots. "Well, I haven't been to town lately, but I can tell you what the women in the river ports have done with their hair . . ."

As they talked, laughing and gossiping, Namina, in the next room, listened and grew even more silent, staring into the black night that clung to the window and sucked the painful thoughts from her mind.

Morning dawned with the same gray drizzle the dusk had brought the day before, and Dion woke early. She rolled over, dragging her blanket with her, and bumped into the wolf, who woke, snorted, and licked her face. She wiped her hand across her mouth and wrinkled her nose. "Thanks a lot, Hishn," she said wryly.

The Gray One stretched, kicking loose straw. *This den smells like dnu.*

That's because it's a barn. It's supposed to smell like riding beasts. And just because they have six legs each doesn't mean they smell worse than you. Dion sat up, pulling the stiff stalks of straw from her hair where they had worked their way into her loose braid. After she combed her hair, she combed the wolf, scowling at the dried mud that had caked into Hishn's fur and had to be crumbled away before the hair would lie flat. With the dust from the loose straw mixing in with the dried mud, the wolf looked more like a stray dog than a Gray One, and Dion had to smile at Hishn's insistence that the wolfwalker help clean out her pelt. It took Dion only a moment to roll up her sleeping bag and tie it onto her pack when she was done, so, glancing around and seeing that only Aranur had woken up at her movements, she dug out her extra tunic and other garments. She was tired, but she could not sleep further. And since Aranur had taken one look out the barn window at the rain, rolled over, and gone back to sleep, no one else was awake, so Dion could take the time to wash her clothes and hair before the others decided to get up and do the same.

She left her straw bedding where it was—it would make too much noise to put all the stuffing back in the bins without waking the others. The work dnu in the corner stall stamped its six legs as she passed, and she murmured to it quietly. She wondered if Jam would take Aranur up on his offer to buy two of his dnu. It would save them a lot of time to use dnu as pack beasts instead of carrying their gear themselves. She sighed and slipped out the door. It would be better still if they could buy seven dnu so that they could all ride. Namina, even when Aranur carried most of her pack weight, could not—or would not—run long distance, and thinking of the girl, Dion scowled as she padded around the corner of the barn with the wolf.

I'm hungry, Hishn broke in. *The smell of the bird pen is making me growl.*

"Go hunt then. But do it in the lower pasture or down in the woods. I don't know when Jam and Byra get up, and I don't want you seen."

Hishn's response was the fleeting image of a gray shadow lurking near a rabbit's burrow, and Dion smiled, shaking her head at the offer of the wolf's meal. She would rather eat Byra's breakfast than Hishn's, and since the farmer's wife had offered to feed the seven of them again, she did not think that

Aranur, who had eaten last night as if he were starved, would turn the old woman down.

There were no lights on in the house yet, so Dion set her clothes down and stuck her head under the pump, stifling a gasp at the cold water that poured over her face and down her neck. She had thought the summer drizzle was chilly as she stepped through the mud to get to the pump, but in the shelter of the eaves, where the drizzle no longer eased into her skin like a thick fog, the pump stream was cold enough to make her shiver. By the time she was done with both her hair and her clothes, her fingernails were purple. But she could see smoke coming from the chimney at the house now, so perhaps Byra would let her hang her wet things by the fire. Without hesitation, she made her way to the porch, stepping carefully so as not to spatter more mud on her rinsed clothes.

"Hello," she said when Jam opened the door. "I was hoping you would let me hang my things by your fire so they could dry before we have to move on."

"Of course. Come in." The old man gestured for her to enter. "Though I was thinking that you're welcome to stay another day."

Dion smiled. "That's up to—uh, Shull. But the way your mate cooks, I'm sure he'll consider the invitation seriously."

"Who is that, Jam?" Byra's voice floated out from a room upstairs.

"It's the woman, Deats."

"Tell her I'll be right down."

Jam squashed his hat on his head and stepped out the door Dion had just entered. "I've got to feed the animals. Why don't you wait in here? You can hang your things by the back fire— there's a line there Byra uses for her own clothes."

"Thanks."

Dion looked around, then sat down on one of the chairs, feeling the softness of the pad against her back and leaning her head so that it pillowed her neck, as well. Except for the previous night, she had not sat in such comfort for ninans— although, if Aranur was right, they would be back in Ariye in another nine days, and she would have as many chairs to sit in as she wished. Nine days—one ninan—and Aranur and Shilia would see their home. If their luck held, she reminded herself. The moons had looked on their flight from Longear's claws with mixed faces so far, and with the news Jam had told them of the troops along the roads, she had no doubts they would have as much trouble reaching the border of Bilocctar as Aranur anticipated.

"Deats?"

She looked up. Byra was making her way down the upstairs hall, her crutches thunking quietly into the carpet as she worked her way toward the stairs.

"Good morning," Dion called. "How are you today?"

The old woman balanced on her good leg and set the crutches into a niche in the wall. "It's good to have company to look forward to." She swung easily down the narrow banister, her bad leg hitting each step with a soft bump. "I see you've been up for a while already."

"I was hoping you'd let me use your fireplace to dry my clothes before breakfast."

"Surely." The old woman reached into another niche at the bottom of the stairs and pulled out another pair of crutches, slipping her wrists into the braces and pointing with her chin toward the kitchen. "You can help me pick the herbs for the omelets. Best to catch them before the sun hits the plants. Don't know why, but the healers always say it's so."

Dion shrugged. "During the day, most of the plant's energy goes to taking in sunlight instead of strengthening the herb's potency. It's during the night that the herbs grow more potent." She followed Byra into the kitchen and, at the old woman's direction, strung her clothes along the line in front of the fire that Jam had already lit. "If you gather the herbs in the morning, before the sun hits them," she continued, "they'll be stronger acting than later in the day. Not much, but it sometimes makes a difference."

The old woman paused and looked over her shoulder. "Now where did you learn a thing like that?"

"My mother was a healer, and her mother before her."

"Huh. Would have thought you'd follow them in the art, not squander around in the mud with the scouts." The woman leaned over the crutches and pushed open the door. "Come on out when you're done. The greenhouse is to the right."

"All right. Be there in a minute."

She finished hanging her clothes on the line, then paused. She could feel the Gray One in her mind, and the images were strong with hunger and the violence of the hunt. The wolf had already caught and swallowed four rodents, but now she was after bigger prey, and the threads of her hunt caught Dion up as well. *Bloodlust, speed. The hare lunges to the right. A swipe, a bat. The short, sharp sound of broken bone. Slide. The rabbit skids neck first into the ground. Hunger. Hard teeth close over its pelt and rip, and the blood, the meat is sweet . . .*

Dion shook her head and pushed open the back door.

As Byra had said, the greenhouse was just outside the door, with a short walkway that protected the entrance from the weather. The door to the greenhouse was ajar, so Dion, after sticking her head in, spotted Byra at one end of the long pole building and went on in. She fingered one of the balms that grew beside the door wistfully. ''This is much bigger than I expected,'' she said, looking around.

''Isn't it though?'' The old woman sounded pleased.

''You've a wonderful variety growing here. I thought you said you grew the usual herbs.''

''I just like to dabble.''

''Garvoset, ansil, wolf's milk, and bugbane? Those are hardly herbs for an inexperienced gardener.''

Byra pinched back the flower buds that had begun to sprout on the lemon balm. ''Well, you recognized them.''

''Like I said, my mother was a healer.''

''Here. You can hold these while I pick the rest of the basil.''

Dion moved up behind the old woman and took the leaves as they were handed back. ''You know, a healer would go wild in an herb garden like this.''

''Huh.'' Byra turned too swiftly and stumbled, and Dion caught her arm to steady her. ''I'm fine, I'm fine,'' the older woman said sharply. ''No need to hang on like that. I'm just clumsy sometimes. Jam says I'm getting old.''

Dion regarded her slowly, then motioned with her eyes at the old woman's leg. ''May I?''

Byra gave her a long look, then sat down abruptly on one of the upturned buckets and lifted her skirt over her knees.

The leg was shrunk and twisted, the muscles wasted to thin strands of tissue and the kneecap protruded from the bony socket as if it had been stuck onto Byra's leg instead of grown as part of it. From midthigh to foot, terrible gashes had healed into raised ridges, leaving the flesh discolored and knotted where the jagged seams had been badly sewn together. Dion, kneeling by her side, touched the flesh lightly. ''These scars—all were caused at the same time?''

The old woman nodded.

"Do you have any use of the leg at all?"

"Well, I can move my toes and shift my knee a bit, but the leg won't stand any weight."

"Can you lift it?"

"Not more than an inch or two, sitting down. The bone was broken up too much to knit."

Dion pressed her fingers lightly against two spots in the woman's thigh. "Do you feel this?"

"Yes, but it hurts."

She pressed midthigh and looked up. "This?"

"Yes."

She pressed the sides and top of the knee separately. "And this?"

"All of what you do causes pain."

Dion sat back on her heels. "Describe it."

Byra stared at the younger woman with a strangely intense look. "It's sharp—and burning, but it doesn't go away," she said finally. "It just turns into a dull fire."

"Does it feel that if only you could rub it, it would be relieved?"

The old woman nodded. "But it never goes away."

"Move your toes as I touch them. That's it. Good." Dion got to her feet and moved beside the older woman. "I'm going to press on your spine now," she said, leaning over. "Tell me what you feel as I do so."

Byra nodded. "Nothing—I mean, no pain. Nothing, Nothing. Oh—oh, that hurts."

Dion tucked the woman's blouse back into her skirt, then leaned back against one of the herb shelves and closed her eyes. When she opened them, she said, "Can you get eucalyptus and marbin?"

"At the apothocary, yes. We have some trade credit left from the spring cuttings."

"I saw camphor in your pantry, you'll need some of that as well, and cut some of your mint, to sweeten the linament." She frowned. "I'll give you a few other herbs that will help ease the pain, and I'll leave a recipe with you, with exact amounts listed," she continued. "When you make the linament, split it into two batches, and add the other herbs I give you to only one bottle. The linament with the herbs will be too strong to use during the day, but it will help during the night. In the morning, it will be easier for you to get up." She let the older woman tug her stocking back up and pull her skirt back down, then helped her off the bucket.

The gray-haired woman nodded slowly. "These herbs you'll give me, what are they?"

"Angelica—not the species you are growing here—curcuma root, water ash, and a very small amount of blue-wing fern. They will increase the blood circulation to your leg, help solidify your bones, and relieve some of the pain. Your leg bones are brittle because you haven't been putting weight on them. You will have to build them back up."

Byra stared at her. "How do you know so much about herbs, Deats? And why do you carry such medicines with you? You're a scout, not a healer."

Dion hesitated. With Ovousibas, the internal healing, she could heal this woman—give Byra back the strength to her legs. But it would betray the rest of the group if she did it.

"Did you train with your mother before you went into Zentsis's service?" the older woman persisted.

Dion shook her head. "My mother died soon after I was born." But she clenched her fist around the headband that hung in the leather pouch from her belt, and it burned against her fingers. Ovousibas—the internal healing of the ancients. And the healer's oath she had taken so long ago. And her oath to Aranur to ride with him as her brother did. Which oath, which words bound her now?

The old woman peered at her. "What troubles you, Deats? Knowing how to use herbs is no crime. And what you know already—you would have made a good healer yourself. Why, from the way you talk, I'd have thought—" Byra hesitated and glanced at Dion's sword and then her forehead, where a faint, whiter line crossed her brow. "You were a healer already."

Dion said nothing.

"Are you? A healer, Deats?"

Dion looked at the hand clenched over her hidden headband.

"You are, aren't you?" Byra got to her feet, leaning against the shelving for support. "And you know something about my leg, too."

"Byra," Dion said, shaking her head, "I know only that the damage to your leg is old. There's always less chance of repairing old damage than new."

"You're a healer, and you think you could fix my leg, and you won't tell me whether what you say is true or not? By the nine moons, Deats, I want an answer." The old woman gripped

Dion by her arm. "Show me. If you're truly a healer, then show me your headband."

Dion wrenched away. "I can't."

Byra looked at her. "Can't, or won't?"

Dion closed her eyes. *Hishn,* she called. *Tell me I don't break my Journey oath to Aranur. I could heal this woman.*

Will you walk in her as you did with the others? The gray voice sounded worried.

Dion stared at Byra, and the old woman leaned forward and slowly pulled Dion's hand away from her belt pouch.

"Moons above," Byra said softly, pulling out the silver band. "You *are* a healer." She stared at the headband, then at Dion, then back at the healer's symbol in her hands. "I don't understand," she said quietly, sinking back on the bucket. "Why do you hide this? Why didn't you want me to know?"

Dion shrugged.

"You're in trouble, aren't you? That's why you became a scout."

"Trouble follows many who don't wish it."

The old woman half smiled, then her eyes fell to Dion's sword and worn boots, and then Dion could see the realization and horror hit Byra's face. "My gods, but you are *she,* aren't you. You—and your friends—you're the ones they're searching for. Three men, a healer, two girls, and a boy." She struggled up and staggered back, knocking over the rude chair. "Those youths—they're girls, not young men."

Dion held out her hands. "I—we—"

"You're not the Lloroi's scouts at all. You're the murderers—"

"No!" Dion was shocked. "No—Byra, by the moons, we are not killers. Believe me. Gods, yes, I am a healer, and on my word as that, I tell you also that we are not murderers."

The old woman looked at her with narrowed eyes, glancing from her warcap to her sword and back to her own hands, which held the intricately carved band of silver. The tiny blue stones set into the design caught her eyes, and Dion stepped forward, stopping as the old woman stiffened.

"Byra, listen to me," she said urgently. "We're a long way from home, and we just want to get back. That's the only reason we're here."

"Why did you come in the first place?"

"We did not mean to. My brother and I were on Journey and were attacked by worlags. The others in our party were killed, but we escaped, and met up with Aran— Shull and the older man and the boy. Their women had been taken by raiders— they were riding to get them back. Byra,'' Dion explained, holding out her hand, ''all we did was follow the slavers to the city. We bought the girls back at a slave market, but the slavers attacked us afterward and stole the girls again. We fought, escaped, and had to fight again, and one of the girls died.'' She balled her fist. ''We ran again, and took to the sea, but we were shipwrecked—''

''Where—where did you go ashore?'' The old woman's voice was faint.

''We never made Breinington. We were driven onto the Cliffs of Bastendore. We—''

''You're lying,'' Byra broke in. ''You can't live through the currents—I've seen them once, long ago.'' She stared at the wolfwalker. ''And there's no way up the cliffs even if you make it into one of the bays.''

''You're wrong, Byra. I'm a rock climber. And so are the men. We climbed the Cliffs of Bastendore and hauled the others to the top. And then we started through the Yew Mountains.'' She shook her head and breathed out, looking up, then back at the older woman. ''By the moons, I swear it is so. I bear the scars to prove it.''

Byra's thin lips tightened stubbornly.

The healer stared at the older woman for a moment. Then she loosened the laces of her leather mail and pulled down her leggings, exposing a long, jagged scar down one thigh. ''That,'' she said bitterly, ''is from the worlags.'' She pulled the leggings up again and shoved her sleeves up to show her forearms. ''And these are from the rocks on the Cliffs of Bastendore.'' She turned over her left hand, and the ridges that crisscrossed the flesh betrayed the mudsucker's teeth. ''And these—they are new scars, Byra, and not the kind a sword or knife would leave. Believe it, Byra. Those marks are the truth of my story. And if you went back to Red Harbor or Sidisport or Fenn Forest, you would see the rest of the truth. There are no scars in those places, but you will see the graves of my friends.''

Gently taking the headband back from Byra, Dion held the other woman's gaze with her own. ''Four men died in Fenn Forest, Byra. Torn apart by the beetle jaws of the worlags that attacked our group. And in Sidisport, a trader gave his life so that the rest of us could escape the slaver's swords. And a young girl died, unarmed and scared and homesick, on the beach just outside Red Harbor. Died because of a raider's greed.'' She gestured with the headband at her sword. "If I fight these things,'' she said quietly, "am I a killer? Do you call it murder if I raise my sword to defend myself or my friends?''

"You're a healer,'' Byra whispered. "Or does the silver band you carry also lie?''

"No,'' Dion said heavily. "It doesn't lie. I am a healer.''

"So you justify your killing?''

"I fight when I must, and I heal when I can.''

The old woman's face closed up at her words, and Dion dropped her hands.

"My county is at war with the raiders, Byra. My people no longer come to me with hurts from predators and rock falls and fires. Now they come missing arms and legs and eyes because a raider's blade is found its way through their guard. Or a slaver had some sport with his prize.'' Her voice shook. "There was a day when I saw four families orphaned, and the children too young to understand. And I couldn't save a single man or woman among them. I could do nothing,'' she said in an anguished voice. "I—we were all too late.'' Her jaw tightened, and she clenched the healer's band. "I took two oaths that day. Two oaths that I swore to all nine moons.'' She shoved the sword back in its sheath and jammed the headband on her forehead. "I don't ask for your judgment, Byra. The moons will judge me soon enough themselves. Neither do I expect you to understand. But I tell you this, I've raised my sword only in defense. Only to protect myself and my friends.''

"How—how can I believe you?''

Dion looked at her for a long moment. "I'm a healer. If that is not enough, then there is nothing more to say.''

The farmer's wife sank slowly down onto the bucket. "Moons guide me, but I don't know what to do.''

The wolfwalker waited, her fists tight and her eyes dark. If the old woman called Jam . . .

But Byra gestured finally at the greenhouse instead. "What I have is yours, Deats. You have Healer's Right here. Take what you need.''

Dion breathed. "I have enough of the herbs I need,'' she said quietly, "but I thank you.'' She hesitated. "There is something I can do for you, perhaps.''

Byra looked at her warily.

"You have nerve damage," the wolfwalker continued steadily. "The linaments I'll help you make will send blood to the areas that are dying, but," she said bluntly, "they cannot heal the damage that's been done."

"I know that. I've lived with that knowledge for fourteen years."

"The damage is not irreversible," Dion said sharply.

"What?"

"You still have use of your leg. The muscles aren't completely shriveled, and you have partial range and motion in all your joints."

"There are no surgeries that can fix what's wrong with me."

"That's true." Dion glanced down at the headband. "But there is something else."

The old woman spoke softly. "Jam's a good man, Healer. He took me all the way to Wortenton to see if the master healer there could help. I still remember what he said. 'No,' he told us. He said the sheaths over the nerves were severed. That the nerves themselves were bruised and frayed. 'We cannot be delicate enough,' he told us. 'We would cripple you further to relieve your pain.' " Byra looked at Dion with bitter eyes. "I'd rather have a leg that drags than no leg at all."

"That is not what I meant." Dion gestured at her own leg. "What I would do would not leave more scars than what you already have—either inside or out."

"Then what would you do?" Byra demanded. "I'm not fool enough to believe in faith healers. All they do is chant and take your money."

"A healer's gift is freely given—"

"As it should be."

"But only if asked for and accepted."

Byra looked steadily at the healer. "I don't know what Jam would do if he knew about you. They say in town that you murdered twenty-six men. And Zentsis's troops—why, they'd burn us out if they knew we put you up."

"I can't tell you what to do, Byra. I can only tell you that we mean you no harm. And that we've defended ourselves only when attacked."

"You're telling me to believe you over the soldiers."

"I'm telling you, as a healer, that what I can do for your leg is between you and me, as patient and healer, not as anything else."

The old woman met her eyes. "I would have to trust you."

"Yes," Dion admitted. She took a breath. "And I, you. My life is in your hands as well, Byra. And the lives of my own brother and our friends. And what must be done, will have to be done now, before the others get up."

"Then what would you do?"

"I'm going to use an old technique—an art, you could say, that was thought lost a long time ago. I think it will work for you."

Byra hesitated.

"It is a chance to walk again."

The woman held her breath only a moment. "All right."

Dion nodded. "Whatever happens, do not be worried. Do not be afraid."

But the woman gasped, her eyes focusing over Dion's shoulder. "Oh, my stars—"

"I will not hurt you, nor will Gray Hishn," the healer continued, sensing the wolf behind her.

"A wolfwalker—you're a wolfwalker as well—" The woman struggled to drop to her knees until Dion caught her arm and urged her back on the makeshift seat. "You honor me—"

"It's all right, Byra." Dion caught the old woman's attention with difficulty. "The Gray Ones honor those who need them. Now, listen to me. I want you to lie on your side here. That's right. Get comfortable, relax, think of nothing, and stay still. No—I want your leg extended. Now, whatever you feel, whatever you think you see, you must ignore. You won't be hurt by this, I swear it, but there is danger to me and the Gray One." The wolf licked her sharp, white teeth and panted easily while Dion shrugged off her leather jerkin and wadded it up into a rude pillow for the other woman. She tucked it under Byra's head gently and gripped her hand. "Do you understand what I've told you?"

The old woman glanced nervously at the wolf. "I think so, yes."

"And you trust me."

"You are truly a healer?"

"Yes."

"All right."

Dion motioned for the gray wolf to sit beside her, and Byra's old eyes glued themselves to Hishn's yellow ones as the wolf padded farther into the greenhouse and sat by the healer.

Ovousibas. Internal healing. Dion frowned in thought and

looked at her hands. It would drain her—it always did—but if she could just repair the nerve damage before she lost too much strength . . .

She smiled reassuringly at Byra and then reached out to the wolf. *Can you take me in, Gray One?*

Her blood is strong, though old, but she smells of fear.

Dion shook off a shiver and rolled the woman's sock down to her ankle. "Don't be afraid, Byra. I used this technique on my own brother. I even used it on myself."

The old woman looked at her for a moment, then nodded.

Dion took a breath, knelt by the bucket again, and stretched the old woman's leg out over her lap. *Take me in, Gray One. Then walk with me, Healer.*

Dion's mind spun down, down, to the left. Her eyes lost their focus, and her hands floated just above the old woman's leg. The wolf's eyes gleamed. A twist, a wrenching of her consciousness, and then they were in. Into the torn and twisted muscles, thin with years of disuse, and the slowly dying tissues.

Tense and silent, Byra lay with her hands clenched. The constant ache in her leg dulled slightly, then flared up, then dulled again; and the twinges that tugged at her leg were odd and deep in the unused muscles. She was afraid to look down. Instead, she stared at Dion's furrowed brow and closed eyes. Taut and strained, Dion's frown grew deeper, and her hands began to tremble up into her arms. Her face went white. The old woman held her breath. The ache subsided, and a new sensation took its place. Something different. Something she ought to recognize . . .

The healer started shaking, and the Gray One's eyes blazed more deeply yellow.

Air—it was the draft in the greenhouse—Byra could feel it on her scarred legs, in the thin hair that grew from her scarred, dead skin. She bit her lip to keep silent, and the healer swayed. And there, that coldness, on the back of her leg—it was the dirt, damp from the rain. By the moons, she could feel it. In a leg that had been dead to all but pain for the last fourteen years, in muscles covered with scar tissue, she could feel the wind and the cold—

Dion shivered violently, and the Gray One growled, and suddenly the healer collapsed back, gasping for breath and shaking against the wolf.

The old woman, sensing a fleeting thought that was not her

own racing through her brain, said tightly, "Is it—are you done?"

Dion looked up blearily, her eyes fluttered once, and then her head rolled limply back, and she toppled slowly over to the side.

Byra looked down at her leg once. Then screamed.

Chapter 6

A gentle touch;
A smile;
Kind words—
By such small things
Are lives changed.

Aranur burst through the door of the greenhouse with his sword bared, Jam a mere second behind him. A bow was in the old man's left hand, and a handful of loose arrows in the other.

"By the moons—" Aranur jerked to a stop before he stumbled over the limp form of the healer, and Jam slammed into him from behind.

"What is it?" the old man demanded. "Is she hurt?"

"It's Dion—" Aranur dropped to his knees. The gray wolf, standing over the healer with hackles raised and a snarl cursing forth, lunged at Aranur, keeping him back, so he could not get close to Dion as she struggled weakly to sit up. She clutched at Hishn's fur, pulling herself up by the wolf's scruff. Aranur, glaring from Byra to the healer, demanded harshly, "What did you do to her? Was it Ovousibas? Did she heal you?"

Byra, crying, was hugging herself and rocking back and forth on the ground. "Oh, Jam—oh, moons of mercy—"

"I'm all right, Aranur," Dion managed hoarsely, but her voice was so faint under the growling of the wolf and the hysteria of the old woman that no one heard.

"Stay back," Aranur snarled at the farmer as Jam tried to get past him to Byra. Wrenching the bow from the old man's hands, Aranur flung the weapon under one of the shelves, and Jam staggered back so far with the force of his motion that the farmer almost fell out of the greenhouse.

"Gray One," Aranur snapped at the wolf, "back off."

The wolf snarled, but Aranur shoved the creature back and she gave way, letting him reach the healer. He knelt and let Dion put her arms around his neck. He could feel the terrible weariness that made her tremble.

"I'm all right," she managed. "I'm okay."

Jam glared at her as Aranur glared back at him. "What did you do to my mate?" the old man demanded. "Why did she scream?"

But the gray-haired woman held her hands out. "Jam— I—I can feel. In my leg—oh, gods, Jam, but she—she healed me."

The old man turned slowly. "What? What nonsense is this?"

Byra clutched his arm. "She's a healer, Jam. She did something—reached inside me—"

"Is this true? That scout—Deats—is a healer?" he demanded in disbelief.

Aranur looked bleakly at Dion, and she lowered her eyes.

"I'm sorry," she whispered. Hishn slunk out of the greenhouse behind them.

"A healer," the old man continued slowly. "And the two young ones: girls?" He glanced at his bow, lying two meters away under the last shelf of herbs, and back at Aranur.

Aranur said nothing, but helped Dion to her feet, catching her as she staggered, her legs buckling under as they felt her weight. But she brushed him off, leaning against the shelves instead.

"Zentsis wants you, doesn't he?" the old farmer questioned harshly. "You're the reason Longear's men've been searching all the towns and outer county." He took a step. "It's Longear's men who're skulking around the taverns like scavengers listening for word of you."

Aranur glanced back at the old man. "We are not afraid of Longear or his dogs."

The old man balled his fists. "If you've hurt my Byra, you're going to learn more than the meaning of the word 'fear.' And there won't be a fingernail left for Longear to have when I'm through with you."

But his mate clutched his arm. "No, Jam—listen to me—"

"We never meant you harm," Aranur said coldly. He

grabbed Dion's arm as she swayed; she caught her breath, took a step, almost went to her knees, and finally accepted his help. "Even what happened here—"

"What did happen?" Jam cut in furiously.

"There was no harm in what Dion did to your mate," Aranur snarled, tightening his grip on the healer's elbow when she would have spoken, too. "Dion would die before she betrayed the healer's band."

The vehemence in his voice made the old man stiffen. "And the rest of you?"

Almost to the door, Aranur paused and turned. "You don't even understand what Dion did for your mate, do you? Look around you, Jam. And look at your wife's leg. Dion is a master healer, Jam. She runs with the Gray Ones." His jaw tightened. "And she knows Ovousibas."

"Aranur—" Dion interrupted.

"Be quiet," he ordered coldly. "You've done enough for now."

But the old man, on his feet, stared at them both in disbelief. "The Gray One I saw, but Ovousibas? Internal healing is a legend. The 'farce of the faith healers' . . ."

The look on Aranur's face silenced the old man abruptly. "Dion knows Ovousibas, Jam. And she did it for Byra. She could have died doing this for you, but she lived and she gave you a miracle. And now your mate is healed, and you stand there accusing Dion of murder instead of blessing her for your mate. How dare you threaten us, and with the name of a maggot like Zentsis."

"Gods," Jam whispered, turning back to his wife as Dion stumbled through the half-open door and Aranur stalked after her. "By the moons, Byra, is this true?"

The old woman nodded. "I could feel her," she returned softly. "And now I can feel with my leg. Look, touch me here. See? I can feel that."

Behind them, Aranur shouldered his way through the half-open door and stalked down toward the barn, half dragging, half carrying Dion, while the Gray One, slinking beside them, whined once, then paced the two fighters silently.

But Dion paused as they reached the barn door. "Aranur?" His jaw tightened.

"I'm sorry."

"You did what you had to do."

"I betrayed you. I betrayed all of us."

He took a breath. "I don't expect you to deny your healing because of us, Dion. I just wish you had better timing."

"Jam—will he tell Zentsis's men that we're here?"

"I don't know. But we can't wait to find out." He pushed the barn door open, sliding it smoothly along its oiled track, and entered the stable where the six-legged work beasts stood in their stalls and stamped their feet.

"Dion?" Rhom was pulling his semiclean tunic on as they entered, and he looked around. "What's wrong?" he asked quietly, noting their faces: Dion's, gaunt and pale, her limbs still trembling with exhaustion, and Aranur's, cold, angry, and worried, his muscles tense as if he expected to feel the bolt of an arrow tear into his back any second.

Dion met his eyes resolutely. "It's my fault, Rhom."

"What is? What are you talking about?"

"I gave us away. I just did Ovousibas. On Byra."

The blacksmith jumped to his feet. "Sweet moons, Dion, do you know what you've done?"

She nodded wordlessly.

"Dnu droppings." He looked down at Gamon, who was only half awake. "Get up, Gamon," he said sharply, nudging the older man's ribs with his boot.

Gamon opened his eyes abruptly, and, seeing the look on Rhom's face, rolled to his feet in an instant.

"Tyrel's out by the pump with Namina," Rhom said. "Shilia—"He looked around sharply. "She was just here—"

"I'll get her," Aranur said. "Get Dion something to eat."

Rhom looked at his sister and nodded. Beside him, Gamon wrapped his bedding into a neat roll in seconds and lashed it to his pack. The older man's tunic hung out of his pants, and his chin was grizzled like a wire brush, but without a pause he started in on the girls' bedding, kicking the straw out of the way quickly as he worked and sneezing at the dust.

Passing her hand wearily over her eyes, Dion sank down to the barn floor near Shilia's bedroll. She was tired. The hunger pangs gnawed at her belly like worms, and Hishn's sympathetic whine only made her feel more starved. The internal healing always sapped her strength—as if the power to heal came from her own body. And then when it was over and the high was gone, all that was left was an exhaustion that wiped out her mind as well as her muscles. She was starved, and she had to eat—a meal that would have fed four people did not sound like enough food for her, and she pressed at her stomach as it cramped again. She felt as if she could eat enough for six.

"Why did you do it, Dion?" Rhom asked quietly as he handed her the cooked meat he had saved from their last night's dinner. He sat beside her and shook his head. "You didn't have to do Ovousibas—they were fine without it."

She tore off a bite of the cold poultry, then rubbed her forehead with her other hand as she chewed. "She was in pain, Rhom. And she'd been that way for over fourteen years. And I knew I could heal the damage . . ."

"They have carrier birds. Zentsis could know in less than an hour where we are."

"I know."

"You had to do it?"

She passed her hand over her eyes. "She needed healing," she whispered.

Rhom stared at her for a moment, then nodded abruptly. He gripped her shoulder.

Dion closed her eyes. "I'm sorry," she repeated. She bit off another piece of the tough meat and chewed it mechanically. It had no taste. Whether that was from its age or her guilt, she did not know, but she offered the other half of the meat to the wolf, her hands still shaking.

Rhom watched her closely. "I don't like this healing, Dion," he said finally.

She swallowed, forcing another bite. "It's a gift, Rhom."

"Are you trying to convince me or yourself? It's too much like a miracle," he returned harshly. "You repeat it, and it drains the life right out of you."

"It's just a skill, Rhom. I can use it, if I'm careful."

"You should have told me—or at least Aranur."

"I thought no one would find out."

The blacksmith jerked open the strap on the pack. "Every time you've done the healing, you've passed out afterward. Then you come to and you eat like a starved lepa. You think we're not going to notice?" He shoved his belongings into his pack and yanked the top string tight.

She shook her head. "It wasn't as bad this time. I'm getting stronger the more I do it. And I didn't need Aranur this time, either. Just Hishn." The Gray One laid her head in Dion's lap, and the woman rubbed the wolf over her yellow eyes.

"I don't like it, Dion."

She tried a smile. "If it gets to be too much, I'll quit."

"I'm supposed to believe that?" He tossed his pack to the side. "You would not make that into a promise, would you?"

"You know me too well," she said softly.

He paused and looked up. "We're twins, Dion." They and exchanged a long look before Rhom picked up his sword, and Dion took up her bow.

Aranur strode back into the barn with the three youths in tow, and in seconds they each had their gear. "Gamon, take them on up to the road," he directed. "I've something to take care of. Rhom, come with me."

Dion got to her feet. "Aranur—"

"Go up to the road with Gamon, healer."

She shook her head stubbornly. "I need to leave some herbs with Byra."

"Then do it here, where they'll find it later."

"She needs instructions."

"Dion, you've done enough today. Now, follow Gamon up to the road."

She stiffened. "Byra is my patient, Aranur."

"And she and Jam are our deaths if we wait any longer."

"What are you going to do?"

"We won't harm them," he said, shrugging her off. "We're just going to insure our safety a little while longer."

"I'm going with you."

He looked at her for a long moment. "As you wish. Gamon?"

The older man nodded and took the other three out the back way, slipping quietly into the early morning drizzle and disappearing. Only the shallow prints of their smoothly worn boots testified to their passage, and as the gentle summer rain fell, water ran across the edges and blurred them until they became only puddles.

Aranur strode out of the barn in the other direction, Rhom and Dion close behind. They found the greenhouse door closed, and the house quiet.

"What do you think?"

Aranur shook his head. "They could go either way. But we're the county's enemies. They have nothing to lose and everything to gain by turning us in."

Rhom sighed and pointed. "The aviary's around this side of the house."

"Dion, where are you going?" Aranur demanded in a low

voice as she turned and jogged through the mud to the house.

"I need to talk to Byra for a moment. I'll meet you around back."

"You can't trust her. Come with us, or go with Gamon up to the road."

Dion shook her head. "She won't hurt me."

"Just because you helped her," he said sharply, "does not mean that she or her mate owes you anything. And you of all people, Healer Dione, should know that." He gestured ahead of him. "Come on. We haven't much time."

"I need only a minute with her, Aranur. I'll be up there and back before Jam even knows I've been in the house."

Aranur opened his mouth, saw the set look of her chin, then pointed up the hill. "Meet us up at the road. If we don't see you in three minutes, I'm coming after you."

She nodded.

She jogged to the porch, hesitated, then ran lightly up the steps and tapped on the door. "Byra?" she called. She opened the door and poked her head around it.

"I'm coming, Healer."

The old woman was in the second room, and Dion could hear her crutches creaking on the floor.

"I just wanted to give you these herbs," the wolfwalker said as Byra came into view. She set the bundle on the table by the door. "They will tide you over until you can get to an apothecary."

The other woman motioned at her leg. "Healer, I—"

Dion held up her hand. "Let me finish, Byra. The others are already gone, and I cannot stay longer." The old woman halted, and Dion pointed out three of the four clumps of herbs. "There is enough here for twelve treatments, but there is only enough blue-wing fern"—she pointed at the last cluster of leaves—"for four treatments. Do not dilute it to make it last, or it will not work."

The old woman nodded. "Healer—"

Dion stopped her again. "One part each of these two, Byra. Two parts of this one, and three parts of this. Steep it in a half pan of water for twenty minutes, then let it cool. It will make a linament that you can rub into your skin." She turned to go.

"Healer, wait."

Dion looked back.

The old woman stumbled forward, dragging her leg as she

hurried on the crutches. "You gave me back my leg—you risked everything for me."

The wolfwalker shook her head slowly. "I did only what needed doing, Byra. You deserved nothing less."

"And the Gray One? I—we—owe you. We owe you everything." She reached for Dion's hand. "Please, wait."

Looking into Byra's faded blue eyes, Dion smiled gently. "You owe me nothing, Byra. The healer's gift is always free."

"Healer—"

"Moonsblessing, Byra." She squeezed the other woman's hand, then turned again to leave. As she opened the door, she glanced back one more time. "But, for your own safety, Byra, tell no one of this healing."

The old woman stared at her for a long moment. "I understand, Healer." She leaned heavily on her crutch, but her foot took weight this time, and she smiled suddenly. "We cannot give you much, but we give you that, at least."

Dion touched her hand again, then turned and slipped out.

Around the house on the other side, Aranur and Rhom strode toward the aviary with chickens squawking and flapping out from underfoot. But as they rounded the corner, a blast of sound beat the air over their head and the thunder of dozens of pairs of wings deafened them.

"Moonworms!" Rhom ducked under his arm, flinging up his sword to help protect his face from the low-flying talons that swept by.

"Look out!"

The two men stared after the carrier birds who fled to the gray sky.

Aranur let his breath out heavily. He looked at the farmer, who still held the master latch to the aviary open in his hand and stood, defenseless, looking back. "So."

Jam eyed them for a moment, then watched the last of his message birds drift off in the rain. "Makes a pretty picture, don't it? All those gray wings in that gray, gray sky."

Aranur dropped his hand from his sword. "How long before the troops arrive?" he asked quietly.

The farmer scratched his chin. "Well, could be two days. But more likely three."

Aranur frowned. "Days?"

Jam waved his arm after the birds. "Always takes a couple for them to come back after they get free, and then I'll have to tag them and send them off tellin' the scouts in town that you been by, seeing as how my work dnu is lame and can't ride me there myself.'' The old man propped the door to the aviary open, then turned back to the two fighters. ''Kind of seems a shame, don't it? Men like you with running boots like those, just standing around in the rain.''

Aranur regarded the farmer for a long moment, until a weary smile tugged at his lips. He nodded slowly. ''We will not forget you, Jaime neKohler.''

''Be better off if you did,'' the old man muttered as he turned away and stomped back toward the house. When he got to the first porch step, he paused and looked over his shoulder. ''Keep those girls hid. The troops are thick around here, and most of them like their women young.''

Aranur watched the old man for a moment, then motioned for Rhom to follow him up to the road. Dion was already jogging up the path, the gray wolf joining her, and as she saw them, she waited for them to catch up. The three of them made their way up the muddy road together.

By the time they joined Gamon and the three youths, the early morning drizzle had slacked off to a light mist that wet their skin more like fog than rain. It was cool at first, then cold as their body heat was stripped away where the water soaked their clothes. As the morning wore on, Dion returned Hishn's occasional growling with her own mental complaints. She wished they could have asked Jam to sell them his dnu, but she knew that Longear would have had Jam and Byra killed if he had done it. Longear would never have believed that the old man had not helped them flee. No, they would have to get riding beasts elsewhere. But Aranur kept them moving, taking them past the next four farms without stopping. They jogged through a shaded woodlot that stretched for thousands of acres, then passed another farm before they reached the first clump of houses in the valley. It was only then that Aranur slowed the group. Two of the buildings faced the road, and the last structure faced east, but he could see no movement in any of the windows.

''Keeping out of sight?'' Dion asked with a frown.

Gamon looked at her. ''Maybe Longear's men? Or Zentsis's troops?''

Aranur shook his head. ''No. We'd have seen signs of the troops. And it wouldn't be like Longear to sit around and wait for us either—cost too many men for too long a time to stake out enough houses in the outer county."

Dion looked back. "A trap in some other way?"

Gamon scowled and shook his head again, more to himself than to the others. "No. I'm just jumpy. Longear's moves just don't make sense to me," he said softly. "There's some pattern I just don't see . . ."

Aranur frowned. "Whatever he's up to, we'll have to figure it out on the run. Right now, we need riding beasts." He strode out into the road moving swiftly so that the fence seemed to march alongside him, its rails pausing only for overgrowth that threaded its way through the wooden poles and overflowed out to the muddy, rutted road. Though the wolf was out of sight, he knew the others followed close behind and that the Gray One was somewhere in the brush near Dion.

Lazy smoke from a single chimney declared the first building occupied. Aranur motioned for the others to stay out on the road while he went up to the house, but there seemed no need for his caution. The young couple who came to the door posed little threat for the tall man. He stayed only a few minutes, then returned, shaking his head at Gamon's raised eyebrows.

"Dnu are highly valued in this county," he reported. "Although I suspect that it's because Zentsis's men are valued poorly, if at all. We'll not find dnu worth buying here."

As the day wore on and the rain slacked off and the mud began to dry into heavy clumps on their boots, they stopped at over six places, each time turned down with distantly polite smiles and the advice to look somewhere else. Four times wagons passed them, but though they asked for rides, none of the drivers even paused.

"Zentsis's scouts are even more unwelcome than Jam led us to believe," Aranur said in a low voice to Dion as they stood in the lee of a tree to scrape more muck from their footwear and rest their legs.

"Well, as long as they think we're Zentsis's men, they don't draw bow." Dion examined Hishn's paw where the wolf had complained of a sharp pain, and found a bickerthorn, which she pulled carefully from between the Gray One's claws. "We'd have no chance against a whole county as well as the army in it." Hishn shifted under her touch, and Dion twitched her own shoulders suddenly.

Aranur glanced at them. "Something wrong?"

"No . . . only that . . ." her voice trailed off, and Hishn whined, then a slow smile broke over Dion's face.

"What is it?"

"A Gray One is birthing," she said softly. "And the pups live." Her face lost its drawn look for a moment as the Gray One passed along their thoughts, and Dion sighed. "Moons bless them with long lives," she said under her breath.

Aranur looked down the road where a clump of rooftops straightened out the horizon in brief spots. "May they bless us with some dnu."

She returned his smile openly, and he was caught for a moment by the depth of her violet eyes.

He shook himself. "We should be able to find mounts in town," he continued finally. "There's supposed to be two stables there, with dnu for hire as well as sale."

"I thought we were going to stop early tonight."

He shook his head. "If we get dnu to ride, we'll need to put as many kilometers between us and this part of the county as possible. The next town is Floren, fifteen kilometers from here."

She sighed. "And from there?"

"An early start east, on the Stirring Road. But we'll tell the innkeeper where we stop that we're heading north to Yozer."

The last of Aranur's words were hushed by a new flush of rain, and he grimaced at the dripping leaves.

As the moons willed it, Aranur bought three of the six-legged dnu at one stable, two at another stable, and the last two from a carver in a market they passed through. The two bought from the carver were half-starved, and with their six spindly legs and thick bodies they looked more like spiders than riding beasts, but Aranur said that their cart-toughened muscles spelled endurance. And then they mounted up and kicked the mud from the road with more hope than they had felt in four ninans, driving the kilometers behind them as they galloped between the farms of Bilocctar.

True to his word, Aranur stopped them at the second tavern they found in Floren. The first had been too close to an armory; the second one, with its half-mud, half-stone walkway and dirt-darkened windows, looked more to their style.

"Noisy," Rhom commented as a sudden roar of laughter broke across the din of conversations that had already spilled into the courtyard.

"It's as good as we'll find this time of night." Aranur swung down and gestured for Gamon to do the same. "We'll be ignored here, and we'd be questioned somewhere else." He looked pointedly at Dion, then at the Gray One who panted by her side. "We'll check inside."

She nodded, signaling the wolf, and Hishn obediently slunk into the shadows surrounding the open corral. The wolfwalker sat like a statue while Hishn sent the images to her; each smell made Dion's own nostrils flare, and the feel of the still-drying mud that clung to Hishn's paws made her want to shake her own hands free of it. By the time Aranur returned with his uncle, Hishn had loped around the inn, then gone through the shadows of the brush behind the building and down one of the streets that led to the next clump of village structures.

"It seems clear," Dion said finally. "Hishn can sense no danger."

Aranur nodded. Then, taking the reins back from Rhom, he led his dnu toward the corral. "Shilia," he said in a low voice, "you and Namina eat upstairs. Keep your eyes down when you cross the room. And don't speak to anyone either."

"We know the routine," his sister returned sourly. She took Namina's reins and handed them with her own to Tyrel. "I swear, sometimes I think I'm not going to be allowed to talk to another woman until we reach Ariye."

Dion raised her eyebrows.

"No offense, Healer," the girl added hastily.

As they reached the door to the inn, Gamon ran his fingers through his silvered hair. "There aren't separate rooms to sleep in," he said in a low voice. "The upstairs is one big loft. You girls are going to have to stand our snoring a little while longer."

"Ought to be used to it by now," Dion teased.

Shilia shook her head. "I'm getting tired of waking up deaf." She ducked the mock punch her uncle threw at her. "I'm too tired to eat. I'm just going to bed."

"I'm tired enough to go with you," Tyrel said, the shadows huge under his eyes. He took Namina's pack, stepped past Aranur and Gamon, and trudged toward the stairs at which the innkeeper pointed. The two girls followed, slipping through the crowd behind him, as Aranur directed the rest of them to a table near the center of the room.

"Keep your ears open," he murmured. "Some of these men will almost certainly be suppliers or service people that support the men Zentsis puts in this area, and an hour here would be well spent."

"Only if your silver's spent, as well," Gamon returned, gesturing peremptorily at the man behind the bar before he straddled the table's bench and looked around.

Aranur put his feet up on the bench opposite, sighed in relief, and pulled a thin silver coin from his purse. Within seconds, two pitchers of ale and four thick mugs had been slapped down on the table, and Gamon, without wasting time waiting for the barmaid—who was quick enough—to pick up the coin, began to pour.

"Ah," he said in pleasure. "Now that's good brew." He sipped from the first mug as he poured the second, and Dion laughed.

"It's the only brew you've had in a month, so it better be good."

Aranur chuckled, and Rhom poked Dion to remind her not to speak where others could hear her voice. She made a face at him, but Aranur glanced around the room, his eyes lingering on the innkeeper a moment longer than necessary. Then he turned back to his beer.

Chapter 7

Throw a shoe, and you throw the race;
It's the leader who sets the pace.

They rode swiftly in the morning. There were already wagons on the streets, and Dion was tense, as if the eyes of everyone in the county were upon them. There was something in the air, and it seemed to infect even the dnu, since the riding beasts pulled at the reins and threw their heads with each gust of wind.

She and the others had heard little or nothing of use the previous night; the only news they had was that Longear had ordered four deserters strung up in a lepa cage, with the bird creatures loose on short tethers. The lepa, apparently, had had a hard time reaching the men. It had taken three of the deserters two days to die; the last man had lived to see one more dawn, though there was little enough left of him to be called human. They were sobering images that Dion took to bed with her, and ones that left her the next morning with nightmares she could not recall. Hishn, who had slept under the steps of the inn, had slunk away earlier, disturbed, too, by Dion's dreams.

The only other item they had heard was that traffic on the bridges and roads was being checked: bags searched, wagons emptied. But they knew that already, having gone one at a time or two-by-two through roadblocks already. Dion, who rode warily, her eyes searching everywhere for signs of a trap, felt as if she were riding along the bars of an unseen cage. She wished she dared to go back into the forest with Hishn, but Aranur insisted on the roads. Time was too short, and it would add a month, maybe two, for the group to travel through the mountains back to Ramaj Ariye. She chewed her lip absently. If Aranur was to stop the raiders from taking over more of Ariye, he must get back soon. And what of Randonnen, her own county? The raiders' attacks there had just begun. She wondered what Aranur thought the elders of Randonnen should do.

That night, as if thinking similar thoughts, Aranur paced their tiny off-road camp like a caged wolf. They were half a day from the nearest town, and he was uneasy. The Gray One was a danger to have around the towns. He knew that, but he knew, too, that Dion's skill as a scout had saved them two ninans in crossing the mountains, and her skill as a healer had saved their lives, as well. But she would not leave the wolf and travel alone with him and the others. Nor, he suspected, would the wolf allow her to consider it if he suggested it again. He narrowed his eyes, watching Dion as she moved around the camp. What was it about her that drew his thoughts so often? Her eyes? Her hair? The way she swung into the saddle as if it were a part of her? The way she wrestled with the wolf when she thought no one was looking?

He swore under his breath. What she did and how she looked was no business of his, especially if Rhom had anything to say about it. Dashing the water from his cup, he strode away to stand where the shadows of the trees were darker than black and the moons' light an unwelcome brightness.

A moment later, Dion's scent warned him that she was near. Aranur's nostrils flared briefly, but he did not turn.

"It is peaceful like this," she said. "As if no thought of war ever crossed that sky."

He glanced down. "Perhaps it was those thoughts which brought the ancients here in the first place."

Dion laughed low. "I think not. If you could cross the stars, would you waste your time fighting or would you explore other worlds instead?"

"When I was young," he said softly, "and the moons rode one behind another like that in the sky, I used to think that if

I could only get my foot on a moonbeam, I could walk across the sky and meet the moonmaids in the west.''

''And now?''

He was silent for a moment. ''Now I think I have a moon-maid right here.'' He looked at her. ''Tell me, Dion. Do you like this fighting you do?''

She looked at her hands. ''It is a skill,'' she returned softly. ''One that I earned with as much sweat and blood as any man.''

''I've met women more vicious in politics than a man could ever be,'' he said finally, ''but I never knew a woman who wielded a sword before.''

The wolfwalker shrugged. ''Our village was small, and there were many dangers in Randonnen—worlags and badgerbears not the least. It was not safe for me to run the forest unarmed.'' She paused and looked at him in the dark. ''And you—do you like sparring?''

''I like fighting,'' he said slowly. ''There's something about it that makes my blood run fast and my heart leap when I face someone at my level or beyond. It's a test of my skill, my strength—sometimes my life. I even like the pain. It makes me feel alive as much as everything else.''

She nodded. ''It's a challenge,'' she said softly. ''Even when I face someone better than me, I can't give in—I can't turn it down.''

Aranur looked at her, the dark shadows angling across his face until he looked strangely unreal. But his voice, when he answered, was wry. ''It's strange to hear that from a lady.''

''You disapprove?'' Her voice was expressionless.

''Absolutely,'' he said gravely. ''If all women could fight like you, we men would never stand a chance in all nine hells.'' His eyes twinkled, and she laughed. He gave her a sideways look. ''Would you care to walk with me in the woods?'' he asked mischeviously.

Startled, Dion stared back for a moment. ''I would,'' she answered finally, ''but Rhom is burning holes in my back with his murderous glare, and my leather mail must be wearing thin if I feel it more than you.''

''But, fair lady and most respectable healer,'' he said with a wider smile, ''I would suffer more than the tortures of the seventh hell to walk one hour with you. Take my cloak.''

''How can I refuse now?'' she asked the skies. ''A man

who's willing to be struck through by a woman's sibling deserves to die with his last wish come true.''

He helped her up, and she dared a quick look over her shoulder before they stepped out of sight. Hishn's tail thumped on the ground and her yellow eyes gleamed slyly before she got up and followed Dion discreetly. Shilia did not bother to hide her grin at the sight of Rhom's widening eyes. Rhom was halfway to his feet before Shilia stopped him with a question. And Gamon had the audacity to wink at Dion before turning back to the fire.

In the morning, Rhom's fury was loud enough to draw a raised eyebrow from the older man, who was going to the stream to refill his water bag. Though most of Rhom's feeling was directed at Aranur, he had plenty to say to Dion about encouraging the man, till she finally pointed out that she was six years past the Age of Promising and, in truth, had always been more discreet than he. The tension between the twins made for a surly ride.

That day and the next stretched into the traffic of many small towns. They were about two days from Zentsis's capital, Wortenton, but they would be bypassing it in the lowlands sixty kilometers to the south.

"Hopefully," Gamon told Dion, "no one will have recognized us. It's the trading season, and there are plenty of travelers to hide among."

"May the moons bless Zentsis's men with slow thoughts for a few more days," Dion returned.

"Or at least for long enough to let us get out of this county with our skins intact. Though with Longear on our trail, that'll take some doing."

The wolfwalker glanced at the older man. "Gamon, why is it that you frown every time someone mentions this Longear?"

He scowled, removing his warcap and dragging his fingers through his gray hair before setting the cap back on his head. "I don't know, Dion." He paused and shook his head. "Well, yes, I do." He looked across the saddle and furrowed his brow even more deeply. "There's something not right with that man. The way his traps are laid—the way he uses other men— he plays games like the tricks Shilia used to play on Aranur. For a man to use other men that way—it just doesn't make sense."

"In what way?"

"I don't know, Healer Dione," Gamon muttered. "I just don't know."

"I don't pretend to know strategy as you do, Gamon, but I do know there is something wrong. Hishn senses it. I sense it. It's as if every sight and sound is telling me that we should turn tail and run, but every kilometer we ride forward, and every kilometer is clear."

He nodded. "Anticipation."

She shook her head. "It's more than that. The closer we get to Wortenton, the more it seems as if I am putting my hand, and then my arm into a—" She frowned, searching for the words. "A mudsucker's mouth."

The older man glanced at her, but he said nothing else, and as he spurred ahead thoughtfully, Dion was left to worry on her thoughts like a wolf on a bone.

It was late afternoon when Rhom's mount decided to throw a shoe. Typically, they were kilometers from the nearest village by their map, and there did not seem to be a single home in sight, just lightly forested hills, growing dry in the summer heat. They dismounted to repack and leave the beast beside the road—they were in too much of a hurry to nurse it along till Rhom could find a forge to make a new shoe. Hishn, panting, took the drink Dion offered and settled down in the shade while the others worked.

Two slow-moving lumber wagons were approaching, their drivers nodding in the heat. It was not until Gamon had gotten all the bags divided and lashed back on the dnu that he realized Rhom and Aranur were not with them at all. Dion winced inwardly, knowing instinctively what they had gone to settle, and muttering something about boys doing men's jobs, Gamon angrily pulled their dnu off the road so the wagons could pass. One of the drivers raised his hand as if to say thanks, but the gesture seemed to break open a hive of bees. Men began pouring from the wagons, their swords out as they jumped down to the road.

"Soldiers!" Tyrel shouted. "Run for it!"

"Hishn—go!" Dion cried out in the air and in her head. The wolf lunged away into the brush. "Find Rhom!"

The two girls jumped into the saddle and tried to break away, but soldiers surrounded them and grabbed the reins easily from their hands. Tyrel, Gamon, and Dion had drawn their blades and managed to swing up onto their mounts to try to charge at the running men, but there were too many. The soldiers just grabbed the riders' legs and dragged them down. Dion struggled uselessly against them for an instant, borne down by sheer weight, until a large fist crashed against her cheek, and in the burst of blackness, she knew nothing more.

Chapter 8

Arguments are heated
Where hearts have lightly tread

"Well?" Aranur demanded, facing Rhom across the clearing.

"We have something to settle," Rhom said flatly. "About last night, about the scouting you send Dion to do, about—"

Aranur's eyes narrowed, and he cut Rhom off with a sharp gesture. "I admit I made a mistake in allowing Dion to backtrack when Longear's men were around, but I can hardly be blamed for using her as a scout. She has those skills, and we need them."

A muscle jumped in Rhom's tightened jaw. "You use her as you would a tool, not a person, Aranur."

Aranur regarded him for a moment. "Since we're on the subject, Rhom, why don't you look at the way you use your sister, too."

Rhom glared at him coldly. "You are the one at fault here, not me." He spit the next words. "Aranur, who lets a woman take his risks and then presumes he's worthy of her favor."

"I'm not going to deny that I think Dion can take care of herself in most situations. As for our . . . evening together, she did not find it unpleasant. You can't protect her all her life, Rhom. She's old enough to Journey with you or without you, so she's old enough to make her own decisions. Give her some credit, man.''

"It's not her decisions I'm worried about."

"What do you mean by that?" They circled, testing each other's strength.

"I've seen the way you look at her. The way you touch her.''

"She's beautiful, Rhom. I'd have been a fool not to kiss her when I had the chance." Aranur meant to lighten the atmosphere, but he knew instantly that he had said the wrong thing. What the hell, he thought, half steel or full steel, a man can't fight a lepa with his sword half drawn. "She has a sweet kiss," he said deliberately. "I'll have to do it again sometime.''

Rhom's eyes went cold. "You moonwormed bag of dnu droppings. You put your hands on my sister again and I'll cut your fingers from their joints and break your face all the way back to Breinington." He launched himself at the taller man, and they grappled.

"You're good, Rhom, but I'm faster, trickier, and I just plain know more than you do." Aranur's foot swept Rhom's leg from under him, and the two men crashed heavily to the ground. Aranur's elbow caught the younger man's ribs and Rhom grunted, but Rhom's fist glanced off Aranur's arm and struck his cheek a jarring blow. They struck each other back and forth till Aranur managed to hook his foot up around Rhom's neck. The blacksmith snarled and drove a vicious kick back into the other man's gut. Aranur rolled, tearing a breath from the frozen air in his gut.

"I don't want to hurt you, Rhom. Your sister—" he grunted as they tumbled over a log and he landed again on his shoulder "—likes me, and I—" He twisted Rhom's elbow and rolled the younger man off. Rhom struck Aranur's gut with his foot, but the taller man took the blow and cracked Rhom a good one in the ribs. "—like her, too." They scrambled to their feet and circled again.

"You're encouraging her in something you have no intention of finishing," Rhom spit out between gasps, standing Aranur off in the grass. "She has lived in a small village all her life. She has no experience with men like you. And, moons help me, I won't let such a rast-spawned worm take advantage of her.''

"Be careful how you speak of someone who has experience you know nothing of," Aranur snarled.

"Whatever the experience, I don't want it brought to my sister's lips," Rhom was incensed. "You don't even think of her as a lady." He faked to the left, and Aranur ducked back, turning the younger man again into the clearing.

"I don't know what—I think of her as," the gray-eyed fighter admitted frankly, warding off another fake and guiding Rhom's steps closer to the heavy brush. "She's unusual, and"—he was baiting the other now—"I've always been—fascinated by the unusual."

Rhom faked another punch and almost caught the older man off guard. "You have no right to play her like a strange prize." His anger sharpened his words as no knife could have done. "She is flesh and blood, and has feelings you wouldn't even recognize—"

"Even if she shared them with me?" Aranur taunted, reminding him of the night in the woods.

Rhom's eyes went icy and he lunged. Aranur slid a kick up under his blocking arms, but it barely stunned the other man. The blacksmith's hands were surprisingly fast, and Rhom faked so that Aranur had to use every sense of movement to counterattack till they broke apart again. Their chests heaved. Blood ran from above Rhom's eye and dripped from his chin. Aranur could feel the swelling on his own cheek and the cut on his jaw. His ribs hurt, but he guessed that Rhom's hurt a hell of a lot more. They looked at each other, waiting like two competing dogs for the next move. They stood for a long moment. Aranur's lips started to twitch toward a smile, and then Rhom's did, too. Then Aranur began to laugh. Rhom straightened ruefully. "You're pretty good."

"So are you."

"You'd have beat me if we'd kept going."

"If I had to."

"But you didn't really try," Rhom said, more to himself as if realizing some measure of Aranur's skill.

"I didn't need to." Aranur caught his breath again. "We've been traveling together, fighting together for a long time. It's natural that Dion and I feel attracted to each other." He stopped Rhom's automatic protest with a raised hand. "This fight—I only wanted you to admit that Dion—that Ember Dione can make her own decisions when it comes to a man's attentions."

Rhom's eyes flashed again, but he held his temper. "You are right," he said finally, giving Aranur a look that said he still would not hesitate to take matters into his own hands if they got out of hers. "The decision is hers to make." He paused, and thought about smiling. "I know her well enough to admit that she'd never ask anyone to take care of anything for her anyway."

"You can say that again." Aranur did smile then, around his swelling lip, and added slyly, "Shilia's a lot like her, you know."

Rhom's face changed as he realized Aranur's own position.

"Yes, I am a brother, too," Aranur said. "I have no complaints about the way you treat Shilia. So far." Aranur let the words hang in the air, and the other man's uncertain smile grew broader as he saw the juvenile threat each of them was holding out to the other.

Rhom wiped the blood from his chin ruefully, then stiffened.

At the expression on the other man's face, Aranur froze, too, listening intensely. That was the sound of—

"Fighting!" Rhom put their fear into words.

Gamon and Tyrel were alone with the girls. Aranur's mind raced. How could they have been so stupid as to leave the others alone on the road— He did not complete the thought; he was already running, Rhom hard on his heels. But they got only twenty meters before the gray shape of the wolf flashed, then burst through the brush in front of them.

Aranur stopped instantly, and Rhom turned back. "Come on!"

But Aranur grabbed the other man's arm. "Wait . . ."

The wolf's yellow eyes met Aranur's, and he felt that shock of another voice in his head. *Leader.* The clear voice had a husky timber to it, and he felt a strange double vision of himself as the wolf saw him, then the overpowering sense of Dion as the wolf felt her struggling even then. He felt the wolf's agony of running from her partner instead of tearing into the soft flesh that attacked her; he smelled the scent of Dion's hair and the acrid sweat of sudden fear as she went down; he blinked and staggered at the blank hole that filled his head as she was struck unconscious. *They have my healer,* the wolf said, projecting a soft worry and an underlying fury in his head. *Now you must stalk them to their lair.*

He cleared his throat. "Wolf—Gray Hishn, you honor me."

Rhom was staring at him. "Aranur," he said urgently. They heard the sounds of men crashing through the brush toward them.

Aranur nodded. They ran.

Chapter 9

Look beyond the coffers
To the men who wield the swords.
The one who rules their hearts and minds
Is the one who guides the wars.
The crown is not the only one
Who writes the songs we sing;
Some games of power, blood, and death
Are played by knights, not kings.

It was a gradual jouncing that woke the wolfwalker, her cheek bruising further against the wood of the wagon as it wheeled over the bumps in the road. She tried to sit up, but her hands jerked her back against the side of the wagon. Pain throbbed up through her swollen wrists where they were tied. Blasts of white-hot needles lanced instantly through her head, and she was suddenly blind. She sucked air and bit her lip, and it was the tiny punishment of that which cleared her mind.

"Dion," Shilia whispered. "Stay still. Don't try to move just yet."

Don't move? She could not move if she wanted to—her limbs were like logs. And where was she? The wooden floor bounced under her, and the wall slammed into her side, and she realized with a groan that they must be in one of the wagons from which the soldiers had attacked. There were guards, too, staring intently at her and the others. The others— It was achingly hard to twist her head, but she did it anyway, ignoring the heavy hammer that pounded into her temples like a hangover. She was probably bruising already, just like Gamon, she thought, seeing the purples and blues darkening on his right cheek. Dion wondered if her face looked the same. With his knees drawn up and his head tucked down against them, Gamon could have been sleeping, except for the fact that the jolting ride would have kept a dead dnu from lying quiet.

A pothole swallowed one of the wagon wheels, and the force of the jerk threw Dion almost into a sitting position. She clung to the slatted wall of the wagon by bracing her feet and shoulders, then worked her way up as best she could. The ropes that tied her hands to the lumber rings were thick and awkward, and did not allow much movement. Another rut in the road threw two of the soldiers against a third, and they straightened each other out with barely a grunt, leaving the prisoners to fend for themselves as their heads rapped back against the bruising walls and their bonds yanked painfully at their wrists.

Besides the guards and the prisoners, the transport was empty. Only lumber shavings, barkdust, and long slivers of wood gave evidence to the previous cargo. Of the ten soldiers who dozed or guarded the prisoners, six or seven were awake and watching carefully. Their swords had obviously seen much use, and their mail was dented, stained, and patched with the marks of many campaigns. Dion did not relish the thought of facing even two of them at once.

They wore no insignia or other signs of rank, but they all had the same look in their eyes and the same air of quiet violence on their shoulders. They did not speak to each other or tease the five who sat bound before them or occupy their hands with games. They were grim, quiet men who did not question their orders, and their leather mail and dark pants gave the shadowed wagon the look of a dark jail.

She leaned toward Shilia. "Rhom?" she whispered. "Aranur?"

"I don't know," the girl breathed back with a tiny shake of her head.

One of the guards motioned abruptly, and Shilia fell silent. Dion looked from one man to another and shivered. Their eyes were shallow, their faces disinterested. But their hands were thick and muscular, and their gaze quick when one of the prisoners moved. Dion did not think it would be easy to escape. But there were always other options, she thought. And Gray Hishn, she knew, was free.

She felt the gray bond tighten as she called the wolf's name, and the creature's images pushed back softly, worried. *The smell of blood and dirt and sweating men. Callused paws padding silently over small sticks. The undertones of the hunt . . .*

The wolfwalker concentrated her thoughts. *Rhom and Aranur?*

Dirty, beaten . . . The wolf sent impressions rather than words, the images creating a shadow of worry and fear that added to the anger that clouded the Gray One's speech. *Crouching, thick brush scratching leather. The sight of a wagon, bouncing over the road like a rock down a cliff. Rhom's voice low and intense. Aranur waiting. Hunting. Waiting. Wood creaks, hooves stomp the dirt. Sweat and dust and dnu and men and blood* . . .

How many soldiers? Dion asked.

Smells that choke the nose. A forest of legs like a herd of deer. Shouts. Voices clog the air . . .

As Gray Hishn sent the thoughts, Dion's nostrils no longer smelled lumber shavings. Instead, her head was filled with scents of men and dnu. Images, not so much of figures as of motion, their faint sounds like a dull murmuring in her head. Motion, and the lust of the hunt.

Wait, Gray One, she told the wolf firmly. *Stay with Aranur. I am not in danger yet.*

The gray shadows gather, the wolf sent back. *We call the hunt. We can tear their legs, tear the throats from them all—*

No! Don't even think about that, Hishn. You cannot fight men like these—not with so many against you—and doing so would destroy you. And that, Gray One, would hurt me more than these slime-ridden tarkens ever could.

A low growl slid through her thought.

Wait, Hishn. It's a long way to Wortenton, and we'll get our chance soon enough.

So the wagon bumped through an infinite kilometer, and then a second and a third. The soldiers drank often from the bota bags that were passed along by their sergeant, but none was offered to the prisoners, and Dion, gazing longingly at the dripping bags, had to force herself to turn her head and look instead at the dusty road. As if the thought of water had brought it on, the realization came that her bladder was near to bursting, and after that, every bump and bounce of the wagon made it worse. Finally, when she thought she could hold it no longer, the driver pulled to a halt, and the soldiers piled out, dropping to the ground with relief and stretching their cramped muscles, leaving only two to watch the human cargo.

"So when is it our turn?" Gamon muttered, shifting his legs awkwardly.

"You, too?" Dion said with a wry glance.

"My tongue's as shriveled up and dried as a dead snake skin," he returned sourly, "but, may the moons curse them all, I've been dying to take a leak for the last two hours."

One of the guards looked over his shoulder as they spoke. "You'll get to relieve yourselves soon enough, so shut up," he growled, "or you'll wish you had."

"Such original threats," the wolfwalker whispered to Shilia. "Almost make you think they're intelligent."

The girl stifled a wan smile as the soldier looked back in, daring them to speak again. Dion shifted, easing her wrists into a more comfortable position now that she no longer needed to use her nerve-deadened fingers to brace herself against the wagon's motion.

"Gamon," she whispered, "these men—are they . . ."

The old man's face was suddenly grim. "Zentsis's soldiers," he confirmed.

"The scouts—they knew where we were even after we left the woods."

He shrugged awkwardly. "Maybe. It does not matter now."

She glanced quickly around. "If these are Zentsis's men . . ."

"Then some of them belong to Longear, as well." Gamon finished for her. "The fact that we no longer have the physical evidence of their war plans will mean little to Zentsis. After all, he just wants us dead before we warn Ramaj Ariye. I have the feeling we should be a lot more worried about what Longear wants."

"But Longear works for the Lloroi, for Zentsis himself—"

Gamon shook his head slightly and stared into the distance. "No, wolfwalker. Zentsis is only one player. And this game," he said to himself, "is played by knights, not kings."

Shilia shivered. Tyrel, his light-colored skin already sunburned, looked at Namina and tightened his jaw. He said nothing, but Dion could almost see what he was thinking. Tyrel's temper was as bad as Rhom's. Dion herself had a temper, but since she had started running with the wolf almost two years earlier, she had had to learn to control not only her outward fury, but her inner anger. The Gray One who shadowed her thoughts reacted to her heart, and if Hishn even thought her wolfwalker was in pain or danger, she would attack with no more thought than a lepa gave before it leapt. Rhom and Aranur together could not control the wolf. Only Dion could. And

Dion had to remember that Hishn could pick up Aranur's thoughts almost as easily as she could Rhom's. If Rhom and Aranur decided to attack, Hishn would lead them in, and the soldiers, with their vicious war bows and barbed arrows, would kill the Gray One before they blinked twice.

But what could Rhom and Aranur do? Create a diversion and spirit the prisoners away? These soldiers would not be easily tricked, she thought. And what if a rescue failed? She was not of Ariye. Her worth to Zentsis—or Longear—must be very small. Unless the Lloroi of Bilocctar wanted to set an example.

The wolfwalker leaned her head back against the wooden slats. Hurry, Rhom, she thought. Whatever Longear's long-term plans, they would not include a stranger like her when better hostages—a Lloroi's family—were available instead.

Ten minutes later, they were finally dragged from the wagon and allowed to sit on the ground, their legs so cramped that they had to be half carried or they would have fallen. The soldiers were hurrying back and forth, some making large cooking fires, some treating the dnu to make sure the riding beasts caught no stones in their hooves. To the side, an officer stood with two soldiers studying a map and a watch. There was no sign of Dion's twin, and the wolfwalker sighed and leaned back against the wagon wheel, closing her eyes in the blessed lack of bruising motion.

But bare moments later, the dust was kicked up by heavy feet, and Dion glanced up tiredly.

"Which of you is the Lloroi's daughter?" The officer looked from Shilia to Namina, his long hooked nose giving him the visage of a raptor. Dion glanced at his sword and noted the worn sheath. His chain mail was not new either, and even his boots, though well made, showed the history of many months of wear.

Shilia swallowed, and Namina looked sullenly at the ground, but Gamon cleared his throat and spit to the side. "When you have properly introduced yourself, I will introduce my niece to you," he stated coldly.

The officer bowed. "I apologize for my insensitivity," he said with slight sarcasm. "I am Generr Didantin neBroddin, captain of the Fifth Squad."

"The Lady Namina maSonan, daughter of the Lloroi of Ramaj Ariye," Gamon returned briefly. The omission of her middle name was not lost on the captain, and the man smiled with bare amusement.

"My pleasure. And this lady?"

"The Lady Shilia maWynron, niece of the Lloroi of Ramaj Ariye."

"Longear will be pleased," the captain said with a tight smile. "However," he added, the smile disappearing, "Longear is not here, and I am in charge for the moment." He gestured for the two girls to be untied, and the guards leaned down to help the girls up. "Ladies, please make yourselves useful. We are tired of our own cooking."

Namina allowed the soldiers to lead her off, but Shilia, after stifling a gasp as her arms were freed, rubbed them slowly without moving away from Gamon.

"Lady Shilia?" Captain neBroddin raised his eyebrow.

"I will stay with my uncle," she said.

"I think not. It would be unfortunate for your uncle if you were stubborn over such a small thing as cooking a meal."

She looked from him to Gamon. "What do you mean?"

NeBroddin smiled, but his teeth were like fangs, and the expression did not reach his eyes. "I mean simply that Gamon will be punished for your actions, as will the boy be punished for those of his sister, the Lady Namina. And vice versa. You are my—guests," he said deliberately. "Do not protest my hospitality too much."

Her eyes wide, the girl looked at Gamon, who shook his head imperceptibly. She nodded, allowing herself to be led after Namina, though she shook off the guard who reached for her arm.

Dion closed her eyes wearily. The throbbing numbness that plunged up through her arms and down to her fingers from the ropes only bolstered her own resolution. If Gamon was hostage to Shilia, and Tyrel to Namina, where did that leave her? Was she hostage to all of them? Or just an extra body to be used later to prove a point? Her status as a healer had protected her before, but by the moons, it was a thin piece of silver to stake her life on here. She wished she knew what to do.

The officer turned to Gamon. "You are Gamon neBentar, weapons master," he stated. "As such, you will be treated with respect, but you will remain tied. If you try to escape, your knees will be broken, as well as the knees of the boy and the ladies."

"I understand," Gamon said.

The captain paused a moment before turning to Dion. "You are a healer and a woman, but you carry a man's weapon. Who are you, and what are you doing in Bilocctar?"

A flash of irritation burned in her gut, and though tempted, the wolfwalker did not even bother to open her eyes. She had spent eleven years becoming a healer just to be insulted by this worlag's son? She resisted the impulse to snap back.

"What is your purpose?" neBroddin demanded again, his voice cold. "What is your position with this group?"

"The lady, as should be obvious even to you, is a healer," Gamon said with equally cold sarcasm. "She merely travels with us to return home."

The man glared at him. "How convenient for you to have a healer along, Gamon," he said finally. "We are so honored by her presence." NeBroddin matched the old man's tone as Gamon had done his. The mime was not lost on the weapons master, whose glare turned to ice as he controlled his anger. "As you know my name, perhaps you would introduce us," the captain continued.

"The Healer Dione of Ramaj Randonnen," Gamon said shortly.

Dion deigned to look at the captain. Games, she thought in disgust. It was all a game, but one they played for their lives . . .

"So. Why does a healer carry a weapon of death, *Lady* Dione?" neBroddin asked, his voice cutting.

"These are dangerous times for women who travel across counties. I prefer to pass as a man in a man's world. It's an odd man who travels without a weapon."

"It's an odd woman who travels as a man," he countered. "Where did you meet these people?" he asked abruptly, trying to catch her off-guard.

"North and east of the Phye River," she said frankly. She knew that they had that information already. "I was captured by raiders, and this man rescued me."

"How commendable of you, Gamon," the captain said without even glancing at the older man. "You have great loyalty, Healer Dione, to remain with them through such dangers and traitorous actions."

"Worlags, raiders, slavers in a merchant's guise—they are the same dangers I'd have faced had I traveled alone."

He snorted. "They are politics, from which these people cannot protect you."

We will speak later." The words were a promise that Dion wished she had not understood. NeBroddin turned to Gamon again. "You have something to discuss with me, Gamon."

Four men moved forward to haul the older man to his feet.

They were not necessary to guard him; his muscles were so cramped that he could not walk—he could hardly straighten as they dragged him to a hastily erected tent and thrust him inside. A guard barked a command at Shilia and Namina to cook, not look, as the girls watched the small procession uneasily, and Dion licked her dry lips. NeBroddin was clever, she thought. He separated them so they could not plan anything, then questioned each of them alone so they did not dare tell anything but the truth.

Heavy voices, muffled by the canvas walls, came from the tent. After a while, one angry voice rose above the others, followed by the sound of blows. It went on far too long. Then there was only silence. Gamon, Dion agonized. It took only two of them to return the gray-haired man to the wagon. He was unconscious, his head lolling across his shoulders, and his face bloody and swollen. But as she watched the two soldiers retie his hands to the spokes, a chill grew in her chest. Which of them would be next? Tyrel? her? And could she take what they had just give Gamon? Silently, the men pushed her shoulders forward and cut the ropes to the wheel.

She steadied her voice. "My turn?" she asked, wincing at their treatment. They helped her up more gently than they had set Gamon down, but her body was so stiff that she, like Gamon, could barely straighten up. "I'm afraid it will be a minute before I can walk."

One of the men flushed as he cut the bonds on her feet. When they cut the rawhide on her wrists and brought them in front of her to retie, she sucked her breath in and held it, but the pain of returning circulation brought tears to her eyes. She ducked her head to wipe her eyes on her shoulder. "It's not often a healer has a chance to see the world from this viewpoint," she said.

The other man looked down at her uncomfortably. "Sorry, Healer, but we're just following orders," he said in a low voice.

She took a step and went to her knees before they could catch her. She winced at the impact, then was hauled back to her feet by her elbows. "Orders such as these for a healer?" She looked down at her wrists, bound so tightly that the leather straps had cut into her skin and stained it red. She looked back up. "I should thank you for the experience. It's been . . . educational."

Both men flushed then, and after a glance at the second man, the first swung her up into his arms without a word and carried her to the tent, the second man striding ahead to hold aside the tent flap.

The tent was already stuffy in the summer heat, and the blast of warm air after the long lack of water made Dion's head swim. The first man set her down gently and held her elbow to steady her as she swayed. NeBroddin just looked at her, her slight form woebegone and dwarfed by the two soldiers on either side.

"Sit," he said, pointing to a wooden crate.

He stared at her for a moment as she did so.

"So. Healer Dione." He looked at her speculatively and picked up the black swordsman's gauntlets that lay beside him on the makeshift desk. "I have no interest in wasting time. Nor do you, I'm sure—this situation must be uncomfortable for you. So I will ask the questions, and you will answer, and soon all this will be behind you." He pulled the gauntlets through his fingers. "What do you know of the people you travel with?"

She met his cold eyes calmly. "What is there to know? I ate salt with them, so I travel with them."

"What a quaint notion," he drawled. "Loyalty based on sharing a meal. I suppose now you will deny that they are spies?"

"Spies?" Dion could not help laughing. "Spies of what? They're just trying to get home. The girls were kidnapped by raiders over a month ago, and their brothers and uncle went after them. They could not possibly be spies."

NeBroddin just looked at her, and the smile died on her face. "You traveled lately by boat," he stated coldly, rather than questioned.

"A fishing vessel, yes. An older boat."

"And before that."

She frowned. "We took kayaks down the Phye at one time."

"You did not board a trading vessel in Sidisport?" He turned away from the healer to study a map spread out on a folding table.

"No," she answered truthfully. Gamon and Tyrel had, but she had not.

"You lie!" he shouted suddenly, whipping around and striding to stand over her. He grabbed her shoulders and shook his fist in her face. "That is not what I hear."

She was startled but stayed her ground expressionlessly. She let irritation slip into her voice. "If you already know what I've done, why do you ask questions you know I cannot truthfully answer 'yes' to?"

NeBroddin's voice dropped to a sinister whisper, and his fingers touched her lips briefly, following them back as she flinched away. "I will know the truth when I hear it from your own lips."

Kilometers away, Hishn growled, and Dion had to resist the wolfish impulse to snap at his hand. *Hishn—no—stay with Rhom—* The wolf was too far away to help her, and she had heard what neBroddin said to Gamon about escape; even if she did get away herself, the caption would cripple the others. He did not care what he did to them. It was their tongues, not their legs, that he needed intact.

"I've told you the truth," she said shortly.

"All right." NeBroddin smoothed his face miraculously, then spoke pleasantly, though his voice was tinged with steel. "Let's examine your position. You traveled to this area but can give me no legitimate reason for being here. You have information which does not belong to you, but you refuse to give it to me. You avoid the police, fight when confronted, and act in a highly suspicious manner. How can I think of you as a legitimate citizen? None of the countries allied with Bilocctar support activities such as the ones you are involved in." He paused and gazed at her with cold hatred. "So I have no choice. You, Healer Dione, are under arrest for espionage." He slapped his gloves against his hip to shake the dust from them, then pulled them on his hands slowly. "I have full authorization to interrogate you and retrieve the information you hold. If you do not cooperate . . ." He shrugged delicately. "Longear has always had a more winning way with prisoners than I. The choice is yours." He turned briefly away as if giving her time to decide while he fit his fingers into the gauntlets. "I have little patience in these things, so I advise you to be quick about choosing."

Dion hesitated. "If you would just tell me what you want to know," she said finally, "I will gladly tell you if I know it."

"A wise decision, Dione," he said without turning. "I am only interested in learning about a certain packet of letters. Letters of war plans, but I'm sure you know that. One of the men in your party might be carrying the packet. Or perhaps it was given to the boy?" He looked over his shoulder and raised his eyebrow. "Hidden perhaps? Stashed somewhere? Handed off to another spy in Bilocctar to deliver across the border?" He turned around and leaned toward her, nodding to the door of the tent. "I could do much to see that you get safely home if you remembered such a thing."

She shook her head slowly and frowned as if thinking back. "None of them has written any letters since I've been with them. In fact, I doubt that the younger boy can write well at all."

But neBroddin took two steps and grabbed her chin in his hand, forcing her head up to look at his tight face. "Don't play games with me, Dione. I am in control here. I can kill one of you every day till you tell me what I want to know, but it will be too late for those pretty little girls, and far, far too late for you. I know you are spies." He spit the words in her face. "How much do you know of our activities?"

"I know nothing!"

"Think." His fingers dug into her chin.

She wrenched away. "I can't tell you what I don't know."

"Perhaps this will help you remember." He struck her brutally across her cheek and flung her off the crate to the ground. The men who had carried her in looked stricken before they carefully wiped their faces of all expression, but Dion did not see. Her mind was filled with a lupine fury that smothered her sight. NeBroddin savagely motioned both men to the back of the tent as Dion crouched on her knees looking up blindly, her breath coming quickly and her hands shaking as she tried to contain her own rage.

—Healer—his blood, his bones in my teeth—
No!—Hishn—stay!

She got to her feet, and he hit her again across the face, then backhanded her across the mouth. "What? No crying from the little healer? Or would it be swearing from the fighter?"

She raised her head slowly and touched her bound hands to her lip where it was torn, the blood leaving a thin trail across her knuckles.

He smiled viciously. "Crude, yes, but effective. And all so needless. The letters, Dione. Who has them?"

"I told you, none of them."

He grabbed her hair and jerked it back so that she was slammed up against his body by his other hand. "Your healer status means nothing to me," he whispered. He forced her back to arch, trapping her hands against his chest. "Your life means nothing to me.'' He crushed his knuckles into her spine and jerked her head back further.

—*Healer—I come—I kill for you—*

No! Stay away!

Her neck muscles stood out like cords; her back strained against his paralyzing strength. ''I . . . don't know . . . anything,'' she gasped.

He shifted to grind his elbow into her shoulder as he yanked her hair further and further back, and she jerked her hands up into his neck as if by mistake, hitting him in the throat.

''Bitch!'' he swore furiously, choking as he shoved her away.

She hit the ground hard, and it was as much Hishn's strength as her own that brought her back to her knees and then her feet. Her vision was blurred—the wolf's fury stained her sight so that she could hardly tell if she was on four feet or two.

''I will have answers, Dione.'' NeBroddin rubbed his throat with a short, sinister motion as he shoved a medallion and chain back into his tunic, then narrowed his eyes. ''If you do not give them to me, you will still be a hostage for the others.'' He reached down and hauled her across the dust by her elbow. ''The letters. Where are they?'' He hit her, then again. ''I want information and I want it now. Who has the letters?''

''I don't . . . know of any . . . letters.''

''Gamon perhaps? Or the lady Shilia?'' His hand came down again. ''The first beating is not the worst, Dione. It's the second time or the third, when you anticipate, that it grows unbearable. I understand that. And soon, very soon, you will, too.'' The blows made her head reel. ''Just one question Dione: Where did you hide the letters?''

She tasted blood, but her mind was fuzzy.

''Does Aranur carry them? Or that other man who escaped our trap with him?''

She hardly noticed when one of his hands dug painfully into her shoulder and the other ground its fingers through her arm until she was lifted off the dirt floor and shaken in front of neBroddin like a doll. ''Speak, woman—before I cut your tongue out!''

''Captain neBroddin,'' one of the men at the back of the tent cut in nervously. ''Maybe she really doesn't know. If she's just traveling with them, they wouldn't tell her anything important.''

NeBroddin dropped her to the ground in disgust. ''Get her

out of here,'' he snapped. ''I'll deal with them both again later.''

Dion was picked up again, and the black spots that now clouded her sight brightened as sunlight hit her full force.

''Heerdon, get some water,'' the man carrying her commanded. When he set her down against the wagon wheel again, the guard named Heerdon had returned with a water bag that he held to her lips, ignoring Gamon, who was watching him closely.

The guard glanced around furtively, then pulled the water bag away. ''Moons forgive us, Healer,'' he muttered as he left.

As the two guards joined the men at the fire where the two younger girls were cooking, Gamon let loose on his anger. ''That stinking, boos-trimmed, dag-chewing, spit-wallowed bastard,'' he swore under his breath. ''If I ever get my hands on him . . .''

Dion cleared her throat, then spit a blob of blood to the side. ''At least I know you haven't lost your teeth to talk with,'' she whispered back.

''Healer, I'm sorry you have to go through this.''

She leaned her head back with a wince. ''We share a Journey, Gamon.''

''No, Dion.'' He let his breath out heavily. ''Aranur and I,'' he said finally, ''we took our Journeys long ago to prove our skills worthy of Ariye. And you, you had your Internship to prove yourself as a healer. Why you travel with Rhom . . .'' He shook his head. ''This is Rhom's Journey, not yours. No one expected you to have to prove yourself again like this.''

She laughed, stopping abruptly as her lip split open again. She coughed and spat, clearing her mouth once more. As she ran her tongue over her torn lip, she leaned her head back against the wagon spokes and closed her eyes. ''I had heard the stories like all the others, Gamon,'' she said at last. ''Rhom and I always stayed up late at the council fires to hear the Journey tales of the youths who left to seek their fortune and came back as men. A healer's Internship seemed so dull compared to those. I used to dream about going on Journey with my twin. The excitement—the adventure . . .''

''The risk.''

She laughed painfully. ''We were heading into Fenn Forest to battle worlags and raiders, not get involved in legends and politics and Zentsis's plans for war.''

Gamon glanced at the now-closed tent, then at the wolf-walker. "Did he tell you anything?"

She shook her head.

"How did Hishn take it?"

Dion bit her lip, then winced. "It was . . . difficult. She is close. Too close."

"Can you reach Aranur or your brother through her?"

She shook her head again. "She is upset. There is nothing but emotions in her right now, and she can't even talk to my twin until she's calm again. Though I think she'll have better luck with Aranur. He seems better able to hear her." She licked her torn lip. "I'm sorry, Gamon. I am not helping much."

"You have a right to be upset, Dion."

She was silent for a long moment. "I almost told him, Gamon," she said in a low voice. "Just to sit there and take it . . . I think I would have broken if he had kept on even one blow longer."

Gamon glanced at her. "No, Dion," he said softly. "You would not have broken." He nodded at the tent. "You are stronger than him. You will never let him own you."

"And Longear?"

The older man looked out across the camp. "Don't blame yourself for what happens, Dion. Human beings can take only so much, and we're going to meet both Zentsis and Longear if neBroddin has his way."

"Do you think Byra or Jam betrayed us through me?" Her voice was harsh, and Gamon, glancing at her, saw the tortured emotions in her eyes.

He was silent a moment. "Only the moons know that, Dion. But if I were wondering about it, I would rather put my silver on the innkeeper where we stayed the night than on the old couple you helped."

She said nothing, but her expression did not lighten. Instead, her jaw tightened; her eyes blurred suddenly. But then the captain shoved aside the tent flap and ordered Tyrel brought to him, and Dion clenched her teeth until she could see again.

Namina cried out and flung herself toward her brother, but one of the soldiers grabbed her and kept her away. Tyrel managed to wink at his sister with a lopsided smile before he went into the tent. Gamon's face tightened.

"That cur will kill him as soon as look at him," Gamon

muttered. "He knows Tyrel wouldn't be given any documents. But he is clever. He gives the girls a taste of what he can do without asking them for the letters. He'll let this stew in their minds for a while, then beat us again later. Maybe kill one of us to show he means business. When they know he's serious, he'll ask them for the letters, and they'll have to tell them what he wants to know or watch us die."

"We've got to get away," Dion whispered desperately.

"How? Look at the guards. Aranur and Rhom would be suicidal to try a rescue."

She shrugged bitterly. "I'm so stiff I couldn't walk even when they let me try. Even if Rhom and Aranur cause a diversion, we would not all escape this camp."

Gamon watched the soldiers around the fire. "Wind carries the lone tree down like a matchstick; only the forest weathers the storm," he quoted softly. "We just have to wait for our chance, wolfwalker. And pray to the moons that it comes soon enough to use it."

Dion leaned her head back against the wheel spokes. It was less than five minutes before they carried Tyrel back out from the tent and retied him to the wagon wheel.

"Healer?"

Dion opened her eyes. It was the guard Heerdon, with three others.

"We'll take you to relieve yourself. Then you can eat." She nodded slowly.

They helped her up—they had to; she could hardly walk. She could feel Hishn in the forest, but the wolf obeyed her, and Dion could not even catch a glimpse of the gray fur across the camp.

Heerdon pulled the flap of the relief tent aside. "In here."

When he followed her in, Dion looked at him with a scared frown. "What, by the second moon, are you doing, Heerdon?"

He flushed, dropping the flap behind him. "You are to be watched at all times."

Relief washed through her. "For moons' sake, Heerdon, I can't possibly escape from you here. And besides, I wouldn't get far with my leggings half down."

The man had the grace to look sheepish before he turned his back.

When she was done, he led her to the fire where Shilia and Namina sat huddled together. Shilia jumped up and would have run to Dion, but one of the soldiers stepped in front of her, while another guard grabbed the healer's elbow and shook his head.

"You eat over here," he said to the wolfwalker, pointing at the ground.

Dion glanced at the patch of dirt silently.

"Over here," he repeated.

She raised her head, met his gaze, then pulled her elbow free of his grip and walked toward Shilia anyway.

He grabbed for her again, but Heerdon stopped him. "She's a healer, Lanton. She can't do any harm just by sitting with them."

The other soldiers stepped slowly aside at Heerdon's direction, and Shilia ran to meet her.

"Oh, Dion, are you all right? I thought—we heard—" The girl hugged her, careful of Dion's face, with its swollen cheek and torn lip, and Dion, her hands still bound in front of her, accepted her hug awkwardly.

"I'm okay, Shilia."

"We saw them take you in after Gamon—and then—" Shilia's voice caught.

Dion shook her head with a nod toward the guards. "It's not worth talking about, Shilia. Namina," she said, catching the other girl's attention, "how are you feeling?"

Namina shrugged. Dion looked sharply at her, but the girl just stared off toward the edge of the fire, her gaze not moving even when Shilia stepped in front of her.

Dion sat down gingerly. One of the guards brought her a piece of old bread and a chunk of dried and salted meat.

Seeing it, Shilia made a gesture of disgust. "Dion, you can't eat that. Let me get you something from over here." She turned to get a plate from the pile of metal dishes the soldiers ate from, but the guard shook his head. "She's to eat this, girl. NeBroddin's orders."

Heerdon looked uncomfortable, but nodded in agreement. "That's so, Healer. Strict orders."

"I understand," Dion said quietly. She raised the loaf and chewed off a piece with difficulty; her lip split again when she bit into the hard crust. "It's fine, Shilia. Tastes just like home."

"But there's fresh food here . . ."

Dion shook her head in warning, and the girl's voice died. Heerdon and the other guards looked down at their feet, their hands, anywhere but at the healer, and Shilia, glancing in disbelief from Dion to the others, sat down slowly. The wolf-walker ate in silence, chewing slowly and mechanically on the dry bread and tough meat; and Shilia, beside her, watched guiltily as Dion took with thanks what Shilia would have thrown away.

Gamon and Tyrel were not allowed to move away from the wagon to eat. Instead, they were guarded there, their rations the same as Dion's.

"At least they let us drink our fill," Dion commented when the guards took her back to the wagon and tied her next to Gamon.

"Enough so that we'll need to relieve ourselves again on the ride," he returned sourly. "They're breaking camp already."

The healer cleared her throat. "Do you think . . . do you think they will try to . . ." her voice trailed off.

"They will question us again," he returned quietly. "Ne-Broddin won't touch the girls yet. He will just let them watch."

"Gamon—"

"You'll do fine, Dion. Just think of your training. Of anything else but the present. Use Hishn, if you can, to let your mind escape." He looked at her. "It's only thirty hours to Wortenton, Dion. All you have to do is survive."

It was evening of the next day when they arrived in Worten-ton, the darkness hiding the suburbs from her eyes, and the pain that shrouded her mind closing her ears to much of the noise of the town. But the city was lit as if in festival. Shouts of parties crossed the wagons, and the dnus' hooves rang on the stone streets in time to the garish music that stomped across the road. Then they drove through a darker part of town, and the driver brought the teams to a halt outside a large gate. A moment later, they drove inside, and the prisoners were hauled out to stand unsteadily on the cobblestones. The pain of the ropes around her wrists and ankles had become a blanket that dulled her mind, then pounded in her head, and Dion shifted her weight from one foot to the other to move her sluggish blood beneath the cords.

NeBroddin looked at them in dissatisfaction before swearing under his breath. "Take them to the third level," he ordered, striding away angrily.

Dion nudged Shilia comfortingly with her shoulder. "That doesn't sound too bad," she whispered.

Heerdon, who overheard her, glanced down. "There are

only five levels, Healer,'' he explained in a low voice. ''The fifth level is only for those who have less than a day to live. People usually last less than a ninan on the fourth level. The third level—'' He paused. ''That's for the murderers and such who might last a month. You might last that long. Maybe more, if the moons ride your luck there, as well.''

''Heerdon.'' Shilia turned big eyes to him in horror. ''You wouldn't take us in there—you wouldn't leave us in there to die.''

The big man's jaw tensed, but as the other soldiers glanced his way, he wiped the expression from his face and took Shilia's arm tightly, pushing her ahead of him toward the prison door. As Dion followed, thrust under the dark gates after Shilia, she hesitated only once, to look at Heerdon and fix his face in her memory as if he would be the last image of a world she might never see again.

Chapter 10

To bring the ax down is easy;
To wait for it to fall can pull your mind apart.

"We've got to do something," Rhom hissed. "We can't just sit here and watch them disappear."

Aranur, crouched in the back of the vegetable cart with the other man, swore under his breath as he watched his sister and the others shoved unceremoniously through the dark gate of the jail. "We need plans," he whispered finally. "We have to see the layout of the prison from the inside."

"Dammit, Aranur, even with plans, we'll never get them out of there."

"There's always a chance we can bribe the guards."

Rhom snorted. "With what? Gamon was carrying most of our money—we've got less than twenty silvers between us, and there must be thirty soldiers around the gates right now—not to mention the guards inside."

"I can see that, Rhom. But there are far too many people in there for us to walk in even with disguises. We just have to wait."

"Like we did on the trail?" the other man said bitterly. "We should have done something before they reached the prison, Aranur. At least we could get close to them on the trail. We can't get within a hundred meters now."

Aranur kept his voice even with difficulty. "Rhom, even on

156

the trail, that captain, neBroddin kept them under so many guards that even with a diversion, we wouldn't have been able to get them all away. We had a rough enough time getting close enough to hear them twice, and both times we were almost caught.''

Hishn, crouched in the night shadows under the cart, whined softly.

''NeBroddin.'' Rhom said it under his breath, but Aranur heard it anyway.

''You could not have reached him without risking your sister's death.''

Rhom clenched his fist over his sword. ''I should have done something.''

''Like what? Tried a rescue and gotten yourself killed instead? They've been waiting for us to try something like that. You heard neBroddin's orders as well as I did. You saw the way he lit the camps, the way he set the guards. They were well prepared to deal with any diversion they saw. If we'd tried to rescue even one of our group, they'd have maimed or killed the others before we could get back out of their camp. No. We've got to be patient.''

Rhom turned slowly and looked at Aranur with a coldly measured stare. ''How patient would you be if it was your sister being beaten instead of mine?''

Aranur's jaw tightened. ''Dion is a fighter as well as a healer, Rhom. She knew the risks.''

''She knew nothing,'' Rhom snarled. ''But now, thanks to you and me both, she's learning fast.''

On the street, the dnu harnessed to the cart perked their ears, and both men froze, their eyes tracking each movement and sound that reached them.

''The driver,'' Aranur whispered. ''He's coming back.''

''We can't leave now. We can see the layout of the courtyard through the gate.''

Aranur slipped to the edge of the cart. ''We can't stay here either. If that driver checks his load and raises the alarm, Longear will have us before we can say 'dnu spit.' We'll move back and around to the other side of the prison.''

But Rhom shook his head. ''You go on. I'll stay here. If he drives off, I'll sneak back into the alley. I could ambush a guard, get a uniform—try to get in by myself—''

Aranur gripped him tightly on the shoulder. ''We're not going to leave them there, Rhom. I swear it. But we've got to get away from here now. The driver's coming back. If he finds us here . . ." He dropped noiselessly from the cart and crouched in the shadow beside the wolf. "Hishn—Gray One," he whispered. "Come with us. You can do nothing from here."

Rhom hesitated, glanced from Aranur to the prison and back, then swore bitterly and dropped to the ground beside the other man. "Come on, Gray One. Aranur's right again. We've got to get out of here."

But the wolf just laid her head down on her paws and whined again.

"Hishn . . ." The blacksmith reached under the cart and grabbed the wolf by her scruff. "Come on. You can't stay here. You'll be seen."

The Gray One snapped at his hand, closing her teeth over his wrist so that he swore and lost his grip.

"She coming?" Aranur whispered as he pulled his meager pack out from between the vegetable bins.

"No."

"Stall the driver. If we're separated, meet me about ten minutes out of town—where the south stream channeled through that broken dam."

Rhom nodded and looked down the street. "What are you going to do?"

Aranur ducked under the cart. "I don't know yet."

"Well, whatever you do, do it fast." Rhom slipped out of the shadows and onto the sidewalk where he hesitated, looking toward the driver of the cart making his way toward the two strangers.

Behind him, hidden by the thick slabs of wood that braced the bottom of the cart, Aranur pleaded with the wolf. "Gray One, listen to me. You can't help Dion by staying here. You've got to come with us."

The massive wolf barely flicked her ears.

"Hishn, I know you're worried. I am, too. But we can't do anything until the guards thin out at the gates. And this hiding place is going to be driven away in a few minutes."

The wolf ignored him, staring instead at the iron gates that walled her off from her healer.

Aranur, seeing that Rhom had reached the driver, grabbed a handful of Hishn's fur and pulled her head around with an effort. "Look at me, Gray One. Look through my eyes."

Anguish—

Aranur almost lost his grip on the wolf, but he forced her head around again. "I feel it, too, Gray One," he said deliberately. "Believe me, it is my fear, too."

My healer—

"We can do nothing until the guards are away from the gates. An hour from now—maybe two—and we can try getting in."

—the distance—her scent is weak—

"It will grow stronger when we get closer. But we have to get farther from here now before we can go through the gates. Please, Gray One. Honor me with your trust."

The wolf whined low in her throat and gazed at the prison gates.

"Please, Hishn." Aranur pulled ineffectually at her scruff. Rhom had not stopped the driver for long, and now he was trudging down the street toward the corner as the driver made his way toward his dnu. "We've got to go now."

He hesitated only a moment longer, then scrambled out from under the cart. With a last mournful whine, Hishn dragged herself from under the cart and, as the dnu on the other side of the cart stamped their feet to greet their master, slunk into the alley after him.

Chapter 11

Keep your strength and keep your pride;
Keep your wits close by your side.
Time will tell, and freedom come
Before the fight is done.

The prisoners stumbled up stone steps, then down a long hall past a guardroom. Lights flamed brightly and futilely on the dank, stone walls. Few glanced their way, but those who did looked long and hard at the way the women's torn clothes barely covered them. Dion kept her chin high, though she could feel the flush on her face match that on Shilia's and Namina's. The hall descended through more steps. They went through an iron grille guarded by two men who exchanged the leg ropes for chains, then stumbled past another grille that led into a hall of cells from which piteous sounds could be heard. Dion felt the blood begin to circulate again in her legs. If she could only free her hands . . . She could see the same thought in Gamon's eyes as they stopped at the third grille and were let into a black and dirty passage.

"NeBroddin wants them separated, but in good condition," the leading soldier said tersely to the guard at the grille. "Those two"—he gestured at the men—"and that one there"—he pointed vaguely at the healer—"are tough."

"Put one of the girls in two, and the other in five, then. Put the healer in number six. The old guy can go in sixteen, and the boy in fourteen. Hey," he called after the guard. "When you

160

go back up, tell Winston to hurry his ass down here. My shift ended and his started an hour ago.''

The other guards did not answer. The one in the lead just looked at the keys in his hand and opened the first cell for the prisoners.

''You,'' he said, grabbing Namina by her arm. ''In this one.'' He slashed the ropes at her wrists and shoved her into the empty darkness, then slammed the door. That clang of metal on metal bars echoed into Dion's skull like the jaws of a trap closing.

The guard unlocked the next one, roughly thrusting back the girl who crowded the door, and pushed Shilia inside. There were already two women in the third, and Dion flexed her wrists to be ready to act when he cut her free. But he chuckled and shoved her inside without cutting the ropes or releasing her from the leg chains.

''You got a reputation, Healer, and I'm no fool,'' he said as he slammed the bars shut with a hollow clang. ''You want those free, you set them up here by the bars.''

As she made to do so, one of the women in the cell launched herself at Dion with a hoarse cry. Startled, Dion twisted instantly, tucking her legs up into a jumping side kick, forgetting how the chains would snag her balance and sling into the other woman. The kick and the metal links caught the filthy woman under her arms, slamming into her stomach. The prisoner collapsed heavily on the stones, and the other one backed off.

''So cut them.'' Dion said coldly, backing up to the bars.

He chuckled again and slashed through the leather strips. ''You owe me two silvers, Cradlon.''

The other guard gave him a dark look and passed the money over without a word. They moved out of sight. Dion stared at her cellmates without shifting, listening to the jail doors close behind Gamon and Tyrel. The stench was still bending her nose as the guards strode away again.

''How long have you been in here?'' she asked the woman she had kicked. The other prisoner huddled against the wall. The jail was quiet except for the moans, so she spoke softly.

''What's it to you?'' the woman snarled back.

''Just making conversation. I'm not planning to stay long, so I thought I'd get to know you while I could.'' Dion was talking to keep from vomiting at the stench. Fear of the dark stone and iron that trapped her deep beneath the city ate at her stomach as much as the sickening smell did, and for a moment she was paralyzingly afraid that she would never see the sky again.

She looked around the cell. Stacked into two beds were four vile-looking pads that she assumed acted as mattresses; there was a hole in the corner for refuse, and chain rings were bolted to the walls. That was all. A month in this place? She shivered. Hishn . . .

"I'm Tehena," the other woman said suddenly. The one on the floor shot her a venomous look, but she ignored it. "That's Morain."

Dion looked at them. "I am Ember Dione. Or Dion, for short." She hesitated, then asked, "So, what brought you two here?"

The one named Morain sneered. "That's a death question in here, Healer. You'd do better to keep your curiosity to yourself." She sat up. "It'll die soon enough anyway." She turned her face to the wall and ignored the new prisoner. In the dim light, the woman looked as if she had good bones and a pretty face, but there was so much filth that Dion could not even tell her prison sores from the dirt.

The wolfwalker slid to the floor and tried to make herself comfortable, stretching her legs out as far as the chains would allow. "What about you?" she asked Tehena.

"What about yourself?" the other woman returned rudely.

Dion shrugged. "Longear has it in mind to . . ." Her voice died away at the look on Tehena's face.

"Healer," Tehena said in an ominously low voice, "if you value what life you have left, do not say that name in here."

Dion glanced at the woman curiously. If there had been more light in the cell, she would have sworn that Tehena's hands were trembling. "Why?" she asked quietly.

Tehena clenched her fists. "There are some things that bring with them their own evil. That name is one of them." She turned away.

Dion tested the bars, and they were as solid as they looked. She could not distinguish words in the flood of miserable noises that filled the prison, but she was no longer gagging so much at the stench of rotting straw and human waste.

Tehena started picking at the parasites in her straggly, filthy hair, then noticed the healer watching her. "You'll have them, too, before the hour goes by," she snarled.

Dion met her eyes without challenge. "Take no offense, I gave no insult."

Morain gave Dion a calculating glance as she took in the healer's band still on her forehead. "Got any root on you?"

Dion's hands went automatically to the herb pouches still at her belt. "Nothing that you would be interested in," she returned quietly. Even in a prison, no one touched a healer's pouches—she hoped.

"How would you know?" the other woman mocked. "I might be interested in a lot of things."

"Morain, shut up." Tehena got up and lay down on one of the sleeping pads. "Want one of these?" she asked Dion. She looked as if she might be twenty-eight or twenty-nine under the filth, and Dion wondered how long she had been in the jail.

"Not yet, thanks," the wolfwalker said with a shake of her head.

"Suit yourself."

A clamor rose and Dion craned close to the bars to see what was happening. The evening guard came by, followed by a scrawny boy in rags who pushed a shallow trough under the bars and set a loaf of bread beside it. The swill looked like a rice stew, but Dion did not recognize anything in it. She swallowed hard. No wonder Morain and Tehena were hostile. The same size trough and loaf of bread went to the other cells, too, no matter how many people were in them.

Dion sensed a movement and turned quickly. Morain had launched herself at the wolfwalker again, trying to throttle her. Dion punched her gut, stomped her instep, and threw her off as Tehena grabbed for the trough. But the wolfwalker kicked it over deliberately, and Tehena cried out, scrabbling on the floor for the liquid that soaked in the straw and dribbled away between the stones.

"You cur!" Morain dropped on the floor with the other woman and frantically scraped small pieces of something horrid-looking into her mouth. Tehena grabbed for the loaf of bread, but Dion snagged it first and backed away. The filthy woman scrambled after the healer, and Dion kicked at her head to keep her away.

"We're going to have an understanding," Dion said harshly, keeping her own chains from Tehena's grasping hands. "I can take you any time I want. I'm not interested in killing you," she said deliberately, "but I will do it if I have to."

"That's all we get." The other woman gnashed her teeth, her eyes locked on the loaf in the wolfwalker's hands. "For the three of us."

"It can be just two of us. Or even one. But I can tell you who the one will be." Dion broke the loaf into three even pieces and tossed one to Tehena. "Here. Eat your heart out." She threw the second piece at Morain. "Call me any more names and I'll not give you any tomorrow."

Tehena started choking. She caught the crumbs that fell from her mouth and stuffed them back in, rocking back and forth and gasping with horrible sounds that Dion finally realized were laughter. Feeling the grinding cramps of hunger in her stomach, the wolfwalker leaned her head back against the cold stone wall and ignored Tehena's howling. Eventually, the other woman shut up.

Chapter 12

Tease the ears with dulcet tones
And thwart the eyes with light;
Obligate the senses
And hide your tracks of flight.

"What about those two?" Rhom nudged Aranur and pointed with his chin at the guard who patrolled the dark corner of the prison walls and the one who stood motionless inside the recessed guard box there.

"Maybe." Aranur squinted. "The lights are still too bright at the main gates. Even with uniforms, we can't go in as guards without a diversion."

"Fire?"

Aranur nodded slowly. "The guard should change within the half hour. We'll have to do it before then. But if we could get in uniform and set the fire before we're relieved, we'll be able to slip through the gate in the commotion without being recognized."

"You want the fire inside or outside the walls?"

"Inside. There are a couple buildings with thatched roofs. We'll use coal arrows so that the tips don't ignite before they hit the thatch. That way, they'll never see it coming."

Rhom glanced at the two guards. "Which one do you want?"

"Give me the one in motion. You take the one in the box. Ready?"

Aranur slung his arm around Rhom's shoulders and the two

men staggered around the corner, leaning drunkenly on each other and wheezing like air bags.

"But Riva wuz hot fer my handful of copperz," Aranur sang out of tune, slurring the last few words into another wheezing cough.

Rhom belched.

"An' I wuz jus' lookin' fer somewhere to turn," the song went on as they staggered up the sidewalk.

The guard walking toward them barely spared them a glance. "Bunch of bottle-sucking maggots," he muttered.

Aranur grinned sloppily at him as they came abreast and Rhom burped grandly again.

"Hey, sodjer man," Aranur said as he held up a half-empty bottle. "Wanna shot of thiz? Guaranteed tuh warm the cocklez of yer heart—"

"Go on home before I throw you in jail for disturbing the peace."

"Throw us in jail? Us? Fer offerin' you a drink like the gentlemen we are?" Aranur looked at Rhom in disbelief and shoved him away so that Rhom stumbled against the wall, close to the guard box. Aranur swayed in front of the guard. "You know, my cousin Upodi's a sodjer man like you."

He swung, and the first guard, caught unawares, staggered back. Rhom dodged into the guard box and slammed the pommel of his knife into the startled man's stomach, bringing his other fist across to the man's temple and then laying him out carefully on the floor. Outside, as the other soldier sagged against the stone, Aranur caught him and dragged him into the shadow. "The uniforms, quickly."

Rhom was already tugging off the sashes and belts from which hung various weapons, logbooks, and whistles. He tossed them in the corner and stripped the jacket off the guard, then the pants, while Aranur kept watch. He could hear Rhom struggling into the clothes, then a loud ripping sound. He flattened himself against the wall.

"What was that?" he breathed.

"Runt's got small shoulders," Rhom whispered, reappearing outside the guard box. He adjusted the sash and swung the guard's sword belt into place, then began stalking along the wall as the other man had done. When he reached the corner, he waved to the guard along the next stretch of wall.

Aranur, dragging the second unconscious man into the tiny room, glanced back at the blacksmith. There was a splash of silvery brown down Rhom's back where his studded leather mail shone dully through the tear. "Don't turn your back on anyone."

Rhom grinned grimly. "When did I ever?"

A few minutes later, Aranur had the hot coals strapped to the arrows with leather thongs. "They'll hold long enough."

Rhom looked down the street. "All clear."

Aranur stepped out and, with a brief glance toward the other end of the wall, shot the first arrow up and over the wall, then ducked back into the guard box.

"Still clear," Rhom said in a low voice.

Aranur shot two more arrows, then two more.

"One of those should have hit," Rhom said.

"I think three were good. But keep walking. We should hearing something in a few minutes."

He was right. A couple minutes later, a narrow column of smoke rose toward the overcast sky, and then a blaze of orange and yellow flames sprouted thinly and spread into a thick column inside the walls. Someone shouted, and an alarm began to wail.

Neither man needed encouraging. They sprinted toward the main gates, getting there just after the other pair of guards who rounded the opposite corner ahead of them. Behind them on the streets, lanterns were being lit and windows opened as people woke and looked at the flames.

"Fire!" "Look there!" "Get the buckets!"

Aranur and Rhom dodged inside the gates and ran toward the prison entrance. Men were dashing back and forth, some running for buckets, some rolling caskets of coal and other supplies out of the burning buildings.

"There isn't much time before the roof caves in," Aranur said as he shoved his way through a thick crowd of men who burst from the jail doors.

"Let's make it quick then."

With Rhom on his heels, Aranur jogged down the wide hall that led into the prison. Smaller openings grew off the corridor, but he was headed for the stairs at the end of the hall. But they got only twenty meters before they were stopped by a group of guards trotting out from one of the other doors.

"What's going on out there?"

Aranur gestured over his shoulder. "Fire in the supply hut."

"You going on down to the levels?"

"Got to check on a couple prisoners."

The lead guard nodded. "I'll clear your papers so you don't have to stop at each station."

Aranur hesitated. "Salbert has the papers. He got caught up in the clean up outside."

The other man frowned. "And you didn't?"

Aranur snorted. "The fire got into the coal. The smoke's so thick out there it doesn't wait for you to breathe in. It crawls into your lungs instead. We would have had to help clear what's left of the supplies, but we figured it would be better to do this instead."

The guard nodded, but the frown did not leave his face. "Who did you say has the papers?" The three soldiers with him glanced at his face, then stepped away from him and formed a loose semicircle around the two imposters.

"Salbert. We were just recalled from the outer county."

"Huh. Who's your commander?"

Aranur jerked his head toward the outside doors. "We're riding with neBroddin."

"Captain neBroddin?"

Aranur nodded and punched him in the stomach. Rhom stepped forward and slammed his fists into one, then another of the guards, dropping one of them instantly. He tripped the other one, stomped on the man's knee, and drove his own knee into the man's face. The guard went down like a brick. Aranur, shoving the lead guard into the fourth man, grabbed the latter by his dress sash, pulling the startled man forward into his fist. The man swung wildly and connected with Aranur's shoulder, staggering the tall fighter, but Aranur slugged him across the jaw, then spun a kick to the man's temple, dropping him against the others on the floor.

He looked back quickly. "They'll be all over us in a minute. Let's get out of here."

"We could still get down into the prisons," Rhom protested.

"And be trapped there before we even knew it."

With an oath under his breath, Rhom gave in, running after Aranur back toward the outside door just as the alarm was raised behind them.

"Stop! You two—stop!"

"Get through to the outer gate," Aranur directed, glancing back.

Rhom nodded and dodged through the smoke. He slammed into a line of men dragging a thick carpet away from the hut, then tripped over a bucket that he did not see in the smoke. He swore, regained his feet, and ducked around a corner. The smoke was disorienting. There—the gates. He jogged toward them, hesitated, and stepped back into a thick cloud of black smog as a group of guards raced in front of him; then he ran for the gates, doubled over with coughing fits. The smoke burned his lungs and made his eyes water so that he was almost blind. Behind him, he could hear the frantic alarm of the guards inside the jail over the din of the fire crews, but he was already outside, knocking down another soldier, apologizing, coughing, and stumbling across the street into the alley, ignoring the other man's shout as he slid into the shadows of the city and fled in their darkness to safety.

Chapter 13

Whip the winds of fury to a frenzy;
Or the pain will kill you first.

Pacing, Shilia glanced at her cellmate and shivered at the
sight of the filthy shadow who still huddled motionless against
the back wall. She heard no sound from the wolfwalker, and
Namina, too, was silent. The only noise that crept into her ears
was a murmur of misery that came from the labored breathing
of prisoners.

"Gamon?" she called softly. "Tyrel?"

In the next cell, Dion got up and, ignoring Tehena's look of
disdain, went to the bars to look down the dark corridor.

"Gamon?" Shilia tried again.

Dion peered through the gloomy light, but due to the curve
of the corridors Tyrel's cell was beyond her sight.

"Tyrel?" Shilia called.

"Here—I'm here," the boy answered thinly from around
the corner.

But from the other end of the dank corridor, there was a
rasp, as if a wooden chair had been scraped along stone, then
a clanking sound, and then the noise of boots slapping the cold
floor.

"Shhht!" Morain hissed. "Tell her to shut up."

In the other cell, Shilia did not hear Morain's low voice. "Are
you okay?" the girl continued, unaware. "Where's Gamon?"

"Too far down for me to see him. Is Namina with you?"

The guard's footsteps were louder now, and heavy.

"She's okay." Shilia continued. "She's two cells down."

Morain scrambled back against the wall, drawing herself up into a piece of shadow as if it were a cloak. "Shut up—tell her to shut up!"

Dion, seeing the fear spreading across Morain's face, moved quickly, reaching through the bars to touch Shilia's fingertips where the girl's hand clenched the bars of her cell. "Shilia—quiet."

"But Healer—"

Dion could see a light in the corridor. "Shhh."

In the shaft of brightness that preceded him, the guard looked like a moondevil who had been dragged from the darkness by the flame of light in his hand. His shoulders were huge. His hulking form blocked the lantern from shining behind him, so that the cells at his back looked like gaping holes that opened onto the seventh hell. His eyes, gleaming in the yellow glow, were like the eyes of a lepa before it leapt on its prey.

He glared from one to the other. "Which one of you is making the noise?" he demanded harshly.

Shilia opened her mouth, but Dion cut in. "I called down the hall to see if my friend was all right."

The guard transferred his gaze to the healer for a moment, then let it rest again on Shilia. His thick fingers tapped the butt of the coiled whip that hung from his belt. "Noise is not allowed."

Shilia swallowed.

"It will not happen again," Dion said quietly.

The guard stood there a moment longer, staring at Shilia until she stepped back from the bars of the cell. Nervously, she sat down beside the stone wall, her face turned away from him.

He snorted, then stalked away.

Dion did not move from the cell bars, staring down the hallway but not seeing the stone that walled her in. The stench was like fingers in her nose, prying her nostrils apart and forcing her to eat its odors of garbage and rot and human waste while she tried to slam her senses shut to its putrescence. She tried breathing shallowly, so that she did not take as much of it in, but the smells crawled farther and farther into her lungs. Hishn . . . If only in thought, perhaps the Gray One's senses could take away this stench. She reached in her mind, but her only sense of the Gray One was a thin and distant worry.

Hishn? she called.

Wolfwalker . . . The Gray One's voice was faint.

Dion concentrated, strengthening the bond until she could almost see a thread of gray running through the stone of the cell. *Where are you?* she called. *Where is Aranur and Rhom?*

Aranur is here. Rhom is nearby. They bring the smoke that chokes and burns. Flames that warm the night in gusts. We hunt as one . . .

Fire . . . Dion gripped the bars more tightly. *Gray One, be careful* . . . In smoke, Hishn could become confused, could panic when she found she could not see or smell. If Aranur was using fire, and the gray wolf was nearby . . . No, he would not be so thoughtless. *Stay away from the flames, Hishn,* she sent with worry nonetheless. *And stay outside the walls of this place,* she added sharply. *You cannot jump these walls like you can leap a downed tree or vault a fence.*

The Gray One licked her lips, and with the odors of the prison clinging to Dion's tongue, the sensation made the wolf-walker gag. *We hunt slowly,* the wolf returned. *But we hunt with our fangs bared.*

The wolf's voice faded. Dion stared into the darkness. Not until Tehena shifted behind her did she straighten and glance at herself. What did she have of use here? Aranur and Rhom—they had their bows, their swords, their knives. Even Hishn had the weapons of her teeth and claws. Dion? She had no weapons. No mail. No warcap. That they had taken her sword and bow was expected, but they had searched even her foot-gear, so her boot knives, too, were gone. They had not been careful, either. Her boots, worn thin by the ninans over the mountains, were slit where the searchers had not bothered to pull her last valuables from their pouches and had cut the leather to get at the gems instead. She owned nothing. She had nothing but the dull silver headband that crossed her brow and the bags of herbs that soaked up the stink of the prison.

"Dion?" Shilia whispered.

Dion stirred, but did not shift her gaze from down the hall. The air was cold. The drops of moisture that soaked the atmosphere carried the odor of the jail into her skin and hair and hands.

"Dion, I'm scared."

The wolfwalker fingered the cold bars wordlessly. As she touched them, the metal chill slid like needles into her skin till it pierced the little warmth she had left and ate away at her bones. Something was happening to her in this place. It was a dream—a nightmare; the only way to escape the pain was to close off her feelings. The bruises with which neBroddin had marked her were already faded and set away from her mind, just a dull and constant backdrop that pulsed with her blood until she moved. She shuddered. Only the thread of Hishn's worry and the long, lone howl of the gray wolf's hunt wormed its way through the blackened stench to give Dion strength.

Shilia's voice trembled as she whispered, "What are we going to do?"

Dion's nose twitched at the pervasive smell. But her eyes were unfocused, her mind ranging across the distance to the wolf. "Wait," she said softly. "Survive."

"Dion—"

"Aranur and Rhom will come for us."

"How can you be sure?"

"They've already tried once."

Shilia pressed herself against the bars, trying to see Dion around the stone. "Did the Gray One tell you that?" she demanded urgently. "What happened? They weren't—moons help them—they weren't hurt, were they?"

"Shh." Dion listened, but there were no sounds from the guard's station, only the shufflings and mutterings of the prisoners who whimpered miserably for release. "They were not hurt," she said finally.

"Dion—"

"It will be all right, Shilia." Dion cocked her head. Her nostrils flared. "Listen."

The girl fell silent. "What is it?" she demanded finally.

"A breeze." The wolfwalker thrust old air out of her lungs and breathed in, and the faint taste of the breeze cut through the stench in her mouth like a cup of clean water thrown in a stagnant pool.

"Dion—"

"Don't think about it, Shilia," Dion said sharply. She paused, then spoke more gently. "Think of home. Think of being greeted by your family. Think of spring. Of your brother—or of Rhom," she added quietly. "And pray."

The girl stared at Dion's hands for a long moment, then sank slowly down against the iron bars. "Oh, moons of mercy, moons of light," Shilia whispered. "Guide me in this darkest night . . ."

Time passed. As Dion's eyes grew used to the dank night,

the shadowy figures across the dim hall grew into the shapes of two women: one lying down; the other hovering, wringing her hands silently over the first. The one on the ground shivered, then her teeth rattled. The one crouched against the wall crawled forward, then back to her post, and Dion watched as if in a dream. Ovousibas. The pain of the dying woman was almost tangible to the healer. Even if Dion was jailed so far as this from the moons' clean light—even if she could still not stop the death of old age, at least she could ease its pain, she thought. She was a healer. The guard would have to let her work.

She was not aware that she had spoken out loud until Morain sneered from behind her. "You can't reach her, Healer. And that woman over there wouldn't let you heal her even if you could."

Dion looked over her shoulder. "What do you mean?"

Tehena stirred and came to stand at the bars, as well. "It's the one blessing of the moons that's left to us." She watched the other prisoner across the hall with jealousy. "Even you, with your high and mighty ways, wouldn't be so cruel as to take that from us."

The healer stared blankly at the other woman. Then, as they watched, the jaws of the prisoner across the hall rattled. The sharp, acrid smell of hot urine cut across the dense air, and the other woman in the cell, gaunt like a string of bones, weakly stripped the body even as its teeth still clattered together. The dying prisoner looked at Dion expressionlessly, her eyes huge and her skin stretched back so far across her cheekbones that it was like leather across a drum, until her mouth opened spasmodically, and her teeth showed her to be barely more than a skull.

Dion turned her head away quickly. Tehena chuckled.

The wolfwalker clenched her fists around the bars, and they seemed to grow bigger and the ceiling shorter and the walls closer as she stared. Oh, sweet moons, she prayed, her lips moving silently. Get us free of this place if only long enough to see your light once more. For this I would give my life. Her knuckles grew white around the prison bars. I swear this by all the moons that ride the sky . . . She pressed her forehead against the bars until their icy touch reached even through her headband. I would rather welcome death now than wait until I welcome the death of another for my sake. "By the gods, hear me," she whispered. "Hear me . . ."

The scrabbling of the rats warned her that the rodents were crawling out of the refuse hole again, and she turned in anger to swear futilely at them to get away, and then froze. Morain and the other woman had dozed off. The two rats that crept around the sleeping figures boldly ran toward the motionless healer for the crumbs and the smell of swill that clung to the greasy stones, and she shuddered at their six-legged bodies and sightless, maggotlike eyes. They were not the rats of the ancients, of those who had crossed the stars, but rats of this world, of the underground jails and filth of Asengar. The creatures stopped, turning their blind heads from side to side as they smelled her. And then a thought rose, unbidden in Dion's mind. Rat bones were brittle. The gray thread that linked her mind to the wolf sharpened at the thought. A large weapon could not be hidden in this bare place, but bone slivers could be made into darts. And darts were small. And rats had poison sacs.

She glanced upward, and even though she saw only the black stone of the cell, she felt as if a weight had been lifted from her shoulders. Oh, moons of mercy, she thought, your light reaches even into this darkness. She did not move. One of the rats took a few steps and sniffed at the stones only a meter away.

Morain and Tehena—would they betray her? Or could she keep what she did secret from both of them? She did not shift her feet, though her heels grew bruised on the hard stone. She did not breathe. The first rat was very close.

She could hear the faint sounds of someone crying. Namina, probably. Dion could count on no help from that quarter, but perhaps Shilia . . . She stopped, shocked at her callousness. That Namina was crying, Dion should at least understand. But that the wolfwalker had given up on the girl—Dion swore at herself.

The movement by her foot caught her attention again. In her head, the echo of gray thoughts gave her a heightened timing of the rat's movements. Could the rodent hear the wolf behind Dion's breathing? Did it know that when Dion struck, it would be as the Gray One on a hare? The rat's ears, huge and cupped, twitched in short, sharp movements as the fanged mouth sniffed the stones. It licked a crumb from a crack in the floor with a long, slender tongue, and Dion shifted her weight. It froze, looked blindly up with its pasty, gray-white eyes, then licked warily again at the stones.

And she smashed her foot down and caught it, breaking its neck with a quick snap. The other rat leapt away. From the one she had kicked, there were not even death throes, and Dion reached for the flea-ridden carcass, taking care to stay away from the poison in its claws and teeth. She tossed it against the wall, out of her way. Behind her, Morain, awake now, watched silently. But the wolfwalker became motionless again, patient as the Gray One who followed her thoughts like a ghost.

The other rat was suspicious. But there was food in the cracks between the stones. And the human thing was silent again, as if sleeping. The rat slunk back a few lengths. Then one more. It lowered its head to the floor. And Dion stomped again, snapping the rodent's back before it could turn and then wiping her foot against the grease and stain-blackened stones as if they would clean the blood from her heel.

Morain rolled over. "Didn't get enough supper?" she taunted.

Dion did not answer. Instead, she examined the carcasses as if she could tell what diseases they were carrying on their fur. They were filthy enough that she was not sure she could force herself to tear the pelt open with her teeth to get at the bones.

Tehena did not even bother to turn over as she said, "Best part's the back and the hind legs. You better eat all you can now. You won't be fast enough to catch them after you've starved a bit like us."

"You can have the meat," Dion said absently, "if you'll save the fang sacs and give me the long bones when you're through."

That did make Tehena roll over. "You serious?" she asked suspiciously.

Dion just tossed the two rats to her in answer. The woman caught them both. Tehena looked at Morain, who swallowed, her eyes intense and staring at the dead rats. The first woman exchanged a long look with Dion, then raised her head a fraction and, though her hand shook with effort, extended one of the rats to Morain. The other woman snatched it in disbelief as if the offer would be retracted any second. She did not take her eyes from Tehena, but scuttled back to the shadow where the wall protected her back. Only then did she tear its fur open with her teeth. The long greasy hairs stuck between her front incisors, and blood dribbled down her chin. The wolfwalker looked away. She was not that hungry yet.

Like the other woman, Tehena stripped the fur away in a

long tube, ripping the pelt away from the ends of the legs when she came to them, and the wolfwalker could hear the two women chewing slowly on the raw meat as she watched unseeing down the stone hall. They chewed and savored each bite so slowly that Dion, never having seen such starvation before, shuddered. They did not finish for a long while.

Hours seemed to pass before the pile of raw bones lay at Dion's feet. Pushing aside the images of the women eating, Dion concentrated on looking the pieces over carefully.

"You know, the new ones always try something as soon as they get here," Tehena spoke softly to the ceiling. "That's why the guards watch them the closest at first. They'll whip at least one of you, maybe two, just to make sure you understand what not to do. Probably you or the girl next door or that boy who yelled back down the hall."

Dion quelled her shiver. As long as she was still alive as a hostage, it would not be Shilia or Tyrel who was whipped. Her joints ached and throbbed from being twisted and bent by Longear's captain. Though one of her ribs felt cracked, it was just a torn muscle resisting the stretch of her lungs. But there was still Longear. And if Longear had more in mind for her to bear, she would rather risk all now than wait for worse to come.

"The guards use norshark whips, Healer."

The wolfwalker glanced at her sideways, but said nothing.

"You'd better rethink what you're going to do, Healer," Tehena said. "If your face says anything about the shape the rest of you is in, you're not strong enough to take a whipping and live."

"How much of a whipping would I get?"

The other woman barked a mirthless laugh. "Ten lashes. Fifteen. Does it matter? I never saw anyone take more than eighteen and live." She paused. "I never saw anyone take more than ten and live past five days."

"Infection?"

"Oh, so calm, you are," Tehena snarled. "Asking this, considering that. It's easy to be brave before you've felt that broken glass cut your back open and have it left raw for the maggots to crawl in."

Dion looked up and shook her head slowly. "Of all things that I feel in this place, the least of them is bravery."

"Judging by what you're doing, you must be feeling stupidity more than anything else."

The wolfwalker stared for a long moment before a smile twitched on her split and swollen lips. "Perhaps. If so, it's hardly contagious." She glanced down the hall.

"That's right, make sure they aren't coming yet," Tehena mocked. "Or better yet, look again and anticipate what you'll get."

"How do you know how many days anyone lasts in this darkness? Do the guards come and spell out the time for you?" Dion retorted.

Morain, looking up from where she crouched like an animal, chuckled humorlessly. "One day, one meal. Unless the cook feels grouchy and we go without. Or unless they decide to see how your flesh feels in their beds first. You can get a good meal out of that, if you know what you're doing."

Dion gave her a sharp look. "What do you mean?"

The woman chuckled again. "You just don't get it, do you? Don't worry, Healer. Right now, your face would scare any man out of bed, not into it. But then, the new guards won't know what you look like in the dark."

Dion licked her cut lip. Shilia and Namina . . . She glanced toward the girls' cells.

"They like to catch the new ones before they get too bony," Morain continued. "The guard will change soon. Then you'll find out. Hells, you might be one of the lucky ones," she said sarcastically. "You might not survive that either."

Dion suddenly felt sick. She looked down the hall, then back at the tiny bones she held in her hands. "How many guards are in hearing distance?"

"How much noise are you going to make?" Morain replied mockingly.

"Shut up, Morain." Tehena turned and addressed the healer, her voice curiously intent. "One guard on this floor and each of the others, three guards and one gofer up the steps in the guardroom."

Dion nodded silently. She started resolutely to clean the bones, scraping them against the cracks and roughened edges of stone as Tehena watched carefully. She had separated the bones and started to sharpen the splinters she had selected when she heard footsteps in the hall. Morain hissed and scrambled toward her. Tehena lifted up the mattress she was sitting on, and Morain and Dion quickly swept the bones under it.

Light from the lantern fell through the bars, starkly illuminating the filth on floor and mattress, as the guard stopped a few meters down and leered into Shilia's cell.

Oh, moons, Dion begged silently, keep them safe for just a little while longer. She shifted the tiny fang sacs between the mattress and the wall so their precious contents would not spill.

"Come on, honey," the guard cajoled Shilia. "I won't hurt you. Much." He laughed and picked out a key from the ring at his belt.

Morain gave Dion a surprising look of pity, then flung herself at the healer. "You bitch of a rat!" she screamed. "This is my mattress, my straw, my cell. I'll kill you—"

They scuffled, rolling across the floor against the bars, Tehena joining in with her own shrieking accusations. The guard, diverted, moved swiftly.

"Get off her, you bitch," he yelled, kicking at Morain through the bars. Dion grabbed his foot and twisted quickly, startling him so that he fell heavily against the stones. Morain shrieked in triumph and grabbed at his ankle to bite him. Dion yanked. She struck his knee hard with her fist, pulling his leg between the bars. The keys were at his belt—

But before she could strike again he thrust hard against the bars with his other leg, breaking her hold and rolling away. He stood up and looked down at the two grimly. The prison was suddenly deathly silent. You moonwormed fool, Dion cursed herself. You idiot. You blew the only chance the moons gave you by reaching for those keys before you took him out.

Morain and Tehena backed away, slinking into the far corners of the cell, but Dion got to her feet. She could not deny what she had just done, and if the moons graced her with another chance to get out of the cell, even if it was for another beating, she was going to take that chance with both hands.

When the guard turned away, surprising her, she let her breath out. But he went only a few steps to retrieve his lantern, returning to hang it from a hook in the ceiling outside the cell. The light made her squint, her eyes watering instantly. If ever she had seen a grim look in a man's eyes, it was then.

"Hey, big and ugly," Tyrel yelled angrily from down the hall. "You always pick on girls? Why don't you try a man sometime?"

The guard did not even look toward Tyrel's cell. "Bad timing, Healer."

"It's all right, Tyrel," Dion called back, trying to laugh. "You never know. I may get a chance to bite back." The words were brave, but their echo in the prison was empty and small.

"Shut up," Tehena whispered. "The more you say, the worse it'll be."

Dion sobered quickly at the guard's expression as he took the ring of heavy keys from his belt. "She's right, Healer. I got orders, and I follow them. You may know some tricks, but if you want your friends to live, you won't use them. And if you use them anyway, you'll answer to Longear, not to me." He unlocked the spring-clip manacles set into the stone between Shilia's and Dion's cells. Then he unlocked Shilia's cell and grabbed the girl, backing her up against the bars. His knife was against her throat.

"Step out slowly. No tricks." He unlocked Dion's cell with his other hand and clipped the ring back on his belt immediately. Shilia looked at the healer with frightened eyes as a small spot of red formed under the tip of the knife and dribbled down her neck, too bright against her pale throat.

Dion had no choice. She stepped out of the doorway, her leg chains sliding noisily across the stones, and the guard kicked the bars shut behind her. Keeping his distance, he backed Shilia away and motioned the healer toward the manacles.

"Put your right hand in the one on the right," he commanded.

Face to the wall, she realized. She looked at Shilia. The guard pressed the knife into the girl's soft skin so that the drop of blood turned into a trickle that ran quickly down her throat. Shilia trembled. Dion reached up and set her wrist into the cold iron; it sprung shut tightly, trapping her arm against the stone. As the notches sank in, click by click, she felt a cold, cold hand of fear close over her heart.

The guard dropped the knife from Shilia's neck and shoved the girl back inside her cell. Dion stood unmoving.

"You might as well put the other hand up, too. You're not going anywhere now."

She thought he would come close, but he paused instead. She twisted to see what he was doing, and the whip caught her across her shoulder, cutting through her tunic as if it were paper. Her breath went out in a hiss.

"I said, put the other hand up." The guard's voice was sharp.

Dion hesitated again, unable to force herself into a position of helplessness. She could die there as a lesson to the others—it was the Lloroi's family that Longear wanted for hostages, not a stranger. The whip cut again, cross the other gash and laying her back open in a long, jagged wound that burned like fire. She sucked in her breath, trying not to shriek. The third time, there was no warning but the sound of the rawhide in the fetid air. She twisted desperately and grabbed the whip as it cracked, yanking it toward her even though it tore viciously through her hand. Gods guide me, she prayed. The guard stumbled, off balance, and she kicked out with both legs at his gut, the fist that was locked in the manacle letting her hang, painfully, to stretch the kick back. She connected, but the blow was not heavy enough to knock him down. Instead, he staggered sideways, out of her reach, and straightened up against the bars of another cell, gagging as his guts rebelled. She snapped the whip back.

There was no contact. The guard had thrown himself aside, farther out of reach. And now all Dion could do was reel the whip in with one hand. She had just blown the other chance the moons had given her. Her eyes met Shilia's for an instant, then she looked away.

"I can understand your hesitation, Healer, but my orders are clear," the guard said almost apologetically. "You should have thought about what would happen before you did that." He unlocked Shilia's cell again and dragged her out. "Drop the whip," he ordered harshly. "Now kick it over here." Dion did as he said: His knife was poised over Shilia's left eye. "Now put your other hand up."

She obeyed. She clenched her fists. And then the whip began to cut again. In the end, she cried out, but even that sound was drowned in the searing blaze that burned its lesson into her back and the gray howl that filled her head.

Chapter 14

It takes a heart of steel
To watch friends die;
It takes a love stronger than steel
To wait to help them.

"No!" Rhom lunged to his feet in one move, slamming against the wall of the inn's cramped room and breaking the bond with Hishn as the wolf leapt away, snarling. "Gods!" His hands clenched against his temples and his face was twisted with pain.

Dodging the wolf, Aranur lunged for the other man. "Rhom, what is it?"

"Dion—oh, sweet moons, I'm sorry." He shoved Aranur away and shuddered. "I could feel her . . ." Hishn whined, then yelped, and Rhom reached down and gripped the Gray One's scruff as if by that touch he would reach his sister, as well.

"What is it?" Aranur demanded. "What's going on?"

Hishn alternately huddled into the blacksmith, then snapped at his arms and snarled.

Rhom tightened his jaw until his words, when he spoke them, were toneless. "They're hurting her."

Aranur dropped to his knees and forced the wolf to face him.

"No, don't!" Rhom said sharply. "She takes you too far."

Aranur barely spared him a glance. "Tell me, Hishn," he ordered.

The yellow eyes swung toward him. And then he was blind

and his back exploded in fire and the frigid touch of icy stone burned through his chest at the same time. He wrenched himself free of the wolf. "Gods have mercy," he breathed.

Rhom, his face taut and pale, buckled his sword onto his belt. "She cannot wait any longer for us."

Aranur shook his head to clear it. "We need time, Rhom. We must have information—floor plans, entrances, chimneys."

"I will go by myself if need be."

Aranur took a deep breath. "By the time we get there, it will be too late."

Rhom froze, his hand on the door.

Hishn glared at Aranur, her eyes a heated yellow in the dim lantern light.

"You cannot deny the truth, Rhom."

The younger man turned slowly. "No. I cannot deny it. But I can change it."

"We cannot." Aranur gestured at the other man's sword. "The moons could not at this point. And—" He paused. "You may not want me to help free your sister, Rhom, but I need you to help free my family. I cannot let you walk into Longear's hands like this."

Rhom stared at him.

"Dion is alive, Rhom." He pushed himself away from the wall, the receding image of Dion's pain strengthening his voice. "And the Gray One can still reach her. And if Dion is able, we know that, sooner or later, she will try to reach us through the wolf."

Rhom gripped Hishn by her scruff until she growled. "You know that they will use her as bait," he said finally, "to draw us in. She has no value to them otherwise."

Aranur nodded reluctantly. "But they do not know that we can speak with her, and that may save all of us."

"We will try now anyway." Rhom stated flatly.

Aranur watched him for a moment, then nodded.

"Hishn stays with us," the blacksmith said.

"No. We cannot afford to be seen with her. We will leave her here, then come back to get her."

"She can tell us what is happening inside."

Aranur shook his head. "She will betray us to any of Zentsis's men we meet."

Hishn howled low, and he flinched at the sound.

"She will follow us anyway if we leave her," Rhom pointed out.

Aramur looked at the wolf. "You are right," he said finally.

Rhom nodded. Hand on his sword hilt, he ducked through the door, the gray wolf on his heels.

"Hells," Aranur cursed quietly. With their luck, he thought as he followed the other two, Dion would try to reach them right when they were at the gates of the jail. At the top of the stairs, Hishn paused and looked back, her yellow eyes gleaming as her gray fur faded into the shadows there. But her low growl reached his ears just the same. He glanced over the railing to the inn's empty dining room below, then strode after the wolf. They needed information. And luck. As his hand found the few silver coins left in his pocket, he frowned.

Chapter 15

The ancient arts are dormant
But never lost;
Those who brave the plague and worse,
Who confront the ancient curse
To pay the cost,
Will carry long the blessing of the moons.

It was hours later when the haze cleared enough to see. What seemed to be darkness was only the black walls of stone that trapped her below the earth, not the blindness she thought was caused by pain. Pain? No, a fire burned on her back, consuming her mind as well as her skin. She blinked with difficulty, shifted, gasped, and lay still.

"It will ease in a few days." Tehena's hopeless voice came from the shadows.

She turned her head slowly against the hot coals of ragged flesh that ate into her shoulders, and looked around the cell. "Where is Morain?" she asked hoarsely.

Tehena looked at the healer for a moment. "She is dead."

Dion closed her eyes.

"She shouldn't have bitten him," Tehena said finally. "But before she died she swore it was worth it."

"Dion?" It was Shilia, whispering from the next cell. "Dion, are you okay?"

"I'm okay." She caught her breath against the fire. "Is Tyrel all right?"

"He's fine. The guard left—he had to have that woman's body taken away. He hasn't come back yet."

"We're getting out of here, Shilia." She tried to shift on the rough mattress. "Just give us . . . one more blessing from the seventh moon and we'll . . . be gone."

"You've done your defiant act," Tehena said scornfully. "If you want to stay alive, you'd best forget about escaping."

"Defense is . . . the art . . . of deception," she said painfully.

"Right. That whipping was really deceptive. I could have sworn it almost killed you, but obviously I was mistaken."

"Drop it, Tehena."

"Why? You can't even sit up. You sure can't shut me up. So tell me, Healer, what did that little act of yours get you except someone else killed?"

Dion stared at the mattress. "I didn't know Morain would die, Tehena."

"This isn't a county fair, Healer. They kill people here."

Dion was silent. After a while, she forced herself to roll onto her side. And then the red fire burned black, and her eyes went blind. For a moment, she thought she felt Hishn lick her cheek, but then her sight cleared and it was only the rough mattress that scraped her skin as she shifted. Tehena's words became clear again.

". . . the guard."

"Did he . . . search the cell?" Dion asked hoarsely.

"He only came in to get Morain. He shoved you back in like you were already dead." Tehena stared at her. "Morain said nothing. Even when she was dying." The woman's eyes were hollow. "I would have. I would have told him everything."

"Yet you . . . didn't. And you pulled me onto this mattress, too."

"False hope, Healer."

"You say you would . . . welcome death if it came . . . But you are still alive." Dion's voice was growing more hoarse. "I'm still alive, too, Tehena. And all I need now . . . is a little misdirection, a little luck from the . . . moons." She managed to turn back onto her stomach without fainting.

"And what will you do this time? Ask the guard for his sword so you can casually chop off his head?"

"Something better . . . than that," she whispered almost to herself.

Tehena ignored her. "Stuck with a raving lunatic in a hell-hole no one remembers." Her voice broke. "With any luck, you'll catch fever or plague and we'll all die and be freed from this place."

"Shut . . . up."

"Lot of good that'll do you," Tehena retorted. But she huddled silently against the wall after that, muttering only once in a while and picking at her hair.

Dion closed her eyes. *Hishn?* she called. She could not think while the whipfire blinded her mind. *Hishn?*

Faint. Frustrated helplessness, relief— Fury at the stone that kept her from the healer . . .

Dion made a picture of Rhom and Aranur in her mind as strongly as she could. *Where?*

Distorted vision of stone walls, impression of padded feet on cold pavement. Two figures beside her, scents of dust and leather and old blood and grease.

An abandoned building? A stable? Dion did not understand the image. *Are you close?*

Tension. Anxiety.

Stifling a sob, the wolfwalker raised her head from her arms and stared into the dark wall before her. What could they do? By the moons, if they did not reach the prison soon—if they could not get Dion and the others out . . .

She could feel the raw skin and the flaps of flesh that lay over the jagged cuts left by the whip. Blood crusted painfully in the open wounds, and it was all she could do to ignore the thought of the vermin that would already be feeding. Whip cut. Her whole back was on fire. If only she could see how badly it really was . . . But she did not have to see, she realized. She could still reach Hishn, so the gift—the art of the ancients— was still with her, as well. Ovousibas. The healing. But Tehena—the woman could betray Dion with a word. And even if Tehena did not give her away, did Dion have the strength to do it by herself? Was it even possible with Hishn so far away? Her back was aflame. She wanted to scream with each pulse of her blood. And in this dimness, she told herself desperately, Tehena might not notice.

Hishn, she called out, *help me . . . Please.*

The Gray One's presence was clear, and instantly the gray voice swept in like a drug, pushing back the pain. Dion let go of her thoughts and sank into the pool of cool gray that the wolf washed over her. And then she could smell the outer streets, the air, the wax from the candles. The sweat of her brother was sweet, and the sound of Aranur's breathing was slow and steady and pulled her pulse along with his. The throbbing of her back faded into a drum that could beat only silently at her consciousness.

Take me in, Hishn, she sent more strongly.

Then walk with me, Healer.

The thought was barely out before her mind spun to the left, quickly. Down. In. She saw her back from the inside out, and the sight chilled her even as the wolf fed her the warmth of her strength. There was little time. Hurry. She could almost see the words burned into the flesh as she worked. She directed the flow of plasma to the slashes, and the impetus she gave seemed to take over. She pulled together the platelets and antibodies— the filth of the prison had already infected her. She sent them to the whip cuts and pulled the skin into cleaner lines. Flesh knitted, smoothed. The wolf pulled at her. But it had been only minutes. She resisted strongly. This was her body—there was still so much to do. The wounds were still ragged, unhealed. She had to stay and finish. But the gray shadow gathered force, and suddenly there was another consciousness with hers. Aranur. And behind him, like sparks struck on stone, Rhom, her brother, her twin. The currents were incompatible, but the wolf held them together, and they shocked her, striking her loose, breaking her hold on the internal world and yanking her back. There was a tearing cessation of feeling and a shocking sense of loss—loss of dimension, loss of depth—and then the roaring in her ears began to separate into sounds.

Tehena's voice shouted in her ear. It faded to a whisper as Dion swam up out of her body and back into her mind and stirred finally.

"She's moving," Tehena said to someone.

"Keep talking to her till she says something," Shilia commanded.

"I—I can't touch her. The skin—it crawled before my very eyes . . ."

"Reach her and make her speak or I'll scream for the guard and tell him you did it."

"You wouldn't."

"Do it. Wake her now!"

"No—"

Shilia took a breath. "Guar—"

"Shut up! I'll do it. I'm doing it now." She touched Dion on the forehead, staying as far from the wolfwalker's back as she could. "Healer?" she whispered tentatively. She hardly waited before backing away. "She isn't moving."

"Keep talking."

"Dnu shit," Tehena muttered. "Healer?" She reached forward again and shoved gently against Dion's temple. "Moonworms!" She scrambled back.

"What is it? Did she say something?"

"She opened her eyes."

Dion tried to speak.

"She's saying something," Tehena reported nervously.

The wolfwalker, her eyes open but her vision hazed with weakness, cleared her throat with difficulty. "I'm okay," she whispered hoarsely.

Tehena stared at her. "You're 'okay'? Are you crazy? Do you know what just happened to your back?"

"I'm . . . okay," Dion repeated, as if to convince herself, not the other woman.

"What in the hells of all nine moons did you do?" Tehena's voice had awe and fear in it as she backed farther away.

"Whatever it is, you're imagining things." That was Shilia, the girl's voice full of just the right amount of scorn.

But Tehena still stared at the healer. "You—your skin— what did you do?"

Shilia snorted. "She did nothing. By the moons, woman, she never moved from that mattress, did she? What could she have done?"

"But—"

"The beating just wasn't as bad as you thought."

But Tehena backed into the far mattress and huddled against the wall, staring at the Dion and not even realizing that Shilia had no way of seeing what was going on. And, faint with pain and a hunger that gnawed on her bones from the inside where, before, the pain had eaten at them from the outside, Dion faded slowly into unconsciousness. The gray shadow that stayed in her mind buoyed her against the swamping waves of dull and throbbing fire.

Chapter 16

You can steal a band from the cooper's hands
And the rabbit from under the cook.
You can walk through a gauntlet of far-seeing eyes
If you hide as a tree in the wood.
You can talk to the deaf man and hear from the mute,
And the blind will be leading your kind.
Deception will save where the sword arm will fail
If you work with your heart and your mind.

Rhom examined the roof carefully as he and Aranur crouched in the shadows of a set of chimneys. "That chimney there, that should lead into one of the larger chambers."

Aranur nodded. He lifted the coil of rope over his head and laid it on the roof. "Brace yourself against the second ridge. Let me down a meter at a time so I can clear the chute as I go. When I'm down, you can tie the rope off on the chimney and follow me down hand over hand."

Rhom pulled a leather pad and some strapping from within his jerkin. "I just hope there's no welcoming committee waiting for us below." He handed the strapping to the other man and stretched the pad out on the chimney bricks. "We need the luck of the moons for this one."

"We'll have it. The moons have been too short on miracles this month, and Longear has had too much of their luck. The security in this place has been tighter than a noose on a dead man." He wound the strapping around his thighs and waist, creating a harness with a loop in front. "According to that map you bought," he continued, "this chimney leads to a chamber in the unused guard's quarters. We'll be able to get in and out without anyone even knowing we've been here." He ran one end of the rope through the loop, then dropped the rest of it down the chute.

"Just don't get stuck in the flue," Rhom returned shortly. He secured the rope with a quick half twist around his waist. Then he braced himself back into the shadow.

Aranur looked briefly down at the soldiers swarming around the courtyards. He was glad he had told Hishn to stay in the alleys. The wolf had been frantic when they tried to leave her behind, and it had taken all his will to impress on her the need for her to remain in hiding. There were soldiers everywhere. If Hishn were seen with them . . . He shook his head. He was worried enough about Dion; he did not need to worry, too, that the Gray One would jeopardize their rescue attempt. That the Gray One would risk everything for Dion, he knew: Hishn had pulled him into the healing with Dion while he and Rhom were in plain sight on the streets. Only Rhom's quick thinking had kept them from being spotted by the guards that patrolled the city as Aranur added his strength to the wolf's—strength that Dion had needed. The wolfwalker's thoughts had not been clear to him, but Aranur had sensed the agony behind Dion's plea. He gripped the chimney bricks, forcing his thoughts away from the wolfwalker. Dion was strong, he told himself. Dion would survive.

But he stared for a long moment across the roofs toward the dark bricks of the prison before hefting himself over the edge of the chimney into the black shaft. "Three tugs mean that it is clear below," he said over the edge, his voice harsh even to himself. "Two tugs, a pause, and two more tugs means to wait. Two tugs by themselves mean trouble." Aranur adjusted his warcap more firmly and ducked beneath the rim. "Don't wait too long."

"You're set," Rhom said shortly.

The chimney was just over a meter square. Aranur lowered himself, bracing his legs and arms against the sides. The chimney widened slightly as he neared the flue. He pushed at the metal flap with his feet. It resisted briefly, then screamed as it scraped past old brick.

"Moonworms!" he swore as the sudden updraft freed old ash and whipped the loose particles into his eyes. The ashes burned, and he rubbed his eyes for several seconds before he could see again. He squeezed past the flue and felt his way down until the shaft widened suddenly into the fireplace. Then he eased his weight onto the rope and dropped to the floor in a shower of soot. The fireplace doors were shut, and the outer room was dark. He could see nothing. No sounds came from the outer room. Taking a stiff wire from his pocket, he eased the fireplace latch up from the inside to open the creaking wooden doors.

Aranur loosed the rope, then tugged twice, and twice more on the line before groping his way to the hall door. The corridor outside was dark and silent. Now he tugged three times on the line. Rhom answered with three more tugs, the muffled sound of the younger man's breathing and soft clouds of drifting ashes announcing his arrival. By that time, Aranur had managed to light one of the lanterns that had been left behind when that wing of the building had been vacated for the summer.

Rhom shook himself off quietly, raised his eyebrows at the door, and pointed toward the hall. Aranur agreed silently. They had studied the diagram of the buildings for two days. It had taken much persuasion and a lot more than copper to get a look at the builders' copy, the one showing the air and sewer ducts, but due to the overly high taxes Zentsis had imposed, almost everyone welcomed money under the table.

With the lantern shuttered almost to blackness, the two prowlers could just see the floor and walls. They crossed a hall intersection, leaving footprints in the dust. The sound of someone snoring reached their ears, and the corridor seemed to grow more light—unless it was only their eyes growing more used to the dark. They left the lantern just inside a doorway and approached the snoring soldier, who was sleeping off some evening revelry where he hoped no one would find him. He did not notice their approach. After Aranur cracked him on the head, he did not notice that they stripped him of his clothes as well.

The uniform fit Rhom better than it would have Aranur, but even so, his wrists stuck out of the sleeves till he rolled them up past his elbows. Still, it was better than the uniform Rhom had worn before when they started the fire at the jail. That one had torn down the back when he had flexed his shoulders, and he had discarded it on a refuse pile outside a tavern.

"What about you?" he whispered, motioning at Aranur's sooty clothes.

"We'll have to find someone else who wants to part with his uniform."

That was not a difficult task, it turned out. The empty rooms seemed to be one of the soldiers' off-duty haunts. A flash of light alerted them to a card game in one of the rooms, and they froze. Peering around the door frame, they saw five men sitting, a lantern shuttered to light only their makeshift table. One of the largest of them was facing the door.

". . . raise you two stars," one was saying in a low voice.

Another tossed his hand onto the table. "That puts me out. What about you?"

"I'm still in. I'll see you." The speaker pushed two stars into the growing pile.

"And I'll see you," said the fourth man, who faced the doorway, "and raise you half a moon."

"Aw, come on, Ferret. Give us a break."

"Put up or shut up," the man retorted.

Rhom glanced at Aranur, who nodded and faded back as Rhom stepped into the doorway and waved furtively at the man facing him. Ferret's expression did not even flicker.

"All right," the first man said. "I'll just see you."

After the third player followed suit, they spread the cards, and the man called Ferret smirked. "That's kind of you all," he said, scooping in the pot, "but it's time for my guard duty. We'll have to finish this game later."

"It's bad luck to take the money and run."

Ferret chuckled. "Since when has it been bad luck to win money off you bums?"

The other man grimaced and waved him away. He pulled two bottles from under the crate. "At least we still have these," he said to the others. One of the other guards began dealing the cards again.

Ferret stepped out into the hall, frowning at Rhom. "Who are—" he started to whisper, mindful of the men still back in the room.

Rhom interrupted him. "Look at this," he whispered excitedly. As the man leaned in, curious, Aranur clubbed him behind the ear and Rhom caught him before he could fall.

"Over there." Rhom gestured with his chin to another empty room. They stripped and bound the man, then rolled him into a dark corner and wedged him between two crates. Aranur changed, and the two stepped out boldly. They passed through the kitchens and grabbed a roast rabbit from under the cooks' noses, then mingled into the crowd in the hall. Aranur was relieved at the lack of attention paid them, but he did not relax his guard. His sister's life depended on him. And Dion . . . He glanced at Rhom. Dion, he prayed, hang on.

They made their way to the corridor that housed the prison guard, and Aranur hesitated inside the entrance.

"A minute is all we need," he told Rhom. He looked at the younger man's empty hands. "The wax?"

Rhom opened his jerkin briefly to give Aranur a glimpse of the small box.

"All right." Aranur nodded. "Let's go."

There were two men in the room when they entered, and for a moment Aranur thought it would mean trouble.

". . . said to make sure," one of the soldiers was saying with irritation. "Don't ask me why, I only follow orders; I don't make them." Then they saw the two newcomers.

"Moonworms," the other guard said. "You never spill a drop, but you dump the keg." He turned to Aranur. "What do you two want?"

"Just here to check the springs on the manacles," Aranur said.

"It took you long enough to get here. I sent in that complaint three ninans ago. Look, I got to take this guy down to cellblock four."

Aranur felt a chill. If the guard left with the keys . . .

The soldier misread his hesitation. "Just start over there with the three on the back of the chair. They're the worst." He grabbed one set of keys and motioned the other to precede him out.

Aranur nodded, swallowing his relief at the sight of the keys still hanging on the racks. Without prompting, Rhom moved quickly to the doorway and listened as the soldiers' boots stomped dully down the hall. Aranur examined the key racks. If only there were time, he could take the keys and free Shilia and the others immediately. He grabbed a key from each rack and pressed it into the wax. Eight keys, one for each of the sizes of the hand and leg manacles.

Rhom hissed at him, and Aranur shut the wax box and barely got the last key back on its peg before the guard reentered. The other soldier continued down the hall. Rhom had stretched the three bad manacles out on the desk, and Aranur quickly turned around and pretended to be looking them over. He sighed, pushed the three together in a pile, and shook his head.

"Well?" the guard asked.

"We need replacement springs. We'll be back."

The guard shook his head. "You're going nowhere till these are fixed, but if you want, I'll get you a beer while you work."

Aranur shrugged. "The spring metal is rusted clear through. You're going to need replacements."

"You didn't bring the replacements with you, and you didn't bring any tools either, I notice." The guard glared at the two men. "What kind of con are you trying to pull? Trying to get out of mop duty or something?"

"Look," Aranur started angrily as Rhom began edging toward the door. "We were just supposed to see how much work you had here, then get Bordon from the main floor—"

Rhom swung his fist, but the guard turned at the last minute.

"Wha—" he started, throwing up his arm. "Hey!" he yelled before they could stop him. At least he went down fairly easily. Fat living in the guardroom, Aranur thought with disgust.

"Walk casually," Aranur commanded. "He won't be found for an hour if we're lucky."

Someone turned down the corridor and passed them.

"We're not," Rhom said shortly. He broke into a run.

"Stop there, you two!" a man shouted. "Hey! Halt! Stop those men!" But Aranur and Rhom dodged into the crowd that now filled the dining hall. Someone grabbed Aranur's sleeve, but he kicked the man's shin and calmly pushed through as if oblivious to the shouts. Rhom was smiling at someone, leaning over as if to get a tankard of ale. He and Rhom dropped to their knees and crawled under a table, disappearing from searching eyes. They scrambled, panting, over the feet beneath the tables as the owners of the feet cursed. Aranur was kicked in the cheek, but the offending foot was drawn back fast when he elbowed the ankle. Aranur grimaced. The grease and table droppings on the floor turned their uniform tunics into serving boys' rags.

A few seconds later, they pushed through the last sets of legs and stood up casually. An expanding ring of soldiers was moving out from where he and Rhom had disappeared. They would see Rhom—and him—any second.

"This way," he said. He pulled Rhom close as if they were drunk, and the two men plunged into the nearest passage, lurching by a guard who was straining to see what was going on in the dining hall.

"Hey, you two!" He put out a restraining hand. "Go sleep it off in your quar—ooof." Two fists hit him the same time, and he sank to the stones.

"Over there!" someone shouted. "By the kitchens!"

"In and out without anyone noticing?" Rhom muttered.

"They haven't caught us yet," Aranur returned grimly, breaking into another sprint. "Through here—"

"Stop!"

"Halt or we'll shoot!"

Four of the guards broke free of the hall and pounded down the passage. Rhom grabbed a tray of food from a cringing servant and flung it behind him. "Might as well grease the hands of luck," he said in reply to Aranur's look.

One of the running soldiers stepped on the flying tray and slid away, crashing to his back on the stones.

"One down," Aranur agreed. "Eight to go."

They burst through the swinging doors into the kitchens. A woman screamed. Aranur grabbed at a cart and thrust it behind him. The guards slammed through the same door, and the cart flipped. Half of the guards went down in a tangle. Rhom kicked a kettle off its frame and dumped its scalding contents across the stones.

"Through there!" Aranur yelled. An arrow whapped by and stuck into a cupboard past his shoulder. "Quickly—"

Two guards had pulled out their bows. Rhom dove between two counters and tackled the cook who stood frozen at the scene. "Get down," he yelled at the man. "They're trying to kill everyone." The cook dropped like a stone, and Rhom rolled over him toward the back exit.

The two men broke for the hall.

"This is a dead end," Rhom yelled over the din, ducking as two arrows followed them into the hall. "There's nothing back here but storage rooms."

"There's an air passage that leads to the roof." Aranur slammed open the third door on his right and shoved it shut behind them, dropping the bolt across.

He turned around. Rhom was looking up at the unbroken ceiling, then down through the fine mesh of a sewer hole.

"There's no air duct in this room, Aranur," he said. "Someone made a mistake on the plans."

The guards outside hurled themselves against the wood, and Aranur glanced back at the shuddering door. He shrugged. "We have little choice. Besides," he added, throwing Rhom a wry grin, "the dung of the worlag comes out in the wash." He shoved the wax box further inside his tunic, then slid the mesh from the dark shaft. "Don't forget to shut the door," he said, lowering his legs into the shaft. The edge was slippery, and he could not keep his grip on it. In seconds, he began to slide. He barely recognized moldy potatoes and oozing greens before the darkness shut them out of his eyes and let him imagine worse.

Rhom, hearing him fall away, glared at the shuddering door. Damn the guards, he swore savagely. He and Aranur had been so close. Just one stroke of luck, and Dion and the others would have been free . . . He sat on the edge of the chute and grabbed the grating. Two more days were gone, and they could no longer count on controlling the Gray One. Without Dion, Hishn was lost. And without Hishn, Rhom could find out nothing more about his twin. He snarled and squeezed between the mesh and the tunnel's edge till he hung from the grating. With a braced jerk, he yanked the cover back over the shaft, his broad shoulders scraping the rest of the leftovers from the chute walls. And then, as Aranur had done a few seconds before, he slid into darkness.

Below him, the tunnel grew steep, and Aranur slid faster and faster. Then he was falling. He could not remember how the garbage chutes were laid out. If they banked hard or turned sharply, his sword could jam, or he could break his legs . . . No, it would have to be smooth. They would not want refuse to get stuck in the shaft.

Weird yells echoed in the shaft from above as the soldiers discovered their escape route. Then Aranur had an instant's warning of dim light ahead, them, *wham*—he sank into a dump of rotting food. He struggled frantically to right himself as dark shapes, that set his pulse pounding further, ran squealing from all sides. A second later, Rhom landed almost on Aranur's head, and then they helped each other struggle out of the waste.

Rhom wiped rotting greens from his sword, stared at Aranur, eyed the dungeonlike hall warily, and then looked down at himself. He started laughing.

"I can't help it," he said at Aranur's expression.

Aranur raised his eyebrows.

"Look at us." Rhom pointed.

Aranur glanced at his leggings. "Well, at least we know where we are," he returned wryly. "Even if we have to fight a hundred pigs to get out."

Rhom brushed something from his shoulder, then dodged aside quickly and swore, staring up at the roof. "Roofbleeders!" The thin tendrils hung from the dark beams of the ceiling, and their barbed tips brushed lightly toward both men.

Aranur looked up and automatically pulled his warcap further down over his forehead. The albino vines had barbed tips that bit, and if not stopped, they could suck a half liter of blood from a man in less than a minute. His uncle had told him once that roofbleeders were related to poison masa, and thinking of that, he curled his lip in disgust. He glanced again at the roof, then halted. Roofbleeders here? In the lower levels? It must be dark there for them to grow, and the pigs must be what provided the vines with enough food to live. But if there were roofbleeders even in this short-roofed level, the vines could hang throughout the prison, as well. If there were bleeders in the dungeon cells and Dion did not notice . . . The wolfwalker had been hurt, and she did not have Hishn with her to sense or fight the dangers hidden in the dark.

Rhom shoved a pig away from his leg and another tendril from his face. He looked grim. "How high are the ceilings in Zentsis's cells?" he asked, echoing Aranur's train of thought.

Aranur shook his head.

"If the roofs are not high enough . . ." Rhom's voice trailed away.

Aranur ripped a thin, dangling vine from the ceiling and dropped it to the floor. One of the pigs grunted and dashed forward, snorting up the twitching growth. Aranur met Rhom's eyes. "We can do nothing from here," he said finally. "We will send word to Dion again tonight."

"If Hishn can reach her."

"She will have to." Aranur pointed toward a crack in the ceiling that laid an outline of light on the floor below. As he strode toward it, the pigs surrounded him, snapping at the tendrils that dropped on their mottled backs.

"At least we smell like we belong here." Rhom moved cautiously between two pillars.

Aranur grimaced. "I don't know how long it'll take for the soldiers to figure out where we are, but I don't want to spend any more time like this." He pushed carefully through another clump of pigs, and two of them turned, snapping at each other until he realized that they were catching and ripping down the vines that stretched toward their backs.

"The door?" Rhom motioned toward the ceiling. A huge sow pushed at his knees and he stumbled, almost going down. The pigs grunted and shifted around his feet. "Hurry. I think the critters are hungry."

"It's got a double bolt." Aranur reached up to slide the

hasp. He was about to breathe fresh air in relief when the whole section came crashing down. "Holy moons—" He staggered to his knees just as the staircase slammed down across his shoulders. Rhom grabbed at the staircase and caught it so that Aranur could crawl out from under its weight. The pigs, after rushing back a few steps squealing, surged forward, cutting his hands with their feet.

Rhom yanked him up. "Hurry!"

Aranur took the steps two at a time, Rhom right behind him. They almost bowled over the old man who stared at them and their swords as they jumped out of the hole in the floor. He had been about to peer down to the open stairs when the two younger men popped up.

"What? What are you doing down there botherin' the pigs?" he yelled, leaning to one side.

"We were checking their feed," Aranur said loudly. "We slipped in the waste."

"Which way? What?"

"No—" Aranur saw the old man's incomprehension and took a breath. "We were checking the pigs' feed," he shouted.

The old man nodded sagely, then grinned. "What did you do, slip in the waste?"

Rhom and Aranur looked at each other. Time was running out.

"We need some clothes," Aranur shouted, trying to wipe some rotted food that he had missed from the hilt of his sword.

"Well, close it then." The deaf man gestured to the stairs. "Ought to know better than to leave the door open with pigs around."

Aranur gestured impatiently for Rhom to close the stairs, then pointed at the stinking uniforms and repeated at the top of his lungs, "Clothes! We need some clothes!"

"Well, anyone can see that. You don't have to yell." The old man turned to a chest and pulled out baggy pants and tunics. "Here, it's all I've got. You can give them back later when you find a shower."

"Thanks," Aranur shouted.

"What?"

Rhom added his voice to Aranur's. "Thanks!" They dropped their leggings and yanked the clean trousers on. Still pushing his right arm through the sleeve of a baggy tunic, Aranur opened the door and looked out into the hall. No one had reached that level yet, but it would not be long before their pursuers knew where they were. Aranur grabbed his sword and pulled two silvers from the money pouch they had stolen from the gambler. He tossed the silvers toward the bed, but the old man caught them midair. He cackled at them again, and Aranur shivered. He did not wait for Rhom, but took off, jogging down the hall. He knew Rhom would be right behind him.

The pigs' holds were the bottom level outside the jails—the third level—so he and Rhom were in one of the second-level hallways. They needed a staircase, then a servants' entrance to get out. But he heard pounding feet ahead of them before he saw a stair. He spun on his heel so suddenly that Rhom almost ran into him.

"Quick," he snapped. "Lie down. Play dead."

Rhom dropped like a stone, letting one of his arms lie at an odd angle and his head loll to one side. He crumpled as if stabbed. Aranur yanked his blade from his side and thrust it along with Rhom swords, out of sight under the blacksmith.

". . . be down here somewhere," the lead guard was shouting.

"Help, help," Aranur cried out as the soldiers rounded the corner. "Two men! They went that way!" He pointed vaguely back down the corridor. "Stabbed Yorik and tried to kill me, too!"

"This way! We've got them now!" They plunged past with a roar.

Aranur hauled Rhom up and they sprinted for the stairs, buckling their swords back on as they did. At the top of the flight, they slowed again. There were stacks of boxes and sacks all over the courtyard they had reached. To the right, three servants stood with heavy boxes on their shoulders, waiting for the guards to open the gates.

"Come on!" Aranur grabbed two of the boxes and hefted them to his shoulders. Rhom did the same.

"Moonworms!" one of the servants exclaimed as the two men joined the line. "Can't they just let us get on with this?"

"Can't believe they'd hold us up here for so long."

"Come on, Deften," the first one pleaded with the guard. "We're going to break our backs if you don't let us get this stuff delivered."

"Orders," the guard replied, eyeing the growing group with discomfort.

"Look, man, I'll give you my ale for a ninan if you just open that gate," another one of them pleaded. "You know we've got to get this to the blockhouse before midnight."

"Come on, Deften. You know us. We're not trying anything with you. Just let us get this stuff out."

"Hells of the ninth moon," the guard swore. "Go on then, but if any of you breathe a word of this, I'll have your heads for it. You owe me, all of you." He unbolted and opened the gates just enough to let the men pass, Rhom and Aranur slipping past with the others and trudging out into the street. Rhom did not glance back, but his face was set grimly. Dion, he thought bitterly, we were so close this time. He trailed Aranur and the other men half a block before shouts rose back at the gate.

"Time's up," Aranur hissed. He dumped his crates and leapt like a shot toward an alley. Behind him, the wooden boxes split and the greenheads rolled out onto the street like balls. Rhom followed suit, dodging into the alley after him.

"Stop those two!" "Halt!" The yells followed them as Aranur bowled over a drunkard and hit the ground rolling, hardly hearing the man's slurred obscenities. Rhom passed him and jumped for the back fence of the narrow passage. He grasped the top of the dead-end wall, hauling himself over and dropping out of sight. The other man did the same, soldiers bursting into the alley entrance as he was silhouetted momentarily against the moons. "There!" But the arrows flew overhead as Aranur dropped down on the other side. Rhom had hesitated, waiting for him before sprinting down the alley. They ran across the street and zigzagged a kilometer before they felt safe enough to slow down.

When they made it back to the inn they had chosen for the night, they tried to enter casually.

"Ale," Aranur called to the landlady, pointing toward their room.

"Stinking gutterwalkers," a diner snarled, his nose pinched at the odor that followed the two men as they passed.

When they got to their room, Hishn was not there, and Rhom, chewing his lip as his sister often did, turned and held out a coin. "I'll flip you for the shower."

Aranur shook his head with a wry grin. "I'd cheat on the toss. Go ahead, but hurry. I'll clean our blades and watch for the wolf."

Rhom nodded, dropped his sword, grabbed a cloth and his

long knife from his pack, and strode down the hall. Aranur was left to stare at the open window. Hishn . . . The wolf had been with them every night. It was not all that late, but that the Gray One was not there yet worried him. Hishn was their only link to the healer, and Dion was their only link to the others in the jail. He picked up his sword, pulled a fresh tunic from his own pack, and began cleaning the blade. He had just started on Rhom's when the other man returned.

Aranur flipped the blade into his hand, then relaxed when he saw it was Rhom. He handed over the sword. "When will Hishn show up again?"

The blacksmith tossed his soiled towel on his bunk and motioned for Aranur to leave and take his own shower. He ran his fingers through his hair to shake it out, but shook his head at Aranur's question. "I don't know. She can find us, if that's what you mean, but it is better to wait for her to return. Her link with us is only through Dion, and Dion . . ." His expression grew even more serious.

Aranur nodded. They knew Dion was alive—the wolf had told them that much. But there was no room in the Gray One for news of anyone else. He could only hope that Shilia and Namina were unharmed. If he could just speak to Dion once more through the wolf. He stalked down the hall toward the shower Rhom had just left. Dion . . . even when the wolf was not around, Aranur saw the wolfwalker in his mind—her face, her body as she had come out of the river, the way she moved in the woods, the way she touched him . . .

He threw his towel over the shower stall, set his knife on the ledge, and pumped the upper tubs full. His sister, his cousins, his uncle—and Dion—were trapped in Zentsis's prisons, and he was taking a shower with a fantasy. He pulled the shower chain almost savagely.

Chapter 17

Fear stalks the sleep of the restless;
Faith will keep hope strong.

Time had no meaning without light, without change. For Dion, there were footsteps and a voice that mumbled in her ears without end. She froze and shivered as if she were sleeping on ice, then grew so hot that she whimpered and crawled onto the stone to stay cool. Once an alarm rang in her ears until she cried out for it to stop, and then she heard that voice again, talking and talking. She chewed twice on a crust of bread, but the effort made her so weak that she lay unconscious for a long time. The water she grabbed at greedily made her choke.

At length, she opened her eyes with clarity. The dank smell of the prison crawled into her nose as it had before, and the dimness of the jail was like early night. She felt firmness beneath her, and she knew she was still lying on the mattress. The vileness of it no longer disturbed her; she smelled as it did, and her nose could not wrinkle more. The cell was as it had been, except that she was lying where Morain had lain before. Before . . .

She closed her eyes again. *Hishn?* she called. *Gray One, are you near?*

Wolfwalker, the wolf answered instantly. Anxiety rode the gray thread like a bird on a rushing wave.

Dion breathed. *Hishn.* She repeated the name for its comfort, and the Gray One, sensing her need, sent a shaft of emotion to the healer that made Dion's senses reel. There was a wild-eyed edge to the gray wolf's thoughts. A hunger that gnawed at her belly and a longing that ate at her chest. It frightened Dion. She felt her own pulse quicken with a tension that clamped down on muscles too weak to respond. She could only shiver. *I have not left you, Gray One*, she sent strongly. *Aranur and Rhom will free us, and we will be together soon.*

But Hishn sent only a long howl in return.

Gray One? Dion called anxiously.

The hunt leaves me hungry, Hishn returned finally. *There are worms of worry in my gut and I cannot eat.*

Gray One, you must eat, Dion sent. *You must remain strong.* She tried to push herself up on her arms, but they did not obey. *Help Aranur and Rhom, Hishn. Follow Aranur's lead—run as his shadow until I am free.*

I hunger.

Dion found her throat suddenly thick and her eyes blurred. *And I also, Gray One.* She closed her mind, but left the gray thread tight between them. The longing Hishn felt—it was not hers alone. Dion ached to bury her hands in the gray wolf's thick scruff, to tug on the ears and smell through her nose. The coldness of the stone beside her made the longing for Hishn more intense, and she knew she must act, or be swallowed by the awful ache. And Aranur . . . She closed her mind to the ache she felt for him. He was only a distant dream in this place, and this place was all too real.

She pushed herself up on her arms, then frowned. She had not moved. She shoved again, and still her limbs did not answer her command. How could she be so weak? A fury consumed her suddenly, and she bit at her silent rage. This helplessness—she had not lived through that whipping only to wait for Longear to laugh at her weakness. She was a wolf-walker, not just a healer. Moons help her if she was going to lie and wait for her death. She forced her arms under her, and managed, at last, to push herself up. Her back found the stone behind her, and she braced herself with her legs until she was sitting upright.

Against the other wall of the cell, Tehena stared silently at her.

Dion became still. After a few moments, when the other woman did not move, Dion cleared her throat. Her voice rasped, but the second try succeeded. "Thank you for the care."

Tehena looked at her for a long moment, then spit on the stones. "I did nothing."

The wolfwalker shook her head; her voice, fed by the anger that still flamed in her chest, was already strong. "The food? And the water?"

"You fought for those yourself. Even in your fever."

Dion smiled crookedly. "Sorry."

The other woman gave her a long look. "For what? Surviving?" But she hesitated, then cleared her throat, and her tone when she spoke again was not mocking but strangely uncertain. "You—your eyes are violet, aren't they? I saw them in the light."

The wolfwalker gave her a sideways look. "Yes."

"And you can fight. Like the guards."

Dion snorted softly, bitterly. "Not well enough," she returned.

But Tehena ignored her tone. "And that thing you did after the whipping . . ." Her voice trailed off.

"The thing—the healing?"

The other woman tightened her jaw abruptly. "Are you a moonwarrior?"

"What?"

"A moonwarrior. One of the ancients, come to put me on the path to the moons."

The wolfwalker looked at her in puzzlement, then shook her head. "I'm a woman, Tehena, just like you. I'm a healer who got mixed up in the wrong kind of politics. If it weren't for Longea—"

"Don't!" Tehena cut her off abruptly, unable to hide her own shudder. "Not that name." She stared at the wolfwalker intently. "You swear, by that band you wear, that you're not one of the ancients?"

"I swear I am as you see me now."

Tehena fidgeted. "Swear that you are not a moonwarrior."

Dion laughed without humor. "Tehena, moonwarriors are legend. Sure, at home, my brother and I used to tease the other fighters that we were moonwarriors, but it was only to get an edge on them. Lots of people have violet eyes. Besides, if I were a moonwarrior and had the power to cross the stars, do you really think I'd be sitting here in jail?"

The other woman flushed. "And your back? I saw your skin crawl together. I saw it heal in front of my eyes."

Dion hesitated. "That is . . . different."

"It is a secret."

"Not one that cannot be shared with a friend."

"I'm not your friend," Tehena snapped.

Dion shrugged. "You can be trusted."

The other woman laughed bitterly. "I'd betray you for an extra piece of bread."

"I think not."

Tehena glared at her in silence.

"Healing like this—it is an art, like any other," Dion said quietly. "But one we thought was lost." She stared at her callused hands and turned them over as if the fingers were even now new to her. "It is Ovousibas."

Tehena stiffened, but her expression did not change. "If it was," she returned harshly, "you'd be dead by now, and not from the whipping."

Dion hesitated, then shrugged. "The curse of the ancients is not always fatal."

"If it was Ovousibas, you'd be dead," Tehena repeated. "And a Gray One, too."

The wolfwalker raised one eyebrow.

The other woman licked her lips. "Do you—do you run with the wolves, as well?"

"Questions, Tehena? I thought they brought death themselves."

Tehena tightened her lips, and instantly Dion was sorry. "The Gray Ones choose whom they will," she answered softly. She motioned toward the corridor and changed the subject. "My friends—are they all right?"

Tehena stared sullenly at the bars for another minute before answering. "They're still here," she said finally.

Dion closed her eyes in relief. She had not realized how much she had wanted to ask that question. "And the bones—the fang sacks?" she asked when she opened her eyes again.

"Where you left them."

"Under your mattress?"

Tehena nodded abruptly.

"Please," Dion said softly; she was still so weak. "Get them for me."

"What am I, your personal slave? Get them yourself."

The wolfwalker just looked at her, and Tehena found herself doing as Dion asked.

"Thank you." Dion turned the bones over and over in the dim light, feeling as much as seeing their shape and sharpness. They had been picked clean. "Is this all of them?" she asked, puzzled.

"I didn't guard your bone pile with my life," Tehena snarled, sitting back against the wall on her own straw tick. "There are other things in here that like to eat, too."

"I meant no offense, Tehena." She picked over the bones until she had just less than a dozen selected.

"A needle gun, huh?"

Dion nodded.

"Look, Healer, you've been sick. And you're still sick if you think you're going to make a weapon out of rat parts."

"But you saved them for me," Dion pointed out.

Tehena turned to stare out at the corridor again. "False hope," she muttered. "Like I said before."

"There's no reason the hope can't be real." Dion scraped one of the dried bones against the stones. "These will sharpen better now that they're dry."

"Moon droppings."

"When I hollow the points, they'll hold a good dose of poison, too."

"You're serious about this, aren't you?"

Dion continued to scrape a finer point to the bone.

Tehena stared at her in silence, then lay down and turned her face to the wall.

Although Dion slept again, she rested only fitfully. She dreamed of Aranur, of Rhom, of the bettlelike worlags, of raiders, and of a blank face behind which sat a man named Longear. She turned finally and reached for Hishn, and the wolf faded from her hands like a ghost. She woke and shivered alone.

As she lay silently in the dark, it was Aranur's voice that comforted her in her head. It took her a second to realize that his worry was real. She snapped awake.

Wolfwalker, Hishn called again, and Dion could sense Aranur's calmness beneath her tones.

Rhom is with you? she asked.

The Gray One bared her teeth. *I run with them.*

Dion sighed in relief. *Hishn, tell Aranur that Shilia and the others are still safe. Tell them that—"*

The gray creature cut her off. *Your hunger is as strong for them as my hunger is for you.* Hishn's voice was full of emotion that Dion could not accept.

Gray One, she sent softly, *you honor me.*

With my life, Hishn returned violently.

Dion balled her fits. *By the moons, Hishn, I swear I will be with you again.*

The wolf was silent a moment, and Dion could sense her struggling with her images. *There is a danger that Aranur can smell,* the wolf sent finally. *It is one that crawls from overhead and bites like the fleas that chew my tail.*

Dion frowned, glancing at the ceiling of the cell. From overhead? That bit like a flea? That could only be a vine, like the roofbleeders. But bloodsucker vines needed short roofs, and the cell ceilings were too high. Unless it was something else that she did not know of. *Is it roofbleeders Aranur is worried about?* she sent back slowly.

The wolf whined softly. *These thoughts are not clear.* She concentrated, sent a fuzzy image of pallid coils, then broke off the image and tried again.

But Dion nodded. *It's all right, Gray One,* she soothed. *I understand. Tell Aranur that there is no need to worry. The ceilings are tall enough. It is rats and parasites that bother us here, not bleeders.*

The wolf hesitated, and Dion sensed her reluctance.

Gray One, she sent, *I am with you always.*

The wolfwalker was stronger the next day, and she finished most of the darts, giving her fourteen with which to practice. The fact that she could hear Hishn and see the daylight through the gray wolf's eyes buoyed her while she worked, so much so that she felt guilty she could not share the images with Shilia. Tehena, who did not know if Dion truly ran with the wolves, did not understand the healer's mood. She watched Dion work, not offering to help, but unable to keep from taunting. Dion ignored the insults. As if Tehena were her pupil, she carefully explained each step in a whisper, and though the other woman seemed to pay scant attention, Dion knew she had memorized every word. Finally, with nothing else to do, Tehena took one of the bone slivers from Dion's hands and began scraping a point to it.

She did not ask about Ovousibas again, and Dion was relieved. When the wolfwalker had learned to do the internal healing, she had not thought beyond using the skill. She had not realized what it might mean if it became known that she could do the ancient healing. She ground another point onto a dart, then looked up briefly. She remembered the old farmer's wife. And as she recalled Tehena's reaction upon seeing Dion's back heal, she realized that the situation could only get worse.

How many people begged the healers for miracles even without Ovousibas? Even Dion herself, each time she had seen a child die, had pleaded with the moons for one more cure, one more chance at life. Aranur had already shown her that she could not resist that fight: it had been he who first pushed her to learn the internal healing, then pushed her to use it to keep his family—and her own brother—alive. But if other people knew? She shivered. There were too many people in the world who needed healing. They could own her. They could destroy her with their will to live. She stared at her hands.

"Healer?" Shilia's whisper broke into her thoughts finally, and Dion started.

"I'm here."

The girl stretched her fingers through the bars, and the wolf-walker crawled over to that side of the cell and stretched her own fingers through until the two could touch.

"Dion," Shilia whispered again finally. "What will happen to us?"

"You'll lose your tan, more than likely," Dion returned lightly.

The girl stared, then choked back a laugh. "You always say things like that."

"Do they make you feel better?"

"Yes," Shilia admitted.

Dion smiled wearily. "That is what healers are for."

As they sat, the damp stone pressed into their shoulders, and the icy touch of the bars on their wrists made the warmth of their fingers unreal. Shapes of others in the dark prison shifted and caught their eyes, but they did not move.

"Shilia . . ."

The girl answered in a low voice. "Yes?"

"How much of the Ovousibas did Tehena realize? Did she talk with you when I was in the fever?"

Shilia thought for a moment, remembering those hours, those days, and reliving her terror that Dion would die only meters away from her just like her cousin had died before. Die and leave her alone. She could not hear or touch Namina, and if Dion were gone . . .

"No," she whispered finally. "I asked her to care for you as best she could, but I never knew if she did, and we did not speak other than that."

Dion was silent. "Shilia," she began again, her voice so low that the girl had to strain to hear her, "what would happen, do you think, if I were to tell the guards that I knew internal healing?"

The girl's fingers tightened, and she flushed slowly, both honored and surprised that Dion, a wolfwalker, was asking for her opinion. "I thought about that at first," she said finally. "And I told myself that they would take you out of here because of it and treat you with the honor your deserve." She paused.

Dion waited, listening.

"And after I was so sure of this that I was going to tell the guards for you," Shilia continued, her voice trembling slightly, "they came by with a man whose hands had been cut off." Her voice shook again. "They said that—that Longear had not liked something he wrote." She caught her breath. "I asked myself what my brother would do if he was here. Aranur," she whispered vehemently, "would never tell Longear that you could do Ovousibas." She gripped Dion's fingers tightly. "They would make you prove it. Then they would make you do it for them, not for people who needed it. And they would never let you free again."

Dion was silent for a long moment. "That is what I thought also."

"Healer," Shilia whispered.

Dion did not answer, but she gripped the girl's fingers, and Shilia let her head rest against the bars. They sat that way for a long time.

Dion used her headband to break a piece of wood from their dinner trough the next evening. Then she rubbed the trough across her mattress and the stones until the fresh break was as filthy as the rest of the wood. No one noticed.

Aside from the whispered instructions and insults, the two women did not speak. They did not trust the other prisoners, any one of whom would turn them in to get an extra ration of food for a ninan, and they never knew when the guards would make their rounds. When footsteps echoed darkly in the corridor, they scrambled to hide their work, living in a constant sweat that one of the guards would search their cell. Twice when the guards came by, Tehena caught Dion on the edge of Hishn's thoughts with her lips curled back and her teeth bared. The healer shrugged it off, but Tehena just licked her own lips and watched silently.

Oddly enough, to Dion, it was not the smell or the dampness or the cold that got to her most, but the way her teeth felt thick and fuzzy and ached with jammed-in filth. The way the grime under her fingernails no longer came out when she picked at them. She could not stand to feel the gray wolf's senses any longer; the clean smells from Hishn only made the odors around her worse, and the clear sound of Aranur's voice brought a bitterness to her laugh to hide the despair in her chest.

Four days. Four nightmares each night. Four breaths in the morning to clear each dream from her eyes. Four bites of bread. Four strokes on each side of a dart to sharpen the point. By those things were her days measured. Finally she began picking threads out of what was left of her clothes, and Tehena, watching her as usual, frowned.

"What are you doing?"

The wolfwalker carefully pulled a long thread free. "The two halves of the blowpipe have to be lashed together. But since the weapon is so tiny, I can use thread rather than rawhide. The pipe will be finished tonight. Then we can practice."

Tehena scowled.

"I won't put poison in the darts for practicing," Dion continued, "but it is ready whenever we need it."

The woman snorted. "Poison from rats takes ninans before it kills. How is this stuff going to knock out a guard in seconds?"

"I added some other ingredients. It'll take a man out instantly." She gave Tehena a sharp look. "Which means that the one thing to make sure of when you use this is that you don't breathe in when you have the pipe near your mouth."

Tehena nodded slowly.

Dion tied the ends of the threads together to make one long string, then picked up the two halves of the tiny blowpipe. She had scraped a gutter down the center of each piece of wood so that when the two halves came together there was a perfect hole through the block. She began winding the thick thread around the ends. "Our darts will be so light that you won't need to blow hard to make this work. Just give it a puff, like this.'' She demonstrated.

Without the blowpipe, Tehena looked like a fish puffing away, and Dion had to turn her head to stifle her smile. When she was done binding the thread, she selected a dart and placed it inside, then aimed and, with a quick breath, sent the dart flying into the corner of the cell. It struck the corner of the mattress there with enough force to bury itself deep in the straw tick, and Tehena, watched Dion swear under her breath and scramble to search the ragged mattress for the bone. The woman got a look of wonder on her face.

"It really works," Tehena said slowly.

"Yes, if we don't lose all the darts before we learn to aim."

"You could use that on a guard."

Dion nodded.

"And he'd go down. Just like that. Without calling for help."

"If your aim is true, then yes."

Tehena got a strange look on her face and said nothing more that day. But when Dion finished practicing with the darts, the other woman held out her hand for the gun. Dion, who let Hishn's voice fill her mind with a dim, gray fog, fell into her dreams, her slipping thoughts punctuated by the soft snapping sounds of the tiny bones sinking into Tehena's mattress.

The next day, they waited for the prisoners across the hall to fall asleep again before they practiced, and in hours, their accuracy increased to the point where they could come within half a finger's width of any spot in the cell.

"Healer," Tehena whispered, putting down the blowpipe after Dion had shown her how to control her breath for maximum distance and force. "I owe you."

Dion did not even bother to look up. "You owe me nothing, Tehena."

"I owe you," Tehena insisted. "And I pay my debts." She glanced at the weapon in her hands and looked at the wolfwalker. "I haven't had many friends. No one's done anything for me since I was ten years old. With this—" she looked down at the weapon again "—I'll get out of this rat hole if it kills me. Then I'll repay you."

"There is nothing to repay," Dion repeated, though she was surprised at the other woman's vehemence. "We are here together. If I can find a way out, I won't leave you by yourself."

She tried to smile in the dank gloom. "Moonworms, I'll need someone to listen to my ravings and tell me how insane the next stunt I'm going to try is."

"Don't make this sound like I'm doing you a favor," Tehena said sharply. "No one does anything for anyone else just to get a moon blessing." She stared at the healer. "I figure you just don't know how things work, that's why you're treating me so nice." She gave a bitter snort. "Just wait till you take a whipping meant for me. I didn't lift a finger to help you against the guard, remember? I wouldn't even blink if you died right now. When you've been here a few more ninans, you'll understand." She paused. "But I do pay my debts, Healer. I pay all my debts."

She broke off. Guards were coming into the prison, as if her mention of them had brought them in. Dion frowned. It was not yet time for gruel, and as Tehena realized that also, she shot the healer a wary look. Down the cell block, doors clanged, and Dion went to the bars to see what was happening. The soldiers had stopped at Namina's cell, and the girl was being dragged out, unresisting. As Dion watched, Shilia was next, and then the guards were at her own cell. They struck the bars with a pipe to make her stand back, then thrust a key into the lock. One of them pulled open the heavy door.

"You, out." The guard gestured peremptorily at her. She stared at him as if he were joking. "Yeah, you. Move it. And hurry. I've no wish to be Longear's lesson-of-the-day."

Tehena, who had flinched at the mention of Longear, watched impassively as Dion was dragged from the cell. The two women exchanged a long look while the guards fettered the wolfwalker's hands together, then pushed her to join Namina and Shilia. The girls had lost enough weight to make their high-boned cheeks too sharp, but they were not nearly as gaunt as Dion. The strain of Ovousibas and the fever that had followed it had taken their toll on the wolfwalker. Her cheeks had hollowed out, and the rags of her whip-cut tunic hung from her shoulders like moss from a winter tree.

Gamon and Tyrel joined the three women, and then they were all ushered out into the hall, up the stairs, and through the guardroom. Dion fought down the urge to slap the leering grins off from the soldier's faces as she tried to pull the front pieces of her tunic together.

At last they were led into a bare bathroom, where the dim

light was still too bright for their near-blind eyes. They were forced into a standing trough that smelled like a combination of burned oil and piss, which the guards said would rid them of vermin, then were taken to another bathroom where the waters smelled more pleasant. At the shock of fresh air, Dion found herself breathing deeply, as if she could not get enough of it into her lungs. But they were given little time to enjoy the experience. They were hardly out of the baths and into cleaner clothes when a door opened and a captain strode in, fingering a bronze medallion in his hands.

"Finish quickly," he ordered the guards. "Longear will see them now. And you," he snapped, dropping the medallion into his pocket and spearing the group of prisoners with disdain, "address Longear as 'sir' if you want to keep your tongues." He turned irritably on his heel and left.

Gamon shot the others a quick look. "I was hoping Longear had gone to the moons for judgment," he said in a low growl.

One of the guards shivered. "That you should be so lucky," he muttered. "That's the name of the post, not the *man*."

One of the other guards gave him a dark look. "As if a man would do those things."

"What things?" Gamon could not help asking.

"Shut up," the first guard said, looking nervously around.

Gamon gave him a speculative look. If "Longear" was the name of the post, then there had not been just one Longear to advise Zentsis. There could have been several men in that post, each with different ambitions . . .

The guards marched the five prisoners in a ragged line down the corridors and through another courtyard. Day was a new experience: the light caused their eyes to cringe, blinding them, and they tripped and stumbled their way between the cool pillars until they were led into another set of halls. As their eyes adjusted, they could make out paintings and maps on the walls, and tables covered with papers in the open spaces. Finally they came to a large room, which opened into dark corridors on many sides, and stopped finally before a desk behind which sat a small woman with a hard, bitter face.

"Sir." The soldiers saluted.

"Leave us," she commanded in a disinterested voice. She remained seated and looked the ragged group over. For all that it was a quick glance, she clearly had taken them in completely in those few seconds.

"So." She leaned back and studied the haggard prisoners

more slowly, her eyes finally resting on Gamon. "Gamon Aikekkraya neBentar. Weapons master of the Ramaj Ariye. We finally meet. I've been a great admirer of yours for a long time."

"The pleasure is mine, lady," Gamon said politely, inclining his head.

Her face darkened for an instant. "*I* am Longear," she snapped. She leaned forward and laughed at their stunned looks.

Gamon wiped his face clear of emotion, but Shilia frowned in bewilderment, and Tyrel's mouth still hung open.

The boy stared at her. "But—"

Gamon poked Tyrel in the ribs, but Dion could see that the older man was as shocked as the rest of them.

"You expected a man?" Longear asked mockingly. "That is natural, but not very intelligent."

Gamon's eyes narrowed, and his face set in a hard line that Dion had not seen before. "It was there in front of me all the time,' he said to himself. "And I never guessed."

Dion felt a chill. Longear a woman? If this woman had merely wanted a position of power, she would have been a elder on Zentsis's council. But to be Longear, the Lloroi's top aide—the woman they stood before would have ambitions stronger than any woman Dion had yet met. The small, bitter woman in front of them could never be Lloroi, but she could wield Zentsis's power from her desk. And, knowing Zentsis's secrets while she held the power of his army, and adding her control over the raiders on top of that, Longear could guide not only the Lloroi's county, but Zentsis himself. Dion glanced at Gamon and saw that the old weapons master had followed the same line of thought. She and Gamon exchanged a long look as Longear watched in amusement.

"Poor Gamon," Longear said. "How does it feel to be outsmarted even in this?"

His jaw tightened, but he forced a smile and edged away from Dion.

"Don't count on heroic actions and dramatic escape," Longear said dryly. "There are guards in each of the openings. And there has been such a succession of people in this office that my death—to ensure yours—is of no consequence. However, I intend to be here a long time. One trick, one move, Gamon, and I will have your legs and the legs of your darling little nieces amputated. You understand?" She paused and looked them over one by one. "I use the same rule for everyone. It is, and I pride myself on this, why the House of Cripples is so popular."

Tyrel flushed as his temper rose. "What do you want with us?"

She leaned back. "Getting to the point, boy? I like that. And that is the question, isn't it? What do I do with you now? I have you, and I know you did not contrive to send any information to Ariye. But I don't have all of you." She leaned forward again. "And I want all of you. My traps have been avoided—cleverly, I might add—and the rabbits still run at large. So what was I to do?" She shrugged delicately. "I've arranged a bit of entertainment for our Lloroi, the great Zentsis." The scorn in her voice was unmistakable. "It will draw your friends, while the public and I will appreciate the entertainment. And I'm sure you'll enjoy it, too. After all—" she paused and looked at the five again, her glance resting longer on Shilia and Namina "—you are the entertainers."

Gamon cleared his throat. "What kind of entertainment did you have in mind?" he asked flippantly. "I can't answer for the others, but I don't dance or play music, and my singing voice is terrible."

"But you don't have to sing for me, Gamon Aikekkraya. I've been waiting years to see you in action." She stalled his automatic protest with a wave. "Oh, I know you're a veritable old man now, but it just gives my guards the chance they wouldn't otherwise have, doesn't it?"

Gamon bowed as well as he could in the chains that still bound him. "I would fight almost any number for the chance to lay eyes on your lovely countenance again, lady," he said deliberately.

Longear's expression darkened further. "I worked many years to reach this post," she said softly. "You will address me as befits this office."

"Most certainly, lady," Gamon bowed again. "But do I address you as Lady Longear, which is a singularly unfeminine name, or lady sir, equally as masculine, or—"

"Enough!" The woman's face paled. "I will be addressed as 'sir' by you as by everyone else. You want to play games, Gamon, well, so be it. Our Lloroi loves a good match, and we need some new fighters for the rings. You and the boy will champion your women against say, five of my men. The winners can take the women for themselves in the ring or elsewhere, and you may watch before you're given over to the dark healers for experiments.''

"And if we win?" Gamon asked with a relaxed smile, hiding the shiver he felt at the mention of dark healers.

"Do you expect to win at such odds? Then I will make it more of a challenge. You may choose the squad you wish to demonstrate your skill upon. We have any number of them and they are of many sizes, as I'm sure you know. Pick one.''

Two men entered the area to the left, and as Longear saw them, her eyes narrowed, but she smiled ingratiatingly. "Ah, Lloroi Zentsis. And Conin neZentsis," she added quickly, with a glance at the younger man.

"Longear," Zentsis acknowledged. He looked at the small group. "These are the spies?"

She nodded. "And also the entertainment for Conin's birthday celebration. I've been saving them for something special, and what better time to bring them out than now, when your newfound son is celebrating his twenty-third birthday and his rise to political power?''

Zentsis looked the group over again, judging and dismissing each one as if too inferior to be of interest. "They will fight?''

Longear nodded. "That one is a weapons master of the Ramaj Ariye: Gamon neBentar.''

Zentsis looked at Gamon's old but proud face. The Lloroi's own face was hard and bony, with heavy lines above his brows. He was a big man, and he had a heavy laugh to match. "This? This old man is a weapons master?" He turned to the young man, who smiled politely at the joke. "What will he be doing? Demonstrating how to use a cane to defend himself?" He laughed, and Longear chuckled.

"I thought of giving one of our squads some exercise, Lloroi. The winner can have the women. It gives Gamon something worth fighting for, I'm sure, to have his nieces as the stakes. You remember that he is the Lloroi's brother?''

Zentsis nodded reflectively. "The woman are the Ariye Lloroi's daughter and niece then? A nice capture, Longear.''

Longear smiled thinly. "I've given Gamon the choice of a squad to fight, but he has not yet chosen. Since you've just gained a son, Lloroi, I thought it fitting that his birthday feast sport unusual skills in areas I'm sure he'll find most interesting.''

Dion had not thought she had heard the woman correctly

before, but now she knew that Longear was serious. The man with Zentsis was his son? Zentsis was supposed to have got only daughters by his wives and concubines. And what did "just gained" mean? Had Zentsis just found out he had a son? Had some whore or poor man's daughter delivered what he had always wanted and hidden the child until he was grown? The son would have to be truly his, she realized, if he was to follow his father as Lloroi. This Conin was twenty-three. Old enough, if he took after his father, to be twisted in thought, she muttered bitterly. What game would he have them play for his birthday feast?

But when Conin looked at Namina, Shilia, and Dion, the wolfwalker was startled to see pity in his eyes. "Father," he protested, "you cannot put the women in the ring—"

"Women have been prizes before." Zentsis waved him off, unconcerned. "They always draw a good crowd. Besides, it's for a good cause: national security."

"Well, isn't that one a healer?" Conin tried again. "It would be a shame to throw away skills we need so desperately right now."

Zentsis scowled. "Is it true, Longear, that the one is a healer? Or is that just a bauble picked up on the street that she's got around her head?"

Dion's jaw tightened.

"It's true, she's a healer," Longear answered, "but one never knows how well a stranger has been trained. She might be more sport in the ring than useful in town." Conin's face blanched at her blunt words and he looked away to study a map on one of the walls.

"Say what you mean, Longear," the Lloroi commanded with a frown.

"She's trained in Abis, Lloroi. The martial art of Ramaj Randonnen. You might get a good fight out of her before she's taken as a prize."

"A healer? Trained in Abis?" He gave Dion a calculating look. "How much does she know?"

It was irritating to be spoken of as if she were not there, and Dion could feel her ire rising.

"I am told she is a fifth, though the source was not reliable. You could match her against one or two, maybe even three of your own men, Lloroi." Longear smiled persuasively "She is not from Ariye, and her fighting style might catch an inexperienced man off guard. I'm sure a well-placed wager would surprise many.''

"I take your point. The boy?''

"A good fighter, but inexperienced. I would suggest the two sergeants from squad eight. It would teach those two a valuable lesson, yet still guarantee the match.''

Zentsis nodded. "A good program, Longear. We'll set the matches for midninan at the height of the feast. Well, son, how do you like the entertainment so far?''

Conin opened his mouth, but Dion cut him off. "A man who wants to win his wagers would do better to hedge his bets,'' she said scornfully, her voice carrying clearly in the room.

Conin looked at her in surprise, and Zentsis looked shocked that she had spoken without being addressed. Gamon nudged her to shut up.

"Keep your tongue still or lose it," Longear snapped. "Lloroi, I apologize for her behavior. She obviously did not understand my *explicit*—''

"No." Zentsis waved her silent as he eyed the wolfwalker speculatively. "I would hear what she has to say.''

"I mean only that you can't expect someone who is starved, whipped, and feverish to fight well. Lloroi," Dion added, inclining her head at him disdainfully as she finished.

Zentsis's face darkened with quick anger, but Conin looked appalled at her words. "Father, you had a healer whipped?''

"Not specifically, no." Zentsis shrugged disinterestedly. "It is a general order for troublesome prisoners. She must have disobeyed, or the guards would have left her alone by Longear's instructions." Curious, he examined the woman with the flashing violet eyes. "How many lashes did she take, Longear?''

"The report said fifteen," Longear answered unwillingly. "Norshark. That would be nine days ago, Lloroi. Exactly one ninan.''

"And moving so well now. This may be worth much to me." He chuckled suddenly. "So be it. The best rooms in the house for my champions.''

"I won't champion you, Lloroi,'' Dion stated boldly. "But if you add my freedom to the pot, I'll guarantee you a show you'd be willing to pay thrice over for.''

Zentsis looked her over as if she were a dnu for a race. He chuckled again, an unpleasant sound. "That would be a wager

I could not afford to lose," he said speculatively, "since your freedom is hardly in my best interest." He made a gesture, and Longear smiled and sat back. "But I accept your offer. Of course, I will expect exactly what I am promised. No less. If the fight—or fights—" He paused maliciously. "—do not meet my standards, I will keep you for my own."

Dion nodded scornfully as if fully confident, but her stomach felt hollow. If she lost, she would be his. If she won, she would still lose, for Zentsis could not allow her to leave the ring alive. But fighting rings were large, and stadiums larger; the chance was worth taking.

"Lloroi, there is also this," Longear suggested, displeased at her loss of control over the situation. "There are two other members of their party. I suspect they're in the city now, plotting a rescue attempt. I would draw them to the fights and see if they will expose themselves to save their friends. Then we will have all of them, and the knowledge they carry will die with them."

"Yes." Zentsis considered that. "If they lose," he added. "The threat of a chancy fight should draw them. Well, old man?" he said mockingly to Gamon. "Would you also fight better for your freedom?"

"I'd fight four times my number for our freedom," the weapons master answered truthfully, his eyes cold.

"Then we'll make it six and let the boy fight with you."

"Father," Conin cut in anxiously, gesturing at Namina and Shilia. "What about those two?"

Longear regarded him speculatively. "They won't be killed, Conin. After they are used in the ring, they will be used again by me."

The Lloroi snorted at his son's expression. "They are the prize, boy. You're too softhearted, Conin. These are the enemy. Take away their pretty faces and all you'll see are the traitorous thoughts of evil women. They deserve no better than they get." The heavy man clapped his son on his shoulders. "It's time you learned what politics is about, son, especially since you'll be taking over from me a year from now. You know I have plans for Ariye. This will start them rolling just fine. By the time you take over, you'll have little to do but guide the action that follows and keep on reaping the rewards."

"A year from now—but you said—the healers said—you have at least three years!"

"Wasted years in a wasted body. In a year I'll want to sit

back and kibitz and make sure you understand what the position of Lloroi means. Because you, Conin, have to learn that there are things that must be done, no matter how unpleasant, for the security of the county. And you'll have to be willing to command them or do them yourself.''

"Yes, Father," Conin said quietly, "and I am willing to do what I have to. But these women—I see no point in putting them in the ring as prizes. They're so young . . .''

"Hells of all nine moons," Zentsis swore. "That mother of yours nearly ruined you. She always was soft upstairs—probably why I was taken with her that time—and on top of that you've got as thick a skull as me." Seeing Conin's face, Zentsis laughed. "If it's girls you want, son, take some from my own house. I have beauties from all over the world.''

Conin looked at him, then at the two girls. "I want them.''

Longear shook her head and was about to speak, but Zentsis cut her off. "Those girls are worthless traitors," he stated flatly. "You'll never know what they're thinking about you. Take Ethona and Lonillin instead. They'll give you pleasure for years.''

Conin's face set. "I want these girls, Father," he said steadily.

"No.''

"These girls, Father. I have not asked anything from you before.''

Zentsis looked him in the eye, but Conin did not back down.

"Be the fool then," the Lloroi said angrily, "but leave me the dark-haired one. She owes me a fight if she's not a liar like all other women.''

Longear eyed Conin narrowly. "They are not in good health, Conin. Leave them with me for a few more days, then you can have them both.''

Zentsis looked at Namina and Shilia as if they were dnu. "They should fatten up all right, Longear, though I doubt they'll have much gratitude for you, boy. You'd have done better to accept Ethona and Lonillin as your birthday present.''

"I will keep these two," the young man repeated.

Shilia started to open her mouth, but Gamon leaned against her lightly as if shifting from one foot to the other. No matter what Conin's plans, the two girls would be safer with him than with Longear. Shilia shut her mouth again without a sound, but her brother was not as discreet.

"Hey you," he said, his temper sharpening his voice.

"That's my sister and my cousin. If you harm them in any way, I'll come for you, and I'll not leave enough pieces for a dozen rats to—"

Zentsis took one step forward and backhanded the boy heavily. Tyrel staggered back so that Gamon had to catch him, the boy tangling awkwardly in his chains.

"Father," Conin started.

"No one talks to you that way," the Lloroi answered calmly. "The girls will be delivered as soon as they look presentable."

Shilia opened her mouth again, and this time it was Dion who nudged her. Longear noticed and merely smiled like a watercat before it pounces.

Zentsis turned back just before he and Conin left. "If I have your word about the fights," he said, "I'll allow you three to remain together."

"You have my word," Gamon said.

Longear gestured thoughtfully for the guards to split the group up, and Dion watched helplessly as Namina and Shilia were taken away. But Gamon cleared his throat as the guards moved toward them.

"One question, Longear."

She raised her eyebrow.

"How did you locate us? We did not enter Bilocctar by any route that could be seen by men."

The woman tilted her head and let a smirk play at her lips. "It was exactly that route that gave you away, Gamon." She smiled more broadly at his puzzlement. "I needed men in Ariye, in Sidisport, in Red Harbor to track you. I needed no men in the mountains. You see, one way or another, I control the raiders, the slavers, and half the merchants in Sidisport. You had little chance there, Gamon. And with my raider fleet, you had less chance once you took to the sea. But when you dared set foot in Bilocctar, you had no chance at all."

"But how—"

Longear laughed, but the sound was short and shallow. "The wolves, Gamon. The wolves." She laughed again at the look on Dion's face. Her fingernails flipped a splinter of wood away. "The Gray Ones can be coerced quite easily, once you know what makes them run with a man. And it is such a simple thing to do, to cause them pain." She chuckled again, then motioned abruptly for them to be taken away.

Dion, stunned, could say nothing, as they were led from the

room. Longear, looking after them, recalled their words with Zentsis and rolled her stylus between her fingers as if she could crush it there.

"You still think you have a chance," she said softly, staring after them. The soldiers behind her shifted uneasily, but she ignored them. "I could see it in your eyes, Gamon," she said under her breath. "Even now, you think to catch me off-guard by bargaining with the Lloroi. Fools. The Lloroi is not the only one who knows the ways of the fighting ring."

Gamon, Tyrel, and Dion were put together in one room. Bare as it was, it was luxurious compared to the cells they had come from, and after a while, the guards threw in three mattresses and the bedding that went with them. They fed the prisoners, too, pushing three trays of food inside the door. There was even a window, though the bars across were heavy enough to keep a herd of dnu in. Starved from the meager prison fare, they fell to the food greedily, though they hid half of it under one of the blankets in case they were not fed again. Their stay in the prison had made them suspicious.

"Well," Gamon said in a low voice as he surveyed the room, "if we can't find a way out in five days, we'll have our chance in the ring."

"With Longear watching every move, just waiting for us to try or for Aranur and Rhom to come get us," Dion said hopelessly.

Tyrel threw himself on one of the mattresses and locked his arms under his head as he stared at the ceiling. "And that will be six against two, anyway. What are you gong to do, Uncle?"

Dion turned to the barred window. "Gods, Gamon, but what about Hishn?"

Gamon watched her thoughtfully. "That Longear is using the wolves to scout for her—we have no way of knowing if that is true or not," he said softly. "And I cannot believe that there are so many wolfwalkers in Bilocctar that Longear could keep them along every border."

"It would take only one, Gamon. And Hishn—"

"Longear does not know you are a wolfwalker, Dion."

Dion paced in front of the window as if she had not heard him. "What if Aranur and Rhom are seen with Hishn? What if Longear captures Hishn and finds out—"

"Finds out what? That she has another wolf in her hands?

She would not be one to speak to the Gray Ones, Dion. She would not find out from Hishn who the Gray One ran with.''

Dion stopped. ''What if it is I who gives Hishn away?''

''You cannot protect Hishn except by not thinking about her, Dion. And the less you think about her, the less chance you will have of mentioning her when there are others around. So stop pacing and start thinking about first things first.'' Gamon gestured at the three of them. ''Let's check ourselves over. Dion, take no offense, but I saw your back during the baths, and I have to say it looks more like you were tapped with a light rope than beaten with the norshark whip I know the guard took to you.''

She nodded, dragging her thoughts back to the way the scars had knit. Her back was still tender, but at least the gashes had healed. ''Hishn helped me with the internal healing,'' she explained slowly, wincing as she mentioned the gray wolf's name. ''But I don't think it's something I want to do again.''

Gamon raised his eyebrows.

She shook herself visibly, as if to remove all thoughts of Hishn from her mind. ''It's different when I do it on myself,'' she explained hesitantly. ''This time I—I almost didn't come back.''

The older man shook his head. ''What you have, Dion, is a skill that should only be used in life or death emergencies.''

''I don't think I'd have survived the fever if I hadn't already half healed my back.'' She flexed her shoulders experimentally. A thought struck her. ''Dammit all to the moons and back!'' she exclaimed.

''What is it?'' Gamon asked.

''Tehena and I had the makings of a good blowpipe. I can't believe I left it behind!'' She tugged at the shallow pockets in her new clothes, examining them irritably. ''I could have found some way to conceal it,'' she muttered. ''There's almost nothing here to make a weapon out of, and I don't even have my herbs anymore to make the simplest drug. They stripped them away with the vermin in my old clothes—''

Gamon listened for a moment and started laughing. ''Dion,'' he said with a chuckle. At the look she gave him, he laughed even harder. ''You are the most unquenchable— Anyone else would be so relieved to be out of those hellholes that they'd forget everything else the nine moons had ever given them. But you''—here his words became lost in his laugher—''you have the gall to be miffed about losing your herbs and some jury-rigged blowpipe when you've barely escaped with your life.''

Tyrel started laughing, too. She stared at them both. Finally, he lips twitched, and then she gave in, collapsing on the mattress beside them in almost hysterical laughter.

"You two," she said, wiping the tears from her eyes, "are the most obnoxious troublemakers *I've* ever met."

"Well, then, we're even." Tyrel rolled over and gave her an awkward hug.

In the evening, the guards took them out, searched them and the room thoroughly, laughed when they found the food that had been stashed, and threw the meager fare out the window, all of it done with one of the three held hostage at swordpoint against the others' conduct. Then they locked the three prisoners back in for the night. Dion, jumpy as a rabbit in a worlag's den, stared out the window for an hour before Gamon persuaded her to sleep. To her surprise, she fell into a dreamless rest almost before her head hit the mattress.

Wolfwalker! The call pulled Dion out of her sleep. *Healer! Hishn!* She got up as quietly as possible and moved to the window, her hands gripping the bars as if she could bend them and escape. Gamon woke instantly, but saw it was just Dion, and seemed to go back to sleep.

Smells of feasting, meats waiting to be eaten, grease from the cooking pots, lupine hunger. An ear-splitting din from the instruments and the heavy stomping of many feet. Nose-choking scents and the desire for the clean smells of the forest. Rhom . . . Aranur . . . The dull brass of a key. Soon, soon, Hishn sent. *Wait calmly, Be strong.*

We'll be ready, Dion promised. *Hishn . . .* She hesitated, and the wolf sent a question in return. *You must not be seen, Hishn,* Dion sent finally. *Longear—* The wolf sent a reassurance, and Dion shook her head. *Longear could use you, Hishn,* she insisted. *You must not be seen by the soldiers.*

I am seen only before I strike, Hishn returned, her worry for Dion clouding her acceptance of Dion's warning.

Moons, Hishn, I do not know if it is true or not, but Longear could be using the Gray Ones by harming their human partners.

Hishn bared her teeth mentally. *You have already been harmed, and your pain is my pain.*

Dion clenched the bars and quelled her thoughts. Hishn was not listening, but Dion hoped the wolf would remember her warning later. She took a half breath and held it, changing the tone of her thought and hiding her worry as best she could. Gamon was right, she told herself. Longear could not control the wolfwalkers. The woman must have been lying. But Dion wished she could touch Hishn and reassure herself that the gray wolf was safe. Hishn—the others were so far away. The image of the two men and the wolf rose up in her mind, and she half questioned, *Aranur?*

Your picture is strong in his mind like a rabbit in the hunt, she said. *I feel his thoughts like yours.* The howl that lingered in Dion's mind was real; it echoed in the empty street where Hishn stood and stared at the walls of stone. Dion's eyes blurred. Hishn, she thought. She pictured being home, with her father and Rhom. With Aranur. But in four days she would be in a fighting ring, and even if she won, Zentsis would have her killed . . .

"The day of fighting will be here soon enough, Ember Dione," Gamon said softly, as if he had read her mind. He rolled to his feet and joined her at the window, putting his arm across her shoulders and pulling her comfortingly close. "Sleep tonight. Rhom and Aranur have not forgotten us. They will know Longear's traps before they come for us."

"Hishn says they—" She paused and steadied her voice. "—that they have keys. That they'll be coming for us soon."

"You see? The moons have blessed us with midnight luck." He chucked her chin gently. "Be strong, Ember. Trust in your skill, trust in yourself."

"I'm not a man, Gamon," she whispered, gazing out between the bars at the forbidden sky. "I like to fight and roughhouse as much as anyone, but I can't stand the killing. I'm a healer." Her voice was almost inaudible. "And I'm a woman."

The older man turned Dion to face him the way her father had once done. "Dion, you'll always be in a different position because of your skills. And you know you won't deny those skills—you worked too hard and for too long to earn them." He shook her lightly. "Don't give in to the lepa before it leaps. There may be a few surprises left for you."

"The only surprise the moons may grant me now is making it through this fight."

"Which will come all too soon if you worry about it. Go

back to sleep," he ordered, pushing her toward her mattress. "We'll be there, too, you know." He smiled. "By the moons, woman, what are you worried about? If you can't count on us and that four-footed, gray-coated friend of yours, who can you count on?"

Chapter 18

Freedom comes costly:
Advice comes cheap:
To pay silver for blood,
The price is far too steep.
Look for the key
That makes the sword keen;
The chains that bind a man
Aren't always those seen.

"It's all set," Aranur said, rubbing his head. He was crouched in the alley with Rhom and Hishn. The Gray One had to understand what they needed from her, or they would get no help from those within the store they were headed for.

Rhom, glancing at the other man, rubbed Hishn and looked into the wolf's eyes until she shook him off. "Did she understand about the keys?" he asked Aranur.

"I think so."

"Are you sure?"

"Dammit, I'm as sure as I can be, Rhom," Aranur exploded. He glared at the younger man. "It's not easy, this talking through a wolf. If you think you can do better, go ahead."

Hishn growled low in her throat, and Rhom took a deep breath. "Sorry, Aranur," he said shortly.

"My family is in there, too, Rhom."

The younger man nodded silently.

"We have to relax, Rhom, or we'll tear each other's throats out before we can do Dion and the others any good. And there's no other way to do this. We didn't even get past the first set of gates last time we tried."

"Longear was just waiting for us, to try again," Rhom agreed bitterly.

"And if Hishn had not dragged me into that healing with Dion before we reached the gates, we would not have stopped and seen that the guards were searching everyone who entered. We would have been caught as neatly as fish in a net." Aranur got to his feet and glanced both ways along the alley. "But it's our turn to do the fishing now. And I know just the fish we want to catch." He led the way onto the street, Hishn remaining behind. In the dusk, she faded into the shadows as if she were an illusion, and Rhom had to squint to tell which shadow was real.

"What about tomorrow?" Rhom asked quietly.

"We split up," Aranur answered over his shoulder. "The feasts are drawing big enough crowds that it will be easy to get lost in them. Longear's men are guarding only the gates to Zentsis's buildings and the county halls. They will never notice two more strangers when everyone and his brother seem to be invited to the celebration." He frowned at the business numbers on the run-down buildings they passed. "This is the place."

He stopped in front of a small bentwood-furniture shop. He hoped the man inside could be convinced to help them; if not, he was sure the man would be open to the kind of coercion he had in mind. After all, according to the wolf, if Aranur had understood her correctly, Heerdon was the guard who had allowed the healer more freedom because of her status. And if he respected Dion as a healer, what would he think when he found out he had helped to imprison a wolfwalker? Already the city was flying with rumors of the wolf. Aranur had suggested that Hishn let herself be seen on the streets, and Rhom had agreed, although reluctantly. The rumors would help give them the authority they might have to use with the guard. They entered the furniture shop.

"May I help you?" The voice floated up from behind a heavy chair as they peered around. Then the woman kneeling behind the chair, fitting cushions to the back, set her needles down and got stiffly to her feet.

"We're looking for Heerdon," Rhom said, helping her up.

She shook her hands free of the fine upholstery thread that was clinging to her and floating in the air currents. "Well, he's in the back, but he's busy. Perhaps I can help."

"It's important that we speak to Heerdon," Aranur said firmly.

She gave him a sharp look and snorted. "It's always important. Well, go on then. Through the door and to the left."

They found Heerdon grunting over a half-finished chair, straining to bend a heavy bough to the shape he wanted. "Just . . . a minute," he managed, twisting the whip string tightly around the bough. "There. She'll hold for a few minutes. Now, what can I do for you? We take orders, if you know what you want, or you can look through the shop out back if you don't see anything you like in here."

Aranur's gaze took in the man's hands, stained with wood colors but obviously a fighter's hands just the same. "We might be interested in hiring you, but it would be for a lighter job than this. We're looking for information."

The man's eyes narrowed, flickering to the doorway. "Information costs."

"Lives cost more."

Heerdon gave them a sharp look, then studied Rhom. "What do you want from me?"

"You were on guard detail the night some prisoners were taken in fifteen, sixteen days ago. An old man, a boy, and three women. There'd be an expensive commission for some work"—Aranur gestured negligently at the spare workbench—"if you could tell us where they are now. Maybe enough to skip guard duty for a month if you could get us in to them."

"What do you want with political prisoners?"

"Let's say I have a personal stake in what happens to them." Aranur shrugged. "I have some money riding on their fate, and I always hedge my bets."

"I say he's one of those that's being looked for," the woman said caustically from the doorway.

Startled, the gray-eyed fighter turned and drew his sword; at the same time, Rhom pulled his own blade out and pointed it at Heerdon. The woman had taken her shoes off and her stocking feet had made no sound as she sneaked up to hear.

She gestured at Rhom with bravado, though her eyes betrayed her fear. "And he's probably the other."

"Our affiliations are of no interest to you," Aranur growled. "Move—over there by him. Now." He glanced out to the hall as she came into the room and edged past Rhom. "Is there anyone else in the shop?"

"I wish I could say yes," she said bitterly, looking at the sword, "but we've been losing business since midwinter."

"Shut up, Auntie, and stay out of this," Heerdon said flatly.

"We don't want to make threats," Aranur said flatly, "but it's your neck if we find our own getting caught in a noose. If you call for help, I'll make sure Longear knows you invited us here." He paused. "You could always help us instead. We're offering tax-free money at no risk to yourself."

"No." Heerdon shook his head. "Longear has many arms and each has many knives. I have others to think of."

"So do I." Aranur glanced at the woman. "How would you feel if you knew that Longear had taken a wolfwalker and a healer to torture and kill."

"A wolfwalker!" The woman's eyes widened. "They say that there's a wolfwalker stalking the streets at night now, hunting. But wolfwalkers are legend."

"They are fact. The healer is a wolfwalker, and—" Aranur paused, "the blessing or curse of a wolfwalker is not something to ignore."

"There was no wolfwalker taken in," Heerdon scoffed. "There's wasn't even a dog nearby. And anyway, how could a wolfwalker curse us here? Get out of my shop now, and I'll say nothing of this—"

Aranur cut him off with a curt gesture. "Use your head, Heerdon. The wolkwalker sent us to find you and expects your help. Her blessing—or her curse—rides on your answer."

"Heerdon," the woman said urgently. "A wolfwalker—"

"They're lying from their own desperation, Mylna," he said, meeting Aranur's eyes. "There was no wolf when we took the healer and the others. Sure, I feel bad about Longear having a healer in that dungeon, but it has nothing to do with us."

"Perhaps more than you think," Aranur said softly.

Rhom tapped the sill of the open window, and as he did, a gray shadow burst through, landing silently on the floor and turning to fix Heerdon and his aunt with baleful yellow eyes. Gray Hishn's fangs were just the right shade of yellow to match her glowing eyes in the failing light.

"May the moons forgive us!" Heerdon's aunt gasped and fell to her knees before the wolf, ignoring Heerdon's clutching hands as he tried to pull her up to her feet. "Gray One, you honor us," she babbled. "You honor our house—forgive us for doubting you—"

"Mylna, shut up," Heerdon said shakily. "They're just—"

You will give Leader what he needs. Hishn met the man's eyes, curling her lips back from her teeth as she spoke.

Heerdon's voice had trailed off and his jaw hung open as the clear-timbered voice snarled inside his head. "You—honor—me," the man stammered.

"Heerdon," Mylna tried again.

Aranur had caught the echo of that voice in his own head. "Wolves speak as the legends say they do." He gestured at Hishn. "The ancients gave the wolves the Voice as a reward for crossing the stars with them. And then they gave the wolf-walkers to the wolves, as well. Wolfwalkers are real, Heerdon. One of them needs your help now. And Heerdon, remember, the legends make it clear what happens to those who cross the wolves and their wolfwalkers."

"Wolves don't lie," Rhom added, "and their curse can follow you to the moons and back."

"The blessing of the Gray Ones will protect you," Aranur persuaded. "You and your aunt, Heerdon. All we want—" He saw the guardsman start to shake his head and began again more forcefully. "All we want is to know where they are and how to get them out. Heerdon, you met the healer, the others. Do you think they're a threat to the county's security?"

Heerdon tried to concentrate on the words as he eyed the wolf warily.

"Use your head, man," Aranur continued. "We've been chased from Ariye to Bilocctar on the basis of some half-baked notion that we know something dangerous. The truth of the matter is that a slaver took our sisters and we went after them. When we got our sisters back, the slaver called Zentsis to help him get revenge. We don't know anything about Bilocctar and aren't interested in finding out any more than we already have. All we want," he finished convincingly, "is to find our sisters, my uncle, and my cousins, and get out of here alive."

Heerdon stared at the wolf again.

Hishn's teeth parted, showing the rows of yellow fangs that retreated into the darkness of her mouth. *I need my healer. You will do as Leader asks*, she sent. She let her tongue curl around the two canines at the front of her jaw, and the woman beside Heerdon whimpered.

"For god's sake, Heerdon," she whispered shakily. "If you love life here and with the moons—"

"Mylna, shut up!" Heerdon rubbed his hands on his pants

as if they were sweating. "How do I know you won't tell Longear anyway if you're caught?"

"You have my word as a man of Ariye, and you have the word of a Gray One to back that up."

The soldier looked away, then met the eyes of the wolf again. Aranur waited a long moment, his sword growing heavy in his hand. Finally the guardsman cleared his throat.

"Longear moved the two men and the healer to the second level of Zentsis's house," he said slowly. "You can't get near them—there's always three guards at the door, and they are checked every other hour."

Rhom met Aranur's glance. "Why those three?"

"Zentsis is putting them in the ring for the midninan entertainment. They'll be fighting for their lives, although it's said that they promised him a show in exchange for their freedom if they win. Longear's making sure they won't get that, but Zentsis has never had someone as skilled as a weapons master in the ring before. He's building up this match as a demonstration for his son's birthday."

"Why Dion with Gamon and Tyrel?" the younger man asked in an undertone. "And where are Shilia and Namina?"

The guardsman cleared his throat again, the words seeming to stick in his throat as he faced the chill in Aranur's slate-gray eyes. "The two young ones were, well, claimed by Conin, Zentsis's son. They say that the healer," he continued, not meeting that icy gaze, "is going to be the prize for the winners of the other match."

Rhom took half a step forward but was stopped by Aranur's grip on his arm. Aranur thought for a moment, trying to ignore the sinking sensation in his stomach. Why had Conin not taken Dion as well? Had Longear been behind it? He glanced at Rhom and said nothing. Dion was not of Ariye, he mused; a mating between her and Conin would bring no strength to Zentsis's bargaining table. Whereas Dion in the fighting ring . . . As a prize, the wolfwalker would not even have a chance. His jaw tightened. And what of Shilia and Namina? How could he get them away from Zentsis's son?

"Can we get in to this fight?" he asked Heerdon.

Heerdon shook his head. "The security is tight. They are expecting trouble. A lot of people are upset with Zentsis for putting a healer up as the stakes—they think it demeans the whole science—and for putting the weapons master of the Ramaj Ariye in the fighting ring. There's easily a hundred people here who have trained with Gamon neBentar at some time in their lives, but you can bet they'll still be there to see the match. He and the boy will be up against six of Zentsis's best.''

"He's an old man, and Tyrel's just a boy." Aranur controlled himself and lowered his voice at Heerdon's nervous look toward the front room. "When will they fight?" he asked flatly.

"Midninan. The house odds are listed at the betting booths."

"And when is their match scheduled?" Aranur asked.

"There's the amateur fighting, then a surprise match, then the weapons master."

"Could we get into the guards' ranks?"

"You might be able to do that," Heerdon said slowly. "There'll be a lot of trainees used to keep the crowds under control. Everyone with rank will want to be in the stands."

"We will need uniforms, orders, and some knowledge of the officers in charge," Aranur said. "Heerdon, get us some uniforms—one of high enough rank that Rhom can pass in the stands without challenge, and one that will pass me as a guard for the fighting ring. We need plans of the arena, and we'll need to know which gates they'll be taken out of."

"But there's only a few days; uniforms have to requisitioned and approved—"

"I'm sure you'll find a way," the tall, dark-haired man said bluntly. The wolf's fangs gleamed as Hishn watched the men, seemingly following the conversation.

Heerdon looked down at his feet. "I will try," he said finally. "But I promise nothing. Be at the Newbuck Tavern at nine, two nights from today."

"If there is a trap for us . . ." Aranur let the words trail off, and the threat hung ominously in the air.

"There will be no trap. You have *my* word as a man of Ramaj Bilocctar," Heerdon returned.

Rhom and Aranur made their way back to their own tavern and spent the next two days waiting, fretting, and irritating each other till they snapped and growled like trapped animals at any excuse for a fight.

The day of the matches dawned gray and uninviting. The uniforms Heerdon brought fit well enough to pass. Aranur's gave him the rank of private first class, while Rhom's made him a lieutenant, and with papers supplied by a local forger they had no trouble posing as guards. Rhom was edgy as a watercat on the prowl, and Aranur could not blame him. The gray-eyed man felt it, too. His fingers kept curling around the keys in his pocket as if the moons might take them from him if he relaxed. Dion . . . His thoughts kept returning to the wolfwalker. With a diversion, maybe she could make it to the stands. And once she was there, Hishn's fangs could clear a path for them both. Gamon and Tyrel would have to get out some other way. His mind ranging on a dozen plans at once, he joined the troops to which his papers assigned him and marched with them to the stadium.

Heerdon had gotten Aranur a post at the gate where the fighters would enter the ring. That had been easiest, since no one wanted tunnel duty on a hot day. And Rhom was in the stands where Zentsis and his son would be sitting. The minutes crawled by like hours. People started filling the stands at noon, hours before the main fights were to start. While others talked about weapons and fighters and sparring styles and ring positions, Aranur watched the demonstrations and amateur sparring matches without attention, ignoring the bets being taken around him.

One of Aranur's neighbors nudged his arm. "Hey, Helvor, you want a piece of this action? The betting closes when the gong sounds."

Aranur shook his head, but the man was persistent. "You can't be saving all your chips for the main matches."

"Maybe." He fingered the keys in his pockets.

"If you are, let me give you a tip," the man said in a low voice, leaning closer.

"Tip one, tip all," the guard called Kirnan said in a loud voice.

"Why should I waste my information on you guys when you waste your stars on the prematches? You probably placed your bets on the main matches yesterday, without even knowing who's fighting. Now here's someone who bets only on a full hand—a man after my own heart."

"Oh yeah, Tekta? Well, I heard you lost three gold pieces on the matches last month."

"And I won five off the side bets," Tekta claimed.

The others laughed and finished placing their wagers. Aranur was amused that so many bettors were placing money on Gamon and Tyrel even though the odds for the match were set at three to one against them. As the amphitheater took ten percent off the top of all winnings, Zentsis would make enough money on the fights to pay half his army for a month.

"Listen," Tekta said, catching the others' attention again. "I got the inside track on the surprise match. For a small fee, I could part with some very valuable information." He paused and jingled two small coins in his pockets. "Information worth a lot of money to anyone who bets on that match."

"How'd you hear this?" another guard jeered. "Get it from the summer moons?"

"I was in the hall, when—" he looked around cautiously and lowered his voice even further "—Longear and Zentsis made a bargain with the fighters."

Aranur hid his surprise at the man's words and leaned in with the rest to hear what the man had to say.

"There were five of them," Tekta started, then stopped. He looked mournfully down at his empty hand. The others sighed and dug in their pockets for a quarter silver apiece to put in his palm. Tekta grinned and continued as if he had never stopped. "The old man, the boy, two girls, and the healer." He paused dramatically. "A woman healer," he elaborated, smirking. "No older than Yurdy here." He gestured at the young man with his chin. "Conin took the two girls for his own, and the healer challenged Zentsis—ssh! keep it down!—and he agreed to let her fight for her own freedom. Then Gamon, the weapons master, and the boy bargained for the same. Zentsis agreed to everything just to see some wild fighting."

"Zentsis is putting a woman healer in the ring?" Kirnan frowned. "That's worse than putting her up as the stakes. It's going to upset a lot of people when they find out."

"Hell, what makes this woman a fighter anyway?" Aranur said scornfully, playing for information as the fear struck his heart like a sliver of ice. "You just said that she's a healer." Moons have mercy on her, he thought with tension.

"She is a healer," Tekta assured them. "But she's also a sixth in Abis. You should have seen the look on Longear's face when Zentsis started ignoring her and started eyeing this black-haired wench."

Aranur kept silent, though one part of him smiled at the man's exaggeration and the other part fumed at his leering words. Then he froze. Longear a she? A woman? What trick was this? He stared at the other man. If it was true . . . it would explain more than he thought: the way Longear had moved her scouts, the way she had used tricks he somehow associated with the childhood games Shilia played on him . . . He was irked that he had not seen the pattern of this woman's thought behind all this, and his face set in a grim line.

"I think it's a disgrace," one of the guards stated with disgust. "Healers are moonblessed. For Zentsis to put her in the ring, that's criminal."

"What's moonblessed about fighting? If she knows Abis, she's a strange healer indeed." Tekta looked around as if daring them to bet on a healer and a woman. "It's said, too, that one of them is a wolfwalker."

There was a general chorus of disbelief and scorn, and then Aranur, shoving aside his shock at the discovery of Longear's gender, cut in. "If any of them is a wolfwalker, I bet it's the healer."

"Yeah? Then where's her wolf?"

"Maybe right here—" He lowered his voice, glancing into the shadows. "—waiting to eat through Zentsis's heart." Some of them laughed at his words, but others made the sign of the moonblessing and looked furtively at the shadows.

"I've never seen a wolfwalker," one of them said boldly. "I think it's all a tall tale. I'll bet a week's worth of ale against the same that there's not a wolf within fifty kilometers to answer a walker's call."

"Mandrake," one of them said with a chuckle, "you'll bet on anything just to get your money out of your pocket and into someone else's pouch."

"So what are the odds on the woman?" another broke in. "How many is she up against? Who is she up against?"

Tekta shook his head. "That I don't know, but I'll give five-to-one odds that the lady wins her match."

"The main gate's set the odds for the surprise match at four to one." Mandrake dug in his belt pouch. "I'll take you up on that."

"Wait a minute, Mandrake," Kirnan said, stopping him from giving Tekta the silver. "How do we know you can cover your bets, Tekta?"

"I always cover my bets," Tekta protested.

"Yeah, but how many paydays will we have to wait for that?"

The others laughed.

"Just a minute." Aranur held out his hand. "I'll lay you eight-to-one odds that the lady takes her man." He got a laugh for that one. But he opened his money pouch and let a flash of gold show. "And I can guarantee your money beforehand." His position in the platoon gained several status notches.

Tekta gave him a sharp look. "What do you know that we don't?"

"I only bet once in a while, and I always bet on the long shots."

"Then I'll hold the stakes," Kirnan offered.

"Aren't you betting?" Tekta asked in surprise.

"I already did," he said curtly. "I bet for the healer, though I didn't know who the fighter was at the time."

A large guffaw went up. "You'd have done better to bet on a wooten race than to put your money on a fighting healer," someone sniggered.

"Helvor," one of them said hurriedly to Aranur, "I'll take you up on your odds if that offer still stands."

"And I," Mandrake said, handing over his silver. The next few minutes were confusion, almost everyone betting against Dion on the fight.

Kirnan was still jamming the money into his pocket when he gestured Aranur aside. The gray-eyed man did not like the way the other man leaned close and looked around to make sure no one was watching them.

"I know you," Kirnan whispered. "It took me awhile, but I'm not blind and deaf like the others."

Aranur's eyes became dangerously still.

"But I won't give you away—" Kirnan held up his hand and whispered deliberately. "—Aranur, of the Ramaj Ariye."

Aranur looked at him grimly for a moment. "What do you want from me?"

"I want nothing. If I win the bets I placed today, I'll have enough to pay off half of last year's taxes on my farm. You see," he said, leaning even closer, "I have no love of Zentsis. Neither do they. Zentsis cares less for his people than he does for the dnu in his stables. One of the larger bets I made was that there would be a rescue attempt today and that the spies would escape." He glanced behind him. "They're upset at a healer being put in the ring. There'll be more unrest when word gets around. Rumors are flying. Zentsis has a delicate hold on the politics of the city, and he is losing that hold ever so slowly."

"He'd have done better to have them killed than put in the ring."

"I know. But then, too, who is going to miss this fight?

He'll have all the leaders here in this amphitheater today. A quiet death or two will be unnoticed in the fray that's bound to occur. And who can pin the blame on Zentsis if everyone's enemies are in the same hall?''

Aranur turned the ideas over in his head. Zentsis was more clever than he had thought, and the political situation more unstable. He gave Kirnan a long look. ''Will you help me?''

Kirnan shook his head. ''You've got to be kidding. I can't risk my position here.''

''I wouldn't ask that. How much do you like a good fight? Or a brawl?'' Aranur gestured out toward the fighting sands.

''I see what you mean,'' Kirnan said slowly. ''The sun is shining, there are six moons in the sky, and the stakes are getting high.'' He grinned slowly. ''It's been four ninans since we've had a good free-for-all.''

''I may live to collect my bets, but if I don't, you can keep my stakes,'' Aranur promised. ''Just see that there's a good group of fighters on the sands when the ring falls apart.''

''You have a deal.'' Kirnan hesitated a moment. ''Tell me, is the healer really a wolfwalker?''

''What do you think?'' the tall man returned with a sly smile. ''Can't you feel even now the yellow eyes of death in the shadows?'' His voice dropped further. ''The heat of lupine breath on your neck? The feel of the fur as it scrapes by your legs?''

''Enough. Enough already. I won't ask.'' Kirnan gave the other man a dour look. ''Though if I were betting, I think I'd bet on you. Just remember who backed you when the stakes were set.''

The guardsmen spent the last hour in idle speculation about the fighters. The prematches started up when the stands were almost full. Only scattered seats at the top of the stadium remained empty. Good, Aranur thought. The more there are, the merrier the melee. They might get out of this yet.

There was some good amateur fighting, exhibiting some different styles that were interesting to watch. If he had the chance, he would have to warn Dion and Tyrel about some of the holds being used, Aranur told himself. Still, the rings were for untested sport fighters, not battle-trained soldiers. Dion should have little trouble—they would not be expecting her level of skill, especially in a healer. Gamon would also have no problem, but Aranur worried about Tyrel: the boy's energy had been badly sapped by the fever he had contracted in the mountains over a month ago, and his stay in the prisons would not have helped his endurance any.

The crowd was boisterous and noisy, warming up for the big fights. Another hour passed. Midafternoon, there was a lull in the ring. The crowd grew restless. They began shouting for the main matches, stomping and yelling so that the stones themselves seemed to shake with their demand.

Finally the stamp of ranks moving in the tunnel brought the platoon to attention.

"Guards *up*!" the lieutenant ordered. Four men including Aranur stepped out to surround Dion as she stood, small and seemingly weighed down by the chains that bound her. She looked at no one, just stared defiantly at the sands of the ring that spread out before her.

"Prisoner guarded and ready, sir." The sergeant saluted.

"Guards *up*!" the lieutenant commanded again. Eight men stepped out to surround Gamon and Tyrel. Like Dion, the boy looked dwarfed; since all the guards around him were wearing leather mail, even the smallest of them looked half again his size. Gamon, with his silver hair, the crow's-feet that made tracks to the edges of his face, and his shoulders stooped like an elder's, looked like an old man. He was already planning some tricks. He caught sight of Aranur's face among Dion's guard, and his eyes flickered for an instant.

"No need to be so formal, men," he said jovially. "You'd think we were guests of the state." The soldiers ignored him, staying in their ranks. From the stands, the chanting seem to grow and to press down on the empty sands, suffocating the guards who stood on the corridor's stones.

Aranur craned his neck to see around the guard in front of him and searched for Rhom in the crowds under the Lloroi's canvas pavilion. There—Rhom was standing only two rows from Zentsis, and only one row from—moons of mercy, Shilia and Namina. What were they doing here? Had Conin claimed the girls only to use them as prizes? Aranur swallowed his uncertainty and tried to see Rhom's stance. But the distance across the heat waves and the press of the crowd was too great. If Rhom could just get to Conin—grab the girls and spirit them through the crowd . . . Aranur was inwardly tense, as though by willing it alone, he could force Rhom's action. Finally Zentsis raised his hands, and the stadium became silent.

"You have joined me today"—his voice rang clearly across the sands—"to see an exhibition of skills never before displayed in our county. Two sets of matches. Three fighters—a surprise match. And then, the match of an Ariye weapons master and his student.'' He paused. ''Who will be my champion against them?''

The answering roar of the crowd separated out into a name: ''Kiyun. Kiyun. Kiyun.''

Zentsis raised his hand again for silence. ''True, Kiyun has won many matches. But he will find these opponents very different. To demonstrate their skill, the surprise match will be fought three times, or until the mystery fighter is defeated. The first round will be against the three who won the lightweight amateur matches: Gustofor, Seckmory, and Kadalif.''

The crowed roared approval.

''If my three champions cannot defeat the mystery fighter, the second round will be against the two who won the lightweight prize matches: Junkan and Worsaw.''

Again, the people cheered.

''Should the mystery fighter win again, she will fight my own champion, Kiyun, for her freedom.''

The cheering died down into a strange silence as the crowd digested his words. A murmur rose, rocking back and forth. The sound seemed to beat at Aranur till it seemed as if the sand itself would rise up and deaden the roar. Zentsis raised his hands, and the sounds died.

''The fighter is a woman. As a spy from Ramaj Randonnen, she would simply have been put to death, but she has challenged the men of Ramaj Bilocctar. I accepted the challenge.''

The voices rose, half for, half against his announcement, but then the lust for the fight overcame the crowd, and they began roaring for the match.

Zentsis let his hands fall, and the sergeant gave the signal to move Dion out into the ring. Aranur pretended to trip, and as the whole group swayed to the side, he managed to grab the wolfwalker's arm. She turned with a snarl that went unheard in the din, but Aranur had already slipped the keys into her belt. Now it was up to her to unlock her chains. Her eyes widened in shock as she realized who he was, but she desperately wrenched the scornful pride back on her face and marched out onto the sands without a backward glance.

The guards left her there, dwarfed by the stands, slighted even by her midafternoon shadow in front of Zentsis's canopy.

''Moonsblessing, Healer,'' Kirnan whispered. ''Watch out for the rixti hold.''

"Moonsblessing," another said in a low voice, adding, "Kiyun likes to use spinning side kicks."

"Moonsblessing," the third repeated, embarrassed.

Aranur said nothing; there was nothing to say. The rest was up to her. He turned with the others and marched away.

The crowd fell silent again, recognizing the healer's band that circled Dion's brow. As the noise quieted, the slender woman raised her hands to speak to the Lloroi, the chains arcing down heavily between her arms.

"I have promised you a fight; you have promised me my freedom," she said defiantly into the quiet, her words ringing against the stones of the stadium. "Bring on your champions, Zentsis, for I champion the light of the moons and the call of the wolves."

A ragged cheer started up, but Zentsis only smiled and motioned to the gates of the ring. The three fighters jogged out, swords in their hands, waving at the cheering crowd. They surrounded the woman and moved in confidently. But Dion did not bring her hands together, or touch her belt. Why had she not unlocked the chains? Aranur clenched his fist. If she could disarm one of the men, take up his weapon, and make a break for the stands, Aranur would start a brawl and give her a chance to escape. But she took a fighting stance, holding herself ready to meet her opponents. When the three men surrounded her, she dodged out of the loose circle, keeping one of them between her and the others. They sparred, faking, stabbing, and cutting, till one of them lunged in. There was a flash of iron, and then he was down, moaning in the sands. Dion did a diving roll away from the other two and caught her breath. The crowd grew almost silent, then began to cheer—she had used the chains themselves as a weapon, and they loved it.

The fighters circled again. Dion whipped the chains in a circle, snaring another's feet as he moved too quickly to avoid the sling of the links. She rolled, pulling him down between herself and the other man.

Soldiers and prisoners alike crowded the entrance to watch the unprecedented fight, their shouts reverberating in Aranur's ears. "That's it, bring him down!" "Get in there, Kadalfi!" Yelling along with the others, he took a chance in the confusion to slip the second set of keys to Gamon. The old man held out his hand and palmed them silently, giving Aranur a sly look as he cheered, "Come on girl, take him out!"

Whipping a ring of metal in blinding speed, the wolfwalker

finally took both men down. She stood before the canopy, her chest rising and falling quickly with her breath, then turned and, instead of saluting Zentsis, saluted the crowd. The cheering rose into a thunder. Several men ran out from the gates to help the three losers out of the arena while Dion casually brushed the sand from her legs. The ring judge raised one of the three flags that scored the matches, and it was blue, for the healer.

The wolfwalker and the Lloroi exchanged a long look. Aranur could see that Zentsis had said something to Dion, but there was no way to know what it had been. Behind Zentsis, Shilia had jumped up, but when Conin spoke in her ear, she subsided and let him pull her down to sit again. Namina had not moved. And suddenly Aranur thought to wonder where Longear was. This was her day of triumph, so why was she not there in the stands with Zentsis?

But the Lloroi had barely waited the required two minutes between matches, and Aranur wrenched his attention back to the sands: the second round had begun.

Dion waited for the two new fighters to approach. Having witnessed the earlier match, these opponents were wary of the chains. They dove in at the same time, one from each side. But Dion leapt up, turned sideways in the air, and swung both sets of chains in a short arc. It was an unusual move that surprised them both; she dropped them in an instant, and it was over right then. The crowd was on its feet, the sands almost shaking with shouts as the ring judge raised the second flag, blue for the healer. Zentsis looked irritated. He held up his hands, and the crowd finally quieted. Aranur barely noticed that Gamon had taken advantage of the excitement to pass the keys to Tyrel. The old man stayed at the front of the group, keeping his loosened wrists and ankles out of sight.

Dion and Zentsis exchanged another set of remarks, which left the Lloroi red in the face. He was about to sit down, but then he whipped around and towered over Shilia, his arm raised to strike. Aranur looked around desperately for some way to reach his sister, but he was too far away. Only Rhom could stop the infuriated Lloroi now.

But Aranur was mistaken. It was Conin who stepped in front of his father and blocked the blow meant for the girl. And Namina, standing beside the young man, linked her arm in his and joined him in facing Zentsis. Aranur stared. No one else seemed to notice anything unusual, but Aranur watched in disbelief as Namina remained beside Zentsis's son, her hand formally touching his arm as if she were Promised to him. Even Shilia, while not quite copying Namina's stance, remained by the Lloroi's son. And unless it was a distortion of the heat waves, Rhom had the same stunned expression on his face that Aranur wore.

Aranur almost missed the beginning of the next match, he was so caught up by Namina's actions. But Dion was already saluting Kiyun, Zentsis's own man, and Aranur found his gaze riveted again to the fighting ring.

Kiyun was tall, broad across the shoulders, and narrow-hipped like Aranur. He stopped just out of reach of the wolf-walker, a spear in his hands, and Aranur, watching, narrowed his eyes. This match was going to be different, Aranur agonized. For if his walk and stance and wariness were any indication, this Kiyun was not inexperienced like the others.

In an instant, the two fighters were at each other, Dion dancing away from the other's spear, and Kiyun keeping just out of reach of her circling chains. Stabbing, twisting, slinging iron, they broke apart and came together until Dion managed to catch the spear in the middle and shatter it with the chain. Kiyun threw the pieces at her suddenly, and as she dove to the side he lunged, getting a hand on the chains around her feet. She seemed to fall, tumbling lightly, but just as the man was about to trap her against the sands, he suddenly flung himself back. The loosened chains from her hands swung out double and caught him on the chest. He staggered back, a splotch of red staining his tunic over the ribs. The crowd roared.

Dion leapt forward, one hand free, and the other holding the chain as a whip. She hesitated as her opponent took a defensive stance, unarmed against her iron whip, then she loosed the chain easily at him. He looked startled for an instant, then caught it quickly as Dion reached down and freed her feet. Now they were both armed with iron whips. The crowd went wild. This was the show she had promised Zentsis and he had promised the crowd. Dion, Aranur realized in agony, was giving away an advantage she could not afford to lose. Kiyun had more experience in the ring than she—and even with the speed of the wolf backing her, she could lose the fight.

The two circled, whipping the bright metal in flashing arcs above the sands, striving to catch each other off guard—one misstep, one mistake, one move too slow . . .

Dion was tiring. She stumbled in the sand, and Kiyun, thinking he had her, jumped in. But with a twist of her body that seemed impossible, she wrenched herself to the side of the metal lash and swept her own links across the sand toward his legs. He jumped to evade the swipe; as he came down again, he rolled in the air in a move that had no equal, and his own length of iron reached out and snared Dion's left leg as she tumbled away. It brought her up short, and he was on her in an instant. The chains were no good in such close quarters, and they grappled, Kiyun's sweat running freely down his muscles in the light. Dion's tunic tore across the sleeve, then at the shoulder as she wrenched away and caught a heavy blow on her arm. Aranur caught his breath. There was a commotion in the roaring crowd. The wolfwalker took another blow on her thigh and her leg crumpled to the sand, tumbling both of them to the ground. Kiyun struck again. Dazed, the wolfwalker barely rolled away, warding off the fist aimed at her neck and striking back at his gut. She caught his wrist and twisted, throwing him away from her. He rolled to his feet instantly, but Dion had only enough time to roll to her knees. Up in the stands, people were scrambling away from the edge of the arena.

Dion froze and looked toward the pavilion, and Kiyun took the chance to smash his forearm across her back and drive her back to the ground. She slammed down in the sand. He grabbed her arm and twisted it up, but she wrenched free, ducking and turning so that he was flung off her. Dion rolled up, lunging at the other fighter and striking at his throat. He missed the block. But, gagging, he grabbed her waist and slammed her at his feet, dropping down on her with his knees to pin her legs.

Suddenly a gray shape plummeted from the stone tiers into the ring. Dion saw the yellow haze cut across her sight, and her mind shouted *No!* as Kiyun looked up to see what could only mean his death.

The lean fighter lunged off the woman just as the wolf hit him. Dion scrambled to her feet, screaming something that was lost in the hysterical roar of the crowd. Zentsis was on his feet, Longear appeared out of nowhere beside him and was gesticulating wildly in his face. The wolfwalker dragged the wolf off the fighter, and Aranur could see the blood running from the man's arms where he had tried to stop the fangs from reaching his throat. The woman helped the fighter sit, and tore what was left of her own outer tunic to make a bandage for his arms. The wolf paced a snarling circle around them. The crowd was in a frenzy; Zentsis tried vainly to control the noise. As Dion helped

Kiyun to his feet, the two faced each other for a long minute, neither moving, the Gray One still snarling between them. Slowly Kiyun saluted Dion.

The ring judge took one glance at Zentsis and raised the blue banner for Dion, signifying a win. Zentsis's face was thunderous. The crowd exploded again, but quieted instantly when Dion raised her own hands in a bid for silence. Aranur, Gamon, and Tyrel waited with the rest of the people, holding their breath for her words.

"I promised you a fight; you promised me my freedom." Her voice rang out, though still breathless from the match. "I have upheld my part of the bargain—" She waited to continue until the cheering subsided. "Now uphold yours."

"You have not earned your freedom," Zentsis said angrily, his face still dark with rage. "You were losing until you had help from that—that cur." An angry murmur rose, and the crowd began to boo its Lloroi. Longear had disappeared, and behind the Lloroi, Rhom had moved toward Conin and was speaking in the young man's ears. Conin nodded swiftly and, with a glance at his father, motioned the two girls to accompany him out of the pavilion. Shilia shook her head and would have pulled back, but Namina said something that made her nod reluctantly. Aranur could not believe it. Namina—siding with the Lloroi's son? No, she was following Rhom's lead. It had to be an act. But it would get them away from the ring.

The Lloroi was shouting over the din, and the people roared in disapproval. Someone threw a fruit at him, and suddenly the stands erupted in an upheaval of bodies. Zentsis, seeing that he was losing control, shouted at his men.

"Guards!" His voice carried just barely over the noise. "Seize her! Take her back to the prison!"

That was what Aranur had been waiting for. He grabbed the two nearest soldiers and yelled, "Come on!" They burst out from the gates along with the guards from the other posts, and the crowds started throwing things their way, as well. Aranur dodged a large melon but was less lucky with a handful of stones that showered down from behind. Ignoring them, he kept going. Dion had taken a fighting stance, back to back with the wolf, as the guards raced out, though how she thought she would fight off twenty men at once was beyond Aranur's guess. Then three citizens jumped over the ring wall and attacked some of the guards. In an instant, the entire stadium was confusion. Dion and the wolf were running toward Aranur, Kiyun chasing them, but other soldiers were closer. "Halt!" "Stop and you won't be hurt!" some of them yelled. A soldier winked at Aranur as they joined the fray, and the tall man grinned before they split around some fighters. He worked his way toward the wolfwalker, and she almost took a swing at him before he grabbed her away from the two soldiers trying to catch her on the other side. Gamon and Tyrel were there, too: the boy had pulled a soldier's tunic over his own, and the older man was stooping by a fallen guard to do the same. Aranur risked a glance toward Zentsis, but Rhom was nowhere to be seen.

"Come on," he yelled over the melee, dragging Dion with him.

"Kiyun, this way," she screamed at the other fighter.

Aranur felt a sudden surge of fury and yanked Dion roughly around to the other side. "What are you doing? Leave him here. He'll turn us in to Zentsis in a hot second."

Kiyun jumped at Aranur from behind as the tough, lean man kept a hold of the wolfwalker.

"Kiyun, no! He's a friend," Dion shouted over the noise, twisting between the two.

Kiyun and Aranur faced each other for an instant, and then the guard who had known Aranur from before appeared at their side.

"Get out now, Aranur," he said quickly. "Try the second gate. They were light on detail this morning." He turned and punched a civilian trying to get at Dion, grinned, and ran after another one who was beating on a downed guard with a stick.

Aranur yanked the wolfwalker around again. They had no time to argue it out. He gave Kiyun a cold look that promised death if the man betrayed them. "Come on!"

They broke into a run, the two men forming a battering ram to open a way through the confusion for Dion to follow. Gamon and Tyrel managed to join them about halfway there, but the mess of people on the sands was getting worse, not better.

"Gamon, get some tunics, helmets," Aranur yelled, sending a guard staggering back. The soldier fell into Gamon's heavy fist and would have dropped like a stone except for the gnarled hands that practically tore his leather mail off. Gamon thrust it at Dion, who pulled it on over her own torn clothes, and Aranur did the same for Tyrel, then his uncle. The fighting ring had degenerated into a massive brawl.

"If we can make the gate," Aranur yelled at Kiyun, tripping

another overeager civilian, "we can march straight through to the outside."

Kiyun nodded, doubled a private over with a punch, and shoved him away. "If we're lucky," he shouted back.

The fighting seemed to press in more closely. Some soldiers mistakenly gave way to the small group and brawled as their vanguard when they saw the uniforms, but there was motion up ahead that looked like a platoon moving in.

"Trouble," Aranur shouted to Kiyun. "Take a hand up for a look see."

He made a pocket with his hands for the other man's foot, and Kiyun stood up on him for an instant. A double line of soldiers had formed on three sides of the stadium and was moving in, slowly swallowing the civilians and gaining more guards from the melee as it passed, until up ahead, close to the gate, it was three men deep. They could hear the shouts. Kiyun dropped lightly back to the sands and stooped for a moment to grab a warcap from someone's lolling head. He thrust it at Dion, and she stuffed her hair up inside quickly.

"Spread out, now!" Aranur yelled. "Act like a soldier and drop through to the back of the line!" Where was Rhom? Could he get the girls away from Conin? Or would he be caught with the Lloroi's son? Gods, but he wished he could see them . . .

But Dion and the others were diving in different directions at his last orders, fighting individually again. The wolf had disappeared. Aranur joined the line of soldiers and, pretending to be hurt, managed to end up in the last file of guards. Tyrel and Kiyun emerged close by. Kiyun, since he was most recognizable, supported Tyrel and Aranur as they staggered toward the gate and passed easily through the soldiers' cleanup crew.

"Can you see Gamon and Dion?" Aranur asked Kiyun in a low voice.

"Not yet," the other man replied, still pulling Tyrel along. "Wait, there they are. They're coming this way."

Dion was looking down to keep her face shadowed and avoid recognition. It was a good thing she had told the wolf to get out of there, Aranur thought with relief. The Gray One would have set them off from the real guards like a blue moon from the nine. The wolf must not have been in trouble though, because Dion did not look worried.

They entered the gate together, their eyes trying to adjust to the dark of the corridor after the daylight. But a sharp command rang out, and Aranur stiffened. The dim hall was filled with waiting soldiers.

"How wonderful to see you again, Gamon," a woman's voice sneered. "And how nice of you to come right into my hands." Longear stepped out from the wall of swords that was facing the small group. "Remain still," she ordered sharply.

Aranur glanced behind, but they were surrounded. He looked over Longear's shoulder, but there were too many men. They were trapped.

The small, dark-faced woman gave him a mocking glance. "No, you can't go that way. And you can't run this way. What will you do now, Aranur of the Ramaj Ariye? You could try to fight your way through my men, but they have orders to kill the woman and boy if you do."

His jaw tightened. "You have the advantage for the moment," he acknowledged, refusing to bow to her authority. Now he knew why the second gate had been light on detail—Longear had pulled her own men in to staff the guard. And what of Rhom? Did she know of him, too? If so, then Shilia and Namina were lost, as well. He forced himself to remain calm.

Longear rubbed her fingertips together in a strange, preening motion. "I have the advantage for the rest of what will be your very short life," she corrected. "You think you have been so careful, Aranur, so far out of my reach, and you have never been more than a half step ahead of me. I might not have the Lloroi's seat, but I control the very heart of Bilocctar. Look around you. These are my troops, not the Lloroi's. I plan for the future, Aranur, and I planned your steps from the moment you set foot outside Ariye." Aranur's jaw tensed, and Longear smiled pleasantly. "How galling this must be for you," she prodded. "And how humiliating."

Aranur seethed inwardly but forced himself to remain silent. Longear, seeing that she could not provoke him, turned to Kiyun, the fighter.

"And Kiyun," she said with mock disappointment, shaking her head. "We had such hopes for you. What happened?"

"Don't play your games with me, Longear," he said. "I'm not one of your pawns."

"You are a pawn as you've always been. As are most people, whether they know it or not." She turned impatiently to one of the troopers. "Is it cleared out there yet?

"Almost sir!" he acknowledged.

"Then take them back out. Watch these three carefully. Has that lieutenant shown up with Zentsis's brat Conin yet?"

"No, sir."

A lieutenant, Aranur thought with sudden hope. She must mean Rhom!

"What will Zentsis do when he finds out you've taken his son?" he asked as two of the guards grabbed his arms.

"He'll do what I tell him to." She smiled grimly. "Just as you will."

"But—you're planning to overthrow the Lloroi!" Dion exclaimed.

"Clever, clever little healer." Longear leaned forward. "I've worked all my life to get where I am now." Her voice was soft, but it held a note that drew chills down Dion's spine. Longear smiled at her expression. "Some gutter-brought child of the country is not going to steal my career. Nor will you help him do it. Take them back to Zentsis!" she commanded. "We'll settle this out there."

Chapter 19

The speaker can lead where the warrior falls;
The people are swayed if the orator calls.
But honor and strength will win you their hearts
When the speaking has faded and the fighting starts.

The guards shoved, and the prisoners were herded back into the stadium like errant children. Zentsis was still standing under his canopy, directing his soldiers from above the ring and sparing the prisoners hardly a glance until the area was nearly cleared and they arrived in the center before him. Then he demanded quiet.

"I am displeased." Zentsis spoke heavily into the restless quiet. "I have made a bargain and been cheated." He waited a moment for the booing to die down. "This is just another example of how treacherous the people from Ramaj Ariye are. This is just another example of their destructiveness." The crowd, puzzled, shifted from booing to listening.

"Whatever else," Aranur said to Dion in a low voice, "he is a good speaker. See how he turns the argument from the match to politics?"

A guard nudged them from behind. "Shut up."

"These are spies," Zentsis stated flatly, gesturing toward them. "Oh, they are good fighters." He paused as the crowd murmured agreement, a few people cheering. "But they are still spies. Do you want them in your county? In your city? In your home? What will happen to them if I let them go? They will stay and try to destroy our county, undermine our government, and convert our children to their evil ways." There was a murmur of agreement across the crowd. "I am not one to help evil grow in our own city. I am not one who will give the hearts of our children to strangers. I am—"

"A liar," Tyrel shouted, breaking in. "A cheat, and a coward! A beater of women and old men—" He struggled against the guards who tried to contain him. "And a defiler of healers—and wolfwalkers!" The boy threw off the gag for a moment and cried out, "You son of a worlag—even the moons will not look on you now!"

It was true: as the heat grew, the sky became overcast and dim, the clouds like a veil across the few moons that shimmered in the heated air.

"Tyrel!" Aranur's voice cracked like a whip above the uproar of the crowd. One of the guards tried to hit him as he struggled to help his young cousin, but Gamon shoved against the guard and took the blow instead. Gags were stuffed in their mouths, and the old man was left to lie on the sand like a corpse.

Zentsis gestured for the guards to drag the boy forward.

"So young to be a spy," he said with mocking sorrow when the crowd had quieted down. "Do you want your children to be as insolent and disrespectful as this? No? Then he will be the first to die." The crowed murmured, upset by Tyrel's youth and their Lloroi's blunt words, unsure of the sentence of death. "But I am not unreasonable," the heavy man continued. "He shall have a last request. Unbind him."

The boy tore the gag from his mouth as soon as his arms were free. "I will fight you to the death to avenge my sisters the shame you have given them!"

The people cheered his defiance, drowning his words again. Another fight would please them, too, Dion thought desperately, and Tyrel would be killed if Zentsis agreed. She needed Hishn, but she had sent the wolf away.

Gray One? she called. *Hishn!*

Here, Healer.

Where are you? Where is Rhom? She could sense the thoughts of the wolf close in on the urgency of her question.

We are coming, the Gray One sent back. *We have the one you need.* An image of Zentsis's son filled Dion's head for an instant, the smells of a corridor and perfumes of luxury contrasting strangely with the sweat and blood of the fighting sands.

"You are a fool," Zentsis was saying coldly to Tyrel. "I can crush you beneath me like a rast of the sewers." Boos and hisses greeted his words, and Zentsis glared at the people around him. "You would do better to ask for something more pleasant," he said to Tyrel.

"I will fight you, and if the moons bless me as much as they despise you, I will give you to them for judgment!" The boy's hotheaded anger fed his tongue, and the crowd loved it. Longear, climbing into the stands to get a better view of the ring, paused to hear the Lloroi's next words.

Zentsis finally raised his hands above the cheering. "So be it." He threw off his cape and removed his state tunic. Even with the grim prospect of the cancer that ate at his body, the Lloroi looked nearly as muscular and toned as he had in his prime. One of the guards drew off his own leather tunic and gave it to Zentsis. The crowed strained to see—this was better than the surprise match. The Lloroi did not fight in the rings anymore.

Zentsis leapt lightly down from the parapet and faced the boy in the sand. Next to the Lloroi, Tyrel's slight figure looked like a child's shadow.

"Moons have mercy on his soul!" Dion whispered in the silence.

It was a pitiful fight. Zentsis toyed with the boy, breaking him slowly, and the crowd, at first enthusiastic, grew silent as he ruthlessly destroyed the youth before their eyes. Dion began to shake with a fury that warred in her with her grief as she watched Tyrel vainly attack again and again till he could hardly move for the beating he received. Only the breathing and blows of the two fighters broke the silence in the ring.

Zentsis finally took the boy by the hair and held him up, slapping him with his other hand till the blood flowed freely from the boy's nose and mouth, drops flying down to stain the sand.

"Stop it!" Dion screamed, unable to stand it any longer. "Leave him alone! For god's sakes, he's just a boy!"

Two of the guards grabbed her, one of them slamming his hand across her mouth while the other one twisted her elbows up behind her until she writhed in pain. In the stands, Longear, having taken a seat near the pavilion, smiled viciously.

Zentsis turned his head and looked at her, his eyes red with the blood lust of killing, then dropped the boy's limp form in the sand. "And you—" He stood before her like the black specter of death. The guard took his hand from Dion's mouth. "What is *your* last request?"

The silence echoed his words, and the crowd started murmuring, uneasy. She was a healer, a wolfwalker. What right did even a Lloroi have to touch her?

"I have no request to make of a moon-spurned rast like you," Dion said angrily, her voice shaking. "I would rather face a hundred deaths than deal once more with a rat like you."

Zentsis's face was dark with suppressed anger. "I am sure just one death will suffice," he said. "And as you feel I cheated you in our previous bargain, we will review the deal. But this time, I will supply the other half of it, and you will belong to me for a time when I am done with you here. Release her," he commanded.

She looked at him for a long moment. Zentsis, the master fighter. The Lloroi, with twenty-five years of experience in battle. And Dion, with her left leg, which had taken Kiyun's blow, barely taking her weight. Her shoulder felt as if it was partially dislocated again, and her elbows were numbed from the grips of the guards. She did not have a chance in all nine hells, and he knew it and she knew it and even the crowd knew it.

Defy him. Hishn's thoughts pressed in on her own, giving the woman direction for her fear. *Get him to fight Leader.*

The wolf's image of Aranur was unmistakable. The guards were stepping away from her, and Zentsis was already advancing.

"You show your people how well you beat women and boys," Dion said angrily, standing her ground. "Are you afraid to fight a man?"

Zentsis merely looked down at her, his eyes still bloody with anger.

She pulled herself together. "Tyrel was right," she taunted him loudly. "You are a coward." Someone cheered her words, and she gained confidence till Zentsis stepped menacingly forward again. She took an involuntary step back.

"You will die for that," he said. "Slowly, but you will die."

"I may die, but I'll die knowing I *earned* my place with the moons." There was more cheering, and a chant started growing with the tension on the sands. "That's more than you can say, false fighter. A coward who is afraid to fight men because he can only win against women and boys."

The chanting grew more fierce in the stands: "*Wolf*-walker . . . *Wolf*walker." Dion caught sight of Longear examining the faces of those who led the chants, and then saw Rhom and Conin pushing their way through the crowd and back to the canopy where they had sat earlier. The girls were not with them—but there was no time to think of that.

"What will your son think of you after this, Zentsis?" She felt like a fish in a shrinking tide pool with a watercat on the bank. "How will he believe in you after you've defiled a healer and destroyed the only wolfwalker the people have seen in generations? Is it not just your body, but your mind going with age? See how he looks at you even now." She pointed to the stands while the chant punctuated her words: "*Wolf*walker . . . *Wolf*walker."

"Enough!" Zentsis was furious. "The first thing I'll take from you will be your tongue." He was slowly backing the slender woman out into the center of the sands, the guards giving way behind her but holding their loose circle to prevent her from running.

"But that does not stop the truth, does it Zentsis? Even a lepa has more honor than you. There is a man to fight you, but you spend your time beating women and boys." *Wolf*walker . . . *Wolf*walker. "You dishonor yourself even in front of your own son."

"Guards, seize her!" he roared. They hesitated, and Zentsis's face turned purple, but then the soldiers broke free of their shock and grabbed her. She did not struggle. The Lloroi took two quick steps and slapped her across her face. His hand was a sledgehammer. The world went black, then cleared into patches, while the chanting died out in the stands.

The woman dragged her feet back under her painfully. "Oh, false fighter," she managed. "You cannot even beat me by yourself. What would you do against a man like Aranur?"

He froze, his breath like a furnace on her face, and his eyes insane with rage. Dion knew she had pushed the luck of the moons too far.

But Zentsis gestured to the guards. "Hold her so," he snarled, "and release *him.*" He pointed to Aranur.

Up in the stands, Rhom was standing closely behind Zentsis's son, speaking into the young man's ear. Dion could see the wolf at their heels. The tension in her own mind snared that of the wolf's, and she sensed, more than saw, Hishn snarling in eagerness to push past the men.

Longear, realizing suddenly that Conin was back in the stands instead of in the prison cell she had prepared for him, took a step toward the pavilion, then stopped. She was obviously furious. Her eyes darted from one side to the other, judging those around her as if to decide whether to try for the Lloroi's seat now or to escape from the wrath she knew would fall if Zentsis survived. And Dion, seeing the look on Longear's face, wondered if Shilia and Namina were safe after all.

In the fighting sands, Zentsis jerked the swords savagely off two of his soldiers and threw one of the blades to Aranur, who brushed off the guards' hands and grimly faced the Lloroi. Without speaking, the two men circled each other. Dion could see Hishn, lunging through the crowd to the edge of the parapet. Hands reached out to touch the wolf as she passed, but no one dared put a limb in the way to stop the Gray One. Hishn jumped from the stone wall down to the group in the ring. As she approached the wolfwalker, the soldiers hesitated, then dropped back from Dion, still guarding but keeping their distance from the Gray One's fangs. And in front of the healer, Aranur and Zentsis circled, feinting their attacks and testing each other. Dion prayed that Aranur had the moons in the metal of his sword, because the Lloroi was one of the best fighters she had ever seen.

The two men clashed, and people stood on their seats to see. "What's the matter, Lloroi?" Aranur growled in a low voice. "Lose your nerve?" He forced a taunting laugh. "That's what you get for practicing only against the women and boys."

Zentsis pulled his lips back from his teeth in a snarl. "I am more than a master fighter. I have never been beaten, rat of a spy. It'll take more than you've got to get close to that with me." Their swords flashed in the light, and the sweat began to run on their faces.

"Perhaps if I practiced more against helpless women, I could come down to your standards," Aranur taunted. Infuriated, the Lloroi lunged quickly in. Aranur turned the attack, dancing away to the side, but a thin line of blood trailed down his arm. Dion's hands were suddenly clenched in Hishn's fur, and the wolf snarled.

"I have first blood," the Lloroi cackled. "I will have last blood, too."

Sand churned as they reached for each other with death in

each blow. Blood laced them both and their breathing was harsh when Aranur suddenly disarmed the Lloroi, sending his sword flying into the sand. Aranur froze with the point of his blade ready to lunge at the other man's heart. The fury of the crowd died instantly, and the tableau held for a long silent moment. Then the Lloroi said something, and Aranur, his jaw tight, threw away his own blade and stepped back. The crowd roared.

Zentsis lunged in instantly, grappling for the other man's throat, but Aranur broke away. He was slowly overpowering the burly Lloroi, dancing away, wearing him down, taunting him to overextend himself. Aranur's own moves were so subtle and practiced that he seemed never to be off balance or out of step in the duel. Zentsis began to look desperate. They fought back and forth, the guards swaying with their movements and the crowd filling the stadium with noise that would drown out a million stampeding dnu.

Dion slipped over to Gamon, who was still lying unconscious. No one stopped her; Hishn's fangs got quick permission from the nervous guards. Reassured that the old man was not hurt badly, she moved to Tyrel. The boy's face was smeared with blood. The swelling of his left shoulder indicated that his collarbone might be broken, as well. And with hemorrhaging on top of the surface loss of blood and the shock that was setting in, Dion was not sure he would make it through the next hour. She sat back on her heels. The sound of the stadium and clash of the fighters faded into a dull roar behind her. Even if Aranur won, she would be healing Tyrel only so that he would face a second death at Longear's hands, she thought in despair.

Death comes when it will. Gray Hishn prodded her with a cool nose. *I will take you in,* she ordered. *We must be quick. Now is not the time for cautious work. The prey*—she shot an image of Zentsis as half man, half worlag— *is cornered and vicious.*

Sensing someone beside her, Dion looked up to see Kiyun kneeling down.

"He's too far gone, Healer," the man said gently. "Zentsis opened his path to the moons."

The wolfwalker set her face and did not answer. Instead, she held her hands out over Tyrel's face and let Hishn take her in. The spin to the left, the drop, and she was in. But gods—the damage. All she could do was relieve the swelling and pressure on the boy's brain and quickly patch his kidneys and spleen before Hishn yanked her out again.

How much time had passed? She swayed, drained, and Kiyun, looking at her with puzzlement, was almost afraid to help her up. Nothing had changed in the ring except that the fighters were moving more slowly in their violent dance, standing each other off with nearly matched skill, their harsh breathing filling the others' ears. Dion was too keyed up with tension and fear to pay attention to the familiar exhaustion that sapped her after Ovousibas.

"What now, Zentsis?" Aranur jeered the Lloroi, ducking a blow and returning it twofold. "You cannot kill me, or even beat me. Even your own people cheer, not for you, but for me."

Zentsis threw him off, twisted, and snatched a knife from a startled guard's belt. "Now we'll see who will win," he snarled.

They crashed together, Aranur's lithe form twisting from the blade as he tried to throw the bigger man over his shoulder. Sand gritted in their clothes and scuffled around their straining bodies as they fell, rolling back and forth to gain control of the knife. Dion's heart stopped for an instant as Zentsis plunged the blade toward Aranur's neck, but Aranur caught the knife with his bare hands against the flat part of the steel, holding Zentsis above him like a guillotine blade about to fall. Zentsis tried to turn the knife and slice through Aranur's fingers, but the younger man, his hands cut and bleeding freely, forced the blade to the side and thrust it into the sand. As momentum carried Zentsis toward him, Aranur flipped the bigger man across the ring and landed on top of him. The knife was still between them, but Aranur was holding it now.

"Guards!" the Lloroi shrieked. The guards began to move in but stopped when Aranur moved the blade menacingly.

"Calling for help because you're down?" Aranur snarled. Sweat dripped from his face, and his muscled arms gleamed where Zentsis's sword had sliced open his tunic. Blood from his own cut hands dripped steadily onto the Lloroi's chest. "Can't even finish a fight by yourself, can you?"

"I will have you thrown into the pits where your flesh will be eaten alive by the rats of your kind." Zentsis's voice was breathless, ragged, but he had enough left to cry again, "Guards!"

"They can come as close as they like," Aranur said, forcing the blade to poke up under the Lloroi's sternum, "but the closer they come to me, the closer this blade comes to you. When they touch me, this knife will be digging into your heart."

The soldiers stopped uncertainly.

"Guards, take him!"

"What will your son think now, his father a coward not just before his own eyes, but before all the people of Bilocctar?" Aranur's harsh whisper reached the ears of the Lloroi, the guards, and even the people watching in silence from the stands. "Will you cheat one more time before you die?"

Zentsis's eyes were desperate, but at Aranur's words a spark of pride seemed to be rekindled in his face.

"You're losing your hold on your city, the strength in your body, and now you lose even your honor," Aranur said deliberately. "You can show your double-tongued dealings to the world now, and die a miserable death later, despised by moons and men, or—" he paused and held the knife touching the man's chest. "—you can release your city to your son and be a hero now."

Zentsis looked startled at the thought.

"The rumors have you dying already," Aranur whispered persuasively. "And the people will accept your son in your place. Look, Zentsis. Look at him in the stands."

Zentsis turned his head cautiously, slowly, and saw his son on the parapet. Conin was leaning anxiously on the rim of the fighting ring, Rhom's hand on his shoulder, and his strong young face blanched as if the knife were already in his father's heart.

"He will be a leader such as Bilocctar has never seen," Aranur repeated. "You can declare him in your stead, now, or—" he paused. "—die a worlag's death here."

The knife pressed in, and Zentsis sucked in his breath. The guards made ready to lunge.

"It is your last choice, Zentsis."

The Lloroi's mouth opened to command his men one last time.

"Your death is facing you. The moons are reaching down even now."

Zentsis let his breath out and drew it in again raggedly.

"How well can your son rule without your blessing? You must declare him before another takes your place by force. Your son, Zentsis." Aranur dropped his voice. "Your only son will lead your people if it is your choice."

"Guards—" Zentsis hesitated again. He looked suddenly old. He took a deep breath. "Stand back."

A murmur rose in the stands, to be silenced instantly as Zentsis spoke again, his words reaching to the last rows of seats in the stadium.

"I am—" he cleared his throat. "—old to lead you." His eyes never left the knife. "Too old to keep the council. I— have been beaten, and—" The words poured out in a rush. "—it is time for me to make way for my son."

The people shifted in their seats, rumbling their uncertainty.

"Conin, my son." Zentsis's voice gained strength, though Aranur's blade never left his chest. "You are Lloroi!"

He suddenly released his resistance and pulled the knife into his own chest. Aranur, unprepared, tried to yank the blade out, but it had locked into the flesh. He could only hold Zentsis's convulsing body as the old man's death throes shocked the stadium. The soldiers lunged in.

"Stop!" Conin's voice rang out. "Halt!"

The guards froze. Conin raised his arms and demanded silence from the thousands who packed the stands.

"I am Lloroi," he declared boldly as the echoes died.

"I am Lloroi," he repeated. "I am your leader." He looked down at the tableau, Aranur holding his father's body, the soldiers frozen to strike him down the moment they were released. "My father—" He hesitated, then gained momentum. "My father has led you for many years, some good, some bad, and it is . . . it is time he reached for judgment."

The people murmured a halfhearted agreement. Conin started to speak again, Rhom stepped back.

"I am new here, but this is my city now. Let me make this my home as my father did."

Someone cheered, and more people joined in till the sound swelled to fill the arena. Conin asked for quiet.

"I am Lloroi," he repeated again. "Let—let the people eat at my feast—" He paused, trying to judge their response. "—for today is a day of celebration."

The crowd cheered approval.

"I am Lloroi! Let the prisoners be freed from the prisons—"

The noise threatened to drown out his words. "—for today is a day of amnesty!

"I am Lloroi!" he shouted. "Let the fighters have their well-won freedom, for today is a day of victory."

He flung up his arms. "Rejoice! For I am Lloroi!"

Chapter 20

Fly, birds, fly,
Before the lepa hunts;
Before its ears can hear your speech;
Before its eyes can see your nests;
Before its mouth can taste your flesh
And take away your children.

Fly, birds, fly,
Before the lepa strikes;
Before its wings of fear stretch down;
Before its claws of death reach down;
Before its fangs of death can find
And take away your young.

Fly, birds, fly,
Before the lepa calls;
Before the last night's hunt is done;
Before the dark breaks into morn;
Before the sky must cry your young
And lead them to the moons.

For hours, the city was still in an uproar. Rumors were flying. Longear had disappeared. So far, there was only slight resistance to the new and unexpected rule of Zentsis's son, although eight council members were thrown under guard and three more killed when they tried to take over some of the Lloroi's inner rooms by force.

Aranur and his group were led, heavily guarded, to quarters where they waited for Conin to receive them. Dion had to force Hishn inside, and once there, the gray creature paced and snarled as if she were trapped in a cage. Dion shushed her three times, and still the wolf could not sit still.

It smells of a trap, Hishn growled.

Dion shook her head. *We have little choice right now, Gray One. We must wait for Rhom.*

The wolf bared her teeth, and Gamon, who was standing nearby, took a step back.

But Hishn was right: this place was just another prison, and Dion was worried. Her brother was still with the dead Lloroi's son, and she did not see how Conin could not know by now who Rhom was. She could only hope that, since her brother had been one of the few men protecting Conin from Longear during those first moments, the new Lloroi would not have her brother imprisoned, as well. And what about Shilia and Namina? Hishn snarled, echoing her worry, and Dion clamped down on her emotions. She was sending too much to the wolf, and Hishn might snap even at Aranur if Dion was not careful.

But even with the link to Hishn damped down, the wolf-walker's thoughts did not stop. Did Conin know how powerful Longear was? Even Dion had sensed the ambition in the woman. She glanced at Aranur, and the look on his face told her that he was concerned about the same things.

She looked at Tyrel then, and her expression grew grim. Zentsis had all but killed the boy, and Dion could do nothing but pray. She was still shaking from the exhaustion of doing Ovousibas in the fighting ring. Hishn, who had pushed her into the internal healing before, glared at her when she asked for help again, and refused to take her in. So Dion was left with nothing to do but pace the room with the others and wait. Finally her thoughts began to run in circles, and, frustrated, she sat down, pulled her knees up, and hid her face in her arms. Seeing that, Hishn slunk over and lay down, her head on Dion's feet.

Aranur watched Dion silently. Her eyes had been worried when he asked about Tyrel, and as he saw her give in to her exhaustion, he hesitated to interrupt. But there were things he had to know. Longear wielded more power than any elder on Zentsis's council. What if Longear was behind more of Zentsis's plans than they had at first believed? What if Longear, and not Zentsis, was their true opponent in this game? If so, he realized soberly, then Zentsis's death meant nothing to them except more trouble. As it was, Conin would hardly be inclined to give amnesty to the people who killed his father. Aranur narrowed his eyes and picked absently at the bandages that wrapped his cut hands. Finally he strode over and touched the healer's shoulder.

"Dion," he said softly as she looked up. "Did you see where Longear went after the fight? What happened to her?"

Dion, her face tight with her weariness, frowned. "What does Longear have to do with us now?" she asked. "Conin gave us our freedom. Longear cannot rescind that. From here on out, she will be his problem, not ours."

Aranur shook his head. "Longear disappeared when Zentsis died. Conin may be Lloroi now, but we don't know how long he keeps his promises. And Longear has enough power that she might have more to say about our imprisonment than we realize."

"You worry too much, Aranur," she protested.

But Gamon shook his head. "For once, Healer Dione," he said, "Aranur is right to worry. Zentsis might have been Lloroi, but Longear is the one who commanded the movements of his troops. She is the one who set the traps and paid the raiders and pushed the pieces in this game."

Aranur agreed. "We've got to find out if Rhom and the girls can move freely. Convince Conin to let us go now—if we can—and get out of town."

"That might not be so easy," Dion said. "Conin thinks he owns Shilia and Namina."

Gamon, who winced and rubbed his head where a lump was swelling rapidly, nodded. "He might not want to let them go. Then, too, if Longear gets to him first, he might want to follow more closely in his father's footsteps than any of us would want."

"And if Longear doesn't trust her hold on Conin," Aranur added flatly, "she might try to kill him rather than use him as a figurehead."

Dion shivered. Hishn looked up and put a paw on the healer's leg, but Dion shrugged the paw off and gripped the gray fur, glancing at Gamon. "Then it would be during this feasting that Longear would move."

"Let everyone relax a little," Gamon agreed. "Get used to the idea of an impressionable and inexperienced young man for Lloroi. Then, while they're mulling it over, bang, Longear steps in, takes over the council, and holds Conin hostage."

Aranur paced slowly. "He would be the figurehead she needs to keep holding the power."

Wolfwalker—

Dion hissed, and Aranur broke off. She rose quickly to her feet. Hishn, leaping up, placed herself between the wolfwalker and the door. Dion nodded at the opening. Aranur and Gamon waited on the balls of their feet.

But when the door swung open, it was Conin who entered, along with Rhom, Shilia, Namina, and the fighter called Kiyun.

Rhom . . . Dion held her breath, but her relief was as palpable as Aranur's when he saw the girls.

Conin's eyes went first to Dion as he caught her glance at Rhom. He nodded. "I know who he is, Healer," the young Lloroi said flatly.

She needed no more urging. Hishn took a step forward, but Dion had already darted to Rhom's side, throwing her arms around his neck. The wolf panted but did not lose the expression of wariness in her yellow eyes.

The Lloroi motioned for all but two of his soldiers to stay outside.

"You trust us greatly, Lloroi," Dion commented quietly.

"I trust you because your fate lies in my hands, Wolfwalker." Conin's face was grim. "Don't make the mistake of claiming friendship because your acts have made me Lloroi. I don't forget who killed my father."

Aranur met his eyes. "I had little choice, Lloroi," he answered heavily. "I know you have no love for me, and I know what the loss means to you—"

"Do you?" The young man strode angrily to the window and looked out. "I grew up without a father. Four months ago, I found out I had one, and that he was the most powerful man in Bilocctar. Now he is dead, and I am without again, though I stand in his bloody footsteps."

"I, too, lost my father," Aranur said softly. "And I lost my mother, as well. Both to the raiders." He hesitated. "I loved my parents dearly, Lloroi," he said, deliberately using the man's new title and meeting Conin's face steadily when the younger man turned angrily at its use. "When they died, it was as if the world had become a black place, a chasm where I cared for nothing and nothing cared for me."

Conin looked at him sharply, and Dion looked at Aranur in surprise. He had told her once how he had felt at the death of his parents, but she had never heard him admit those things to any other person.

"It was years before I could hear their names without the grief engulfing me." Aranur spread his hands. "Now, I've made a place for myself. I love my parents still; their memories have never faded. But I have my own life, too."

"So, you understand," Conin stated in bitter acknowledgment.

Aranur nodded. "It took me many years to admit it, but the passage of the moons will dim the grief eventually and lighten the memories you have."

Conin snorted. "And in the meantime, who guides me? Who counsels me? Who can I trust?"

Aranur spread his hands with ironic humor that the son of the man whose blood was on his hands was asking his advice. Conin knew as little of this place as the man from Ariye did. "You must have friends."

"Not in this city," the Lloroi returned sharply. "The politics are so twisted I can't tell who is a friend for friendship's sake and who just wants to step on the hoe of my grave."

Dion glanced at Aranur, then spoke quietly. "There are two men, one Kirnan and one Heerdon, who support your values among the guards today." Aranur had told her of the man named Kirnan, and as Aranur did not stop her, she continued. "Appoint them and ask their advice on other men and women. You might not get the most experienced people, but they will be indebted to you and will work hard to please you. You'll learn soon enough who you can trust."

Conin stared at her. "Why should I take your suggestions?"

Aranur's face tightened, but Dion said, "Why should you not?" She met Conin's gaze steadily. "They are good men. You have my word as a wolfwalker and healer that I speak the truth. If you are as honorable as I think you are, then you will win their loyalty quickly."

"I am Lloroi. Their loyalty is already mine."

Dion's face became still, and she gripped Hishn hard as the wolf growled. Aranur felt his anger flare.

The young Lloroi turned from the window and stared grimly at them for a long moment, then addressed Aranur. "Longear has disappeared."

The tall, lean man controlled his anger. "She has power," he returned steadily. "And ambition."

"You are saying I shouldn't trust her?"

"Are you asking my advice now? She will not give up so easily what she almost had in her hands. Did you agree with her views when you talked with her before?"

"No," the other man answered slowly, his eyes troubled.

"Then choose someone else for the position."

Conin looked a little surprised. "I can, can't I?" He paused, then asked awkwardly, "How is the boy?"

They both looked at Dion. "He might live," she said bleakly. "The next few hours will tell."

"I brought your sisters," Conin said abruptly. He gestured at Namina and Shilia, still guarded at the room's entrance. "I have not touched them," he reassured Aranur. "They can go with you or stay with me."

In spite of himself, Aranur admired the young Lloroi's courage. If the common people learned of Conin's humble gesture to strangers and enemies of their county, he would lose face in the city.

Conin spread his hands. "If they stay, they will have an honorable place in my home."

"We thank you for the honor, Lloroi," Rhom said, "but Shilia is already Promised." Shilia looked at him over Conin's shoulder and blushed, smiling.

"And Namina—" Aranur began.

"Is staying." Namina's flat voice startled them, but Conin's face relaxed at her words.

The young Lloroi offered his arm to the girl, and she touched it formally. "Honor is satisfied," Conin said with a curt nod.

Aranur stared blankly at the girl. He must have misunderstood—or Namina must have been forced into it. There was no other explanation.

Dion touched the girl's arm. "This is what you want?" she asked quietly.

Conin's face showed irritation, but the girl nodded. "It is."

Gamon closed his mouth with a snap and strode across the room. Conin instantly stiffened, and the two soldiers in the room took their swords from their sheaths. Gamon ignored them. "Namina, what in the name of the nine moons are you thinking of?" he began heatedly. "What about your brother? Your father?"

Conin stepped in front of the old man. "Gamon, you are now my uncle, as well; but you are still in my city."

Gamon was suddenly still. His gray eyes flicked from Conin's face to his niece's. "I see," he said quietly. He stepped back.

And Dion, who found her hands twisted in Hishn's fur in tension, realized why they had not been thrown back in prison. Why Hishn had been allowed to stay with her. Why Rhom had not been harmed.

Namina had Promised to Conin neZentsis. The girl had given them their lives—and their freedom.

Behind Conin, Namina blanched at Gamon's words but met his eyes. "Tell my father what you like," she said flatly. "I will not go with you now. I am Promised."

Dion nodded slowly. Namina was seventeen. She was old enough to choose. And if Namina was doing this for them as well as for herself, what right did Dion have to belittle the girl's courage now that Namina had found it? "May the moons forever bless your union with their light," she whispered.

The girl nodded and fumbled blindly for the door; one of the guards finally opened it for her.

"Namina," Shilia called softly, halting the fleeing figure in the doorway. "Nine moons blessing on you here."

"Thank you," Namina whispered, and was gone.

Conin spread his hands. "I will treat her well," he assured them. "You need have no worry about her comfort. I . . ." He hesitated. "I have no sister to give you in her place—Zentsis did not acknowledge the girls born of his mistresses—but I have returned to you your own sister Shilia."

"Honor is satisfied," Aranur acknowledged formally, his voice bleak. "A wronged Lloroi's daughter for a wronged Lloroi's son."

A bare smile almost reached Conin's eyes at the other man's words.

"We have safe passage to the border?" Aranur asked.

"Safe passage, mounts, what supplies you need. You can choose your dnu from the Llor—from my own stables. I want you away from here, away from me by morning." The sounds of revelry could be heard from outside as more people joined the feasting below.

Aranur nodded. "The less seen of us, the safer your position will be."

Conin turned to leave, then remembered the fighter waiting patiently behind him. He turned back. "Kiyun has asked to travel with you, Aranur. He wishes to train in your fighting style and has, shall we say, fallen out of favor with Bilocctar after his actions in the ring. It would be a small payment in your debt to me."

Aranur frowned at Dion, then gave Kiyun a hard glance.

"*I* have no objection," Gamon said, as Aranur hesitated. "He's a good fighter, and the raiders are still roaming in large groups."

Kiyun nodded his thanks. Conin nodded and left, the guards stalking out behind him.

"I've always wanted to visit Ramaj Ariye and train under your weapons master," Kiyun said in the awkward pause that followed. "Even here, we talk of Gamon Aikekkraya neBentar and his teachings." He looked at Tyrel still unconscious on the bed. "The boy is only fifteen? And yet he proved himself twice over just by facing Zentsis. And you, Aranur—I would not have believed it possible to beat the Lloroi had I not seen it with my own eyes. You knew he was an eighth in laki, a master in our own fighting system?"

"I knew."

"He was a master in almost all weapons and open-hand arts, yet you bested him three times, with and without weapons. If I didn't know that Gamon"—he nodded in deference to the older man—"was your weapons master, I would have asked to study under you."

Aranur said nothing, judging the fighter silently while Gamon's eyes twinkled.

Kiyun cleared his throat. "I have little gear. I can leave as soon as you're ready."

"We'll go in the morning—at least as far as the city limits," Aranur said curtly. "When Tyrel can travel, we'll leave the county. Dion?" Looking at her, he raised his eyebrows.

She shook her head. "Not for at least two days. Maybe more."

Kiyun shrugged. "I am to stay with you till you go, and the guards will send food up for all of us. The adjoining rooms are for us, as well."

Aranur turned away, to stand at the balcony and stare at the crowds below. Kiyun paused, then spoke to Dion in a low voice. "Healer, I hope there's no hard feelings about earlier. I had little choice either."

She smiled briefly. "I'm glad you're with us now, and not against us."

But he hesitated again. "That—thing you did in the ring," he said uncertainly. "With the boy—what was that?"

At Kiyun's words, Aranur looked around, and Dion asked him with her eyes for permission to speak. He stared at her for a moment, then shrugged bleakly and turned back to the balcony. Hishn bared her teeth. Dion glanced at the Gray One.

"It's a form of healing," she said finally. "I learned it in the mountains."

The fighter frowned. "But you did not touch the boy."

"I touched him internally," she corrected. "It is just not

something you have probably seen before," she added simply.

Her twin chuckled humorlessly, and Kiyun regarded him with a thoughtful expression. Rhom raised his eyebrow. "You'll see her do it again if you stay with us, Kiyun." He gathered his gear. "If it's all right with the rest of you, I'm going to turn in. After"—he looked at Aranur's sister—"Shilia and I do a little talking."

Shilia nodded, flushing at Rhom's look. "I'll help you look after Tyrel in a bit, Dion."

Dion shook her head. "There's nothing you could do besides worry, Shilia. And I'm doing enough of that for both of us."

Gamon tactfully excused himself to the next room, and Kiyun followed. Aranur, his expression unreadable, turned from the balcony and passed Dion without a word. Rhom glanced after him, then smiled at Shilia and moved with her to the balustrade Aranur had just left. The two did not return until the cool night air drove them in. When Shilia finally left to go to her own bed, Rhom remained with Dion.

He dropped to the floor beside her, leaning back against the sofa and scratching Hishn on the ears. He glanced at his sister's face. "Life seems to have taken a turn for the better," he commented.

"For most of us," Dion said, glancing at the still form of the boy on the bed. She passed her hands wearily over her eyes.

"What do you think of Shilia?" he said finally.

She managed to smile. "I think you'll be very happy together." She did not want to think about the Waiting Year she would have to spend with Aranur, taking Shilia's place in his family while Shilia got to know Dion's father. Rhom had always teased her that she would get Promised first, and that he would get a new sister or brother to break in. But now it looked as if it would be Dion who went to live with a new family.

"Dion, Shilia wants to come back home with me immediately to meet our father." He hesitated, and Dion looked down at her feet. "I don't want to leave you alone in a strange county, especially with Aranur, and especially since I know you want to come home, too, but," he said, squeezing his sister's arm, "you know Aranur and half his family already, and as soon as Shilia meets our father, you can come home again, at least for a while."

Dion squinted as her eyes threatened to water. Rhom's year

of joy would be her year of exile. Tradition, she thought bitterly.

Wolfwalker? Hishn sounded worried as she nudged Dion's feet.

Gray One, Dion sent back, gripping the scruff of the beast. *We will not be going home for a while.*

Hishn gazed up, her yellow eyes troubled. *The pack is your home.*

Dion stroked the gray fur. *The pack will be with us in Ariye, but not my other family, Hishn.*

Ariye. Tradition demanded that she take Shilia's place in the other girl's household for the Waiting Year. If Rhom had had no sister, he could have paid Year's Price in place of Dion's staying with Aranur. But they were twins, and she had no choice in this without dishonoring both families.

Rhom looked at her closely. "Dion, you can't say you don't like Aranur."

"We do nothing but fight when we talk," she returned in a low voice.

He regarded her with irritation. "So maybe you should talk less and kiss more," he retorted. He laughed at the look on her face.

"It isn't just me," she protested.

"I know," Rhom said slyly, deliberately misinterpreting her. "And if I'm any judge of the looks a man gives a woman, Aranur would rather you talk less, too. With Kiyun here, Aranur will have to decide how he feels pretty quickly—don't think I didn't see the way that fighter looked at you tonight." He grinned. "Aranur didn't miss it either."

"Don't tease me, Rhom."

"I'm not. I wanted to wait till we were home again to tell you about Shilia and me, but . . ." His voice trailed off.

"But I really knew about it anyway."

"You love him, don't you, Dion?"

"It shows so much?"

"I'm your twin, remember?" He looked thoughtful.

"Rhom, don't go getting any ideas," Dion started.

"Don't worry," he said, getting to his feet. "I'll be discreet."

"About as tactful as a worlag at a dinner party."

"But much more effective. I'll see you tomorrow. I've got girls on the brain."

"Well, that's nothing new," she retorted. "Just make sure Shilia doesn't find out about them."

He made a face, then left.

For a long time, Dion listened to the sounds of the feasting and let her thoughts curl about themselves. Finally, she leaned against the wolf and dozed into restless dreams.

In the darkness, she was in the prison again, but this time Hishn was with her, and the barred door of her cell was open. They tried to run out, but as they came close, Longear appeared from the shadows and laughed and pulled them out from the cell into the hall. But the hall was just another cell with another open door and another Longear beyond it. They turned and ran the other way, but Longear appeared again, pulling them through the next barred door into yet another prison cell until the dream blurred and all they saw was darkness with streaks of iron.

A small sound woke her, some sense of danger made greater by Hishn's sudden awareness. Dion lay still, calming her ragged breathing as she reached out to the wolf. *What is it? Who is there?* she asked.

The door. The Gray One rose silently to her feet. *There is danger.*

Dion sat up. She groped for her sword and realized it was across the room. Idiot, she snapped at herself. She had only her knife in its sheath, and already the door was inching open. She pulled the short blade free, keeping it down behind her leg where it would not be given away by a glint of light. *Can you call Rhom?* she asked in her mind.

Hishn growled low in her throat. *His mind is not open to me,* she sent. *His feelings are—*

A match flared. Hishn's thoughts broke off as Dion saw the oil lantern in the soldier's hand. *Wha*—Dion did not complete the thought before the dark man threw the lamp across the room. She screamed as the oil cast liquid flame across the carpet.

"Aranur! Rhom! Fire!" She lunged toward the bed where Tyrel still lay unconscious. "Shilia! Wake up!" As the blaze seared the rug, the wolf leapt, snarling toward the window, her animal fear of fire even stronger than her need to stay with her wolfwalker.

There were cries in the other rooms. Dion tried to pick Tyrel up, but her leg was still weak and his dead weight caused her to stagger. And then Aranur and Rhom burst into the room.

"Give him to me," Aranur snapped. "Get the bedding off and smother the fire."

Rhom jumped the flames and broke into Shilia's room as Dion tore the blankets from the bed. The blaze had already crawled up the tapestries against the door and was beginning to blacken the ceiling even as she hurried. In an instant, Gamon and Kiyun were beside her, trying to flatten the fire with sheets and blankets.

"We'll have to go out the window," Gamon said. "They've locked the doors from the outside!"

Rhom returned with Shilia, shielding her from the flames as they made their way to the only window in the three rooms. But as they stepped outside, Rhom swore and dodged a wicked arrow from across the courtyard. Aranur lunged back in from the balcony, banging into Kiyun.

"What—" Gamon shouted through the smoke as another arrow skittered into the flames at his feet.

"Someone wants to make sure we stay in here to fry." Aranur set his cousin down quickly but carefully beside the wall as the boy groaned and whimpered. "Longear's making her move, and no one's going to remember that we're in here till too late. Or else maybe Conin wants us to fry, too—be an easy way to get rid of us without scandal." And Namina would not suspect a thing, he thought bitterly.

They were beginning to cough as the fresh air from the balcony fanned the fire inside the room, creating huge black clouds of smoke. The music from the feast had stopped, and as another flurry of arrows flashed through the opening, people below began shouting at the smoke.

Dion's arms were tight around the wolf, forcing the wild-eyed beast to stay. She shoved Hishn's head into her jerkin, where the cloth of her tunic would help protect the wolf from the smoke. "Where did the shots come from?" she demanded, coughing.

"The roof across the way." Rhom pointed, holding a cloth over his face. "We're a watercat's easy supper if we step outside."

"If that sprinkler system doesn't come on damned quick, we'll have to chance it anyway." Aranur broke toward the other room. "And those archers are serious. We're going to need weapons." He returned in a moment, coughing and bent double, with two bows in his hands. "I couldn't get the others," he said, closing the door between the rooms quickly and slapping at his smoldering pants. "Flames are too thick." The heat was getting fierce, and their efforts to stop the fire's advance were futile now. Aranur tried to string one of the bows, but his coughing bent him over again. "Fire!" The cries rose from the courtyard. "Fire on the third floor!"

Dion strained to keep Hishn down as the blaze crackled into the woodwork. The Gray One's mind was incoherent, and all she could sense was panic. How much of it was herself, she could not tell; only that the wolf was beyond their bond, and she could not control her.

Seeing that Dion could not help, Kiyun grabbed the weapon Aranur was trying to string and took the arrows from the other man's hands. Rhom left Shilia and grabbed the other bow.

"On three," the fighter said to Rhom. "One . . . two . . . three!"

They dropped to their knees and took an instant's advantage to sight in on the men across the roofs. One toppled slowly, falling into the courtyard below, but two more got off another volley of shots. Kiyun did not move as an arrow gashed across his arm; he merely took aim again with Rhom at a dark figure in the cover of a chimney. Both shots missed.

Men yelled at them from below. "Jump!" "Hurry!"

"They can't," others countered. "There's someone on the roofs firing in!"

"Get that table over here," Aranur commanded. "We're going to make a diving shield."

"That fountain's only a meter deep," Kiyun protested. "You'll break your neck if you try to dive from here."

"I'm not going to," Aranur returned grimly, tying a cloth around his face like a raider. "Rhom is."

"Sure," the violet-eyed twin said with a sooty grin. "I'll do it. I've always been reckless. But do I get to take this with me?" He held up the bow.

"You'll take it with you and use it." Aranur flashed a black smile as he and Gamon dragged the table toward the window. "And if any of those shots miss, you'll be dnu meat when I see you next."

Kiyun looked at them as if they were crazy to be joking at such a time. Then he lifted the table end away from Gamon and thrust it through onto the balcony. There were two thuds, and the tips of two shafts stuck through the wood of the table.

"They'll be expecting us to shoot from around the sides,"

Aranur said, "Rhom, dive from underneath." He paused to cough violently. "Make it quick, okay?"

"I am fast as the lepa, unseen as Aiueven," the younger man replied, dropping to his knees on the floor where he could thrust off from Kiyun's feet like a racer from the starting block.

"Okay." Aranur paused and looked at Kiyun; the fighter nodded. "Now!" They lifted the table a fraction, and Rhom burst out from underneath, bow in his hands. Two arrows whipped by on either side of the makeshift shield, and an instant later, two more drummed almost through the wood as Aranur and Kiyun dropped the table down again.

"That table isn't going to last much longer," Gamon said. "What say we send a few more of us off below?"

Aranur turned to his sister. "Shilia, remember last summer at Green Lake? This is exactly the same. Don't be afraid, just do it."

She nodded nervously and took her place on the balcony.

"Kiyun, we're going to have to give them something else to shoot at now that they know our trick," Aranur said. "I'll show a shoulder on this side, Shilia will go down, then you show a shoulder on your side, and Dion will dive." He paused, as if struck by a sudden thought. "Dion, you do dive, don't you?"

"You have a bad habit of asking me if I can do something just before you tell me to do it." Dion coughed. "But, yes, I can dive." She tried to add something, but she coughed again, and her words were lost.

"Then get going," Aranur said over his shoulder. "Rhom's going to need help, and we're not going to last much longer up here. Gamon," he warned, "you're going to be next." Without a pause, he moved to reveal one shoulder, and as the enemy archers took aim, Shilia dove off. Dion dragged Hishn with her to the balcony, but flung herself and the wolf back when an arrow shot between her legs under the shield. Gamon hauled her to the side as she looked wildly around for the wolf.

"Moonworms!" Aranur swore. "Dion, you'll have to go out over the top." As she bent with another spasm of coughing, he took her arm from Gamon and looked into her eyes for a long moment. "If you know any tumbling, you better do it on the way down, too."

Dion wrenched herself free and grabbed Hishn, who was crouched, snarling, against the wall. *You're going to have to jump too, Gray One,* she insisted as Aranur swore again. But the wolf's mind was incoherent, seething with trapped and panicked thoughts of fire. *Come,* Dion sent urgently. *Hurry—*

Hishn resisted, and Dion pulled with all her strength at the gray wolf's scruff. *Come—*

"Dion, don't wait." Aranur grabbed at the woman and yanked her toward the balustrade. "I'll throw her to you if I have to. Now get going!"

"She won't jump without me!" Dion tore free. *Come, little one. You've got to do this. I won't lose you here—* Aranur's hand closed on her arm again like a steel trap, and she took a sooty breath, doubled over coughing, let Aranur drag her toward their wooden shield, and lied. She projected an image of water, cool water, just two meters on the other side of the table. *Water, Hishn, water. Come with me.*

The wolf hesitated.

Aranur jerked Dion close as another arrow skittered by her feet. She tried to calm her thoughts. *Gray One, look—no flames. No smoke. Only water.*

Hishn yelped as a brand touched her back, and she jumped forward, only to stop, cringing, at a gust of heat just before Dion could grab her.

Aranur looked at Dion for a long second, then kissed her hard, pushed her away, and put his hands together with Kiyun. The wolfwalker stepped up into the pocket they made, crouching down before flinging herself over. *Hishn!* She cracked the command at the wolf, and the Gray One, with a howl, lunged up with the woman. Dion shot out in a double barrel roll, then twisted into a flip. The wolf howled again, a terrified sound as Hishn realized Dion's lie. She was falling three stories. They separated. An arrow passed through the twist they made on the way down, and Dion was bruised by the shaft of another before she hit the water and arched along the bottom of the fountain. Hishn landed with legs spread and claws and fangs extended. People leaned in to help the healer out of the water, but Hishn's furious snarling and lunging scattered them on all sides.

Shilia stepped back as Dion was hauled out. The girl was wrapped in a blanket, her eyes huge in her dripping face. Looking back up at the wall, Dion could see why. The table Aranur and the others were still holding up against the balcony railing was cracked, and a column of smoke poured from the opening. The orange light of flames could be seen stretching out behind them. Where was Rhom? Dion thought desperately.

"They won't make it," a man standing next to the healer predicted.

She whirled, snarling, "Shut up!" He looked at the expression on her face and backed away.

And then her brother yelled from the roof behind her, "Aranur! It's clear. Get on down and join the fun."

Dion's knees were weak with relief.

They did not wait any longer. The table was flung aside, and Gamon dove cleanly down. Kiyun followed quickly. Aranur, with Tyrel in his arms, edged out coughing and hacking onto the balcony and leaned against the wall for a moment to get a breath of air. A man ran into the courtyard with two blankets, and several people grabbed them from him. They doubled the blankets and stretched them out between them, shouting, "Throw him down! We'll catch him!" Aranur held the boy's body out over the railing and let him fall. There was a soft thud, and Dion ran, Hishn at her heels, to pull the boy off the pad and get him away from the smoke, thankful for the gleaming yellow fangs that parted the crowd for her passage.

"Jump, now!" they yelled at Aranur. He did.

"Dion? Healer?" he shouted as he struggled free of the wool blanket. He finally saw her and dodged his way through, demanding, "Tyrel—is he all right?"

She was looking at the boy's eyes. Finally, she nodded. Five minutes later, smoke began billowing even more darkly out of the window.

"The hoses must have gone on," Aranur said, answering Dion's question before it was asked. "Where is Rhom?"

"Hey, Dion," Rhom called, answering for himself as he swung down onto the steps that led to the upper story. Shilia ran to him. "I found a friend of yours," he went on. "She helped me clean up the roof." He helped another figure down, and Dion squinted, her eyes still watering. As she and the others made their way toward the pair, she recognized the gaunt figure as Tehena, the woman from the prison.

She was startled. "Tehena?"

Hishn reached her nose forward to sniff the other woman, and Tehena froze, staring at the massive beast. She breathed finally, as the wolf turned away, then she held up the blowpipe they had made in the prison.

"I owed you one," she said, gesturing at her clean clothes.

"Then they set you free, too." Dion smiled and touched the other woman's arm. "I'm glad."

The other woman stiffened at the contact, but she did not draw away. She shook her head at Dion's words. "I would never have been let out of jail," she said flatly. "I used this and got away after they freed almost everyone else."

The healer frowned, puzzled. "How did you know we were here?" she asked instead.

"I've been trying to reach you for hours. Everyone knew where you were, but there were guards at your door to keep everyone away." The woman leaned toward Dion, pressed something into her hand, and whispered, "Longear has something against you, Healer." She straightened. "I figure we're even now."

"There was never a debt to pay, Tehena. But thanks." Dion looked at the bronze medallion in her hand, then glanced up and saw that Aranur was standing beside her with a grim look on his face. "Aranur Bentar neDannon," she said quickly, "this is Tehena—" she paused, expecting the older woman to supply the rest of her name.

"Just Tehena." The woman gave Aranur as hard a look as he was giving her.

He bowed coldly. "The pleasure is mine." He could not help his manner; the glimpse he had caught of the tattoo on Tehena's arm warned him more than instinct ever could that she would be trouble. But Dion looked from one to the other, baffled by their hostile manner.

"Healer," Tehena said, turning back to Dion. "Get out of town tonight. Don't wait. The word is already out, and Longear is setting up for your party."

"How can she?" Dion protested. "And how do you know this?"

"Haven't you learned yet that curiosity kills the careless?" Tehena gave Dion a sharp look and gestured at the medallion she had pressed into Dion's hand. "Those medallions came from the necks of the men on the roofs. Those medallions have Longear's seal on them, and that means that the men who wore them are in Longear's secret service. I'm doing you a favor, Healer. Longear didn't disappear today like everyone thought; she took her men with her and just waited for her chance— there was an attack on the new Lloroi already, but the rumors say it failed. And Longear's put the word out on you—you made her look like a fool in front of all Bilocctar and she wants you dead." A quick, furtive look crossed Tehena's face as more people entered the courtyard, and she crouched closer to repeat her warning. "Get out of town while you still have the chance."

"If this is a trap—" Aranur began.

"I owe *you* nothing," the woman snarled at him unexpectedly. "Healer, Longear wants you dead. Get out of the city tonight." She whirled, dodged between Gamon and Kiyun as they came up, and was gone.

"What was that all about, Aranur?" Dion snapped. "She's a friend—and doing us a favor."

He frowned. "We'll talk about it later," he said, stopping her protest with his hand. "Conin's coming."

". . . men kept shooting anyone who got near the pumps," a man was saying as he trotted beside the young Lloroi. "Three wounded, one badly, two dead."

"Are you all right? Was anyone hurt?" Conin demanded.

"No one was hurt," Aranur answered calmly, "but we will need clothes and supplies again, and it's sure that those rooms are totally gutted."

"I don't care about the rooms or your clothes," Conin said shortly. "I suppose you know it was more than simple arson."

Dion looked at him. "Longear?"

Conin, still throwing orders over his shoulder, answered briefly. "Her attack against me failed—I was prepared for her to try again tonight—but she had four men down at the pumps keeping everyone away till we could rally a guard and chase them off."

Aranur nodded. "She made sure there were some on the roofs, too, to keep us inside till we fried."

Conin looked grim. "I'll have you moved to more secure quarters."

"Thank you, Lloroi," Aranur said, smiling faintly, "but if you don't mind, we'll just get some mounts and take ourselves away before anyone is the wiser."

"All right."

Aranur stopped him before he could turn away. "I would like a word with you before we go, Lloroi."

Conin regarded the other man. "Come with me." He motioned for four men to go to Rhom. "Get him what they need. See that they aren't bothered."

"Sir!" they answered with a salute.

Aranur touched Dion's arm as people started moving again.

"Come with us," he said in a low voice. "Having you along ought to keep the sparks down."

Gray One, she said to the wolf, *stay here with Rhom*.

The wolf ignored her, following her and Aranur as they strode after Conin.

Gray One, you will not lose me. This is important. Stay with Rhom. Hishn whined, and Dion met her eyes briefly. I know, Hishn, but I cannot afford to feel through your senses when Aranur and Conin talk. She gripped the wolf's scruff hard, then shoved the creature away. *Stay with Rhom. You will be safe with him.*

Hishn slunk back, whining in her throat, but she went.

Dion had to run to catch up and Aranur frowned as she joined him again. Walking quickly, Conin led them through several hallways and finally into an empty room where he told the rest of his men to stay outside.

"Now." He turned to the two foreigners. "What is it?"

Aranur regarded him thoughtfully. "How much do you know of Longear's dealings?" he finally asked abruptly.

"I don't think you have the right to ask me that," Conin returned.

"I think I do."

The two men faced each other grimly.

"By what authority?"

"I am nephew to the Lloroi of Ramaj Ariye," Aranur stated flatly. "If Tyrel dies, I will take his place on the seat as Lloroi."

Conin stared, realizing suddenly that the man before him had as much rank as himself. But Aranur continued, his voice filling the small room with stern authority.

"And I," the gray-eyed leader continued, making sure Conin's attention was riveted on him, "not Gamon Aikekkraya, am weapons master of the Ramaj Ariye." He paused to let that sink in before letting loose the last telling shaft of truth. "If you are planning war, Lloroi, it will be I, not an old man, who will face you when the moons look over your battlefield."

Dion's face must have shown as much shock as Conin's. Gamon—retired? He was old, but hardly old enough to step down from the post of weapons master. And then she stared at Aranur. Aranur neDannon. The weapons master. And it suddenly made sense. His attitude toward Tyrel and his cousins and sister. His use of Rhom and Dion. His authority. His skill. Gamon talked a lot, but it had always been Aranur who gave the orders. And he was barely twenty-eight. To be accepted so young by the other weapons masters of Ariye . . .

"I am not planning war," Conin said finally, shaking the disbelief from his voice with difficulty. "I've only just taken the Lloroi's seat today. I have much to correct at home before I start fixing the world outside my own county."

"What about the fact that half the raiders of the central world are on your payroll?"

"You're mad. I've never even spoken to a raider."

"You didn't have to." Aranur gestured at Dion. "Why do you think we've had to come so far to rescue our sisters?"

Conin found his own cold authority as the two men bristled at each other. "That's a good question, Aranur of the Ramaj Ariye. Suppose you answer it for me."

"Raiders stole the women from our Lloroi's family to sell to Zentsis. You didn't think they wandered into Bilocctar by themselves, did you?"

"Aranur," Dion said in a low voice, trying to keep the accusations down.

"Sorry, Lloroi." The apology barely sounded sincere. "What I'm trying to say is that while we were fighting to get our sisters back from the raiders, we found evidence that Zentsis and Longear were in the first stages of a war designed to take over Ramaj Ariye just as they took over Prent's rule three years ago." Aranur raised his hand to forestall the other man's protest. "Lloroi Conin, listen for just a moment. Zentsis and Longear were paying the raiders a bounty in gold for every farm they destroyed, every high-caste woman they stole, and every leader they killed. If Longear has disappeared with her own guards, she's going to stir up more trouble than you're going to be able to handle right now, because from what we learned, the raiders dealt with Zentsis through her. If she says they'll be paid for doing something, they'll do it."

"That's ridiculous!" Conin sputtered.

"Is it?" Dion asked softly. "I was there, Conin. I saw it, too."

He stared at her. "I have your word as a healer on this? As a wolfwalker?" She nodded.

The young man sank down on the sofa. "It could be possible."

"It is not just possible. It is happening," Aranur corrected forcibly.

"Lloroi," Dion cut in, seeing him stiffen at Aranur's insistence. "Did you never hear Zentsis mention anything about expanding his territories? About his plans for the future? Even in Ramaj Randonnen—that's where I'm from—we've had six times as much trouble from the raiders lately."

Conin tore his eyes from the Ariye man and looked at Dion as she continued.

"I saw the letters myself," she said gently. "I read the words. Lloroi Conin, in two years, the plans will come about by themselves as long as they have just a little push to keep them going in the right direction. Longear is that push."

"Then I am already in a war," he said slowly.

"You are in a situation, not a war," Aranur said flatly. "You will not be in a war until Longear leads your troops into one."

"I lead my troops where they go," the other man snapped.

"Are you sure? Do you control all your men? Or does Longear pull the strings? You could stop this insanity now, before you have to test that. After all, it has only just begun."

"Begun where? And with whom?" Conin asked desperately. "How can I stop something I don't even know is happening? I've only been Lloroi for half a day, and I find out I'm starting a war I don't even know about! By the moons, I don't even like fighting!"

"More the reason to stop the senseless killing before it goes any further." Dion sat beside him and touched his hand. "Conin, Lloroi, you have the people of Bilocctar behind you. They are ready for someone new to take the Lloroi's seat, and that person is you. What you ask of them, they'll give."

"But what would I do?"

"You could try to cover this up, but word is going to leak out anyway," Aranur said quietly. "It might be best to be honest. Tell the people that you've discovered plans to make war on another county. You can tell them that they will have to pay no more war taxes because you have decided to throw out those plans and use the money to rebuild and better their lives at home."

There was quiet for a moment and Conin stared at them both. "You are persuasive, Aranur of the Ramaj Ariye. I have no love of you, but you talk sense. Even if you *were* a spy," he said slowly, "I would listen to what you say."

Aranur spread his hands. "What we thought was a simple rescue of our sisters from the raiders' hands turned into a nightmare for all of us. All we want is to go home again."

Conin was silent for a moment. "It is best, as you say, that you leave tonight. When I speak to the people, I don't want you hanging over my head like a lepa, drawing fire from even the most conservative men and women."

Aranur nodded.

"Those men you suggested," Conin said suddenly. "I met them. I think they're good men."

"I'm glad," Dion returned sincerely.

Aranur bowed politely. "Perhaps you will visit us in Ramaj Ariye when your own household is settled."

"Perhaps," Conin said, barely recognizing the offer of political peace in the face of the news he had just had. "The guards will see you back to your friends—you look as if you could both use a change of clothes."

Aranur glanced at Dion in surprise, then smiled wryly as he realized she was still sopping wet from her dive into the fountain.

Dion stood. "May the moons bless your leadership with wisdom," she said softly.

"I won't pretend that meeting you has been a pleasure," Conin said flatly, "but I will do what I can to make your passage from this county swift and sure."

Aranur chuckled without humor. "As will we, Lloroi. You can bet on all nine moons for that."

Chapter 21

Go home to your fathers, go home to your sons.
The battles are over; the war is near done.
Now watch for the riders who meet you at dawn,
At dusk and at night, for their war is not won.

Their spirits are keeping the roads for your ride;
Keep on and don't greet them or they'll stay by your side:
The faces that lost, the faces now maimed,
Will haunt you forever till judgment's dark day.

Kill not when the need is not there for your sword;
Take not when the need is not there for your word.
Repay all your debts before you have gone
To meet the nine moons and sing the moonsong.

"I don't know if you've done me a favor or not, Aranur," the soldier, Kirnan, said as he grasped arms with the lean, gray-eyed man. "But I appreciate your prompting my new position." The new uniform made the former guardsman out to be a lieutenant in the Lloroi's bodyguard, and though young, Kirnan was eager to start directing the Lloroi's security.

Aranur stifled a grimace as he reached up to tighten the saddlebags on the dnu. His hands throbbed where Zentsis's knife had cut his palms, and the fight had not left him a single muscle or bone unbruised, he thought. He wondered how Dion—who had to be at least as bruised as he—was going to take the ride. "Just keep Conin out of trouble. Like you, he's young to hold such a position."

"And there's plenty who'd like to take it from him, too. Don't worry. He'll be a hell of a lot better than Zentsis. You know, you didn't have to give me half your winnings; we made a bundle on those fights. You wouldn't be interested in setting the wolfwalker up for a rematch before you go, would you? Or fighting one yourself?"

Aranur chuckled. "No," he said definitively. He swung

284

stiffly up into the saddle and glanced back down at the other man. "Kirnan, I've been meaning to ask you something since we met. Just how did you know who I was? What was it I said or did that gave me away?"

Kirnan gave him a sly look. "Do you remember a man named Siteva neAman? He trained under Gamon six, maybe seven years ago."

Aranur thought a moment. "Wait a minute. Yes, I do. He wanted to learn double sword fighting and was pretty good once he got the hang of it. He had a lanky boy with him, too. One of his brother's sons—a clumsy one, but I figured the boy would grow into a good fighter once he discovered where his arms and legs ended."

"And it only took me three years to do that," Kirnan said with a grin. "Go on, get on the road." He laughed at the look of dawning comprehension on the other man's face. "And watch your backsides. No telling who waits in the woods with all the turnaround in the city."

As the group pounded out of the Lloroi's courtyards, the night air was still warm with the day's heat, and Dion felt incredibly lightened with relief at their freedom. Tyrel had regained consciousness, and she was sure now that he would be all right. With the saddle basket she had arranged, he would travel even easier. She wondered what Namina's letter to Tyrel said. The girl had tucked it in the boy's belt pouch for him to read when he was better, and the thought made Dion tighten her jaw. Aranur would have to teach Tyrel how to curb his mouth and handle his fists better. Bravery accomplished little without the skill to back it up.

She glanced over her shoulder. Behind her, Rhom rode beside Shilia, and each rider trailed the reins of an extra dnu, Shilia holding the reins of Tyrel's beast, as well.

Hishn caught Dion's look and grinned. *Will you run with the little one's pack brother as well?*

The image of Aranur was clear, and Dion, with an involuntary glance at the man whose dnu was loping ahead of her, flushed. *It's a good thing you can't talk out loud,* she told the wolf, *or I'd be spending most of my time getting you out of trouble.*

Hishn sneezed, and the yellow eyes gleamed, but Dion pointedly ignored her.

At the rear of the group, Gamon and Kiyun led the last three dnu. Lloroi Conin had given them the extra dnu for breaking custom, he had said, and for keeping Namina when he had no sister to give in her place, tacitly ignoring the fact that with the extra beasts, the small group could switch saddles from one dnu to the other and ride for days without stopping except for short breaks. Conin was shrewd enough, Dion acknowledged. His "gift" would get them out of the county in mere days instead of a ninan. And, with the moons riding their trail, they could reach home in a little over two ninans. Eighteen days, she thought. Home.

Ahead of Dion, Aranur rode with a bleak look on his face, for all that they were free of the city of Wortenton. He could not help feeling that he had somehow failed. Namina, he berated his cousin silently. What will I tell your father?

His thoughts lingered behind him in the city, and his expression darkened further. That woman—Tehena, Dion had called her—the one who had helped them out in the courtyard. Rhom had said that he had seen the woman on the roofs as he traded shots with one of the archers. She had taken out the other man he could not get to, but had given him no explanation of why she had done so except to say that she owed Dion a debt. How Dion could be mixed up with anyone from a dator drug cult was beyond Aranur.

And then there was Longear—still hanging about in the shadows and waiting to strike. She might have left town, but Aranur was sure that she had not given up her ambitions; whatever trouble she had in mind for Conin, he could not guess. He paused and narrowed his eyes. Longear might still have trouble in mind for his own group, as well.

But the countryside was quiet. Conin had drawn up papers to assure them safe passage through to the border. Aranur, who had not seen the next county since it had been taken over three years earlier, wondered what Prent's land looked like now that it was part of Bilocctar. Perhaps Conin would reassess the value of simply draining that devastated land and try rebuilding it instead. Prent's old county would soon be more of a burden on the young Lloroi's coffers than Conin could handle—even if he began rebuilding immediately, it would be years before that county recovered enough to support itself again.

The scattered light from the moons broke through the overcast sky and printed the clouds with oranges, reds, and yellows as night rolled on into morning. Shilia was nodding off in the saddle, and Aranur could see that Gamon, too, was having a hard time staying awake. He did not mind. They had a long way to go, and he had a lot to think about. Even if Conin reversed the raiders' plans of harassment and destruction, the elders still needed to be told. The raiders would not give up their activities just because Conin told them to; the only hold Conin had over them was through Longear, and Longear would no doubt encourage them with gold till her own coffers ran dry.

Dion rode up beside Aranur as they topped a small rise. "How about stopping for breakfast?" she asked.

"I'd rather put a little more space between us and the outskirts of Wortenton," he answered.

She nodded and, with a slight motion, sent the gray wolf off to hunt its breakfast alone. As she dropped back, she tossed the news over her shoulder to Rhom, who passed it on to Gamon and Kiyun, as well. Aranur, glancing over his shoulder, frowned darkly. He did not actively dislike Kiyun, but he was not sure he liked the idea of having the fighter travel with them to Ariye. The idea of teaching the man the martial art of Abis did not sit well with him, either. Irritated, Aranur spurred his dnu faster, bringing the whole group into a trot and waking Shilia up with a start.

They rode for two days, stopping only to eat and snatch a few hours' sleep off the road, avoiding taverns and farmhouses alike. Aranur did not want to risk their being trapped indoors until they reached Sidisport, the coastal city at the end of Wyrenia Valley, at which point they would turn north, back to Ariye. He also ordered Hishn to stay out of sight near towns, and Dion fumed silently. She had thought he would have given up that overcaution, but he made clear that he was taking no chances. So when they rode through villages, Dion sent the wolf into the woods, fretting irritably until the Gray One met them again beyond each town's borders. She thought Aranur was too worried about safety. After all, Conin had given the whole group safe passage, and besides, no one would intentionally harm a Gray One.

Except perhaps Longear, she acknowledged. Or raiders. But Longear, she told herself as Hishn nudged her hand before she mounted again and galloped after the others, was two days and ninety kilometers away. Surely they had little reason to worry anymore. But Aranur continued to be tense and cautious.

Two days later, trouble came in the small form of a single rider.

It was dark, and they had just stopped in the road to debate whether to camp and make dinner for the night or to go on another couple of kilometers, when pounding hooves were heard. Aranur immediately motioned them all off the road and down into the brush. But the lone figure who rode into view was neither a raider nor a guard, and as Aranur frowned, trying to remember what was so familiar about the face of the rider who pounded through on the road, Dion made a startled sound and spurred her dnu past his.

"Dion, wait!"

But she was already out from under the trees, calling out, and the rider, startled, hauled his dnu to a stop and turned the beast around to face the wolfwalker.

"Tehena," Dion exclaimed, urging her dnu up to the road. "What are you doing here?" The gray wolf leapt up to the road with the wolfwalker and trotted around the other dnu to sniff its hindquarters.

Tehena. Aranur's mouth shut and his face grew closed. The woman from the prison. He had not remembered to ask Dion about that woman, and at this point he had no choice but to join Dion on the road as the others rode out from under the trees behind him.

Tehena flicked her eyes at him, but greeted Dion with a wary smile. "I thought you'd be riding this way."

Dion was still looking at her in surprise. "But we're two full days from Wortenton."

"I know. You people ride fast and sleep little."

"You were trying to catch up?"

Tehena shrugged. "There wasn't any reason for me to stay in town, so I thought I'd look you up. I can ride, and I can use this fairly well now," she said, holding up the blowpipe. "I'd pull my weight." She gave Aranur a challenging look.

"Of course, join us," Dion said.

"I think not," Aranur said coldly.

The wolfwalker looked at him in puzzlement, then turned back to Tehena. "It would be no trouble," she corrected.

But Aranur shook his head. "No trouble, like a lepa in a rabbit pen."

Dion twisted in the saddle, staring at him. "What is the matter with you?"

"You heard me. That woman is trouble. More than we need right now."

"Tehena's a friend," she returned quietly. "She helped get us all away from Longear, and you know it."

"And maybe I don't. Maybe she works for Longear instead.

Did you ever think of that?'' he asked. Dion was being unreasonable, he thought. She knew nothing of the history that was tattooed on Tehena's arm. ''If I'm any judge of people,'' he said, staring coldly at the woman, ''this one is trouble.''

''Maybe you're not the judge,'' Tehena said calmly, glancing at Dion.

Aranur's anger grew colder. The woman wore a long-sleeved tunic that made her seem less thin and, he reminded himself, also covered that tattoo. ''And maybe you're taking advantage of your 'friend.' ''

Dion cut in. ''No one is taking advantage of me, Aranur—''

But Aranur cut her off grimly. ''You know what I'm talking about, don't you, Tehena? You carry the picture of it straight from the rotten heart of the city.''

''Maybe I do, maybe I don't.'' The woman was infuriatingly casual. ''What's the problem with letting the healer decide if I should stay?''

''Dion is a little naive when it comes to dator dealing.''

Dion frowned. Dator? That drug was one of the most dangerous to be addicted to. If Tehena really took dator . . . But how could she have done so in prison? Dion had seen nothing to indicate drug use.

''Perhaps we should make camp and discuss this further,'' Gamon suggested in a hard voice.

''We'll settle this now,'' the wolfwalker said sharply.

''Dion,'' Aranur said warningly.

She opened her mouth, then closed it with a snap and dismounted angrily, leading her dnu back off the road and following Gamon and Rhom to a small clearing. They did not speak as they set up camp using an old fire pit left over from the war for Prent's rule. It was not until dinner was nearly over that Dion brought up Tehena's request.

Aranur shook his head. ''I'll share a meal, but not a road with this one, Dion. And you should do the same.''

Tehena merely smiled. Rhom gave Aranur a sharp look, and Dion's violet eyes smoldered with suppressed anger.

''Then tell me why,'' the wolfwalker demanded.

Aranur met Tehena's eyes coldly, though he spoke to Dion. ''Drug dealers do not belong in Ariye. And I will not be the one to help bring a dator dealer to my home.''

''Aranur, you know nothing of Tehena's past—''

''Don't I? Ask her yourself.''

Dion stared at him a moment, then snorted, and turned to the lanky woman who waited arrogantly to the side. "Are you really a dator dealer, Tehena?"

"That's a question that brings death in the city," the woman answered with that casual smile. "Remember?"

"I'm asking as a friend."

"Maybe Aranur knows best," Tehena replied mockingly, giving him a sidelong look. "After all, he seems to know what he's talking about."

"Aranur—"

"Look at her left arm, Dion," he said in a hard voice. "Tell me what you find."

Tehena made a point of examining her nails. "Do you really want to know, Healer?"

"Don't make it worse," Dion said sharply. "Let's just get everything out in the open."

Tehena raised her eyebrow. "I thought you were a friend."

Dion just looked at her.

The thin woman shrugged finally and pulled back her sleeve. The tattoo, red as blood, stained her forearm in a pattern of smoke and twisted roots around the image of a skull.

The wolfwalker frowned, and Shilia shook her head at Dion's unspoken question, but Kiyun spit instantly.

"She's a member of a filthy dator drug group," he said into the silence, the disgust plain on his face.

"That can't be!" Dion turned to the other woman, waiting for her to deny the accusation.

But Tehena shrugged her sleeve back down over the tattoo. "Why not? You saw the tattoo before. Now you know what it means. So I duped you. Here you thought the world was all grins and smiles again, and then you meet me." She sneered. "Well, don't worry, Healer. It isn't as if you can't leave me here and go back to your pretty home and happy family."

Dion's face blanched.

"Dion," Aranur started gently.

"Oh, believe it, Healer," Tehena said sarcastically. "Aranur knows what he's talking about."

"Shut up, woman," the tall man snapped. "You've said and done enough."

But the wolfwalker stood up, suddenly angry, and Hishn, who had been sitting beside her, scrambled aside. The Gray One's teeth were bared, but it was Dion who snapped, "Aranur, perhaps it's you who should shut up and listen to what she has to say for a change."

He got to his feet and faced her. "You think it'll make a difference in taking a drug dealer back with us to Ariye?"

Tehena nodded slowly, mockingly, looking from one to the other. "You see, Healer, I don't think anyone here really wants to hear any explanation I'd give. Tattoos like this don't lie."

Dion tightened her jaw and glared around the small group. "You judge this woman before you know her—even though she helped you in Wortenton at the risk of her own life. Is this the kind of welcome that any stranger could expect to receive in Ariye? If so," she said scathingly, "then I can see that my Waiting Year in your county will be one of hell." She glared at Aranur. "Were it not for the fact that it would dishonor my own brother not to ride there with you, I'd rather not set foot in Ariye even if the moons themselves begged me to."

Aranur glared back at her for a long moment. Gamon cleared his throat, and Shilia looked at her feet. Finally Aranur motioned curtly for them to sit. "Speak, Tehena. We'll hear you out."

Tehena leaned back and picked at her nails with a twig. "Really?" she drawled.

"You wanted your chance," Aranur said sharply. "You have it now. Don't waste it."

She shrugged. She paused and glanced at Dion, but then saw Aranur's hard expression and wiped all expression from her own. "I was ten when I was kidnapped by a dealer and held for ransom," she began.

Gamon snorted.

She ignored him. "The ransom was paid, but I wasn't returned. The dealer tattooed me and kept me for himself."

"But surely you had chances to escape," Shilia said uncertainly. "Why didn't you leave him?"

Tehena smiled, but the expression held more pain than humor. "I tried twice. But I was tattooed. Even my family closed the doors on me when they found out. They said I was dead to them—even held a fake cremation for me. No harem would have me, and the army would have put me in jail before putting a uniform on me." She looked at Aranur. "Word got around, and I couldn't get work outside the cult. By the time my dealer found me again, I didn't care anymore. So I went with him."

She stared at the fire, unseeing. "He promised me food and clothes. Told me he cared. That he loved me. He said I was like a daughter to him, and that he had tattooed me so he wouldn't lose me." She snorted. "I was just a child. I fell for it so fast I got dizzy. And then he started me on dator, and a few ninans later, he asked me to help him out with a friend. Then another friend. And by that time, I was hooked, and he owned me as sure as if I wore chains. You understand how the drug works? First peace, then euphoria, then delusion, then nightmare? By the time I had gone through the first three stages, I was eleven. In the cult, I was old enough to have a baby. But I'd been sucking root for a year. I didn't get the peace anymore or the dreams. Instead I got the nightmares. I couldn't stand them, but . . ." She shivered, then focused her eyes again. "Withdrawal was worse." She shrugged, her face hard. "I had to have the drug. One night, I—" She choked on a word and cleared her throat. "I killed my dealer and—and cut my baby's throat."

Shilia gasped.

Tehena gave her an unreadable look. "It was easy. I saw her as she would be when she was older." She picked at her nails again with the twig. "The authorities were called, of course, and no one protested. It was an easy way to get rid of a poor producer. So I was hauled away and left to rot in prison."

"How old were you?" Rhom asked with a frown.

"When I went to prison? Thirteen. I'm sixteen now." She smiled indifferently. "You thought I was older, didn't you?"

"How could you have a baby so young?" Shilia asked in horror. She had guessed Tehena's age at twenty-eight or twenty-nine.

"It's the drug," Kiyun answered quietly. "It ages the body four times as fast as the natural turn of the moons. I remember those years," he said slowly. "There were children disappearing all over the city then, though not many were ransomed. Parents were afraid to let their children go to school, to their friends—even the older ones. I had to walk my own sister to her classes every day before I went to work, and she had to wait till I got off every evening to walk her home again."

Aranur stirred, moved in spite of himself by the woman's story. "How do we know we can trust you?"

She laughed in his face. "You can't."

Dion just looked at her, and Tehena's smile died.

"How do I know I can trust *you*?" she returned. "This tattoo is guaranteed to get me into any prison or slave detail in the continent. Will your healing rid me of this?" she demanded of the wolfwalker.

Dion looked at her feet, then back at the other woman. "I don't know," she admitted quietly. Hishn nudged her hand.

"All you have to do is call the police or soldiers," Tehena pointed out, "or even an honest citizen, and you're rid of me. I'd have to go to a lot more trouble to get you out of my hair."

"Dator is a hard addiction to break," Aranur said in the silence that followed that statement.

"Not so difficult when there's none around for three years. That's how long I was in that stinking cell of a rat hole before Dion gave me a way out."

"You said you'd paid your debt."

"So I forgot to thank her for the blowpipe lessons." She turned to the wolfwalker. "Thanks."

Dion met his eyes. "Aranur, we cannot send her back there."

Though he was put off by Tehena's hard bravado, he had seen her empty pack when she joined the camp for dinner. He knew she had no gear, no food, no extra clothes in the flat saddlebags on her dnu. Hells, but she had probably stolen the dnu and the clothes on her back, as well. What would she do if they left her now? Go back to the drug cult? He glanced at Shilia, and it struck him that he would not have hesitated about his decision if it had been his own sister in Tehena's position.

Tehena looked around the group and stood up abruptly. "I can leave if you need privacy to make your decision. Or I can just leave, since it's obvious that you've made your minds up already."

"There's no need to ride out tonight," Aranur said finally, hoping he was making the right decision. "We can decide in the morning if anyone has doubts about it."

"Suit yourself." She shrugged as if she did not care, but she sat back down warily and, for an instant, though he could not believe it, looked lost.

Aranur watched the woman from the corner of his eye. If the moons were still guarding over the group as haphazardly as they had been doing, Tehena might be mixed instead of just bad luck. But one can't tell the future without a direct line to the moons, he told himself.

In the morning nothing more was said, and as they went through the motions of breakfast and then packing, Tehena remained silent, though it was clear there was a struggle in her to speak. When they were ready to ride, Rhom glanced at

Aranur and then, receiving an imperceptible nod, checked Tehena's mount as he had the others, ignoring the way the woman's face tightened as she controlled her emotions.

Rhom offered her a hand into the saddle, and she stared at it as if it would bite. Finally, he motioned to the dnu. "It's a long way up," he commented. She gave him a strange look, but allowed him to help her mount.

"You'll be riding behind Shilia," Aranur said mildly as he checked the line. "Take one of the extra dnu from Kiyun to lead. They've been getting bunched up too much because of those lazy men in the rear."

"Lazy, my foot," Gamon snorted, winking at Kiyun. "He just wants to keep as much space as possible between us and the girls."

Tehena's face tightened further, then relaxed when she realized she was being teased.

"Take this one," the old man said, handing the reins across to her. "It bucks too much for me."

"Thought you said no one bucked too much for you, Gamon," Rhom called back.

"Get on up there and mind your mouth," the old man shouted back. "Or I'll teach you some manners."

Hishn had already loped up to the road, and Dion urged her dnu after the wolf while the others fell in behind her. Kiyun would be watching the back trail that day, and he had sharp eyes, so she and Hishn could relax for once. But her own eagerness to leave Bilocctar was sensed by the dnu she was riding, and it loped faster and faster till she began to crowd Aranur and was forced to rein in. They would reach the border soon enough without her racing time to get there, she told herself wryly.

They stopped at noon for lunch, and Dion asked Kiyun to show her some of the moves he had used on her in the fighting ring.

"Kiyun, you did several things I'm not familiar with," she said as they cleared a small area of sticks and branches. "One of them looked something like this." She demonstrated on her brother.

"The rixti hold," Aranur said as she helped her twin back up.

Kiyun nodded, "I used that hold, but you countered with something that threw me off like a hot brand from the hand."

He shook a mock fist at the woman. "I want to know what it was, too."

"I'm not sure I remember what move I used, but I think that one was from the Cansi style." She turned to Aranur. "Aranur knows a lot more about Cansi than I do. You'd better ask him for a demonstration. I'm still sore from the runaround you gave me three days ago."

Kiyun grinned at her. "Not that I wouldn't want to tumble with you anytime, Healer."

"Let me show you that counter, Kiyun," Aranur broke in. The Bilocctar man moved into the rixti hold, and instantly Aranur flung him across his hip into the dust.

Dion stifled a laugh. "Yes, that's the move," she agreed as Kiyun rolled to his feet and gave Aranur a look as hard as his landing had been. "It was definitely from a Cansi style set." The Gray One snorted, and Aranur could swear the wolf was laughing at him again.

A ninan later, they crossed the outer borders of Prent's old rule—the last place where Longear could stop them within Conin's rule. And three days after that, they skirted Sidisport and went on up Wyrenia Valley without mishap. But Aranur, in spite of the relief he should have felt once they entered the valley, felt his restlessness turn to tension. He had promised Shilia that they could stay at inns along the way, but with his irritability increasing every kilometer they rode, he wanted to change his mind.

"You feel it, too?" Dion asked, noticing the way he kept looking back over his shoulder as they left another small town behind them.

"I keep telling myself I'm just eager to get home," he answered. "But it's just been too easy."

"I know what you mean. I keep expecting Longear and her raiders to pop out from behind every corner, jump out from behind every bush. And Hishn keeps telling me I'm wrong, that there's no one on the road but us, and I'm still nervous."

"Longear has no reason to come after us now," he said with a frown. "But the raiders have not been called off, and she could still be behind them. I trust your instincts more than mine, Dion. Let me know if you get any other feelings."

She looked him in the eye. "About Longear or the raiders?"

Looking at her, he smiled suddenly. "About anything," he said.

But still, nothing happened. Aranur had no excuse not to allow them to stay at inns overnight. They traveled upriver at a leisurely pace, stopping almost every day on the banks of the Phye for lunch and a swim in the river to relieve their saddle-sore muscles. There were dust clouds behind and before them—traders and farm workers traveling along the Phye. Aranur was almost surprised to realize that it had been only two months since they had traveled in the other direction looking for their sisters. And they were returning with only one, he thought, suddenly depressed.

One day, Tyrel reined in beside Dion, a set look on his face, and rode beside her without speaking for several minutes.

So, she thought, it was time to talk about Namina.

"It's like a rock in my throat," Tyrel said suddenly.

Dion glanced at him sideways. "It can be hard to accept the judgment of the moons, Tyrel, but it has to be done."

"It's not the judgment of the moons that worries me," the boy said bitterly. He pulled Namina's letter from his pocket. "I can't accept what she's written here." Dion said nothing, and the boy turned on her angrily. "You're a wolfwalker. A healer. And Aranur listens to you. Why didn't you talk to him? Make him stay and fight? How could you let her stay with that—that—"

"That man, Tyrel," she supplied steadily. "The man who is now her mate. Legally Promised. Legally bonded. Mated."

The boy shook his head. "Did you even talk to her yourself? How could you let her walk into Zentsis's own house as a mate?"

"It was not my decision to make, Tyrel. Namina reached the age of Promising over three ninans ago, and she said it was what she wanted."

"But why? Look at this—" He held out the letter, but Dion did not take it, and Tyrel eventually crumpled it in his hand. "She says she could be happy with—" He struggled with the name and got it out in a rush. "Conin. But Dion, it has to be a lie. The man is Zentsis's son. He can't be trusted to treat her as she deserves."

"He seemed honorable to me."

"But how do I know she's all right? What do I tell our father when we come back and he sees that we couldn't bring back *any* of his daughters?" His voice broke. "Both my sisters are dead to me."

A shadow fled across Dion's eyes, and when she answered,

her voice was heavy. "Tyrel, you have lost only one sister—Ainna—and she is with the moons now. As for your other sister, Namina, she is promised, not lost. Even the miracle of Ovousibas could not bring her back now. What has happened is for me as a healer and Aranur as the leader of your group to explain, not you."

The boy looked at the ground. "I'm sorry, Dion," he said finally. "I have no right to complain." He took a deep breath. "Namina says she will be happy," he said, pausing as if to hear the healer reject that and encourage him to return to Bilocctar for her.

Dion said nothing.

"She says that this mating might be important for our people, too."

Still, the wolfwalker remained silent.

"If you accept this—" The boy hesitated, giving Dion one last chance to deny his sister's letter. But Dion nodded instead, and Tyrel looked down at his hands, clenched on the reins. He took a deep breath and straightened his shoulders, the scars from Zentsis's fists whitening as he tried to control his emotions. "I will accept it, too, then."

"It's not easy to know what the moons want of you, Tyrel," she said quietly, "but the way you accept the challenges is what will make you a man."

The boy nodded without looking at her, but he rode straighter after that.

Aranur did not want to stay at another tavern. They had already stayed at one each night in the valley, and he felt nervous, as if they were pushing the luck of the moons too far. But Gamon, who seemed to know every innkeeper along Wyrenia Valley, assured them that the next inn up ahead was safe. He had known this particular innkeeper since boyhood.

When evening finally dropped its shadows over the road, they stopped at the place Gamon had recommended, put their mounts in the corral with the other guests' beasts, and made their way inside. Dion, dismounting, rubbed her tired thighs and accepted a lick from the wolf.

Do you want to go hunting, Gray One? she asked. *There is time.*

Hishn snorted softly. *The smells of this place are not pleasant.* She looked with longing at the dark forest out beyond the inn's barn, but said instead, *There is death in the air.*

Dion frowned. *What kind of death?*

Old death. Musty death.

The wolfwalker shivered and gripped the wolf's fur. *Then stay with me, Gray One.*

You could not lose me, Hishn retorted. She butted Dion on her aching thighs, and the wolfwalker grunted, cuffing the creature lightly to make her stop. She looked around, but Aranur and Gamon were already talking to the innkeeper, a fat man of forty years who looked little like Gamon's description of the man he had expected. She made her way to the door, holding it open for the wolf so that Hishn's tail was not caught as it swung shut.

Did Gamon sense anything wrong? But the older man was smiling, glancing around the half-filled room, and Dion was sure she was imagining things. "Are the east rooms taken?" Gamon was asking as she joined them.

The innkeeper smiled widely, his eyes flicking to the wolf at Dion's side and then back to Aranur and Gamon. "You're in luck, sirs, they were vacated just this morning. And that a Gray One honors this house is a blessing from all nine moons. If there's anything I can get for you sirs and ladies—or the Gray One—let me know."

Aranur glanced over his shoulder. "Then we'll get our packs. And make sure we're not disturbed, understand? We're tired and want some quiet."

"This is a very quiet place," the innkeeper assured him. "Very quiet."

Dion frowned at the innkeeper's tone. She caught Gamon's eye, and the older man nodded, touching Aranur's arm as if by mistake. Aranur motioned for the others to wait inside while he and his uncle went back for their packs; then Dion and Hishn followed them out.

"It's quiet." Gamon remarked thoughtfully. "Like the calm before the storm. Wouldn't you agree, Wolfwalker?"

She shivered. "I don't like that man. There's something wrong with his eyes."

Gamon glanced at her sharply. "An odd observation, Healer."

Aranur glanced back inside. "I thought you knew the innkeeper, Gamon."

"I did." Gamon chewed his lip thoughtfully.

The other man nodded slowly. "I see."

Dion, who had one hand in Hishn's scruff, said softly, "Did you notice his hands? They were callused like those of a fighter, not a farmer or innkeeper. And he was clumsy with his fingers—not a skill you would want if you handle glass or silver."

Aranur scowled. "Could he have just bought the place from the old innkeeper? He could be unused to the work."

Gamon grinned without humor. "You know you don't believe that. Besides, old Tecorra, who owned the place, would not willingly have left his inn to someone not of his family. Whoever that is, he did not come by this place legitimately."

Hishn growled. "Longear," Dion said flatly.

"It makes sense."

Aranur thought a moment. "We'll go to bed anyway—let them think we've settled down for the night. We can slip out the windows then and be down the road ten kilometers before he even knows we're gone."

"I'll tell Shilia and Tehena," Dion agreed.

"Take Rhom along to stay with them while you join us again. What about Hishn?"

"She stays with me."

Aranur nodded. They turned in as expected, but Rhom made his way noiselessly to the women's room, and it was Dion and the wolf who returned in his place.

"The hall is clear," she said quietly.

Gamon nodded, then rolled back the meager carpet that lay in the center of his room.

"You've been away from home way too long if you have an urge to clean house, Uncle," Aranur said, eyeing with distaste the dust and debris that had been tucked under the long and faded carpet instead of picked up and thrown out.

"This inn was built by old Tecorra's great grandfather nearly a hundred and sixty years ago," Gamon said in a low voice. "He put in an escape tunnel, as many people did then, as protection against the raiders and bandits."

Dion looked at him sharply. "I wondered why you asked for specific rooms."

Gamon chuckled. "Tecorra's son loved to gamble, and we used to sneak out to the barn to play cards with that little cheat. Our fathers were always in the front room, drinking and passing the evening, so we used the tunnel to get to the barn so they couldn't see us go out the windows. I know all the inns along this river—and how to get into all the betting rooms, too, of course."

"I don't doubt it," Dion retorted.

The trapdoor was light, made of a dry, sturdy wood that

shrank and hardened as it aged. It was a good thing they rolled the carpet all the way back, because the cobwebs and their creepy denizens scattered on the floor as they lifted off the cover. They looked down the dark shaft.

"Kiyun, take a lantern and see if the tunnel still goes through," Aranur ordered. "Tyrel, how are you feeling?"

"Good enough."

"Then keep watch out the window. See if any other guests arrive."

"The innkeeper may not know of these tunnels," Gamon said thoughtfully, helping Kiyun down the shaft. "The rugs haven't been moved in ninans."

Aranur looked at the piles of dust on the floor. "If you're right, it's a bonus for us."

Ten minutes later, the glow from Kiyun's lantern came back into sight, grew, and then was suddenly cut out as the fighter appeared at the ladder again.

"It goes through," he whispered loudly, coming out as gray as the cobwebs he had crawled through. He stifled a sneeze. "It's almost big enough to stand up in the center. There's a sort of room with emergency supplies, but they haven't been touched in a long time. The dust is a centimeter thick, and," he added, grimly brushing the dust from his pants, "there's a body—torn apart by the rats already, but recent—within a few days recent. It looks as if the man was badly wounded—two broken legs—and crawled into that chamber from the barn entrance to die. The rats would have cleaned the bones off pretty quickly, judging by the amount and size of their trails I found down there."

"Could you tell anything about the body?" Gamon asked.

"It's small, and what's left of the skin looks old, though I didn't get too close. I think it's an old man or woman. I found only a few teeth. The healer would have a better idea of its age than I."

"Tecorra would have been ninety-six this spring," Gamon said slowly, "and he was never a big man."

"And we're in land that raiders make frequent stops in," Dion finished for him.

"So we're sitting in Longear's lap," Aranur said softly.

Tyrel frowned and looked over his shoulder from the window. "But why would she come after us now? Conin knows of her plans. It's only a matter of time before he stops them."

Dion looked at the boy, a thought taking shape in her mind

like a dim nightmare that would soon be alive. "Why," she said slowly, "does he *have* to stop them?"

Aranur gave her a sharp look. "What do you mean, Dion?"

"What proof do we have that Conin will not encourage Longear?"

"We have his word," Kiyun returned steadily.

"We have his Promise to Namina. That is all," she corrected.

Aranur regarded her thoughtfully.

"We do not know Conin," she said. "We do not know his advisors. And we do not know how far Longear has already gotten with the war plans. If Longear and Conin begin working together as she and Zentsis did, then nothing has changed for us." She glanced at the others. "We've been telling ourselves that we're safe now that we crossed the border of Prent's old rule and are beyond Conin's reach. But we have put distance only between us and Conin, not between us and Longear. If Longear could reach so boldly into the heart of Ariye, what will stop her from doing so again? Why should she give up years of planning simply because we managed to ride away from Bilocctar once? What guarantee do we have to that she will not worm her way back into Conin's house within ninans, if not days?"

Dion shook her head at Kiyun's frown. "Longear is clever and ambitious, Kiyun. And Conin is inexperienced and young. Longear need speak with Conin only once or twice to convince him that he cannot lead the county without her. After all, she knows the secrets of the Lloroi, controls her own troops, and controls the raiders at the same time. She even claimed that she used a wolfwalker to track us when we first entered Bilocctar. She has the means to direct power at any county, including Bilocctar, if she did not get what she wanted out of Conin. She could give him years of grief, if she does not destroy him outright. And as for us," she added, motioning at the group, "we are still the only ones who know of Longear's—and possibly Conin's—plans. We did not write letters since we were carrying the news home ourselves. We did not send a single carrier bird with the news because, with the predators in the valley, birds cannot be trusted over such a long distance. And so here we are, riding up the valley along the predictable route, stopping at inns, taking our time, congratulating ourselves that Longear has given up . . ."

The men stared at her.

"Dion," Aranur said slowly. "Do you know what you're suggesting?"

She gripped Hishn's fur, and the gray wolf nudged her back with a low whine. "Longear would not need to touch Namina," the wolfwalker continued, as if she had not heard him. "As Lloroi, Conin could control Namina easily, and Namina would never need to know what really happened to us. What a feather it would be," she added softly, "for Longear to catch us and kill us now—before we become a threat. Or keep us until she controls Conin and we become hostages again in Ariye."

"And to Randonnen," Gamon said slowly. "Aye," he said at Dion's look of surprise. "Longear now knows you are a wolfwalker, Dion. If she controls you, she controls Hishn. Even if she did not use you to force Hishn's actions, she could still use you as hostage to any county. Both threats are real."

"But Dion would know if the wolves were being used," Tyrel protested.

She shook her head. "The Gray Ones don't dwell on reasons, but actions, Tyrel. And the bond between a wolfwalker and wolf is private. Unless I asked directly of each one, I would not know if a Gray One was acting because its wolfwalker was held in pain or coercion or if the wolf was acting because the wolfwalker had simply asked it to help. A wolf would not be disturbed to be used as a tracker—most wolves who run with wolfwalkers do that at some point anyway." She bit her lip. "There is no way of knowing—there *was* no way of knowing," she corrected bitterly, "when we crossed into Bilocctar, if Longear used the Gray Ones against us." Hishn growled at her and closed long teeth gently on Dion's arm. Dion, squeezing Hishn to her in response, laid her face on the gray fur. "But the Gray Ones will not run far from their wolfwalkers. So, at least Longear cannot control the wolves here or in other counties," she said. But her words, even to herself, sounded more like a prayer than a statement.

Aranur paced the room, his expression icy. "Tyrel," he said abruptly, turning on his heel so sharply that the boy jumped, "any sign of movement?"

"Not a thing," Tyrel returned. "But—" He hesitated, then shrugged. "I'm not going to hear much with all the noise from the front room."

Aranur gave him a sharp look. "That might be a ploy to keep us from noticing the arrival of other guests. Gamon, get

Rhom and the girls and bring them here.'' The older man left almost before Aranur had finished speaking. ''Kiyun, start taking the packs to that chamber you said was down there. We'll meet there before going out through the barn.''

Minutes later, Shilia and Tehena were in the room and their packs had been tossed down into the corridor. Rhom, and then Shilia, jumped down to help Kiyun, grabbing two bundles and disappearing after the fighter. A few moments later, Tyrel and Gamon followed. Dion took the boy's place at the window, while Hishn bared her teeth and sent the wolfwalker the sounds of men in the night. Aranur caught a glimpse of the expression on Dion's face and drew his sword, and Tehena grabbed the remaining packs and began to throw them down the shaft.

Hishn whined suddenly, and Dion stiffened. ''Aranur,'' she said urgently, ''they're coming. Maybe twenty of them. And there's a woman in the lead.''

''Longear,'' Aranur breathed. ''They knew we would have to travel this way—it's the only road up the valley this side of Fenn Forest. They just waited till we showed up, like rabbits in the noose.''

Dion motioned the Gray One toward the underground shaft, and with a whine, the wolf tried to crawl down the ladder. But her paws were too big, and halfway down, she lost her balance and jumped, banging her back on the opposite side of the shaft. Her yelp made them all jump. But they could hear the raiders in the courtyard by then, and without hesitation, Dion dropped down after Hishn, while Aranur turned to help Tehena.

But the other woman shook her head. ''Wait a minute—''

Voices were raised in the outer room. They had no time to waste. Aranur turned to shove Tehena into the shaft if he had to, but she pushed him into the opening instead.

He hit the ladder with bruising force, only to be knocked off as Tehena threw the last pack down on his head.

''They don't know me,'' she snapped as he flung the pack aside and leapt up. ''Someone's got to cover the door with the rug.''

He reached the top rung of the ladder and lunged up just as she dropped the trapdoor on his hands. He barely stifled the curse that leapt from his lips.

He hung there for a moment, uncertain. Tehena had made sense. But he stayed on the ladder anyway, listening as she quickly rolled the rug back across. The tiny line of light that had outlined the door went out. There was a minute of quiet in the room above as the raiders argued with the innkeeper. From the tunnel, Aranur could not quite distinguish the words.

"Aranur," Dion whispered almost imperceptibly, "where's Tehena? Come on."

He hesitated, then dropped to the floor of the tunnel. There was a roar of male laughter from beyond the room above them, and they heard a man's high voice pleading, and then a horrible cry. Dion blanched. Aranur drew her close where he could speak in her ear without the sound carrying, but he froze, and they both heard the heavy footsteps that grew louder as they came closer to the room above.

"She's covering our tracks," he breathed. "We may not get to take the dnu with us when we leave, so lighten the packs as much as you can before you make for the woods." He pushed her away down the tunnel, but she turned back.

"Aranur, they know how many of us there are, and they've got to know that she's one of us. They won't believe that she's the only one left."

"She's buying us time, Dion, and we need every minute we get. She knows what she's doing."

"You can't let her pay for that time with her life," she whispered urgently. In the room above them, the door burst open. His hand clamped instantly over Dion's mouth and they froze again, not daring to breathe.

"What?" That was Tehena's frightened voice. "Who are you? What do you want?"

". . . only one in here," the muffled voices sorted out into a man's tones. "Must not be the right room." There was a comment, then a laugh, then the voice continued. "Check the other rooms. Take them alive if you can. I think Longear can wait a few minutes to see this one."

"Take your hands off me!" Tehena demanded. There were some muffled bumps, then the footsteps faded heavily.

Aranur pushed the healer toward the barn. "Get back to the others. Tell Rhom to lead everyone out to the woods. If it looks like you could get the dnu, do so, but don't take any risks. Longear has more men than we can handle right now."

"What are you going to do?"

"Retrieve some stolen goods," Aranur answered grimly. "Now get going. I'll be right behind."

Dion made an odd throat sound at the wolf, and Aranur realized that the Gray One had not left either; and then they were gone, the only sound of their passage being the barely audible scuffling as they crawled quickly through the dust. He waited a few minutes, straining to hear anything more. There were cries, but not many people had stopped at the inn that night; there were few for Longear to vent her frustration on. And Tehena would be one of them, he thought. He could barely hear some confused babbling, some wild pleading, and a rising scream that cut off almost instantly. It was Tehena's voice. Whatever they were doing, he told himself, it was guaranteed to make the woman talk.

He dropped soundlessly to the floor of the tunnel and crawled out after the rest of his group. He caught up to them at the east end of the barn and, after glancing back at the inn, signaled for them to break for the woods. He held Kiyun back, trusting Rhom to make sure the others made it out together. "Get the dnu from the corral," he whispered to the fighter. "Start a run up the road. That should draw them off."

But the fighter hesitated. "Aranur, I'm not good with animals. I only get near them because I have to. It'd be better if you got the dnu and I went around to get the girl."

"No, I'll stand a better chance with Longear and her men. Just step lightly and talk to them softly."

"I don't think you understand, Aranur. If you want the dnu to come quietly, I'm going to let you down. Use the wolf-walker instead. She's best with animals. And I can cover her from any fire on that side."

Dion cleared her throat, and Aranur realized that she and the wolf had stayed behind while her brother led the others in a furtive sprint to the tree line.

"It would work, Aranur," she whispered. "But I can take the dnu out by myself."

"I told you to get going with the others," he ordered coldly.

"If neither of you make it back," she said bluntly, "that leaves only Rhom and Gamon to fight against the raiders later. We need Kiyun in the woods a lot more than we need me. And I'm small enough not to attract as much attention as he would in the corral. I am good with animals, Aranur."

"This is dangerous, Dion."

She snorted. "I haven't noticed this to be any different from the rest of our journey. And besides, I'll have Hishn with me." The wolf's yellow eyes gleamed, and a wet nose nudged her hand until she rested it on the furry back.

Aranur hesitated. "All right. Kiyun, go with the others. And Kiyun," he said, stopping the fighter, "good luck."

The other man crouched and ran quietly across the clearing. As he ran, the bundle of packs on his back made him look like a strangely hunched demon in the moonlight. But Aranur was watching the inn again.

"You'll have to distract their attention from the rear windows as much as you can," he whispered. "Dion—are you sure about this?"

"It's not for myself that I'm scared, Aranur."

He looked at her sharply, then nodded: Tehena. "How long will it take you to get our mounts and start a small stampede?"

She glanced toward the corral. "Give me four minutes to get enough of their bridles on, and another minute to open the gate and get them started."

They squirmed onto their stomachs and started worming across the dirt. The Gray One slunk to their left, and Aranur envied the grace with which the wolf crossed the ground. "If you can," he whispered, "circle the dnu in front of the inn and make a lot of noise before you take off. I'm going to need some time to get Tehena out of there."

"We'll come back around one more time when we've drawn them off. That'll give you a chance to catch a ride out of there if you need it." She squirmed into a wagon rut behind Hishn, then edged toward the corral, disappearing into the shadows with the wolf.

Aranur rolled up against the wall of the inn and froze. Longear's voice was angry. He could hear her clearly as she alternately berated her men and coaxed Tehena to talk.

". . . beginning to feel the effects now, aren't you? I could make this much more pleasant for you if you told me what I wanted to know."

"I know nothing. I came here alone to meet my new dealer."

"You've traveled with that group for days," Longear said coldly, "and I'll make sure you're with them when I destroy them all. Don't worry, little addict, I can be patient. All I have to do is wait; the drug will loosen your tongue for me."

"I came here alone." Tehena's insistence faltered as her voice began to slur. "All . . . alone."

There were quick footsteps across the floor.

"Damn you to the hells nine times over, Varley," Longear snarled. "If you hadn't lost your head and killed that slob of an innkeeper, I'd have the information I needed by now. Now we waste our time on this addict when we could have had them in our hands."

"Longear," another raider interrupted, "she's starting to slip into the euphoria. If you want to question her anymore, you'd better do it soon."

"Happy little addict," Longear said mockingly. "Can you feel the dator?" Her voice became menacingly smooth and persuasive. "Feel the heaven in your veins, feel the world go away and the moons take you up in their arms."

She paused, and Aranur edged up against the window and peered in. Longear had Tehena's slack face in her hand and was leaning close. "But you are all alone. Where are your friends? Heaven is so much nicer when your friends are with you. Friends. Wouldn't you like to have your friends with you?"

Tehena's head lolled back and she looked vacantly at Longear. "No friends. No friends." She tried to concentrate, a small frown appearing on her face. "All alone."

Hurry, Dion, Aranur thought silently.

Longear was becoming frustrated with Tehena's lack of comprehension. "What about your girlfriends?" she pressed. "Two girls; one with black hair, one with brown?"

"Hair . . ."

"That's right. They're hiding from you. You'd like to find them, wouldn't you? To play with your friends? Let us help you find them."

Tehena's eyes rolled to the window. "Find . . ." She tried to push away from the raider's hands that held her sitting up. "No . . ." she protested weakly. "No friends. Have no one. No one."

"She'll tell within ten minutes, or I'll have your head for giving me weak dator," Longear snarled to the raider beside her.

"It is pure," he said grimly. "I picked up this load myself—" He was cut off by a shout and then Dion's wild yelling from the front of the inn.

The raiders looked up, startled. "The dnu! They're out at the corral!"

They leapt from the room, Longear running with them, and Aranur quickly flung the window up and slid in. The roaring of the frightened dnu and whooping of the wolfwalker shattered the tension of the night. Aranur could hear the deep pounding of the stampede across the dirt as he reached for Tehena. The drugged woman gave him a blank look, her smile frozen on her face. He swallowed his disgust.

But someone pounded back down the hall, and he dumped the woman unceremoniously on the floor as the door burst open. Aranur whirled to face his new opponent, and the huge raider's eyes narrowed. Aranur reached for a knife, and the other man did the same, moving into a fighting stance. And Longear stepped into the room behind him.

"So, Aranur." She eyed him speculatively. "You return to me again." She stepped away from the dusty raider and motioned negligently at the raider to take the young weapons master on. "I wondered if your honor would force you to a trick of this kind. Well, go on. I won't stop you from your heroic deed. Rescue the girl if you can."

"Sorry," he returned. "I don't have time to play." He threw his knife suddenly, and the raider flung himself to the side as Aranur lunged. But in an instant, Aranur had Longear by her throat, dragging her in front of him while the raider rolled to his feet with a grunt. Aranur's short blade was sticking out of his shoulder, but the raider wrenched it free.

"Uh uh," Aranur cautioned the raider, having ripped Longear's knife from her sheath. He held it to her throat. "You wouldn't cut off your gold supply, would you?" Grimly he dragged Longear toward the bed where Tehena sat leaning against the bedstead with a fatuous grin on her rubbery face.

"How will you get the girl and keep me at the same time, Aranur?" Longear whispered viciously. "You can't keep me forever, and in a few minutes, my men will return."

"Shut up," Aranur hissed. "Another sound, from either of you," he warned, gesturing warningly at the raider, "and I'll start by slicing the right side of your throat." He used the hand with the knife to press Longear against him, while with the other he dragged Tehena to the window. She giggled as he tried to push her over the sill. Longear, thinking his attention had wavered, hit his elbow and thrust herself away. The raider took that chance to make a break for it.

Aranur grabbed Longear by the hair and yanked her back tightly, causing the raider to stop in his tracks. Longear gasped. A line of red started dripping from her throat. "Not too smart, Longear," he whispered. "Not too smart at all." He shoved Tehena the rest of the way over the sill, and she collapsed with a limp thud against the ground. He hoped vaguely that she had not hit her head too hard. "For now," he whispered, the sounds of pounding hooves and shouting still getting louder, "you're coming with me."

"I'll have your head for this, Aranur," Longear said in a calm voice.

He felt her chest expand as if she was gathering breath to call out, and he jerked his fist against her stomach hard. She lost the air in a woofing sound, giving him time to swing one leg over the sill, but then she kicked her legs quickly and they both fell through the window, landing roughly on Tehena. The drugged woman merely oomphed and giggled. Longear shouted for her raiders, breaking free and rolling away on the ground.

Aranur had no time to fight her: Dion should be rounding the back of the inn at any time. He whirled and scooped up Tehena just as the dnu thundered around the corner. Longear's eyes opened wide and she scrambled back against the inn, her orders drowned out by the sound of crashing hooves. Aranur's heart seemed to stop. He did not see Dion with the dnu. Did the raiders have her?

"*Dion!*" he yelled over the thunder, leaping to catch the mane of a charging beast. With Tehena in his arms, he did not make it, bouncing back down beside the dnu. He hit the ground with jarring force as he clung to the animal's mane, and then he flung himself over onto its bare back. A dark head popped up on another dnu, and he realized with sickening relief that the wolfwalker had been lying low beside the dnu, one arm and one leg hooked into its hair so she could ride without making herself a target. He could not see the wolf.

Dion caught sight of him and waved. Four raiders had run around the inn in front of them, swords out. Dion started to veer, then changed her mind and charged the herd right down on them. The raiders scattered, one grabbing at a dnu as the stampede passed. There was a scream, but neither rider looked back. Aranur tried to settle Tehena's form in front of him, hunching as low as possible as they swept back across the front yard toward the road. Dion had about eight dnu by the reins; there were bridles on three more, and full gear on the ones she had stolen from the raiders' pack of beasts. A nice stampede, Aranur thought with approval, though his heart ached for the beasts he knew would be hurt in the rush. The raiders had their bows out and were shooting. Two more dnu screamed and fell. Longear was shouting from the porch, screaming to be heard over the pounding hooves of the wild-eyed herd. The clouds cast strange shadows; none of the raider's arrows came near the crouching, dnu-hugging forms, though at least five beasts went down.

"They're cutting their own throats," Dion managed to shout back at Aranur.

They cut into the field from the road and headed into the woods, and suddenly the wolf was loping beside them again.

"Rhom should be close," Aranur called, the noise lessening as they crashed through brush and slowed. Dion was having a hard time with the beasts she was trailing.

He heard a shout from the right. "Aranur! Dion!"

They veered through the trees, the shouts of raiders close behind. Dion stayed mounted, trying to hold on to the stamping, snorting dnu. Rhom grabbed several traces from her hands. "We're all here. How far are they behind you?"

"Minutes only."

Kiyun threw Shilia up onto a dnu, and Gamon leapt up on another. Without hardly stopping, they were mounted. Aranur still had Tehena, and Dion had two extra dnu by their reins.

"Bring them along as long as you can," Aranur directed, shifting the drugged woman in his arms. Tehena's body had begun to twitch, and he was having a hard time keeping her on the dnu. "The fewer there are for the raiders, the safer we'll be."

There was crashing several hundred meters away in the woods. "Over here!" a raider shouted. "They came through here!" Arrows skittered through the brush, and one found a tree trunk beside Aranur's head.

The wolf flashed by him, and Aranur jabbed his heels into the dnu's flanks. It leapt after the wolf. "This way," he cried. They plunged through the brush. In moments, they left the raiders behind again and fled after the massive gray shadow that dodged through the brush. Suddenly the wolf veered off, and Aranur almost followed until he realized that they had come to one of the larger game trails. He slowed their crazed flight to a safer lope. The wolf, with a snarl, dropped back to Dion's side.

"What's the matter with Tehena?" Shilia called.

Aranur answered in a low voice. "She's so high on dator right now she's probably speaking to the moons."

"Aranur!" Shilia was shocked.

"They did it to make her talk." He ducked under a low branch, guiding his mount more with his knees than the reins, since his arms were full of Tehena. "We can be thankful she didn't."

"How much did they give her?"

"Enough to vacate her mind and start her body twitching." He shifted again. "Rhom," he called back, "take the lead. Tyrel, follow him. I need another hand to keep this woman here." As he dropped back, Rhom's dark form and Tyrel's slight one plunged up beside him and then passed.

Dion was breathless as she ducked through the brush beside Aranur, trailing the extra dnu like two awkwardly bouncing balls while the Gray One seemed glued to her mount's side. She leaned precariously in the saddle trying to keep their reins untangled.

"Aranur, dator addiction doesn't ever really heal," Kiyun said, telling the gray-eyed man what he already knew. "If she worked up to the nightmare stage years ago, she'll still be affected the same way now." They split around a clump of trees, the low growth whipping against the dnu's legs.

"Then I wish," Aranur got out, grasping the woman tighter as she flung out her leg, "she would have a delusion of sleep. It would make it easier to carry her. As it is, she's getting harder and harder to hold on to."

"It's going to get worse, Aranur," Kiyun called back. "She'll become unpredictable."

"Like all women?" Aranur answered wryly, then grunted as he was caught on the chin by one of Tehena's flailing arms. They were still thrashing through the underbrush too fast for comfort, but they seemed to have lost the raiders in the black shadows. Beside him, Dion jumped a gully that opened up in the night like a giant yawning mouth, and gasped as she landed. He wondered why she said nothing about Tehena's condition, but perhaps even Ovousibas could not heal a drug addiction.

Kiyun glanced back. "She's going to get hysterical when the nightmares start," he warned. "She'll become incredibly strong for a while, and you won't be able to hold her and ride at the same time. Knock her out while you can still hold her."

"I can handle this myself, Kiyun," Aranur said, tipping dangerously on the dnu as Tehena shuddered and kicked out again. But the woman convulsed, and he had to throw back his head to avoid her wild arms. Another branch hit his face, cutting his cheek. "On second thought—" He freed an arm for an instant, and Tehena started to cry out in a garbled voice, struggling hard against him. "—I think I'll take your advice." He backhanded her on the jaw, and she went out like a light.

For an hour they fled through the night like wraiths, the heat from the sweating dnu warming their legs while the cold evening air made them shiver. Brush whipped and cut them; they lost Gamon's dnu to a rodent hole when its leg drove suddenly through the crust of earth and broke. Dion hauled up instantly, and Gamon rolled free, leaping back on one of the extra mounts she was still trailing gamely behind her. One after another, they jumped the dips and ducked through the hollows along the game trails behind Rhom. Aranur could see flashes of Tyrel's shirt in the night, and Shilia's quick form just ahead of him. Dion brought up the rear. Twice they interrupted the night hunt of a lepa; once they came to a shuddering halt at a deep ravine that cleft the forest with a deadly rock bottom. The wolfwalker started to fall behind, and Aranur called back at her. She spurred her mount and they slowed finally in a clearing to count themselves and check their bruises.

"Is everyone all right?" Aranur asked, coming to a pounding halt where Rhom, Gamon, and Tyrel were already dismounting. Their harsh breathing cut the thick night air as he slid off, Tehena still in his aching arms. He laid her on the ground and started to shake his arms out. The thin woman might not weigh much, but she had gained a kilogram every minute. Kiyun was helping Shilia down. Dion was—

"Dion!" Rhom cried out as the Gray One bared its teeth and howled. Aranur turned. The wolfwalker was sagging, eyes closed, slipping slowly off her mount as it halted, the reins of the panting beast dropping from her nerveless fingers as she collapsed onto the ground. Aranur died a small death, and then she was in his arms, Rhom beside him and the Gray One pacing circles around them both.

"Aranur?" Shilia asked, frightened.

"She was hit," Rhom said tersely. "She was riding drag, and took an arrow from one of the raiders. She's lost a lot of blood."

Gamon dug a lantern from his pack and hurriedly poured in the oil. Its light shone yellow in the clearing, casting their shadows on the forest like macabre dancers in the night.

"She never said a word," Aranur snapped, furious at himself for not noticing the dark stain that had spread across her back. The arrow had pierced between her ribs and broken off. No wonder none of them had seen it. Dion breathed shallowly in his arms. Around him, Hishn's snarl reverberated in his ears until he felt half deaf.

"It's going to have to come out," Gamon said, looking at the wound. He rolled back the sleeves on his tunic and Aranur started to lay Dion on the ground, but she moaned, and the Gray One growled, and he froze.

"I mean her no harm," Aranur said to the wolf in a low voice. He shifted the wolfwalker in his arms again, but she cried out involuntarily, and the Gray One closed her teeth on his arm.

He could feel the sharp white fangs pricking at his skin as he resisted and tried to put the woman down anyway. "Look, Hishn—" He cleared his throat. "We have to take the arrow out." The teeth did not relax, and the yellow eyes gleamed. He reached no thoughts with his own gaze, only jumbled emotion and rage. "Gamon," he said hoarsely, without turning away from the wolf, "can you do it?"

"Maybe, but the wolf had better understand what we're going to do before we do it. Otherwise . . ."

He left the words hanging, and Shilia frowned in puzzlement, but Aranur understood. Hishn would not let them hurt Dion even to help her. If Dion were to live . . . well, they might have to kill the wolf to save the woman. "Rhom, talk to her," he asked quietly. "Make her understand."

But the blacksmith got to his feet slowly, a strange look on his face. "She will not hear me in this state, Aranur."

"Rhom . . ."

The blacksmith's hands clenched. "You are the only one who can reach Hishn through Dion right now, Aranur. My twin and I—we are too close, and Hishn is holding Dion right now." His face twisted in bitterness. "My touch in Hishn's mind would burn my own sister."

Aranur stared at the man, then nodded abruptly.

Gamon took the cloths Tyrel tore from one of their last extra tunics. "You better talk to her soon, Aranur. Dion can't wait much longer."

The Gray One's teeth were still on his arm, and Aranur stared deliberately into the yellow eyes. There was a dizzying flash of pain and he knew he had touched the wolf's mind. *Hear me, Hishn,* he thought strongly to her. *If you want Dion to live, let us help her.*

Dion moaned again. "Gamon, she's losing more blood," Rhom said urgently.

"I know." The old man took his knife from Tyrel, who had quickly lit a tiny fire to sterilize the blade. But the wolf tensed, and sweat dripped down Aranur's forehead.

Steady, Aranur said instantly.

Gamon flicked his eyes to the teeth that surrounded Aranur's arm, then carefully edged the skin away from the arrow's shaft with his knife. He slid the blade in. Dion cried out. The wolf clenched her jaw. Aranur gasped in spite of himself.

"Easy," he snapped. *Easy.* A new flow of blood obscured the silver of the old man's knife, and the Gray One snarled around Aranur's sleeve.

Gamon pressed the knife against the arrow head, and the knife slit her skin easily. The wolf almost tore Aranur's arm off to get at Dion, but Aranur cracked the command in his head. *Down! Back!*

She is in pain. Hishn's lupine lips parted and her teeth snarled at him dully.

Aranur cleared his throat. *The arrow must come out or she will die,* he said into the yellow eyes.

You're hurting her, the deep-throated snarl insisted.

Only to heal her, Aranur stated urgently. "Dion, forgive me," he breathed to himself. How could he have let her get into this?

Gamon slipped another knife on the other side of the arrow-head and began to ease it out from between Dion's ribs. The wolfwalker cried out again, her eyes opening wide in pain. "Aranur?" she gasped.

"Just another minute, Healer," Gamon said quietly, "and you'll be good as new." He lifted the blades gently, trying to keep the wicked barbs from tearing her flesh further. Aranur sensed Hishn reaching out, telling Dion what to do as the wolf picked the image from Aranur's mind. It was as if the Gray One had suddenly stepped beyond her emotions and taken charge, and Aranur barely breathed as she let go of his arm.

The wolf touched Dion gently with her nose. *Relax the muscles on your back. Breathe in deeply,* she commanded.

Trusting the wolf completely, Dion shakily breathed in once, then took as deep a breath as she could and held it, though her body shuddered with unspoken sobs at the pain.

"That's it!" Gamon said with relief. With her chest expanded and the muscles relaxed, he was able to cut the arrowhead neatly out from between her ribs, lifting the gory piece of metal away. Rhom quickly held up a pad to the open wound, catching the blood as it flowed out. It took only a moment to tightly bind the tear.

Dion clung to Aranur, one hand dragging on the wolf's scruff as Hishn pushed herself under the woman's hand.

"We've got to move on, Dion," Aranur said gently. Gods of the light, how had he not noticed that she had been hurt? He rose with her in his arms, his face bleak. He did not notice the look that passed between Rhom and Gamon.

Tyrel separated the dnu. "I'll take the extra," he said, mounting again and making a quick loop of the reins to fit his hand.

"Gamon, Rhom, you lead," Aranur ordered flatly.

Rhom helped the grim leader up onto the beast he had ridden before, then picked up Tehena and gave her to Kiyun, who was already mounted. Shilia tied the extra packs together and slung them in front of her on her own mount. With the wolf making Aranur's dnu as jittery as a rabbit that ran beside a lepa, they started out again. The woods had quieted down while they had stopped, and now the screams from disturbed night creatures were less shrill as they rode slowly instead of thrashing through the brush.

Chapter 22

Summer, fall, and winter solstice,
The moons fade in sun-turned hills of gold
And still waters reap the harvest of the tides.
Full eyes, dark eyes;
Wet sky colors fill the dawn.

Summer grasses fading dry,
The heat of drought brings hardened soil.
Balance calls the earth to grow again:
Dark earth, rich earth;
Life from seeds of death.
The watercats cried and the Spirit Walk heard:
Two alone, two together;
To the end.

Dion was being held by strong, hard arms and softly rocked by the smooth gait of a long-legged dnu. Her head rested against a man's shoulders, and she was confused for a moment; then her eyes opened to look into Aranur's stained and dirty tunic. He smelled of old blood and dust and dnu. His face looked gaunt, his skin haggard.

Wolfwalker? The green and dusky morning clogged her nose, and she realized that Hishn's image was strong with worry.

Hishn? she returned. Then Aranur shifted, and, lost in the drums of the pulse that beat at her ribs, Dion closed her eyes again.

Some time later, she woke, and at her slight movement arms tightened instantly around her. She struggled, trying to raise her head to see where she was, what time it was, but a sharp stabbing pain in her shoulder dragged a moan from her lips and made her sink back.

"Dion?" Aranur asked. The skin was taut and tense around his eyes; his face was dark with unreadable emotions.

She tried to speak, but only a whisper came out. "Where are we?"

The lean man controlled the dnu with his knees, resting the reins only lightly in his hands. "About fifty kilometers from the main valley road."

"Raiders?"

"We lost them for the time being. If we keep heading east, we can circle around to Ramaj Ariye from the northeast and avoid them entirely."

She managed one more question. "Tehena?"

"Kiyun has her," he answered. "Lie still and be quiet." He softened his words with a smile that did not quite touch his dark eyes. "You're heavy."

She closed her eyes obediently and knew nothing more till she was wakened hours later by the throbbing pain.

It was midmorning when they stopped to eat. They had had little food in their packs when they quit the inn so quickly, so it was a light meal even with the two birds Tyrel had managed to bring down. Hishn had not left Aranur's side as he rode, and now she sat, panting, waiting for him to set Dion down so she could lie beside her.

Exhausted, Aranur slid down the flanks of his tired beast and staggered under Dion's light weight. She bit her lip to stifle the gasp when her feet hit the ground. Rhom was instantly by his sister's side.

"It's all right," Aranur insisted, shaking his head. But he released Dion to her brother anyway, watching as the blacksmith helped his twin to a fallen log so she could lean against it while the others dismounted and stretched.

Hishn licked Dion's hand and laid a furry head in her lap.

A half hour later, when Tyrel went to collect the dnu, Dion would have risen, but Rhom's light hand on her shoulder easily held her down. "Whoa there, twin," he drawled. "Where do you think you're going?"

"I can ride," she said, irritated.

"Maybe half a kilometer," he corrected. He reached down to help her up, but Aranur reached her first.

"I'll take her," the leader said shortly.

Rhom flicked his glance over his shoulder. "I guess Kiyun already has a passenger," he said slowly, looking over at the fighter.

Aranur's jaw tightened, but he said nothing as he helped Dion up on the dnu and mounted behind her.

When they rode out, Aranur let Dion shift into a sitting position in front of him, her head resting on his shoulder, his arms around her protectively. Kiyun still had Tehena's limp form in front of him. The other woman would not regain consciousness till midafternoon or later, Dion had told him, so with two of them riding double, he knew they would have to ride easily or run the dnu into the ground.

Rhom set a medium pace, breaking into a distance-eating lope as soon as they hit the main road Hishn had directed them to. By the time the first big drops of rain hit, Dion had sunk back into a throbbing state of semiconsciousness. She struggled to sit up, but Aranur balanced her with one strong arm and gently pulled her cloak up over her head. "Rain," he said briefly.

It took five days to ride the rest of the length of the valley. Tehena, who was caught in the addiction of dator again, spoke little. When she did lash out, the others said nothing in return, knowing how she had risked her life for them at the inn. Aranur, his face hard-bitten and his gray eyes plainly showing his exhaustion, carried Dion for three days till she had healed enough to ride by herself. Hishn would not allow her to do Ovousibas again—she was too weak, and the Gray One did not trust Dion's stamina—so the healing was slow and painful. But heal she did.

At last they reached the mesas, and there they camped together for the last time, for Rhom and Shilia would split off the next morning to ride for Randonnen. Dion had a decision to make. By tradition, since Shilia would ride first to Randonnen to meet Dion's father, Dion should ride on with Aranur to Ariye. Once she had met Aranur's family, she could return to Randonnen without dishonoring the Promise Rhom and Shilia had made. Dion longed to see her own father. This Journey had been long—too long.

And Aranur had not spoken to her in days.

Hishn whined and butted her thigh, and Dion clenched her jaw. Finally, fleeing the campfire where the others were talking softly among themselves, she rubbed at her temple and stared bitterly at the stars. It had been bad enough when she and Aranur were fighting constantly, but this silence—if it was like this now between them, what would it be like in Ariye? He must think her useless, she realized bitterly. Getting shot, being unable to ride . . . There would be no honor to his family in taking her into his home.

Hishn, standing beside her, whined again softly. The gray coloring of the wolf melted into the night shadows so that only the yellow eyes were visible, gleaming in the moonlight, and Dion stared at the stars that tried to hide in the moons' glow. She could not hear the campfire anymore; she was far enough from it that even Gamon's voice was lost in the sound of the night insects. Hishn nudged her hand. She gripped the wolf's fur, and the Gray One leaned her head against her. They were close to Ariye, was that it? She turned the thought over in her mind, realizing suddenly how she must look to Aranur. What if it were not just her weakness that repelled him? Had he lost interest because they were only days from his home? Close enough for Aranur to remember that he would have to introduce Dion to his family. The Lloroi had acted as a father to Shilia; and Lady Sonan, his mate, treated her as a daughter, too. How would Aranur tell them that Dion would be their daughter in place of Shilia for the Waiting Year—a woman who carried both a sword and a healer's band? It had been hard enough for her own elders to take; what would Aranur's family think? Uncertainly, her hand clenched Hishn's fur so that the wolf snorted. Dion touched the healer's band softly, then rested her hand on her sword. She was not ashamed of what she was. She had earned the right to wear both sword and band. She would not give them up. And if that was what Aranur wanted, for her to hide her skills, then she would have to reconsider her feelings. Was that truly what he wanted? Or had his interest in her been only passing? Now that he was near home again, were there others whose pursuits were more acceptable to an Ariyen weapons master?

Dion tightened her jaw. She had no reason to deny her skills. No. Nor would she dishonor Rhom by returning home with him instead of going to Ariye with Aranur. If that was what it came down to, that Aranur was ashamed of her in the face of his family, then she would bear it. Aranur would have to take her as she was. But her eyes blurred, and she stared at the sky unseeing.

The voice, when it came, made her stir, and she realized that she was intruding on someone else's night.

". . . we have to talk." Rhom's voice was low.

The wolfwalker stood still, not wishing to interrupt or ruin a mood with her passage. She was surprised, however, when Aranur, not Shilia, answered.

"Haven't you done enough already?" the leader answered bitterly.

"Not enough by far if you haven't yet come to your senses."

"We had a conversation like this once before, Rhom. I can end this one the same way. Say what you mean, or mind your own business. I've left your sister alone. Isn't that what you wanted? The moons know I feel bad enough about her now without you adding to the burden."

"Aranur, our fearless leader," Rhom said mockingly. "Brilliant with his enemies and blind with his friends—"

"Rhom." The other man's voice interrupted her twin like hard steel coming from a sheath. "I'm tired of games, and I'm tired of your talk. Say what you mean or shut up."

"Dion has been spending little time with you lately," the younger man taunted.

Dion stiffened. Hishn cocked her head as if listening intently, and Dion would have moved to break up the argument, but something held her in place.

"You like that, don't you?" Aranur's cold voice betrayed his growing anger. "Anyone—even a foreigner from Bilocctar—would be a better mate for her than me."

"I don't know if anyone else is better—" Rhom paused deliberately, "—but at least others have more guts."

There was the sound of feet moving, then she heard fists thudding into flesh. Scuffling. Thrusting. Branches broke and fell to the ground.

"So I finally got a rise out of you, Aranur the—" Rhom grunted. "—sightless, Aranur the blind—" He woofed as something found his gut, gasped, and caught his hoarse breath. Feet scraped in the dust.

"I don't know," Aranur grunted, "what you're trying to—do—" There was more scuffling. They seemed to be circling now. "—but I'll take your face off for what you've said." There was more grappling, then thudding sounds. Rhom was not getting the better end of the deal; he should have known better than to taunt a weapons master like that.

"Why don't you admit it?" Rhom managed to wheeze out after a scuffle. "You're jealous."

Aranur snorted. "Of what?"

"That Dion sits with everyone else and enjoys their company, not yours." The younger man barely got the words out before landing on his back on the hard earth. He had no breath with which to say anything for a few moments. He was too busy trying to save his face from the other man's fists while Dion tried to figure out just what her brother was trying to prove.

Aranur seemed to get Rhom in a lock hold, and Dion could hear her twin's hoarse breathing as the other man whispered in the heavy dark. "Dion has no more use for me than for a worlag's son. You're the one who told me that, remember? Only now I believe it. I nearly got her killed again, just one ninan ago, remember? You've made your point, Rhom, though why you need to drive it home so many times is beyond me."

There was a choking sound, as if Rhom was trying to say something, and the wolfwalker almost broke and ran to stop them before they killed each other. But Hishn was not worried, and Dion hesitated. Rhom's voice, when he answered, was barely a wheeze.

"I have to make the point because you will be—taking Dion home with you when we ride tomorrow."

"What are you playing at, Rhom?"

"Just the truth. I want my sister to be—happy."

"Then be satisfied that I'm leaving her alone to despise me at will in my own home."

"But she'll still have to be with you, when Shilia lives in my home for the Waiting Year."

"What do you want me to say? Lady Sonan and the Lloroi are as parents to Shilia and I. Do you want me to break tradition and refuse Dion's presence in their—in my—home? Disgrace my own sister to keep you happy?"

"Do you hate my twin so much?" Rhom's whisper managed to mock the man one more time.

"By the moons," Aranur groaned, "I love her."

"You fool," the other man whispered. "You blind and sightless fool. Dion has eyes only for you. She loves you so deeply that she will do anything rather than let you know it."

There was silence for a moment. "What game are you playing now, Rhom?"

"This is no game, Aranur. Dion loves you."

There was a moment in which nothing could be heard but the harsh breathing of the two men, and then Aranur broke the silence. "She has a funny way of showing it." His voice was closed again, hard and cold, but there was a new note there, too.

"She's a woman," Rhom replied obliquely.

There was a pause, then more scuffling. She could hear them brushing the dust from their clothes.

"If I were you—"

"You've said enough, Rhom," the leader said, cutting him

off curtly. "Shilia rides with you to Randonnen tomorrow, and Dion does not have to remain with me. It is her choice."

They moved back to camp, and Dion stayed under the moons, watching the stars climb around the sky and circle with the moons. There was much to think about, and the night was very short.

Camp was quiet the next morning. No one spoke as they packed for Rhom and Shilia's leave-taking. It was understood that Tehena would go with the healer, and that Kiyun had a place with Gamon and Aranur in Ramaj Ariye. As Shilia mounted her dnu, Aranur said nothing, just kissed his sister and exchanged a long look with Rhom before stepping back and letting Tyrel and Gamon do the same. Gamon pressed a small bag in Shilia's hand and wished her moonsblessing, while Dion kissed her new sister good-bye and then rode with Rhom to the edge of the mesa where the paths split east and west. They sat quietly for a moment watching the desert light play across the sand and stone formations. Rhom broke the silence. "So, you've made your choice?"

"Were you ever uncertain what I would decide?"

"No, but Aranur was."

"I know."

Rhom gave her a sharp look. "Last night? You heard?"

Dion smiled wryly. "That's some tact you have."

He chuckled. "It worked, didn't it?"

"Tell Father I'll be back soon," she said, her voice breaking a little.

"Shall I tell him anything else?" Rhom teased lightly.

"I'll—we'll," she corrected with a glance at Aranur, "tell him ourselves when we get there."

"Then I'll tell him to hold his breath."

"Just tell him he just doubled his family," she said lightly. She looked at him, her eyes blurring until she dashed the moisture away angrily. "I'll miss you, Rhom."

He touched her hand. "And I you, Dion."

She pulled away and sat very straight in the saddle. "Ride safe."

"With the moons," he returned quietly.

She wheeled and rode back to the other group, reining in beside Aranur. She met his eyes steadily, then smiled.

The gray-eyed man looked at her face, then glanced after Rhom. Seeing his hesitation, the wolfwalker shook her head. "I ride by choice," she said softly. "Not obligation."

A strange look crossed Aranur's face, but Dion only raised her eyebrow, and suddenly Aranur threw his head back and laughed as if a weight as heavy as a dnu had been lifted from his shoulders. And Gamon, his eyes twinkling in the background, was smugly satisfied when Aranur leaned across the saddle and pulled Dion to him.

In a few minutes, Rhom and Shilia disappeared from sight behind an outcropping of orange-striped stone, leaving the others on the mountain steppes. In the thin, clear air they could see hundreds of kilometers in all directions, the flat mesa colored yellow, orange, and brown around them. Far away, the curve of the world hid the beaches of the southern coast. To the east, the range stretched out in deep forest till it dropped out of sight into the valleys of the other counties. To the west, the desert crawled up against the foothills and lay, dried out, till the dark line of Randonnen broke its border with trees and green growth. And to the north, beyond that last peak, lay Aranur's family and Dion's new home.

The sun leaned against the mountain peak, bathing Ramaj Ariye in the evening colors of Asengar. No one greeted Aranur, Gamon, and Tyrel as they rode into the town. Their weary faces already told their story. A healer rode beside Aranur, and—the people made the sign of the moonsblessing—a wolf ran beside the healer's mount. Two other riders were with the small group, but of the girls the men had gone after, there was no sign. The news sped ahead, fleet as wind and grim as famine. The elders gathered with Tyrel's father and mother, and his parents' faces were bleak as they recognized only their son, their nephew, and their brother. The men had been gone for months. Were their daughters and their niece lost to them?

The small group reined in. Tyrel swung down first, striding to greet his father. With surprise, the Lloroi sensed the new strength in his young son, the authority and experience that had aged his eyes. He grasped the youth and pulled him to his chest. "Tyrel, my son . . ."

"Father." The boy turned then to his mother and pressed an envelope into her hands as she hugged him. The woman's eyes glistened as she recognized Namina's writing on the paper. "Ainna?" she whispered. He shook his head. "Shilia?" Her voice broke. Tyrel smiled, and she started crying and turned to Aranur, who hugged her and motioned for the healer to come forward.

The woman dismounted, stepping up to kneel with Aranur before the Lloroi and his wife. Lády Sonan's eyes spilled over again as she took the blue Flowers of Promising and the purple Flowers of the Waiting Year and heard the healer's soft words: "May I bring happiness to your home as your daughter, Shilia, does to mine. May your daughter be as happy in my home as I will be in yours." Lady Sonan cried as she folded the younger woman in her arms and blessed her.

And across the desert, where the wind tumbled summer clouds over Randonnen peaks, two riders topped the pass that led to a mountain village. People gathered to watch them, and someone ran to the forge to get the blacksmith as they recognized his son in the pass. A woman rode with the man, but she could not be his twin, the healer—where was her wolf?

Kheldour watched them come in silence, ignoring the murmur of the growing crowd. The riders' clothes were clean but stained and battle worn, proof of a difficult Journey, but the two rode proudly with no hint of sadness in the gait of the dnu. Kheldour searched his heart for his missing daughter. He had felt fear for them so many times, waking in the night to the sound of distant swords and faded fighting, stopping his hammer when the ringing metal broke into his thoughts like battle, and praying to the moons as his daughter and son reached out across time and distance to one who could hear but not answer.

The murmuring rose, and Kheldour squinted more closely at the woman who was riding alongside his son. Two bright spots of color, purple and blue, marked her hands, and as they drew near, he realized that they were flowers. The Flowers of Promising and the Flowers of the Waiting Year. He felt his heart expand, and he drew in a breath as if to hold that sudden joy in him forever. Had it been only the Flowers of Promising, then his son would have mated; had it been only those of the Waiting Year, then he would have known that Dion had chosen her mate. No, this woman who rode so straight beside his son held two bouquets. Then his daughter and his son were both Promised.

"A double blessing," he told himself. And Kheldour strode to greet his children home.

About the Author

Tara K. Harper grew up in Cedar Mill, Oregon (before the stop light was put in). She went camping often as a child and discovered many things, such as the undertow is always stronger than one thinks, sea lions are not friendly creatures, and dry stream beds are not good places to sleep on rainy nights. In spite of these adventures, she made her way through school in a relatively calm fashion. She went to college, and eventually graduated from the University of Oregon.

Since college, Tara has been a technical editor and writer in various fields. Currently she works for a small company in high-speed wafer probing. She continues to study the sciences in her spare time, plays stringed instruments, and creates elaborate costumes even though there is no more room in her house to store them. She camps, hikes, rock climbs, and enjoys water sports such as swimming, water polo, and kayaking. Aside from a small library, her house is filled with drawings and paintings she has made from photos she takes while camping. She lives with three cats, two dogs, and a handful of fish.